FORCE IN THE MOUNTAINS

FORCE IN THE MOUNTAINS

DAVID SHERRILL OAKS

TATE PUBLISHING
AND ENTERPRISES, LLC

Published by Tate Publishing & Enterprises, LLC
127 E. Trade Center Terrace | Mustang, Oklahoma 73064 USA
1.888.361.9473 | www.tatepublishing.com

Tate Publishing is committed to excellence in the publishing industry. The company reflects the philosophy established by the founders, based on Psalm 68:11,
"The Lord gave the word and great was the company of those who published it."

Book design copyright © 2015 by Tate Publishing, LLC. All rights reserved.
Cover design by Eileen Cueno
Interior design by Joana Quilantang

Published in the United States of America

ISBN: 978-1-63418-029-0
Fiction / Historical
15.09.29

The Sherrills of America

This book is dedicated to the Sherrills of America. The Sherrills were among the first families to start settling the Western frontier during the early 1700s. This helped start what would become a free and independent country known as The United States of America.

Adam Sherrill, known in North Carolina as "The Pioneer," was awarded the first land grant on the western side of the Catawba River in 1748. He and his wife Elizabeth started their line of Sherrills who now live throughout America.

This book describes my thoughts on what Samuel Sherrill, my fifth great-uncle, and his family faced in their life and journeys in the southern Appalachian Mountains. His daughter, Catherine, became the first First Lady of Tennessee.

1

1760

The unrelenting force surrounded the mountain, making itself known to everything in its path. It would not let go of what it captured. Nothing was able to block the pressure of its grasp. Nothing known to man had ever stopped it. This power created an increasing tightness in Samuel's body followed by a rapid intake of breath. A sense of impending death flashed in his mind as he almost lost his balance while leaning into the force, as it had ever so briefly—vanished. It was the last of September. The chill he felt before getting on the rock was now enhanced by the all-encompassing unseen power. An involuntary shivering ran through his body as he thought about how close he came to meeting his maker on the rocks at the end of a three-hun-dred-foot fall. *My guardian angel musta' been watching over me,* he thought as the near-falling experience pushed hard through his mind.

He placed his rifle butt in a weatherworn depression on the rock surface and gently leaned on the barrel to, once again, steady his position. He looked deep into the vastness of nature's panorama before him. The view, left and right, showed waves of increasingly higher hills rolling toward him from the heavily for-ested low-lying lands. He let his eyes wander over the endless for-est with all its splendor as it seemed to melt into what appeared to be a hazy, far-off unknown ocean. At this elevation, the leaves of a few maple and dogwood trees were starting to show their tinge of red color heralding the approaching fall season. His alert eyes spotted a soaring hawk showing its mastery of the winds as it slowly completed circles in the sky. The uncomprehending power of what he was experiencing gave him a feeling of a deep-felt soul-fulfilling reverence. Many thoughts passed through his mind and one in particular kept surfacing, *Doesn't take too much thinking to figure out why the Indians fight so hard to keep it.* Samuel Sherrill is thirty-five years old and his tall lanky hard-muscled frame and calloused hands show he is a man used to hard work. His face has the look of soft angles and the twinkle in his blue eyes is that of a mischievous boy.

"You gonna come down from that rock or are you just trying to catch some kind of consumption in all that wind?" questioned Samuel's brother, Moses, nicknamed Mode, as he moved closer to the large rock protecting the camp from the wind. *Wonder if this wind blows all the time,* thought the eighteen-year-old Moses who, like his brother, possesses a square-shouldered six-foot body containing a noble-looking face set off by penetrating blue eyes.

Samuel came back into the sheltered campsite saying as he started to sit down next to the fire, "I'm here to tell ya that wind will knock you down and throw you away if you aren't careful. If that isn't enough, it's gonna be a colder one tonight. We need to get off this mountain to some warmer weather down below."

"You got that right! We gotta get on with hunting meat for our tables and smoke house back home and not play around all day looking at the sights," said Frank Travis, twenty-five years old, the son of Mike Travis and Saka, a revered woman of the Catawba people. Frank has a faint appearance of some of their friends in the western mountains who call themselves Melungeons. His ever alert brown eyes, black hair, and slender body were more his mother's genes than his father's, but his mind was like both his parents—quick and decisive.

"I sure don't want to get some deer or elk this far from home. I don't want to carry that meat any further than I have to. I'm gonna go back up top for one last look," said Samuel.

Moses and Frank looked at each other, shrugged their shoulders, and watched Samuel start back to the rock shelf to do battle with the fierce wind.

Moses said while thrusting his hands in the air, "Great day, Frank! Just listen to that wind moan and groan! Sounds like those winds blowing through the trees during those summer storms we get at home except it doesn't seem to ever quit up here. Wonder why that is? And just what is it that Samuel is trying to prove?"

The sun was slowly setting behind him and the deep blue sky of early evening was dispersed with towering white-topped clouds as Samuel again surveyed the grand spectacle in front of him. His eyes swept from the northeast to the southwest. He saw two separate and distant cloudbanks with what appeared to be slowly weaving delicate curtains reaching to the ground. One of them had bolts of lightning streaking through the clouds. He knew these curtains were made of rain. His eyes briefly lingered on another shadow of rainfall and passed on in the southwesterly direction. He abruptly came back to the shadow. Squinting his eyes while trying to sharpen his focus in the dwindling light on the shadow, he thought, *That's not rain! It's smoke!* He continued to watch it and thought, *I hope it's not someone's cabin or barn or both. Must be a big one to have that much smoke. Must not be too windy there.* Then in a deep fear of what and where it might be, he called out to Moses and Frank to come quick to his side.

"What do you think that is? Seems to be close to our farms, maybe a little north of our place. On the other hand, could it be...one of...ours?" said Moses in a fear-tinged, hesitant voice. He then slowly sat down on the rock rather than battle the wind in a standing position.

"Yeah, Mode, I think you're right about that other place. I'm fairly sure it isn't ours since we aren't close to the first high hills.

We oughta get over there to see what we can do to help. Might be somebody we know that is hurt or needs some other kind of help," said Samuel.

"That's gotta be a day and a half walk for us to get over there and what if it's a forest fire? We can't do anything about that!" exclaimed Frank as he gestured toward the smoke.

"Yeah, it's a far piece for sure. I'm beginning to think it's where we saw that new cabin being built last month, and if someone is in trouble, I think we gotta help 'em out. You both know our Pa's would do such a thing," said Moses nodding his head in Frank's direction.

Samuel said, "Might belong to some new settler or Catawba, but I doubt it being so far from their land. Then there's the British who want all they can get their hands on and tell us what to do with it and threaten us if we don't. Not only do we have to fight the Indians, it's beginning to look like we'll need to fight our relatives from England one of these days."

Moses said with a thoughtful and frowning look on his face, "Yeah, you're right, brother, I never thought about it like that. Just think about that for a minute, Samuel. One of these days, one of our Devonshire cousins could be looking down his sights at us as he pulls his trigger. Something's not right about that."

"You got that right, Mode! The sad thing about that is we've never met our kin from over there. And you know something else, it ought to be that the men making the decision to fight should be the ones doing the fighting and getting shot at or knifed. Betcha that would put an end to all the killing and maiming going on," Samuel said in a low wistful voice as he slowly shook his head.

"Whatever we're gonna do, we best be moving on and quit wasting time with all this talk. Can't do nothing about those British anyway," said Frank. "Let's get moving," as he picked up his backpack and rifle.

Moses picked up his pack and rifle, and while adjusting the load on his back said, "I don't like someone across a big ocean that I've never seen, telling me what I'm gonna do and how to do it! Hang it all, they don't even know what this land looks like. I think all of us should have a say about how we live."

"Dream on, brother! Seems guys who can help us wind up thinking about how to keep their positions and forget about the little man. Isn't anything any of us can do about that except tell them to go back where they came from and I don't think that is gonna happen," said Samuel.

"Y'all just gonna talk all day about things you can't do anything about! I think we better do something that we can do something about and that's to get off this mountain," said Frank.

They all slowly nodded their heads in agreement and started following known game trails down the mountain. *Wonder if the buffalo or elk, or both, made this trail; seems to have been here for a long time*, thought Samuel as he could see how parts of the trail bed were worn down below the level of the surrounding land.

2

The three prepared their camp for the evening next to a creek and started fishing from its slow moving clear cold water. They casually watched their lines hoping to see if a fish would start nibbling at their grub-baited hooks.

"Talk about clear water! This creek is so clear I can count the stones in the bottom even in this dwindling light. I can see the fish and you know darn well they can see us," whispered Frank. "Wonder what they are thinking?"

Moses gave Frank a sideways glance, shook his head slightly, and said, "Fish think? I declare, Frank, I think your mom dropped you on your head when you were born especially when you come up with those crazy thoughts. You'd better wonder on how you gonna catch some so we can have a decent supper." Frank caught Moses smile and shook his head with an "I'm not even going to try to comment on that" look.

After a time of watching their lines and watching trout inspecting the baited hooks, Samuel finally caught the first one. "Looks like I'm gonna have a mighty good supper. What y'all gonna eat?" Samuel said, as he looked for a response from the others.

"Most likely we'll have to get some of those vines over across the creek and tie you up while we have your fish," Moses said in a smug manner while gesturing and looking across the creek.

"Yeah, uhhhh huhhh. Y'all better get an army to help you then," Samuel said with a look of "I can take on you two any-time." He noticed Moses was taking a lot of time looking across the creek. "Thinking about those honeysuckle vines and what you're gonna do with 'em, Mode?"

"Nawww, I'll just catch me a fish and be done with all this blather," said Moses, while giving the others a worried brow look. "Let's fish."

In a low, almost whispered voice, while not taking his eyes from his line, Moses said, "Hey, boys, don't flinch when I tell you this. But I don't think we're alone. Something or somebody is watching us across the creek. Behind that big hemlock."

Nobody looked up or said anything as they absorbed what Mode had just said. A short while later, Frank slowly got up, stretched himself, and casually said, "I gotta knock some bark off a tree. Be back in a minute," and disappeared into the woods. The other two continued fishing but were considerably more alert and tense. They knew that Frank intended to find out what, or who, was watching them. His stalking skills were about as good as his Catawba cousins.

He was hidden in a laurel thicket growing under a huge hemlock tree while watching the men trying to catch their supper. A smile crossed his twenty-five-year-old face as he thought, *I'm gonnu' have me some fun now. They won't know what hit 'em. I'll wait 'til he gets back and then let go at 'em.*

Frank had quickly moved upstream around a slight bend that hid his crossing of the creek. His inborn instincts took over his movements and he became like a shadow moving in the woods— silent and breathless. He knew he was close to the hemlock tree as he cautiously peeked over a long ago fallen moss-covered log. The evening's light was dimming making it difficult to see with any degree of accuracy when he saw his quarry lying on the ground. *There he is....I got 'em! He looks like....naww, couldn't be. Too far from his place.* Frank eased into a crouch and put his rifle sights on the man.

He sure is taking a long time. Then, with a flash of immediate understanding, he knew what the third man was doing. He placed his hands underneath his body to get ready to silently stand up.

"Move and your dead," Frank said in a matter of fact steady voice as he pointed his rifle at the stranger's back.

"Great day in the morning, Frank. You sounded like a wounded bear crashing through the brush," said the stranger as he started to turn to Frank.

Sounds like him but can't make 'em out good enough. "Don't move a muscle, don't turn around! You may know me, but I don't know you! Now start walking to the creek and don't say another word. This rifle's got a real nervous trigger," said Frank in a low menacing "don't mess with me" tone.

Moses and Samuel stood up when they saw Frank and the other man emerge on the opposite bank. Moses, with a suppressed "time to have some fun" look on his face leaned toward Samuel and held up one finger while mouthing the number "one," held up two fingers, "two" and then on "three," they shouted at the top of their voices, "Boone!"

The man they shouted at was startled to the point of losing his footing on the creek bank and while trying to keep his rifle above his head, attempted to keep from losing more of his unsteady balance. He fell into the creek. He slowly stood up in the creek and just as slowly looked at each of the others with a menacing glare. He then stalked out slinging and wiping away water from his face and deerskin coat and pants while slapping his wide brimmed hat hard against his leg. He slowly stalked up to Moses, laid down his wet rifle and hat, leaned his face close to Moses, and looked him in the eyes with a stern unyielding force.

"Uhhhh, you all right, Dan'l?" said Moses in a questioning "what's gonna happen next; you ain't mad, are you" manner.

A cold, dripping wet, slightly mad Daniel Boone grabbed Moses in a bear hug and said, "I ain't gonna be the only one who is wet around here!" and fell back into the creek taking Moses with him.

Moses swishing the water away from his face, Daniel doing the same, and Samuel and Frank doubled up with laughter made for a free and uninhibited scene. "Hangfire, Daniel, it's good to see you again!" said Moses.

"Yeah, me too, but let's get out of this creek before we catch our death of some kind of consumption," said Daniel. "I thought Frank had lost his mind when he said he didn't know me. But I sure wasn't gonna mess with him. I learned long ago he means what he says."

"Yeah, I thought it might be you when I first saw you. But the poor light in there made me careful like. Best be safe than otherwise, wouldn't you say?" said Frank with a slight smile and shrug of his shoulders.

After catching more fish for their supper, the four men sat around the campfire getting ready to eat. They looked up in a surprised yet somewhat casual manner when another man emerged from the woods across the creek, waded through the creek and sat down next to the fire. Not a word was spoken. No hostile moves were taken by anyone. After a moment or two, Moses said, "Don't know how you can be so quiet, Carlo. Just like your pa. How is Santee these days? Can you believe it—we haven't seen each other in over a year and now—it just beats all."

"Well, my flatland friends, I coulda ridden up on a buffalo and you wouldn't have known it with all the cat'rwalling going on here. I'm on a hunting trip and got close to this place and thought I would drop by for a quick visit. Better be glad no raiding Cherokees are around," said Carlo. "And I wanted you all to know that I've changed my name to Carl. Makes it easier to say."

"Whatcha doin' that for?" asked Daniel. The others nodded their heads signifying agreement.

In a questioning wondering way, Carl said, "My pa and some others are saying people like you are starting to take a lot more notice of where we live and don't really know how to get along with us and don't want to find out. Since we have been here for a long time, they think we are part of some Indian tribe. That makes 'em think they can just take over and shove us out of the way. Try and figure that one out. See what I mean?"

"Sounds like what we are doing with the Indians. That why you changing your name?" asked Samuel.

"That's most of it. My folks think it is time for us to start becoming a part of what is happening to this land. Pa says what you Sherrills and Boones have done around the Catawba lands will be done around us and we had better get set-up for it. Most people don't or won't understand names like Santee, Carlo, and Franco, which makes us somehow different to them," said Carl shaking his head in frustration.

"This means we can't say 'O-Carlo' anymore. Now it's just plain old Carl," said Moses with a slight smile. "Think I'll change mine to Saint," followed by a laugh.

"Saint you ain't! You'd best leave it to what your ma and pa gave you, Moses," said a smiling Frank. "Now do like the first Moses did and go part us that creek so we can get to the other side nice and dry."

The group of men laughed and kidded Moses to part the water. "Don't have them Egyptians to cause me to do that," said Moses, "so I'm just going to let y'all get wet."

"I'll go back home and get you one of those guys who claim they came from Egypt and bring 'em back here to watch you part those waters," said a laughing Carl.

The five men, representing different backgrounds, were proving the theory that people could survive and grow lasting friendships by getting to know each other and accepting each other's way of wanting to live.

Daniel said, "Well, my good friends, I'm getting some shuteye tonight. Who's gonna take first watch?" They developed the watch plan for the night as they checked their weapons making them ready for action. Moses took the first shift.

"By the way, Dan'l, did you come up here in the last day or two? We're on our way to check out what looked like a fire. Might be a neighbor in trouble," said Samuel.

As he motioned with his head back over his shoulder, Daniel said, "Nope, been over the mountains to do some hunting and look at some land to settle down with my Rebecca and our boys. Getting too crowded around our place these days. And it is getting worse by settlers coming back here from around the Ohio River."

"Coming back? That doesn't make a lot of sense," said Moses. "Too cold up there?"

Daniel said as he casually pointed toward the northwest, "Seems that war up there between the English and French keep the Indians up there all riled up. And we all know some of those northern tribes, especially the Iroquois, are helping the French. I guess that means anyone speaking English is an enemy to those Indians."

Carl said, "Yeah, I hear of that happening from some of our Cherokee friends. Bad enough fighting the Indians but when you add in some Frenchman shooting at ya makes a body think twice. That, plus those French got so far into the Cherokee's land that Attacullaculla, somehow or other, got the governor of South Carolina to build him a fort at their main village, called Chota, for protection. Things are just not right. Fightin' going on all the time."

Samuel said, "That chief got the governor to build a fort? That Attacullaculla must be some man all right. Wonder where they met?"

"That Indian blood makes a man a mighty smart feller. Just look at me," said Frank with a smile, "beside that building forts is not usually the Indian way."

Samuel said, "I've been told that some guys a few years back, out of Virginia, going down that path the Indians made a long time ago, helped 'em build a fort. Seems like I remember it being built at one of their villages. I'm thinking it was Chota or something that sounds like that name.

Daniel said, "See what I mean! People all over the place over there and I want to be part of it. Anyway, I need some space to do what I want to do. Saw some mighty fine-looking bottomland and buffalo like you've never seen before and nobody around, except some Cherokees or Shawnees, who didn't take too kindly about my being around. Had to hide under a waterfall to lose 'em," said Daniel.

"Hide under a waterfall! You musta made 'em really mad. That was some fast thinking," said Moses. "How long did ya have to stay there?"

"Wasn't too long by the clock. But it seemed like forever to me. I could hear 'em talking and walking around the creek bank. But they soon left and I slowly crept outta there and was mighty careful in leaving that place. I was trying to be real quiet to the point of hardly breathing," said Daniel.

Samuel said while looking at each man and finally to Daniel, "You best be mindful of those Cherokees. I kinda feel for 'em 'cause I sure won't want some stranger stomping around my land without my knowing it. And, let's face it, boys, they've been here forever and they're just protecting what they think is right-fully theirs."

"You got a point, Samuel. But there aren't many that think like you do. Most men are so wanting of their own land that they'll do most anything to get it," said Frank. "And I'm half Catawba and have often talked with my kinfolk about this same thing. It's tough to get people to live together and accept each other's ways."

Moses, wanting to change the subject, said to Daniel, "Looks nice over there, you say. Probably looks like it was around the ford when Pa first crossed the Catawba back in '29. Betcha ya didn't know he got the first land grant west of that river, after moving back in '47. Brought some Robinsons and others with him to help settle the place for good."

Samuel rolled his eyes saying, "I oughta remember all that 'cause I was there." Carl shrugged his shoulders and Frank indicated a "not-again attitude" with a slight movement of his hands and said with a smile, "C'mon, Mode, we've all heard this before. Whatcha want—a monument saying that happened?" The others joined in kidding Moses about what to write on a monument.

Soon afterwards, the kidding died down and everyone turned their attention to Daniel as he said, "Well, boys, y'all know I settled around the Forks. Y'all ain't the only ones who have wet legs in their family's past," said Daniel.

"Awww, c'mon guys, we've about beat that subject to death a long time ago. C'mon, Dan'l, tell us about what you saw over there," said Samuel nodding his head back over his shoulder to the west.

"Most likely you're right 'bout that land," said Daniel. "The big difference is the low valleys and high mountains surrounding them. It sometimes makes me stop and just do nothing but look at the greatness of that land. Makes a body want to settle there."

Samuel said, "I'm going over there and take a look around. I agree with Dan'l. It's getting to be too many people over at our place around the ford. It's getting so bad that a man can't even go into the woods to wet down a tree or bush without thinking someone might be around."

"Well, ol' boy, if you do go over there, ya' best be careful about firing your rifle. Sound carries a long way. Come to think of it, maybe that is why those Cherokees started after me," said Daniel in a pensive manner.

Carl said as he looked into the eyes of each man while making emphatic gestures with his hands, "See what I mean! More people are starting to move to the lands where we and the Cherokees live in peace, but the new settlers come on in and take root without even thinking about us! And, boys, that just ain't right!"

"You have a point, Carl. But how do you stop people who want to make a better life for themselves and their families? From what I heard, Pa says we sure don't want to be like they are in England. No one has any freedom, got a tax on nearly everything, most people can't own land and...well, things just aren't good for a man trying to do better for his family," said Moses.

"Talk about a tax! What about that Molassess Tax we've been having to pay! That's not right for us to have to pay for something we grow and make! And especially sending the money back to England to a bunch of men who only care about themselves!" said Samuel.

Everyone murmured agreement but made no comments how to solve an ever increasing problem. One by one, they prepared their places to sleep for the night.

After moving back from the fire, Moses let his eyes become accustomed to the dark. He moved to the edge of the woods lining the creek bank and looked to the heavens and looked for, and found, one of his favorite constellations, the Swan, and lost himself in its beauty and simple symmetry. *I can't wait to see it standing upright in the sky at Christmastime. Looks like the Cross then. The power of God's creation is more than my mind can figure out. What is His plan for all of this?* Carl's father, Santee, had taught him a lot about stars and their guideposts to the seasons and even earthly travel. His thoughts drifted to Carl and his people and his situation of having to adjust his lifestyle to the things developing around him. *I see why Carl is worried. But he and his family, like the rest of us, can't control what is happening. Even Samuel is thinking of crossing over these mountains to settle close to where Carl and the rest of the Melungeons and Cherokees live. Might be some tough times ahead for all of us.*

He turned his attention to the sounds of the forest and knew that as long as those sounds continued, they were most likely safe. Frank's mom, Saka, had always told him about the way a forest has many sounds all its own. The sounds tonight were of owls sending out their chilling screeching calls, whippoorwills whistling their clear calls, distant elk bellowing, and crickets sending out their unique call, but when the forest became quiet then it was time to be increasingly mindful of your surroundings. At times like those, silence could be almost deafening. He continued to listen to tonight's unique language of the forest. A peaceful warm blanket feeling settled around him while he fought the impulse to shut his eyes.

3

The sun's first rays were just starting to brush their startling hues of red and pink on the morning's high clouds. The colors were gently blending and folding into each other when five men were on their way to check out what caused the smoke Samuel had seen two days ago. They paused on top of a hill and each strong-willed and strong-bodied man looked to the East.

Frank said in an almost reverent whisper as his eyes slowly drifted over the skyscape, "Not often you see a sunrise like this one."

Carl, who seemed to be lost in the splendor of the moment, said, "I agree. This is awesome. Just wait till you get over to my place and see the sunsets slowly slide behind the mountains. The colors just slowly fade and then grow together into an ever deepening purple and then the stars start turning on and then in almost a blink of your eye it is dark night. I've never seen the equal. None better."

Samuel said as he turned to the rest of the group, "That does it! I'm going over there and find me a place to settle down for good."

Toward early afternoon, they could smell the faint odor of smoldering wood and followed its scent trail. Moses saw it first and stopped at the edge of a partially cleared ground. He motioned the others to join him. They kept back in the woods next to the clearing and then dispersed in a circle scouting for potential problems. The cabin, or what was left of it, had wisps of smoke slowly curling up from a few smoldering embers. The grass around it was scorched and the oak leaves on a branch over-hanging the cabin were singed from the heat. An odor of death lingered in the air.

Five men stood in what had been the middle of the cabin looking at the burned bodies of what appeared to be two men. "Got to be a helluva way to die," said Carl. The others silently nodded their agreement with grim, tight-lipped faces.

"Wonder what happened and wonder who they were?" said Daniel. "Chimney or fireplace sparks catching something on fire is about the only thing that mighta happened. Musta been asleep and the smoke got to 'em first."

Carl said, "You Sherrills are all over the place around here. Seems to me some of you had to know those guys were here."

"You would think so," said Samuel, "but none of our kin has mentioned anything about this to me or Mode. And this isn't the place we saw a few weeks ago."

"We gotta bury these poor guys," said Moses.

After the brief service over the graves, Frank said, "Are you two sure you want to move over the mountain? Seems to me these guys were far out from where anyone lives and look what it got 'em."

Samuel tilted his eyes to Daniel and they both looked at each other silently thinking about what Carl had just said.

"Might wanna stay at the ford you two. Got to think about Mary, Sam Jr., Susan, Catherine, Uriah, Adam and William, my old brother. And Rebecca, James and Israel for you, Dan'l," said Moses.

"You gotta point, Mode. I'll think on it some more," said Samuel as he picked up his pack. "We best get on home. I don't feel right about what happened here. Two people dying in a fire like this just doesn't make sense. Mighta had some hard drink with 'em, but somehow or other, I kinda doubt it."

✑

Some miles away, Newt Taylor was thinking, "*Them two guys didn't have no shillings or nothin' else I could use. They died and I'm still broke. I've got to find someplace where I can get some money.*

Mary Preston Sherrill thought, *Just when are those men coming home? It's been five days now and Lord only knows where they are and if they are all right.* The more she thought about it, the more worried she became about her husband and if something had happened to him. What would that mean for their sons and daughters was an ever present concern for her. Samuel Jr., age twelve; Susan, age eight; Catherine, age six; Uriah, age five; Adam, age two; William, age one; and another child was expected very soon made up the Samuel Sherrill family. With exception of Catherine and William the rest were visiting their grandparents, Adam and Elizabeth. Mary knew the Sherrill brothers and wives would make sure she and the children were cared for, but the fact of no father or husband was something she did not want to face. *This is a wonderful place to raise a family and grow old. I'll try to teach my children to try and make a difference in this land and leave it a better place than they found it,* she thought as she picked up the clothes to be washed in the outdoor iron pot.

Catherine's face was, even at her early age, a sculptured beauty that contained a pair of breath taking blue eyes which showed their youth-driven sparkle when her mom said, "Want to feed Jack and Betsy?" Catherine was always ready to do anything to help with their horses. She loved it when her pa picked her up and placed her in the saddle on Betsy's back while he held the bridle. She longed for the day when she would be given the bridle's reins and the command of such a large and beautiful animal. She loved Betsy and cared for her as best a six-year-old could do. Betsy loved to nibble the apples, or sometimes a rare sorghum candy treat, out of Catherine's outstretched hand. The horse and

young girl had a special bond between them that her parents found to be a blessing due to Catherine's driven approach to life. Her parents soon found out after she learned to talk that she was going to enjoy life to the fullest extent. Betsy was her current method of finding that enjoyment in her life.

Mary stepped out of the log barn holding William on her hip and, while glancing around their property, saw a man crossing over their split rail fence at the edge of the pasture. "Catherine, do not come out of the barn until I say so!" while wishing she had some type of weapon to defend herself. She watched with increasing anxiety as the man approached her.

She saw that the man was dressed in worn buckskin pants and what appeared to be a ragged linsey-woolsey shirt that needed washing and much mending. He walked with a slow, almost to the point of falling down, pace until he was about twenty feet from Mary and stopped. Mary saw that he was painfully thin, almost like he had been starving. She then realized he did not have any weapons. *Strange that he's been in the woods but has no rifle or even a knife that I can see. Musta lost them.*

Mary could almost feel the "touch" of his brown eyes as they searched her face as if trying to decipher if she had any intent to cause pain or harm.

He finally said in low halting manner, "Afternoon, ma'am. Name's Isaac Logan. Been lost for weeks in the woods after escaping from them Cherokees. They jumped me after I got out of Fort Loudoun back yonder over them mountains. I'm trying to get back to South Carolina. You're the first person I've seen that most likely won't hurt me." He then reached up and started to remove his sweaty, stained, dirt encrusted hat and, after hesitating, dropped his hand to his side.

Mary could hear in his monotone voice that he was, as they say, "some place else" when talking about people who just don't seem to be fully aware of their surroundings or themselves. She shifted William to a more comfortable position and said, "Are you hungry? Want a drink of water? You look tired, Mr. Logan. Come sit down by the fire." She motioned him toward the fire pit where water was gently boiling in the iron wash kettle. She was not about to let down her guard and maintained a safe distance from him.

Isaac Logan sat down on a log beside the fire and looked with sad eyes into the fire and said, "Thank ya kindly. If you got somethin' to eat, I sure would be grateful to you for it. Can't really recall when I had a decent bite to eat."

"Kate, go in the cabin and get some biscuits and fried ham and bring them to me," said Mary in a low commanding voice without taking her eyes off of Isaac.

Catherine knew that when she was called "Kate" that things were not as they should be or was about to be scolded for not doing something like her chores. She walked out of the barn, paused, and said "Hi" with a little girl's cheerfulness while waving her hand to the stranger. "I'm gonna get those things, Mama." She kept her eyes on the stranger while turning to go into the cabin.

Isaac Logan seemed to come out of his "some place else" attitude when he saw Catherine. He smiled at her, stood up and then bent down toward her saying, "Hi, yourself, pretty little girl," and without hesitation, removed his hat as most well-mannered men do in the presence of ladies.

Mary's immediate gasp of breath and hand abruptly brought to her mouth compounded her wide-eyed reaction to the sight in front of her. Catherine stopped in mid-stride as she looked with startled fascination tinged with horror at the vision in front of her. "Oh, my heavens!" exclaimed Mary as she slowly dropped her hand from her mouth to hold William even tighter to her body.

The top of Isaac's head showed a hand's length of exposed skull starting just above his forehead. He was momentarily surprised by the reaction being displayed in front of him and then realized why. "I'm sorry for letting you see my head. I just plain forgot about it when I saw your little girl. Reminds me of my little girl back home."

Mary could not contain her startled attitude and said with an incredulous voice, "Ahhhh, Mr. Logan, what in the... world happened...?"

Isaac said while pointing to the west, "I was captured by some Cherokees over at Loudoun across them mountains. They were letting some of us go and I thought I'd better escape when I had the chance. I started out one night and one of them caught me"—he hesitated for a long moment and with a low trembling voice said—"and scalped me. He musta thought I was dead." He touched his skull and then seemed to go back to his "some place else."

Mary slowly regained her composure. Catherine continued her wide-eyed stare. "Kate! Do as I told you. Get that food and bring it to me and in a hurry!" said Mary in a level voice.

"Yes ma'am," said Catherine as she slowly walked to the cabin never taking her eyes off the stranger while her mother moved to the fire and the kettle. Isaac sat back down on the log while putting on his hat.

Catherine set the basket down in front of her mother. She looked at her mother with an intense stare and said, "Here it is, Mama. Hope this is what you wanted."

Mary hid her surprise when she reached into the basket to take out food for Isaac. A cloth was covering their pistol. A flood of "thank-yous" for a six-year-old girl thinking and doing such a thing swept through her mind as she handed a biscuit laden with ham to Catherine. "Please give this to Mr. Logan, Catherine."

◠◡

Newt Taylor smelled the faint odor of burning wood. He followed the odor until he saw a clearing containing a cabin, barn, and a couple of smaller buildings. He instantly made up his mind to rob these settlers since his last attempt netted him nothing except a fight with the two, now dead, men. He walked out of the wood line into the head high, ready for harvest, corn crop toward the cabin. He held his rifle in the crook of his arm positioning it to use it at a moment's notice.

While savoring the remaining bit of his first real food in weeks, Isaac saw Mary's reaction on seeing another stranger walking up to them. Mary got up while saying, "May I help you?" while wondering if these two men were friends. *I don't like this!* she thought as she reached for Catherine's hand. This man's small brown eyes were constantly searching, making Mary think he was looking for something or someone. *He sure is acting peculiar. Like something is really botherin' him.*

Newt said, "You needn't get up on my account. Name's Newt Taylor. I'm just traveling through to Polk's place. Can I get some water and maybe a bite to eat and I'll be on my way." He cast a wary eye to Isaac who had barely glanced at him when he had walked up to the group. He also noted Isaac was holding a biscuit.

"Thet biscuit good?" Newt asked of Isaac and sat down. Isaac didn't even acknowledge the stranger's comment as he kept looking at the fire and munching on his biscuit.

Mary noticed that Newt had placed his rifle so the barrel was pointed such that it could be rapidly moved to cover either her or Isaac's position. Her face paled when she realized the danger that this man posed to her and, more importantly, Catherine and William.

"Kate, take the basket to Mr. Logan so he can get another biscuit and then hand it to Mr. Taylor so he can get a biscuit."

While Catherine was picking up the basket, Isaac quickly looked up into Mary's eyes and just as suddenly looked away. Mary wondered what had just transpired between them. "Kate, just leave the basket with Mr. Logan and go quick and get Mr. Taylor a gourd of water."

Newt Taylor decided the man sitting across from him was "not all there." He also decided this was the opportune time to set his robbery in motion. Sliding his hand toward his rifle's trigger housing, he said to Mary in an even no-nonsense tone, "Go git me yore money! I'm keeping yore man covered, and if you want him to be alive for another day, you'll do as I say and no funny business either. Where'd that little girl get off to?"

"She's gone to get you a gourd in the barn so she can get you a drink of water," said Mary hoping that Catherine would take a long time to find the gourd. Mary was thinking, *I've got to find a way out of this. He thinks Mr. Logan is my husband. Maybe I can use that somehow.*

"Pass me that basket!" demanded Newt while looking at Isaac. "Nawww, on second thought, just hand me one of them biscuits. Now, you best git into yore cabin and git me some money! Like I said, no funny business either!"

Isaac reached into the basket for a biscuit and barely felt the pistol. He knew some type of weapon was in there since he saw Mary's earlier reaction when Catherine brought the basket to her. His fingers circled around the butt of the pistol.

Samuel, Moses, Daniel, Carl, and Frank stopped walking when they saw the gathering around the fire in front of Samuel's cabin. Moses said, "Something just ain't right over there, Samuel. I don't recognize them two guys."

"You're right, Mode. Wonder if they're the ones who killed those two and burned their cabin," said a worried Samuel.

"Hey, boys, let's spread out and walk up on 'em one at a time," said Frank.

"Good idea, Frank. Nothing like five surprises!" said Carl. They all drifted apart. Samuel started walking toward his cabin.

"Pa!" yelled Catherine when she saw her father. She started running toward him as fast as her legs would carry her. Mary felt a flood of relief when she saw Samuel. Samuel saw one man holding a rifle at a threatening position toward Mary. His blue eyes became steely as he readied himself for any unexpected or suspicious movements. He thought of nothing except to protect his family.

Newt turned to see what was happening and saw Samuel walking toward them with a purpose-filled stride. He got up, turned toward Samuel, and started raising his rifle. The click of a trigger being pulled back in firing position followed by a "don't even think about it," purpose-filled voice from Isaac stopped him with a cold shiver running through his mind.

Isaac said in an even-toned voice, "Don't turn around! Raise your rifle above your head with both hands and hold them there! I don't know if this pistol has a hair trigger or not! You even breathe deep and I'll blow your spine outta your back!" Newt Taylor did as he was told.

Samuel heard Catherine, saw the actions at the fire pit and slowed his pace while readying his rifle and with worried thought, *What in the world is goin' on here? Where are the rest of my children?* He saw Moses walking up to the gathering from another direction and then saw Daniel coming out of the woods further along the wood line.

While running toward her pa, Catherine exclaimed, "Ohhh, Pa! I'm glad you are…" She stopped running and talking when Samuel, by small side-to-side movement of his hand, signaled her to stop.

"It's good to see you, Kate. Stay away from me and those men," Samuel said in a level commanding voice as he held his eyes on the scene around the fire pit.

Mary saw the other men coming up to the fire from different sides. Newt and Isaac were also aware that five men were now assembled around them. The five men held very stern looks. Mary was so relieved to the point of an overwhelming weakness in her legs. She, still holding William, sat down on the chopping block and called for Catherine to come to her.

In a slow determined voice, Samuel said to the man holding the pistol aimed at the man holding his rifle over his head, "Mind telling me what's going on here?"

Newt, realizing this might mean a way out of his current predicament, said, "This feller is threatening to kill me!"

Mary immediately said, "Not true, Samuel! That man was going to rob us and it looked like he was going to take a shot at you when Mr. Logan stopped him."

"Where's Sam, Susan, and the others?" Samuel said to Mary as he kept his eyes on Newt Taylor.

Mary said, as she looked down the path leading to the woods, "They're over at your pa's. They should be getting back here soon."

Samuel momentarily took his eyes off of Newt when he looked at Mary as she started speaking to him. Even though it was a slight chance at best, Newt figured that a slight chance was better than none at all as he quickly sidestepped to his left and started bringing his rifle down into firing position intent on aiming it at Samuel's chest. He thought, *I'll get the drop on this feller and make 'em let me go.* Moses's unthinking immediate reaction started the swinging of his rifle toward Newt's head. Newt's finger was finding its way to his rifle's trigger when he felt the full force of Moses's rifle butt behind his ear, and a split second later, Isaac Logan pulled the pistol's trigger. Newt staggered back two steps while his world became of mass of splitting stars spiraling into a darkening void. Everyone held their position as they watched the light in his eyes slowly dim.

In a calm voice belying his inner feelings, Samuel said, "Anything you want to ask your Maker forgiveness for before you die?"

With a halting pain-filled voice, Newt Taylor said, "I just… needed a…little bit of money. I…didn't…want to…hurt them… two of my buddies…" He slowly let go of his rifle and fell to the ground.

After a long silence where all were looking at the fallen man, Samuel looked over at Isaac and Moses and said in a low voice, "Thanks for what you did. I owe ya." He then looked at the others and saw their looks of wondering how a man's life was so suddenly ended. Nothing they could have done would have prepared them for the development they had just witnessed.

Moses said in a slow manner while giving an uncomprehending stare at the body of Newt Taylor, "We better get the sheriff here so he can make the right reports. And just who are you?" while pointing his finger at Isaac Logan and, at the same time, slowly thought, *I've just killed a man. What was I thinking?*

Issac put the pistol on the ground and stood up. "I just happened to be here when that feller came up figuring on robbing the missus' here. That little girl sure helped. Smart one she is. And my name is Isaac Logan." On saying his name, he pulled off his soiled hat.

In a disbelieving trailing off voice, Carl said, "Good gosh almighty! What happened to you? You...you've been scalped!" He couldn't believe what his eyes were telling him.

The other men were equally astounded at the sight. Frank said in a low voice while slowly shaking his head, "I've heard my mother's uncles talk about men living after they were scalped. I never thought I would ever see one."

Daniel did not take his eyes off of Isaac's exposed skull and said, "Mind telling us how it happened and who did it?" while thinking, *How in the world does someone live through that?*

Isaac said, "Won't mind a bit tellin' y'all. Already told some of it to the lady. But can I have some more of that biscuit. I'm awful hungry." He looked at the man he had just shot and briefly shook his head thinking, *Why me O' Lord...why me?*

Mary became very aware of the possible negative impact of seeing a man killed would have on Catherine's mind. She said, "Kate, come with me and help me find something."

Catherine did as she was told and followed her mother into the cabin. Mary said, "Let's find a big enough blanket to cover that poor man out there. It isn't right to not cover him up."

"He was a bad man, wasn't he, Momma? He was going to hurt us, wasn't he?" said Catherine with a voice filled with fear and wonderment.

"Yes, he was, and if it hadn't been for Mr. Logan and Uncle Mode, we just might be the ones on the ground. I hope you will not think bad about what has happened. There are some people who just don't know how to follow the rules and live peacefully with other people," said Mary while holding Catherine in her arms. "Do you want to talk about this some more?" as she looked at that special innocence that can only be held by a six-year-old girl. *I pray that she will understand this one day. This is too much for my daughter to have to figure out at her early age.*

Catherine said, "No ma'am, I want to see Pa and then go see Betsy. She might need me just now. Maybe the gun noise scared her."

Catherine and her mother walked out of the cabin holding a blanket. Mary gave it to Samuel who covered the fallen man's body.

Catherine, after witnessing all that had gone on, walked up to Isaac, grasped his big soiled hand in her little hand and said, "Thanks for saving my pa." And in a matter-of-fact tone, she said, "That man is dead, isn't he?"

Samuel glanced at Mary and both recognized they had to help Catherine understand death and why it happened the way it had today. Samuel kneeled down so he could look into Catherine's inquiring eyes and after a moment said, "Catherine, you know what it is when someone dies, don't you? She shook her head up and down and looked over at Newt's body and said, "He was a bad person, wasn't he?"

"Yes, he was and if it had not been for Mr. Logan and Uncle Moses here then you and Mom might have been hurt by him," said Samuel.

Catherine turned to Isaac and said in a solemn voice while still holding his hand, "Thank you for keeping my mom and me alive."

Isaac slowly took his hand from hers and knelt down to her saying, "You are welcome. I hope you don't feel bad about me."

A small smile broke out on Catherine's face and said, "You will always be my friend."

Isaac looked over at Samuel and then to Mary and back to Catherine and smiled as he said, "You are a bonnie lass, aren't you?"

Samuel looked at Mary with a quizzical look and Catherine looked at her mom and said in a quavering voice, "What did he call me?" She thought Mr. Logan was trying to make fun of her or make her feel bad about the events that happened today.

Isaac immediately recognized Catherine's hurt feelings and said, "No, no, Miss Catherine, you must understand that in my country across the ocean a bonnie lass is known as a beautiful and smart girl. And that you are on both counts."

Through eyes that were just starting to mist up, Catherine looked at her mom and said, "Is that true, Momma?"

Daniel said, "Yes, it's true, Catherine. I have heard the people from Scotland say that about their lady folks. I think Mr. Logan really likes you."

Samuel then held out his arms for Catherine who ran into them saying, "Ohhh Papa, Mr. Logan thinks I am beautiful."

"He is right, Catherine. And I thank our Maker that he has seen fit to let us have you," said a smiling Samuel. He looked into Mary's eyes and saw a loving warmth for her family.

"Uncle Mode, what do you think about all this?" said Samuel.

Moses smiled as he looked at Catherine and said, "Well, my little niece, I guess we will know you by three names now—Catherine, Kate, and now Bonnie Kate. You know what? I think that name fits you very well."

Samuel stood up and said, "Well, Mr. Logan, it looks like you have made quite a knowing on me and my family today. I am very glad you came by when you did." He held out his hand to Isaac. While shaking his hand he said, "What can we help you with?"

Everyone, except Catherine, recognized the talk about Bonnie Kate was a way to relieve the tension of killing a man. Stark reality manifested itself when Frank said, "We had better get all this over to Sheriff Clark."

"Why waste time with him? said Carl. "Let's just bury him, say a few words over him and let it be. No one knows him anyhow."

Samuel, aware that Catherine was hearing the words, said, "We must be mindful of the laws. Never know when somebody might come looking for this guy and find out what happened here today."

Everyone shook their heads signifying approval. Daniel said, "I've got to be getting on my way to Rebecca and the boys. I'll drop by Clark's place and let him know to come out here."

"Thanks, Dan'l. I appreciate that. Sure wish you didn't have to leave us especially under these circumstances." said Samuel.

"Hey, boys, no problem. It could've been a lot worse and we need to be thankful for that, if nothing else. I'll bring Rebecca and the boys back for some of Mary's bacon, biscuits, and coffee real soon. In fact, I just might have me another boy or my first girl when I get home," said Daniel as he picked up his rifle and pack and started toward his home.

Catherine said as she waved her hand, "Bye now, Mr. Boone."

Daniel came back and picked Catherine up in his arms, gave her a squeeze and said, "Bye now yourself, Bonnie Kate." He put her down and walked down the wagon road that followed a small creek and disappeared out of sight at the wood line. *Having a little girl would be a good thing*, he thought.

Mode said, "Dan'l is quite the man, isn't he? Bet Rebecca keeps him at home this time."

The others chuckled at Mode's comment with Frank saying, "That man is always wanting to find out what is happening on the other side of the next hill. Some of us can settle down, others can't. I think Dan'l is a can't."

Samuel turned to Mary and said, "You have been through a lot today. Why don't you rest and me and the boys will cook up a mess of supper."

He couldn't quite believe his ears when he heard Mary say, "I think I will just let you do that. C'mon, Catherine, let's take a much earned nap."

Mode looked at Samuel and with a small laugh said, "Whatcha going to do now, brother?"

Frank said to Carl, "Help me move this body outta here. We'll wait 'til tomorrow for the sheriff. We'll have bury him tomorrow regardless."

Mary said, "Let's wait for Grandpa and get his idea on what to do. He and the others should be getting here soon."

Everyone shook their heads in agreement thinking that any postponement of a decision, even for a short period of time, was the easiest way out of the present situation.

Daniel saw the wagon topping a long sloping hill and recognized the driver as young Samuel Jr., holding the reins while seated beside him was Susan and Uriah. Their grandfather was sitting on some bags of corn with Adam, who was named after him. Daniel waited by the side of the road for the wagon when Sam recognized him and with a hearty wave said, "Hi, Mr. Boone!"

"Hello, Sam. And another 'Hi' to you, Susan, and to you, Uriah," said Daniel as he tipped his hat.

"Gonna say something to me? Or am I just like one of these sacks?" joked their grandfather, Adam Sherrill, while holding out his hand to Daniel. "Might want to say something to young Adam here, too."

After shaking Adam's hand, Daniel told them about what happened back at Samuel's place and that everyone was all right except Newt Taylor.

Adam slowly shook his head full of gray hair from side to side while looking at nothing in particular in the forest and said in a slow, thought-filled manner, "Too many people coming in here and some of them are just plain bad. Things were different back in '47." He thought about the time he had gotten his first land grant on the Catawba River. "What's a body to do, Daniel?"

"Don't rightly know, Adam. Sure does make one want to find a place to settle down where no one can bother him," said Daniel.

"Well, Dan'l, that might be easier said than done. But in the meantime, we best be getting on to Samuel's place and see if there is anything we can do to help what's going on there. Wish we had more time to talk about things. Maybe you and Rebecca and the children can drop over to our place soon. Elizabeth would really like to see y'all. One more thing, how ya getting back to your place this time?" asked Adam.

Daniel said, "I'm taking your path, you know everybody's been calling it Sherrill's Path these days. Just look what you've done and it sure makes it easier for me to get over to the Yadkin and home."

Adam said in a musing way, "Who woulda thought it? Using that path some animals made and then named it for me. Does beat all, doesn't it? But it is close to the way I first came into this land. Thank goodness for the elk and deer trails, right, Dan'l?"

As he slapped his hand on the horse's rump Daniel said, "One might say that Mr. Sherrill. Bye to both you Adam boys." He waved his hand as he watched the wagon leave then he turned to continue his walk to his home. *Hmmm, I just might have to go back for another look into that land. If that man Walker can do it, so can I.*

Samuel Jr. stopped the wagon at the barn's entrance and helped his brothers and sister down. "Be sure and curry down the horse, Sam. Must be mindful of taking care of our animals. We take care of them and they take care of us and that makes it good for all of us…wouldn't you say?" said his grandfather in a musing sort of way.

After Adam was quickly told about the events of the last two days, he looked over at the prone body of Newt Taylor and said,

"Did anyone search his pockets to see if he has any kinfolk so we can let them know what happened?"

The others looked at each other with a "why didn't we think of that" look and Moses said in an apologetic manner, "No, sir, we didn't think about that."

Adam walked over to the body, bent down, placed his fingers on the corner of the blanket and slowly pulled it back. He looked at Newt's face trying to determine if he had ever seen him somewhere else. The others saw Adam's head snap back while dropping the blanket. Newt Taylor slowly opened his eyes and focused directly into Adam's widening almost fear-filled eyes. While his arms and hands remained in their startled position, Adam said in a low even tone, "Boys, get some water for this man."

The men rushed up to gather around Newt not believing what they were seeing. A man they thought was dead was living. Newt Taylor barely mouthed the word "water" while slowly raising one hand to his chest.

Adam said to no one in particular, "I said someone get some water! Do it now!"

"Here's some water, Grandpa," said the small level voice of Catherine standing between Sam Jr. and Susan. No one had seen the children join the group assembled around Newt.

Adam knelt down and put his hand behind Newt's head, tilting it so he could drink from the gourd. Newt then raised his hand to his head feeling the bloody knot where Moses had hit him. He did not say anything and continued to stare at Adam as he stood up and looked at the others saying, "Guess Mode knocked him senseless. Didn't I hear someone say he was shot?"

Moses pointed to Isaac and said, "Yes, sir, Isaac shot him just about the time I hit him."

Isaac said, "That's right! But it sure didn't kill him," while thinking *Thank you Lord, for keeping this man alive.* I've been having a tough time thinking about shooting a man in the back.

Carl said, "Shouldn't we look for a ball in him? Might need patching up."

Mary walked over and looked into Newt's eyes and saw a meanness of character that made her say, "He is a smart one, he is. Trying to make us think he is not all there. I say that if he has a ball in him then let him say so. I just soon let him lie here until the sheriff gets here. Just don't turn you back on him."

Samuel looked at his wife, pursed his lips in a thoughtful manner while barely nodding his head up and down, "She's right. Good thinking, Mary. This man is not to be trusted. Thanks again, Mode, for popping him. No telling what would have happened around here if you hadn't done it."

"Let's keep a guard over him until the sheriff gets here. I'll take first watch. Two hours apiece oughta do it. What do y'all think?" said Frank.

Mode said, "Sounds good to me. Maybe he will want to sit up or something. Can't stay on the ground for too long I wouldn't think."

4

At the same time of the events unfolding at Samuel Sherrill's home, fifteen-year-old Patrick Ferguson was reading a manual on military tactics while sitting on a stone bench in his mother's flower garden at their Edinburgh, Scotland home. His father, Lord James Pitfor, entered through the gate to his home and saw Patrick and decided to resume his talk a couple of days ago with his son about his future.

"Hello Patrick, my son. What be you reading?" asked James.

Patrick said, "Just reading some points about military tactics on battlefield maneuvers. Looks as if I shall be getting more of this training. I have been told I will be posted somewhere in Germany."

"Ohhh! That's too bad," said his father with a wistful tight-lipped look. "I was hoping you would be able to stay somewhere in England until you got a little older."

"Do not worry so much, Father. I will be safe. After all, we have the best trained and equipped army in the world, and I don't think anyone in their right mind would try to enter into combat with us," said a confident-sounding Patrick.

In a deliberate pensive manner, James said, "That's just the thing that greatly concerns me. I'm hearing all sorts of problems are heating up things in America. Those people could cause a lot of problems for the King's forces. and I fear our new King George isn't the leader we need at this time."

With a somewhat indignant tone, Patrick said, "Father...I can't believe you are thinking those thoughts, much less saying them! Aren't you loyal to the crown?"

"Yes, my son, I am. But I am also thinking of the adverse consequences that can result from our actions. But never fear, your ears are the only ones to hear my statements. Feeling free to talk about our leaders is one luxury we don't have, and we may learn too late that this freedom means a lot to the King's subjects over there," said an even more pensive James. "Well, enough of this, my son, let's see what your mother has prepared for our dinner." He put his arm around Patrick's shoulders and walked with him to their two story limestone-faced home. "Aren't mother's roses looking pretty? She puts a lot of time and effort into these plants," said James as he cut one, put it to his nose, inhaled deeply of its fragrant aroma and gave a brief smile as they resumed their walk to the house. Patrick was somehow struck with a chord of melancholy while watching his father. *Why do I feel this way?*

Samuel turned to Isaac saying, "Anything we can do to help you along with your plans? I want to make sure you feel that you are welcome to stay here, but I can see why you want to get back to your home."

"Yeah, I tell ya I want to get back home and try to get my life back together. I'm not sure how my family is going to take the way I look now," Isaac said as he slowly felt his exposed skull. "I'll start in the morning."

Samuel said, "I would be thanking ya for staying until the sheriff gets here. Might help set in his mind what to do with that sneaking snake of a man," He nodded his head with a disgustful look toward Newt.

Isaac said, "That's a good idea. I'll do it. The extra rest might be good for me."

Newt Taylor thought, *I'll just lay here until my chance comes along. I'm gonna git outta here!*

The next morning found Catherine feeding her horse when she saw Sheriff Andy Clark riding a buckboard up the road.

After much discussion about yesterday's events, the Sheriff walked over to Newt and bent down to look into his eyes and thought, *Crafty ol' fox, ain't he.* He reached down with his hand to Newt and said in a gruff commanding tone, "Gimme your hand!"

Newt automatically extended his hand and immediately wished he hadn't. Clark took it and with a hard yank pulled Newt to his feet. "Thought ya would get one on me, eh?" said the Sheriff as he started tying Newt's hands behind his back. He then gave Newt a push making him fall to the ground and while holding his feet together started wrapping a rope around them.

Sure ain't gonna get out of this fix, thought Newt.

Sheriff Clark said, "Hey, Samuel, help me lift this no count on to the back of my buckboard."

Samuel said, "Andy, something Taylor said has been running around in the back of my mind. Just after Mode hit him, he said something about 'two buddies' and then fell to the ground."

"I'll keep that in mind when we put him on trial," said Andy.

"Thanks much. Let us know how the trial goes," said Samuel.

"Sure will. Ohhh, by the way, have y'all heard about the new King of England? George the 3rd. Just heard about it myself a few days ago," said Andy.

Samuel said, "That's the first I've heard of it. Hope he is better than his pa." At the same time, thinking *Maybe this one will have more sense about us over here.*

The sheriff, who owed his job to the King's agents, gave Samuel a hard look and said, "God save the king, wouldn't you say, Samuel?"

"Yeah, Andy. God save us all," said Samuel while looking into the sheriff's eyes with an unwavering penetrating "don't mess with me" stare.

They watched as the sheriff drove out of sight. Samuel said, "Glad to get rid of that problem, both of them. Guess one or more of us will have to go to the trial next week."

Mode said, "He'll be found guilty by the jury and then hung by the end of next week is my guess. Swift justice for sure. Got a new king, eh? Wonder what that means for us?" He then turned to Isaac and said, "Mind telling us about what went on at that fort?"

Isaac said in a quiet voice accompanied with a far-away look, "Don't mind tellin' y'all what happened." Then he looked around at Catherine and the rest of the children and said, "Not sure the young'uns need to hear it though."

Mary said, "We can't keep them ignorant of the facts of living in today's world, especially around here. Things are starting to grow as more and more people start coming in here, and I just know the Indians aren't going to give up their lands without a fight. Never have, never will. Wars for land are a constant thing and it sickens me to think of the killing always going on for some cause having to do with land. My children need to know what is going on, be part of getting them schooled. Part of getting them prepared for an ever changing life."

Samuel said, "She's right...as usual. So, Mr. Logan, if you're a mind, tell us what went on over there."

Isaac sat down and while absently focusing on a lichen-covered rock a few feet in front on him said in a slow-halting manner, "I...want to forget what happened; but, I'll tell y'all... then I'm gonna try to forget it. Even though I got this constant reminder," as he ran his fingers across his exposed skull.

The others sat down around Isaac and Mary said, "Just take your time and if you don't want to tell it then don't."

Isaac took his time in looking at each person and then in a very earnest manner said, "I'm beholden to you for that. Well, here goes. Like I said earlier, I'm from over around the Waxhaws area. Been a smithy all my life and was asked to help out at the fort at Chota by a man that had been asked by Captain Demere to find somebody like me to go with them. That was over a year or so ago."

Samuel said, "You gotta be kidding me! There really is a fort over there and in the main Cherokee village? How many of us are there? Why in the world did the Cherokees allow such a thing? They're not too happy with us settlers anyway. And who is Captain Demere?"

"Maybe you have heard of their Chief Attacullaculla. You know, he's a smart man. He's even been to see ol' King George. At any rate, he got our Governor Lyttleton, ya know, in South Carolina, to agree to build a better fort than what they had. Seems some guys from Virginia built a small one which didn't please the chief at all. And before you ask, I don't know much of anything about those guys from Virginia," said Isaac.

Samuel Jr. said, "Isaac, why build a fort for the Cherokees? Nothing over there except them, right?"

"A lot of people, even me at one time, think that's right, but y'all know the French and English are at each other's throats, and the French have gotten some of the northern tribes to side with them. Seems like they're getting closer and closer to the Cherokee land and that's what made Attacullaculla nervous and he thought a fort was a good idea."

Moses said as he looked around the group, "Guess he feels like he is getting hemmed in from all sides. People like us just starting to go across those mountains and the French coming at 'em from the north. Guess if I was in his shoes, I'd be worried about what is going to happen to me and my people."

Carl said, "Yep, and it seems like nobody wants to let on they know about us Melungeons. We've earned the right to live where we are and the Cherokees, Shawnees, and Yuchis have always gotten along with us, as far as I know about."

"C'mon, guys, let Isaac finish his story," said Mary. She felt her baby move and thought, *Won't be long now. I best be getting things ready for his, or her, arrival into our family.*

Isaac, realizing he needed to finish his story, nodded his head in agreement to Mary and said, "Well, 'bout a year ago the killing of Cherokees by the whites was really getting out of hand. Weren't nothing being done about it to satisfy the chief's demand to stop, ain't no law folks over there anyway. So they figured on getting back at us since we were white. That made us more of their enemy, I reckon. At any rate, around the first of this year, they jumped us and took over the fort. Then they made a lot of us, including Capt. Demere, leave the fort taking us to one of their places. I can't believe what happened next and I don't wanna tell it neither." He turned and stared at the fires smoldering embers and everyone could tell he was totally alone with his thoughts.

The others slowly looked around at each other with questioning looks and turned up hands of "what's next?" Mary walked over to Isaac and laid a hand on his shoulder and gently said, "Never you mind now, if you don't want to tell us then so be it. It musta been hard on you."

Isaac looked up at Mary. She saw his trembling tight lips and tears in his eyes. He started crying in uncontrollable sobs and shouted between sobs, "They…they scalped him! Made him dance! Then they—o dear Lord—they cut off his arms and then his legs! It was horrible! I can't forget it! And I couldn't even help him. I thought I was gonna be next!" He put his face into his hands and continued his heaving sobs.

Everyone sat in stunned silence, absorbing what they had just heard. Thoughts of, *Did I hear what I thought I heard? Cutting up a living man! What in the world is going on? Are they all crazy? Is there no hope of getting along with them?* smashed into their unbelieving minds.

Puzzled expressions, wrinkled brow concerns and tight lips were displayed on each other's faces. After a few more moments, Moses said, "Are you serious? Cut off whose arms and legs?"

Isaac looked at Moses and shouted through his anguish, "Captain Demere, that's who! They made him dance around even after they scalped him. The more they made him do things, the more they seemed to get caught up in their wanting to hurt him. Cut his arm off with knives and hatchets. Blood was everywhere and after that…" Once again he fell into shoulder heaving sobs.

Mary's wide-eyed response to the story was followed by her saying, "I think we have heard quite enough. Let's let Isaac gather himself and if he wants to complete the story, then so be it."

Samuel looked at each of his children whose open mouths and fear-filled eyes were startlingly evident. *Might have been a bad idea to let them hear this. But who would've thought such a thing would be told.*

"I was one of the lucky ones they took back to the fort. We sealed it up as best we could and then they came back," said Isaac.

"How in the world did you get out?" said Carl.

Isaac said, "We were pretty near starved and they knew it. So they made a deal with our leaders and we were allowed to leave. We could barely walk 'cause we were so weak. Some thought they heard we were being taken to that land of peace in the middle of the Hogohegee river."

Moses said, "Yeah, I remember Pa talking about that land. He and Santee were over there. Right, Carl?"

"Yep, that's right. Been there myself on some hunts. But why didn't you stay with the group going to the Hogohegee which, by the way, is now called the Holston River. Seems a guy named James Holston living up that river decided to take it as far as he could. Got to a big river that headed south, I think," said Carl.

Isaac said, "I figured I best escape the quickest I could 'cause I was afraid they were going to cut me up. One early morning before dawn, I sneaked off and that's when I started for home and soon after I got jumped by one of them Cherokees that had been tracking me. Like I said, he scalped me and left me for dead. And now I'm here. You wouldn't believe the mountains and valleys I've crossed to get this far, been eating roots, nuts and some berries, and I'm grateful for y'all putting up with me." After few silent moments, he said, "I think I best be getting on home tomorrow." He lowered his eyes to the fire and seemed to drift back into his "other place."

Mary said as she got up and looked around at the others, "I think we need to leave Isaac to his own thoughts. He has been through enough to make anyone lose their wanting to exist."

Later that evening, Moses said to his father, Adam, "I've been thinking that I want to go with Isaac to his home to see some new territory. And besides, he still needs help."

"I agree he needs help, but I think he can find his way back home and his family would know what is best for him. Anyway, it seems you have enough to do around the farm. And you're at the age you need to start thinking of settling down," said Adam.

"C'mon, Pa," said Moses with a small smile building across his face. "I'll settle down one of these days. Who knows, I might meet the right girl on my trip. That, plus the fact, I still think Isaac needs someone to help him on his way."

Adam reluctantly said, "You got a point, son. But give it some more thought, and if you are still wanting to help him, then I'll help you on your way."

At the next morning's first light, Moses and Isaac were standing by the barn, getting ready to leave when Samuel said, "Why don't y'all take Betsy. You can ride double until you get to William's place. He'll let you borrow one of his horses to get on home."

"Good idea, Samuel," said Moses. "But what about Catherine seeing Betsy leave? And that means I'll have to lead William's horse back."

"Then why can't I go and ride Uncle William's horse?" asked Samuel Jr. who had just walked up to the group at the barn.

All three men turned to Samuel Jr. with looks of "somewhat on the young side," but it might work when Moses said, "Not a bad idea, brother. Why not let him go with us? It's about time he was starting to see what's around here anyway."

Samuel looked at his firstborn son and saw that he was eager to go on the trip. He thought, *Yeah, I guess Mode's right. Time for Samuel to learn some more about things.* Then he looked his son in the eyes and saw a determined, unafraid look in them. He clasped his hand on his son's shoulder and said, "All right, my son, but you got to tell your mother where you are going and about how long you will be gone."

"Aww, Pa, do I have to?" said Samuel Jr. with a look of doubt on his face. He knew it wasn't going to be easy to get his mother's blessing on this idea.

"Yes. Now get going and get your things for the trip. Time's wasting!" said Samuel. Samuel Jr. took off in a run to the cabin thinking all the way Mom's not going to like this.

Moses said with a slight turned up grin, "Got out of telling Mary, eh? Good move brother, I hope it works 'cause it'll be good to have him along on the trip."

Isaac said, "Seems to me y'all are going to a lot of trouble just to help me get home."

"No problem, Isaac. It'll be a learning experience for young Samuel and I know how Mode is good at camping in the woods. I think it is a good idea," said Samuel. "And I'll tell Catherine that Betsy will be helping her new friend and uncle, so all will be right with her."

"Well, it's not too far to the Waxhaws anyway and we just might get some more meat for curing this fall," said Moses.

Samuel said, "That would be good. And while you are away, see if you can find some more salt. We're getting a little low on it."

Samuel Jr. ran up to the group and said, "Mom says it is all right for me to go with Uncle Mode and Mr. Taylor! Wow! And, Pa, she wants to see you. In fact, here she comes now."

"Thought that was pretty smart, didn't you?" asked Mary with a stern gaze. "Sending a boy to do a man's job. You oughta be ashamed."

Samuel, with a wide-eyed feigned innocence looked into his wife's eyes, "Never thought such a thing. And, anyway, he's got to learn how to handle situations like trying to convince someone of his point of view. Wouldn't you say that is a good thing?"

Mary, with an "I give up" look, said, "You beat all, Samuel Sherrill." She turned back toward their cabin. "I know he has to grow up, but why so fast worries me a lot. And, one other thing, why is it y'all can't build a boat and float that river out there to where you're going?"

Samuel, Moses and Isaac looked at each other and each could tell they were thinking the same thing, *That's a good idea. Why didn't I think of that a long time ago.* "Well, hang fire, why not?" exclaimed Moses, "Let's get to it."

"Anybody around here know 'bout boat building?" asked Samuel. After a moment or two, the others shook their heads and Moses said, "You got a point brother. Guess we best be getting on our way. Still a good idea though."

"I know some guys who built a raft and floated down the river. I'll get them to talk with us when we get home," said Isaac.

After stopping at William's cabin, Moses, Samuel Jr., and Isaac were on their way to Isaac's home in the Waxhaw region of South Carolina.

5

"What's bothering you, Samuel? Something's been eating at you ever since you got back from your hunt three weeks ago. I'm thinking you're worried about our living here because of what happened with Taylor and it could happen again," Mary said while looking intently into her husband's eyes over their breakfast table.

"You always have a way of peering into my inner most thoughts," said Samuel with a small smile coupled with a look of "you're right, I do have a problem" in his eyes as he looked at his wife. "Truth be known, I'm getting the 'Boone itch' to cross the mountains and take a look at what is going on over there. There could be a lot of good stuff for us over there and I've got to find out about it."

"Mind telling me what kind of opportunities are over there that we don't have here?" said Mary with a slight wave of her hand and a small look of exasperation.

"How can I tell you that when I haven't even seen it? Pa's been there and he talks about the broad valleys with fertile ground next to some nice rivers and creeks. Dan'l tells me the hunting over there is something you wouldn't believe. Got all sorts of game for a family's table," said Samuel. "And I must admit, I would love to have some buffalo meat in our smokehouse. Carl and Dan'l tell me they are over there in many numbers."

"Well, mercy me, you and your brothers always talking about having to carry a woods dressed deer or elk and how heavy it gets in bringing it home. Now, what about these buffalo? You gonna carry that much meat back across these mountains? I don't think so," Sarah said with the look of feigned sorrow as she slowly moved her head from side to side.

Mary, who after marrying Samuel, found out that even though most of the Sherrills were a clannish lot some of them had the need to explore and move on to new places. *Why is he so set about that land? I think I'll talk to Rebecca to see how she handles Daniel's exploring ways.* "Well, my husband, it looks like you have almost made up your mind about over there. When you going? And, do you have any idea of how to get over there?"

"Most likely go after spring planting. Got to think about the way to get over there some more. I'll talk with Dan'l and get his map and study on it. And anyway, the snow will be in the mountains soon and I sure don't want to be there when that is going on," Samuel said as he got up from the table. "Gotta go check the corn mash. Might be getting close enough to run the still."

Mary said, "Yeah, I'm getting low on the stuff to clean the children's scrapes and such. And you and your buddies certainly get to do a lot of talking when you first make it. I just don't see how y'all can swallow that mess! And it seems like y'all do a lot of talking about the English, making all sorts of laws for us but nothing ever changes!"

Samuel said with a hard-eyed squint, "And it continues to get worse for us. One of these days, something good is going to happen for us about our own land. I'm here to tell you now that I'll be there when it happens! I want it better for all of us and especially our young'uns and especially for Susan and Catherine. Women folk need lots more help than the men,"

Susan and Catherine were playing on the second story floor and could hear things they weren't supposed to hear. Susan said in a loud whisper, "Catherine, you hear that? Pa wants us to be better than Samuel and our other brothers!"

Catherine looked up at her sister and matter-of-factly said as she turned to put her doll into its bed, "I will be."

The next day was a special one in the family. Mary gave birth to George whose lusty cries were heard by a proud father and his daughters. Susan and Catherine were directed by their mom in how to help her and their new brother at this special moment of birth. Samuel said as he held his new son, "He will help us all build a new place in this land. I've got a feeling he will help this country be better than it is now."

Catherine looked at her new brother and thought about what Pa had just said, *I'm going to be helping out this land. Between both of us, we'll make things right.*

6

He sat looking at the fire. It was always a marvel to him how so much fire could be stored in a piece of wood. How did it get in there was something that ran through his mind from time to time. His camp was on a slight hill in the middle of a long fertile valley. A meandering clear, cold, smooth surfaced river divided the land between the two mountain chains like a silver necklace casually laid on the ground. The river has always provided excellent fishing and beaver trapping for his friends. His gaze slowly drifted from the river and crossed the forest containing trees that had been growing forever, or so it seemed to him. His favorite was the widespread chestnut tree that provided a constant source of wood and edible nuts. He slowly raised his head as his gaze wandered up increasing heights to finally rest on the top of one of the higher mountains. The sun was disappearing for the day and its dwindling light was gradually causing the colors of the valley to blend into varied hues of gray that were slowly giving way to the dark purple of night. His eyes took in everything, yet nothing. The tops of the mountains were still lit by the sun's fire. He followed the graceful effortless glide of a wehali whose white-tipped wings and head feathers stood out in the fading light as it searched the river surface for one last meal for the day. This magnificent bird was known as an eagle to the white man. The far-off call of an awiequa, an elk to the white man, added to the total experience and all that he saw and heard created in his mind a grand and glorious feeling. Yona lost himself in thought, *the*

Creator has made a great place for all of us. Why is it that the whites want to make it for themselves? Why can't this stay like this forever... this land...I would die to keep it.

His musings ceased when he saw his best friends, Tawadi and Yanisa, approach the camp. They acknowledged his wave with nodding heads. Not a word was spoken. Tawadi was carrying two rabbits that would be cooked for their dinner. He sat down on a log by the fire, leaned his rifle across it, and looked into the fire. Yanisa took the rabbits and with skillful cuts peeled the pelts away and said in a low murmur, "These will make good linings for our winter moccasins."

Yona said, "What's the matter with you two, especially you, Tawadi? No greeting or even a 'good to see you' from either of you. You're acting like someone stole your last horse."

With a heavy sigh and a gesture of upturned palms, Tawadi said in an even-toned, halting manner, "Elawii (Quite one) and Tsiya (Otter) are...dead." He continued to look into the fire.

Yona sharply raised his head and gave a disbelieving questioning look at Yanisa and with a small gesture conveyed the question of "What does he mean?" Yanisa looked into Yona's eyes and slowly shook his head in an "I don't want to talk about it" manner.

A few moments of silence enveloped the three friends. While he continued to gaze into the fire, Tawadi finally said, "They were killed by two white men who were hunting on our land! Elawii and Tsiya had captured some horses that were living free in the forest and had gone to get them and take back to our village."

"Isn't that the same thing that started the war at the fort called Loudoun?" said Yanisa.

"Yes, that was one of the reasons why Ostenaco attacked the fort. But you must tell me more about Elawii and Tsiya. When did this happen and where are the white men who killed them?" said Yona.

"Happened yesterday. No one found the white men...yet!" said Twadi.

"Then how do you know it was the white man who killed them? Could have been a Shawnee raiding party," Yona said with a rising voice while looking from one to the other.

With a quiet yet firm voice, Tawadi said, "Had to be the whites with their messy ways. Scalps were taken but not like we would have done. The Shawnee would have also taken scalps like we do. Most of their hair and skin were taken which is not what we do."

Yona's face became calm with only his narrowing eyes showing his anger. "I understand what you say and it makes sense," said Yona. "And what we have to do is find them and satisfy the need for our brothers to rest in peace."

Twadi and Yanisa looked at Yona and slowly nodded their heads in agreement. Yanisa said in a voice ending in a high-pitched screeching sound, "We avenge our brothers! Yeeee iiiii ahhhhhh!"

The warrior battle cry carried along the river and reverberated among the mountains. A black panther turned his head toward the sound, owls looked in the direction of the sound and blinked their eyes while other creatures of the night stopped their hunting to listen again for a sound that did not belong in the forest and might represent danger. A rabbit silently scurried out of its hiding place in the tall grass. Little did it realize it was about to become the panther's meal before the arrival of the sound. The forest became silent. Some late season crickets started hesitantly calling each other, and just as quickly as the silence happened, the forest came back to life.

"I'm tellin' ya now, Luke. I know you don't like it but we shouldn't taken their scalps," said Wilbur while checking the coffee brewing in a pot. The sun was low on the horizon signaling the end of a day for the two men. They were tired after a hurried walking through the forest. They wanted to put as much distance between them and the killing ground of the two Cherokees.

Luke said, "I'm not favorable of doing that. Makes me right sickish. Just ain't right anyway."

Wilbur, with a questioning look, said, "You got something against money?"

With a penetrating look into Wilbur's eyes, Luke said, "Naww, I don't have nothing against money, but I do when I have to scalp someone I just killed. Then I gotta cure it and take it to some place to collect bounty on it."

"Well, I'll be danged fer shure! Gittin' a mite almighty, ain't ya?" said Wilbur with a quick look to Luke. "Shoot, I jist mite take yore hair and sell it claiming it is some Cherokees."

"Aww, c'mon, Wilbur. How many red-haired Indians have you seen lately? I can see you now telling someone you got it off a Indian," said Luke. "I sometimes wonder if you do any planning at all."

"The only planning I'm doing is how to get some money. And I know that Jake Courtney up in Virginia territory pays for scalps. And from now on I'm gonna start gittin' some more," said Wilbur with a shaking of his head for emphasis.

Luke said, "Yeah, I've heard about him. I hear tell that when he gets enough of 'em he takes 'em to Pennsylvania and sells 'em for a hundred pounds each. I hear tell their governor started that pay-off idea. That's a lot of money and I hear white guys are getting their hair lifted by other whites because of it. Killer claims they's Indian scalps."

Yona was the first to smell the brewing coffee. They had gone to the place where their friends were killed and picked up the trail of Wilbur and Luke just as the dusky evening light was starting to slowly evolve into many variations of grey color.

"Yanisa, get as close to them as possible to keep them from running away. Twadi and I approach them with the sun at our backs," said Yona. He knew that the sun would tend to blind the enemy for a moment and that is all they would need to get ready for the kill.

The three friends started their skillful soundless advance, taking advantage of every tree trunk, bush, and tall grass. The smell of coffee was becoming stronger and then they started hearing their enemy talking to each other. They saw the two white men.

Yona looked at Twadi pointing to him and then pointed to the man who was getting ready to get up from his log seat. Twadi nodded his head and while raising his rifle sighted through the notched front sight and centered the muzzle sight on the heart of one of the men who killed his friends.

As Wilbur got up from his seat on a log and stretched his arms out from his side and said, "Well, ya see wot I'm talking 'bout? Might be easy money and I'm...ughhhhhh!" His eyes grew wide when he saw Tawadi aiming a rifle at him, his mouth dropped open in a soundless surprise. He heard the thud of the .47-caliber ball tearing into his throat severing his spinal cord, but he didn't hear the crack of the rifle. Wilbur was dead before he dropped to the ground.

Luke stared dumbfounded at Wilbur as he slumped to the ground and, just before regaining his senses, was dead when a ball from Yanisa's rifle shattered his brain.

Clouds, stained with varying depths of burnished gold were motionless in the low light of evening, witnessed the violent deaths of two men. The rifle shots caused the forest to become silent for a moment and then slowly crept back to life with its unique sounds. As the two men searched their victims and took their scalps, the color of the clouds slowly turned to a deepening bold red as if to match the blood spilling from the wounds of Luke and Wilbur.

Yona observed his friends holding up Wilber and Luke's scalps while giving a brief yell of victory. Yona thought, *I hope this doesn't keep growing to where we have a war that never ends with these new people.* He waved to the men and said, "You sure these were the ones who killed our brothers?"

Tawadia said with a wild eyed look, "Who cares? They are white men, aren't they? They are all our enemies who kill our people just because they think they can take what we have had forever!"

"Yes, and who asked them to come into our land? Things have been good for us for as long as anyone can remember. They don't know our language or our ways of doing things. They are bad people," said Yanisa in a quiet but firm manner. *I can't wait to show the red-haired scalp to the village.*

Yona said, "Let's leave this place. We've got to get some meat for the winter." He took one last look at the men on the ground, looked at his friends, and turned away to start toward their village. *What has been done here will be repeated many times. This is not good. I see more and more sadness in time before us.*

7

1761

The Presbyterian church sat just below the brow of a hill and was bordered by a clear cool creek on one side and a small well-kept graveyard on the opposite side. It was sturdily built of large chestnut logs sitting on a foundation of limestone rocks. The roof was covered in oak shake shingles held down by long poplar saplings which, in turn, were held tight by oak pins along its length. The early morning breeze carried the pleasant distinctive odor of the forest after an all night softly falling rain. The leaves on the oaks, chestnut, and poplars were waving at each other as each gentle zephyr brushed against them. A more peaceful setting was hard to imagine. The land was on part of the land grant obtained by Adam and Elizabeth Sherrill. The church served not only the members' need for a closeness and connection to God, it also served as a meeting house for what was becoming a community that some were calling Sherrill's Ford.

At any other time, this meeting would have been a Sherrill family reunion ending in a church service but the reunion had just happened three weeks ago. The reunion was held just before the crops had to be harvested and not too much tending the fields was needed during that time of year. This brief respite was filled with getting ready for, and holding, the two-day reunion.

However, some serious issues had to be addressed among the family members which was why Adam had asked his son's and their families to attend the meeting. No one was going to refuse the invitation as it was well known that the Sherrills were very much family-oriented and when one needed help, the rest pitched in to do what was needed to solve the problem. Help in the form of building a barn, making a dam for a pond, providing meat for the table, or clearing some land were a few of the things needed most by the families.

An occasional display of rifle marksmanship was held in the form of hitting specific targets. More often than not, targets were placed at varying distances where the one hitting the farthermost target was declared the winner. This was one of those days.

Adam and Elizabeth sat on the log bench with their backs resting on the church wall. "My word, Adam, just look at all we started," said Elizabeth as she let her gaze slowly travel over her children, their wives, and their grandchildren.

With a voice tinged with heartfelt feeling, Adam said, "It is truly a miracle that coming from our beginnings in Maryland, through Virginia and then to here, that we survived those times. It still scares me to think that I almost lost you the first time we came here," as he reached out to grasp her hand.

They were lost in reviewing times past when William walked up and said, "Before we get started on the meeting, we'd like to have a shooting match, Pa. Is that all right with you?"

Adam said, as he slowly stood up, stretching his six-foot frame, "Only if I am the last to shoot."

"This is by elimination," said William in a trailing off voice when he saw his father's no-nonsense tolerated look. "Well, I guess we can make an exception for the head of this outfit," he said with a slight crooked smile.

"Don't take too long for this match. We have to talk about some important things," said Adam.

Eight brothers ranging in age from thirty-seven to eighteen were being watched by their parents and a seven-year-old granddaughter, Catherine, who had left the cooking fires tended by the wives and other girls to be with her grandparents.

Aquilla and Uriah proved themselves the best shooters in today's match with each splitting a white oak shake shingle propped up on a tree stump 150 yards away.

"That's some mighty fine shooting," said Jacob. "I got to 125 yards and missed by just a whisker."

Moses said in an off-handed way, "Close is for horseshoes, ol' boy."

"I can take you at that one, too," said Jacob as he swung his arm around his brother's shoulders. "Just because you are the youngest boy doesn't mean you got the sharpest eyes. I can beat you any day guessing distances."

"Yeah, yeah, I know. But just don't get too uppity with me. I'm gonna beat you yet one day," Moses said with a lopsided grin and cutting his eyes to Jacob.

The shingle target had been placed 175 yards which was almost to the edge of the field. The fresh cut white oak shingle was clearly outlined yet was getting smaller and smaller due to the increasing distance.

"Quil, Uriah, show us some good ol' Sherrill shooting," said Isaac who had also missed the 125-yard target.

Another rifle shot. The smoke cleared. The shingle was still standing. "Step aside, my brother," said Uriah with a false show of bravado. "Let me show you how it's done."

Uriah's shot splintered the shingle. "Whoa, there, my son. That's some mighty good shooting. Now you're going to see why none of you growing up went hungry for lack of meat on the table," said Adam as he walked up to the firing line. He turned to Uriah and said, "See that dead pine just beyond the wood line, on the right?"

"Yes, sir, sure do," said Uriah while looking dubiously at his brothers.

"See the dead limb sticking out the farthermost?" questioned Adam.

"Yes sir, sure do," said Uriah and thought in a worried manner I sure hope he's not wanting us to shoot that limb off the tree. "That's gotta be two hundred yards!"

"You always were pretty good at figuring things," said Adam as he broke into an I-gotcha smile. "You first, my son." He backed up from the firing line. "Don't get nervous. Take your time," Adam said with a small smile of his face.

Another rifle shot. The smoke cleared. The limb was still on the tree. "Dagnab it all, that branch didn't move. Pa, show us how it's done," said Uriah as his face displayed an "I betcha can't do it" look. The others joined in giving encouragement to their father, but most of them felt there was no way he would be able to hit the limb.

Adam knelt down and worked his way into a prone position behind the log used to support the rifles. He lined up the sights on the barrel and concentrated on the tree limb. He took three deep breaths and held the last one, pulled back the hammer, and set trigger and while slowly tightening his finger on the release trigger, he just as slowly let out his held breath. The rifle fired. The smoke cleared. The limb was still on the tree. Silence ruled the moment as no one wanted to say anything that might hurt their father.

Adam casually got up and while dusting himself off looked at the limb said, "Give it a few more seconds."

All were looking at the limb as it slowly started slowly folding back and stopped as it rested against the tree's trunk. "Pine wood is always a little stringy, isn't it, boys?" said an amused Adam.

"Great day in the morning! That beats all! How you do that, Pa?" said an unbelieving Uriah.

"If you had grown up firing those old smooth bore muskets, you would really get to know all you could about these rifles with their grooved barrels. I couldn't be counted on hitting much of anything beyond fifty yards but with these rifles…Well, you can see for yourself," said Adam as he motioned with his head back toward the pine tree.

Isaac said, "I'm thankful those guys up in Pennsylvania started making these rifles. Doggone, if Pa couldn't hit anything at fifty yards, I doubt if I could hit anything at ten with a smooth bore."

"All right, boys, enough of this. We've got some serious things to decide on for us," said Adam.

"Grandpa," said Catherine as she walked up to the group. "Mind it I give that limb a try?" She tilted her head toward the targeted tree limb.

"C'mon, Kate, you're just starting to get used to a rifle. Hitting a target at long distances takes years of practice," said Uriah as he looked into his niece's eyes where he saw an unwavering confidence in them.

"What's the matter? Afraid your brother's seven-year-old daughter is gonna be the best shot? I won't tell anyone," Samuel said while looking at his daughter whose slight tilting of her head and smile meant everyone within the next six counties would know of her beating her uncles if she was successful.

"Ohh, all right, Kate. Here's my rifle. It's ready to go," said Moses.

"Thanks, Uncle Mode, but I want to use Pa's if he'll let me. I'm used to it," said Catherine.

Samuel handed his daughter his rifle and said, "Show 'em how its done Bonnie Kate."

Catherine stood beside the log and placed the rifle butt on the ground. She looked up to the tip of the barrel extending above her head. *Sure is awfully tall.* Samuel Jr. then stepped in beside Catherine saying, "There is no way I will allow my sister to do this! The recoil could hurt her bad! Besides, she isn't old enough!" The others were thinking all sorts of thoughts and mostly about her even being able to pull the rifle's trigger and finally Uriah said, "Samuel is right. And it looks like he is wanting to take Kate's place. Right, Samuel?" This was all that Samuel needed to help Catherine out of what could become a very embarrassing problem. But Catherine laid the rifle down across the log and then got into shooting position. Samuel exclaimed in a loud whisper, "No, no, not now. Wait. Not now!" She looked over the field and tops of the trees to see if any wind was blowing. A few breezes were moving through the treetops but nothing of major importance. She sighted down the barrel across the brass tipped front sight to the target and then turned her head to Samuel saying, "It looks like a shot you can do, brother," and then moved over to allow Samuel to get into position. As Samuel was getting into position, he looked at Catherine with a brief smile. He put the notched sight on the limb, pulled back the hammer and set trigger, placed his finger on it, let out half his breath and ever so slightly started a steady press on the firing trigger. The rifle fired as if it had a mind of its own. Pine bark flew off the base of the hanging limb and it dropped to the ground.

Catherine got up from her position, looked at her astonished uncles, smiled and said, "Thanks, brother, I knew everything was going to be all right. And Pa, thanks for the use of your rifle. I hope it belongs to me one of these days."

Isaac said, "Great shot, Samuel. I'm glad both of you are Sherrills," while giving each of their back a congratulatory slap.

Adam said, "Enough of that! We don't strike ladies like we do our men friends and brothers!"

All the brothers nodded their heads in agreement. Catherine was all smiles at being called a lady and her willingness to take a shot today would be talked about many years.

"All right, boys, enough of this. Let's get inside," said Adam.

The Sherrills sat on the wooden benches made by Adam and all seemed to be talking at once. The talking faded away when Adam slowly got up and walked to the podium and said, "Who will lead us in prayer?"

Isaac said, "Mode will do it," while looking at Moses who was showing a tight-lipped response to the offer.

Adam said, "Well, thank you, Isaac. Since you spoke up first, I would be obliged if you would please lead us in giving our thanks to God for allowing us to meet here today and giving us wisdom to make the right decisions."

Moses suppressed a smile knowing that Isaac was somewhat surprised at being called on for the prayer. Isaac stood up, glanced at Moses with an "I owe you one" look and opened his prayer. The more he prayed, the more he added to it.

Uriah punched Moses and whispered, "Will he ever quit?"

Isaac was warming up to the prayer and soon one after another would sneak a look in his direction in hopes he would soon finish. Finally, at a point where Isaac paused to catch his breath, Adam immediately said in a loud resounding voice, "Amen!" All the others followed suit. Isaac looked around the room with an "I'm not finished" look and was getting ready to start up again.

"Take your seat, Isaac. Good prayer. I'm sure the horses, cows, and pigs appreciate your mentioning them and feel blessed," said Adam. "Now, boys, let's get down to figuring out some ways to solve some problems. Some things I heard while over at Tom Polk's place a couple weeks ago really rile me up if they are true."

"What sort of stuff, Pa?" said Aquilla.

Adam said, while looking into Aquilla's eyes with a stern glare, "Seems that new king, Georgie boy, is studying on getting ready to issue another of those British laws for us! Can you beat all, that boy has never seen us except in some drawings. Remember what they tried to do with their Iron Act tax? Having someone across an ocean telling us what to do when he doesn't know squat about us is just not right!"

Jacob and his brothers could see that their father was getting ready to launch into a tirade about his feelings of being governed by a country half a world away and said, "Well, Pa, just what is this next law you heard about?" The others nodded agreement.

"Boys, you aren't going to believe this! But talk is that he is going to tell us that a line will be drawn across the tops of these mountains behind us and then telling us we can't cross it and, to add to his stupidity, he's gonna make those who settled over there come back on this side!" Adam exclaimed while giving a frustrated wave of his arms. "That, my sons, is beyond stupid and if I want to go back across those mountains, I will do it regardless of what that boy in London says! And now, since they ran the French out of lands up north plus capturing some country on the other side of the world, they are saying the sun never sets on their lands they call an empire! Hmmmphh, let 'em come over here and see their land for the first time and, most likely, their last!"

The others were looking around at each other not quite believing what they heard. *No way could anyone keep us from walking that land!* was a common thought among all of them.

William said, "Pa, I totally agree. But you gotta keep your feelings to yourself. If that English-loving Sheriff Clark or some of his buddies heard you talking like this they would throw you in jail."

"Good point! But what is said by this family in this church stays here! That, plus the fact, we are family and, I say again, what is said in here stays in here when we leave. You got that, boys?" exclaimed Adam as his eyes with their gleam of purpose penetrated into the eyes of each of his sons. There was no misunderstanding in each mind as to what their father had just said. "And just let that sheriff try to put me or one of you in jail. He would soon find out hell hath no fury like a Sherrill made mad! He ain't seen nothing like a bunch of riled up Sherrills."

Catherine quietly walked away from her hiding place beneath one of the windows thinking Grandpa is awfully mad about somebody named Georgie boy—whoever that is. Maybe I oughta tell Mom.

8

Oconostota, the War Chief, and Attacullaculla, the Peace Chief, looked down with drawn tight-lipped faces at Chief Kanagatoga's body at the same time Adam was venting his feelings during his meeting. Oconostota softly said, "Here lies a great chief of the Cherokee people. He will be missed by our people."

"He did many things for us. Whoever thought we, the mighty Cherokee, would become friends with the white man enough to help them in their wars? He asked me to lead us into helping the English against their French enemy," said Oconostota as he looked at Attacullaculla with a puzzled frown. "And what did it get us except more of the white's broken promises and walking on the land of our people and killing our men!" he said with increasing tone of frustration mixed with harshness.

"You and others crossed the ocean to see the English Chief George when you were just a young man. I'm sure that was still on the chief's mind and had something to do with his decision to help them," said Oconostota.

Attacullaculla said, with a thoughtful stare at nothing in particular and said in a hesitant manner, "Yes...I guess you are right. I remember them telling us in their great hall that we will be friends 'as long as the mountains and rivers last, and the sun shines.' I've been thinking, for a long time, that their sun is starting to get dark clouds over it for us."

Oconostota said with an exasperated gesture, "Can you blame them? What Ostenaco did last year at the fort called Loudoun was enough to create war with all white men! He was a fool to do that! But at the same time, it is difficult for me to see how we are going to live with the never-ending numbers of the white man unless we both adjust our ways. There are some whites worse than what they call the copperhead snake such as their chief in Pennslyvania who buys scalps taken from our men, even our women and children, which means we are forever hunted down and killed with no reason except our hair. And they are the ones who started the scalping of their enemies, but we get blamed for it. And we are like the disappearing yanssi! And when you see what their pox has done to all our people, it is no wonder we are angry!"

Attacullaculla said, "What you say is true. And our having to adjust our ways is not going to be an easy thing to do. We've been our own people for as long as anyone remembers. Change is hard to accept if we can't see how it will help us. Even though they tell us they want to live in peace, they continue to do what they want to do and when they want to do it. It is no wonder some of our men lose patience."

"Enough of this talk. We must make ourselves ready for mourning the death of our chief. You must be the one to tell the council that Kanagatoga has gone to sleep," said Oconostota as he turned and walked out of the single room hut.

The last rites for Kanagatoga were comprised of much mournful sobbing and crying, known as the Funeral Cry, by women of the village. The Funeral Cry lasted four days.

At six years old, this was the first time Little Quail had watched, or remembered watching, a funeral for a chief. She asked her mother, "Why is everyone sitting in all those circles around Chief Kanagatoga?"

Ulagili said, "Let me tell you about these things, my little daughter. You know all of these people and can see that the first ring contains Kanagatoga's family and, the next two circles around them are his friends and others from other villages. There will be much talk about him around our fires."

Oconostota slight nod to Attacullaculla caused him to get up and move to the covered body of Kanagatoga. It was generally acknowledged by the village members that Attacullacula was an excellent speaker. He looked around at the assembled people and gently turned his palms toward the sky and said, "We are here to mourn and honor a great leader of our people, the great Cherokee. But you also know that we believe that all life is special and not one of us is greater than any of the Creator's creatures yet we are here to honor one of our great chiefs. We are taught that the Creator made us all. We know all life is equally important to each one of us. We are simply one part woven into the blanket of time by our grand Creator. The wind is our breath, the sun our eyes, the waves lapping on the shore are our heartbeat, the rivers and streams our veins, through our eyes we are no greater than the wolf, the butterfly, or even the mighty tree. All creation is connected to us and we to it. We are one." All people in the circles nodded their heads in agreement and waited on the next words of Attacullaculla who said, "It is time to place Chief Kanagatoga."

Yona said to Yanisa as they were getting up from the second circle, "When I last talked with Kanagatoga, he told me that he had been told that the great chief in England wants to keep his people from coming over here."

Tsi'yu-gunsini, the twenty-three-year-old son of Attacullaculla, strode up to the two men saying, "He is missed already and we must determine our next chief." Tsi'yu-gunsini, later known as Dragging Canoe, has the "I am always ready to deliver" demeanor about him at all times and is considered to be a leader of men. The scars on his face, left by the white man's small pox, added a ferocity to his manner that intimidated his enemy. He was not aware his good looks had been destroyed by the pox until seeing himself in a still pool of water. From that point on, he harbored resentment for the white man for bringing the sickness to him and his people.

9

1762

Catawba Chief Hagler motioned Samuel to sit by his fire. "Hello to my good friend Samuel Sherrill! It has been too long since we have talked. What brings you to my village? We need to talk of many things."

"It is good to see my friend, the great leader of the Catawba," said Samuel. "Since my father first met your people, we have steadily grown in learning how each other lives so we can continue to live in peace. We are using the strengths of each of us to help each other."

The chief drew on his pipe, slowly nodded his head and continued to look into the fire. Samuel knew he was thinking and when the chief was ready to talk again, he would initiate another conversation. Samuel turned his eyes to the fire, *What a great way to live. It really must have been even greater before we got here.*

Soque, the chief's wife, walked up to the fire bringing with her a jug of water and some parched corn for them to eat. It was difficult for Samuel to keep from staring at her face. She saw his look and put her fingers on her cheek and slowly felt the deep scars left from the white man's smallpox.

"Her skin was a smooth as a water polished stone in the river. It is now forever marked with the plague of the white man," said the chief as he held out his hand to hold his wife's hand. Soque looked at her husband with loving eyes and knew she was his mate for life. She said, "As you know because you saw them, many of our people were killed by this dreadful thing your kind brought us. But, we somehow, will survive this terrible thing," as she turned her eyes toward the sky.

Samuel knew she was lifting a silent prayer to her Creator and remained silent until she turned to him and said, "I do not blame you, Samuel Sherrill. I do blame your kind that followed after you. It is almost as though they gave us this thing to kill us all. We are half of what we used to be when I was young"

"Is it any wonder I have problems controlling my young braves who want to seek revenge on your kind," said Chief Hagler. "Even our enemies have been felled by your pox. Is there nothing the white man brings us that will cause my people more problems? Why can't it be like it is between you and me?"

Samuel said while pushing a stick further into the fire, "That pox is a terrible thing that doesn't care who or what you are. Many whites have gotten the pox and, like your people, have died from it."

"I have heard that some of the whites give the Indian blankets that have the pox in them so the Indian will get sick and die. What kind of people would do that?" said Chief in a rising voice.

"Just like your people, there are some different thinking men who will stop at nothing to get their way. It is a harsh world. Even that king in England continues to make it difficult for us with his various laws and taxes," said Samuel.

"What is this thing—taxes? You have talked about them before. Is it another of your dreaded smallpox?"

Samuel half-smiled at the reference to it being a dreaded disease. "Yes, it is a way for the leaders of our people to get money from everyone which allows for the buying of things they feel is needed to run the country," said Samuel. *Never heard of taxes! Wish that was the case with me and my kin.*

"It appears to me that the rulers get to keep this thing you call tax. Is tax a way of stealing from your own people? It cannot be any worse than the paper, you call treaty, that, in time, is used to take our land. The paper always says that no more will be taken from us. Why does the white man lie to us when they know they will not make the words on the paper true," said Chief Hagler while he looked intently into Samuel's eyes.

Samuel said, "I wish I had some words that would make sense to you and to me about the things you say are lies. But I don't have such words. All I know is my small part of this vast land. There is land I want to explore over the mountain."

"See what I mean," said Hagler in an I-am-not-pleased voice. "Even my white friend is wanting more land from us. This is not good."

"No, no! That is not true! I do not want any more of your land. You have been very generous to me with what you and your father have given my father and me," said a troubled Samuel. "All I want to do is look over some of that land across the mountains to see if I should be moving over there. My friend, Daniel, is telling me it is rich in game and bottom land for farming."

"I do not understand how you can leave here and move over there without getting the agreement of the Cherokees," said Hagler. "Does this mean you will give me back the land here that my father gave your father?"

Samuel in a hesitant voice said, "Well, uhhhh, my friend. I have to have time to think about that." *What if I decide to come back after a year or two?*

They both fell silent and turned their attention to the fire and lost themselves in thinking about what they had just said. *The white man always wants more than he needs. Taxes! I think Samuel thinks it is a type of pox*, thought the chief.

He's right! Why do I need to keep this land if I move my family across the mountains. I'll never be back to see it anyway! I'll give it back, thought Samuel.

Samuel said as he waved his hand toward his home, "I must go. Next time, we will sit on the bank of the river and catch our supper."

Chief Hagler nodded his head as he continued to look into the fire as Samuel stood up and waited for a gesture or some other acknowledgement of his leaving—he didn't get one. *He doesn't want to answer the hard questions about his kind always wanting more land,* thought the chief as he looked up to see Samuel walking back to his home.

10

1764

The spring was slowly turning to the first days of summer. Wildflowers at the edge of the pasture were being visited by what seemed to be thousands of bees, varied shades of green were on the trees in the vast forest, and the smell of newly plowed earth all contributed to a seldom known feeling of peaceful existence for Samuel. He stopped plowing, wiped the sweat away from his eyes and hat brim, leaned on the plow handles and looked around at the wonders of nature. He let his eyes drift across the landscape until they settled on the high hills and even higher mountains west of him. *I'm gonna go over there and soon. I could care less that the idiot king's proclamation saying we can't cross over the tops of those mountains. I'm gonna go when I'm good and ready!*

"Hello, the plow boy," said Daniel with a wide grin as he walked out from the edge of the woods. "Whatcha planting? Corn, beans, weeds?"

"Ahhh, my good friend, it's corn I plant. Look at those straight furrows. Am I good or what?" said a half-smiling Samuel as he gave a small gesture with his hand toward the rows.

"Yep, looks straight to me. Wonder if you could plow that good growing ground across those mountains? I've gone up there to see if ol' Georgy boy has some soldier up there to stop me from crossing his proclamation line. Didn't see a soul. Sure saw a lot of elk and bear wondering back and forth over that line and you know what? They didn't pay any attention to it any more than I did," said Daniel with a big grin and look of self-satisfaction.

"Yeah, know what you mean! And he said he is gonna put outposts along the line to keep us out and then he thinks all of us on this side of the line are going to somehow pay to keep those posts open. I think Georgy and his guys in his parliament are drinking out of the same well of crazy water," said Samuel shaking his head in disgust.

"Well, wouldn't ya know! Sherrill and Boone lollygaggin' around here like there's nothing to do," said Sheriff Clark in a half shout as he rode his horse up to the field.

"Gotta watch what we say," whispered Samuel. "I hear he's a mite touchy about people kidding him about the line and you know he is sheriff because of Georgy boy's men around here supporting him."

"I heard that!" whispered Daniel through tight lips with a slight nod of his head.

"Get down from that saddle and lend me a hand with this plowing," said Samuel with a little mocking smile building on his face, "or does hard work make you ill?"

"Better watch it, Samuel, or I'll have you in the stocks before nightfall," said the sheriff with a look that he can do it, too! "Anyway, what's this I hear about you picking up and moving across the line?"

Samuel, with a feigned look of disbelief and motioning with his hands the area around them, said, "And leave all this! Whatcha been into today? Some stuff outta my still?"

The sheriff paused a moment, giving Samuel an "I'm not going to put up with much more of your guff" look and said, "I'm here for two reasons and both you had better give me some careful listening!"

The two friends didn't move a muscle and with unwavering eyes looked at the sheriff who immediately knew the two men in front of him were not thinking pleasant thoughts about him.

"Not only am I reminding you to keep on this side of the proclamation line, but I'm here to tell you about…what the heck, where is that paper?" He searched his pockets.

Samuel and Daniel looked at each other with a look of "here we go again" suspicion.

"Here it is," said Clark with a half now-I've-got-you smile as he unfolded the paper and with a show of bravado said, "Lord of His Majesty's Treasury Grenville and Parliament have made some changes to the Molasses tax. It's called The Sugar Act and it will be the law everywhere around here. This act means sugar, wine, coffee, pimientos, some kind of printed calico cloth, and shipping of lumber and iron will be taxed. And it cuts the tax from sixpence to threepence on a gallon of molasses. Well, whatcha boys think about that?" He held out the paper to the other two men.

A stony silence ruled the moment as two men continued looking at Clark with narrowing eyes as they adsorbed what they had just heard. *More taxes and for what! How much is this going to cost me? Blithering idiots!* were just a few of some thoughts coursing through their minds.

"And my sheriff, why is this being done?" asked Samuel while giving him a look of stony disbelief.

"Those things I ain't privy to. But I hear tell that it's to help pay for the posts on the line plus payback to the Crown the money it is costing to make sure the colonies do what they are told to do," said Clark with a feeling of not being sold on the tax either. But he had to enforce the laws given to him.

Daniel said in an even-toned I-don't-believe-this manner, "You mean to tell me that I have to pay more tax to you because someone, who has never been here, thinks we're gonna pay their soldiers to keep us from crossing that line—wherever it happens to be up there. And, on top of that half-baked law, they are adding more taxes on us! Who is over there from here to tell Parliament what it really is like here? Nobody that's who and I don't like it one little bit. I can't wait to see the first man you arrest for stepping over that line up there! And another thing—"

Samuel put his hand on Daniel's arm to try and stop him from saying too much more and said with as much control as he could muster, "If that is it, Sheriff, just give us that paper as you leave so's we can study it some more. You don't have to be told the bad feelings this is going to cause around here and probably more so in cities like New York and Philadelphia."

"Never been to neither one and I have no need to go to anyone of them. Got enough to do on my own," said Clark as he climbed back on his horse. "But you two best be studying that there paper I give you. I sure don't wanna put either one of you in my stocks." He laughed the kind of laugh which implied "I would really like to do that."

As the sheriff was riding off, Catherine rode up holding a bucket of water and gourd to give to her pa. She handed the bucket to Samuel and jumped off Betsy's back with the fluid grace of confidence and said with a smile, "Good morning, Mr. Boone. Hi, Pa. Brought you some of the best tasting and coldest water in these parts."

Daniel said with a small grin, "I declare, Miss Catherine, you look prettier every time I see you. You must be getting on to eleven or twelve, right?"

Catherine blushed at the comment. She knew she was taller than the other girls her age and had the strength, even though not evident, of a boy her age. "Thank you, Mr. Boone. Would you like a drink of water, too? You're close to being right, I'm going on eleven."

"And I can't believe it either. Seems just yesterday she was crawlin' around the cabin floor," said her father with a proud look in his eyes. "And, just think, if it wasn't for me, Kate would have never gotten near a horse. Isn't that right, Kate?"

"Yes, sir, it is. Not to brag, but I can outride any boy my age. And they don't like it either," said Catherine while displaying a wide grin.

Samuel, as he had done many times, noticed his daughter's self-confidence trait, and why he said, "Daughter of mine, do you want to ride up to the tops of those mountains with me?"

Daniel slowly turned his head and, while looking Samuel in the eyes, said, "Mind repeatin' that Samuel? I don't think I heard ya right."

I sure can't get out of this without making it seem I don't think Kate can do it, thought Samuel as he looked at his daughter and said, "You heard right, Dan'l. I've been thinking for quite some time now that Kate needs to get some idea of what it's like to camp in the woods. Never know when she might need that knowing. Heaven forbid, what if she got captured by a bunch of Indians and escaped—knowin' what to do would get her back safe to us."

"Ohhh, Pa, I can hardly wait! I'm goin' to tell Ma what we're going to do! Maybe Uncle Mode and Mr. Boone will go with us!" Then with one stride, she jumped on Betsy's back, grabbed the reins, leaned forward, and spoke something in her horse's ear. Besty was at full gallop after her first step taking her Kate back to the cabin.

Samuel and Daniel watched as a rider and horse, that seemed as one, grow smaller as they crossed the plowed field and jumped over a split rail fence into the pasture. "Did ya know she could jump fences?" asked an amazed Daniel while continuing to watch Kate ride Betsy home.

After a couple of deep breaths, Samuel said with an I-don't-believe-this voice, "Uhhhhh uhhhhh, I sure didn't. Wot's Mary going to say? I think I'm in trouble."

"Well, my good friend, it looks like you have quite a girl who can ride plus one who is going to the top of the mountain with us," said Daniel while giving Samuel a wide grin. "Come to think on it, let's take my Isreal along with us."

Samuel looked at his friend for a long moment and was ready
to agree when Daniel said, "Might want to rethink that a little
bit. She sure doesn't need a boy along to try and outdo on her first
campout. Maybe the next one after this one. What say, Samuel?"

An inwardly relieved Samuel said with a slight nod of his
head, "Might be the best and, by the way, I sure do thank you for
agreeing to go with us, Dan'l."

"Well, I gotta be getting on back and tell Rebecca we're off on
a hunt for a few days. Uhhhh, when we goin'?" said Daniel.

"Let's see now. Got two more days of plowing. One day of
convincing Mary. Two more days of getting things ready. Seeing
how this is Tuesday we'll leave Sun...day," Samuel said with a
trailing off voice. "Sunday is not good. That's the Lord's day."

Daniel said, "Next Monday it is! Just might bring Rebecca
and the boys with me on Saturday and we can go to church with
y'all and afterwards, we can cook up a mess of cornbread to take
with us. That bein' all right with you?"

"Dan'l, my man, why is it you are so good a thinker? Let's do
it!" said a smiling Samuel. "And, while you are gone, I'll go over ol'
George's new law. He thinks we're gonna live by, so we can kick it
around and decide what we're going to do about it." *Use the paper
for starting a camp fire on the line would be the best thing for it...*

⌒

At that moment, Patrick Ferguson propped his leg on the foot
stool next to his chair thinking, *Will the pain ever stop? Had this
for two years now and it doesn't seem to be getting any better.*

His mother entered the parlor overlooking her flower garden and walked over to her son and said, "How does it go today,
Pattie? Feeling any better?"

"Seems to come and go, but I'm a fighter and I'm going to
win this battle. Just wonder what it was I got in Germany that
caused my leg to be on the lame side all the time. Just doesn't
make sense to me," said Patrick while rubbing his leg. "I've been

looking over your garden, Mother, and I can see some first green of your plants."

"Oh, my yes," said his smiling mother, "those are my flowering currants. Aren't they just what is needed to get your spring spirits soaring?"

Patrick said while pointing out to the edge of the garden's rock wall, "I know you've told me many times what that bush is with all those pretty yellow blossoms, but I just can't remember its name."

"Ahhh, ha, Pattie. One would think you've been in the house too much these last two years," said Mrs. Ferguson. "I've got to make sure you get outdoors and do some gardening with me. Walking and bending will be good for you. Makes the blood run true."

"Well, if you insist, I'll go out and dig around your garden, but you'll have to pay me to do it," said Patrick with a half-crooked smile on his face.

"Well, my son, if that's the way it is, then I'll pay you with a good dinner each day. Seems more than fair to me. Hmmmmm?" said his mother while she raised an eyebrow at him while tilting her head at Patrick in an *I have got you this time look*. "Oh, by the way, that is a forsythia bush. Bet you didn't know it was named for our friend William Forsyth. Wonder how he is doing? Haven't seen him in a long time."

Patrick said in a wistful manner, "I'll never forget your love of plants. I always think about your roses and their fragrant smell. Flowers and my mother were made for each other."

"Why thank you, son. That's such a nice thing to say." She patted him gently on his head thinking, *Why do they have to grow up so fast?*

❧

Samuel opened the cabin door and saw Mary sitting at their dining table, stirring mashed potatoes with a fury he had never

witnessed. "What in the world are you beating, Mary? Better be careful...you just might break that stirrer," he said with a worried look.

Mary quit stirring and gently placed the stirrer into the bowl and with a "don't mess with me" look on her face looked deep into her husband's eyes and very slowly said, "Just what do you think you are doing by telling Kate she is going to those mountains with you? I think you have been out in the still too much today."

Samuel backed a few steps toward the door as he said with a trailing off voice, "Ahhh...'cause she needs to learn...the ways of...the woods?"

Mary slowly got up and just as slowly started walking toward Samuel with her hands on her hips and said, "The way of the woods it is...just what are you talking about? She has been living around and getting to know the woods fairly well all her young life and now you want to take her to a place that everyone knows is dangerous! I'll not hear of it anymore!" She turned back to the table.

Dear Lord, please give me the words to say. Show me the way to make Mary understand why I think Kate needs to go on this trip. Samuel, in hesitant steps, walked to the hearth, reached up and took his flintlock from the pegs, and stood inspecting the flint that was locked in the hammer mechanism. "Mary, as you know so well, our children need our guidance as much as we can give them. They need to know how to react to things that could possibly harm them. And the only way I know how to do that is to give them as much experience as possible to help them in later life."

"Go on my husband. You may be making some sense...finally!" said Mary.

Samuel, seeing that his words were making some headway with his wife, said, "Remember when we let Samuel Jr. head out to the Waxhaws with Mode and Isaac? You weren't all that much in favor of it, but you gotta admit that it was good for Samuel Jr. And I'm just as convinced this will just as good for Catherine."

"Well, all right, I can see a small part of your reasoning. But you've gotta ask Susan. I'll not have any of my children thinking they are thought of as better or worse than the others," Mary said while looking at her husband with a tight-lipped smile.

Samuel, with a look of relief, called out to his daughters, "Susan, Catherine…I know you have to be close by so come on out and let's talk."

Catherine looked at her sister with a "we've been found" look and whispered to Susan, "Guess we best get on down there. Why wait? They know we are here." Then she called out, "We're on our way, Pa."

∽

At that moment, Yona, Tawadi, and Yanisa were closing in on a deer. They had decided they would use the bow and arrow because they did not want to lose their ability to use them. They realized they were becoming increasingly dependent on the muzzle-loaded rifle and needed to make sure they could use their time-tested weapons if the rifle didn't work. Their stalking skills were unbelievable in that the sound of their steps was barely a whisper, if that. It had been decided that Yanisa would make the first shot while the others backed him up. The bow Yanisa used was capable of propelling an arrow through a deer at fifty paces. There were stories told around their fires that the first white men who came into the Cherokee country over two hundred years ago were afraid of their powerful bows. They could penetrate their metal helmets and breastplates. He and his two friends crept toward the deer so that it only had one way to run if they showed themselves. The buck was pulling at leaves on a low lying willow branch.

Yanisa knew he was close enough to the buck to make his shot count. He ever so slowly stood from this crouching position and ceased to move, or hardly breathe, when the buck quit eating and turned his head to Yanisa. Yanisa could almost feel the buck's eyes as they locked on him. He had been told from an early age

to never look a deer in the eyes as they could sense danger and run. Yanisa slowly lowered his eyes to the ground where the deer stood but could still see when the deer stopped looking at him.

The deer was motionless for a long time as if trying to figure out why he hadn't seen the object he was looking at before now. Yanisa did not move either. The deer turned his head back to the willow branch and resumed his eating. Yanisa slowly pulled his bow up into firing position, aimed at the spot above the front legs, pulled the arrow back as far as the bow would allow, held it steady for a moment, and released the arrow toward its target. The deer felt the arrow pass through his chest wall piercing his heart as it continued its path out his other side and stuck fast to a nearby pine tree. The deer felt a momentary pain as he backed up one unsteady step and died on his way to the ground. The three friends stood by the fallen deer and started a chant to the Creator thanking him for the deer in its giving his life to them so their village could have meat to keep from going hungry. No comments were made to Yanisa about his excellent marksmanship as it was expected to be so by the others and he knew it.

As they were carrying the deer back to their village, they talked about heading to the mountains to the east to do some turkey and elk hunting. "I like elk meat, but bringing it back from those places is not an easy thing to do," said Yona. "Turkey is bad enough if you have a lot of them."

"But those animals living in the higher country seem to be better tasting. I say we go as soon as we can," said Tawadi.

Yona said, "Then it will be done. We will make sure our village has enough meat to last them while we are gone. I think we will be gone at least fourteen suns."

The three friends had satisfied themselves that their village was safe and had enough to eat for the anticipated time they would be away. They picked up their rifles and food as started toward the high country. It was Sunday in the white man's world.

Tsi'yu-gunsini came running up to them just as they were about to leave the village and said, "Are you hunting the deer and elk or the white man?" His demeanor was one of total hatred of the people encroaching on land that had been with his tribe for many generations. That, plus the fact it appeared the settlers were always trying to change any Indians they met to their ways and not even thinking about how to meld the two cultures where they would take the best of both to make a peaceful situation.

"We go to hunt meat for the village," said Yona. "Why don't you come along with us. We could use Tsi'yu-gunsini's mighty hunting skills and make it so we can get back here quicker." Yona looked deep into Tsi'yu-gunsini's eyes in an effort to keep from looking at his pockmarked face.

Tsi'yu-gunsini's look was one of respect for Yona and said, "I go but from now on, use my name of Dragging Canoe. All of you know that I've been called that since I was a young boy." He turned to get his rifle from his lodge.

The four men left their village in a single file with Yona leading the way. Much later in the day, they stopped by a waterfall and fished for their meal from the large deep clear pool at the base of the falls. Yona watched his line waiting for it to become taut when a fish took the bait. Tawadi held a spear, just made from a sapling, readying it to strike out at a fish swimming within range. As Yona fished, he let his gaze wander over his Creator's work when he looked at the top of the waterfall and followed a few drops of water falling apart from the main stream. They seemed to be falling in slow motion when they suddenly caught a beam of sunshine and, for a brief moment, Yona felt he was caught in a mist of golden colors. He watched the drops hit the pool. *They are now where they belong. Among their own kind. We want to be among our own kind. Why can't the white man understand that we don't want to be like them.* His line tugged and a quick flick of his wrist caught the fish and when it broke the surface, its scales seemed to have absorbed the golden-colored waterdrops.

11

It was barely enough morning light to see as her father and his friend were following a dim game trail beside a fast-flowing stream, then through vast limb thickets of rhododendron and around long-ago felled trees. They emerged from the forest and found themselves standing in a wide clearing devoid of trees that tapered down to a slim ledge that contained an eroded path made by various animals, and maybe even local man, over years of use. Catherine was grateful for the stop as she was doing her best not to let on that her legs were protesting the torture of extreme effort to keep up the pace set by her father. There was no way that she was going to let them know she was in pain. Before venturing out on the path, they could see where a misplaced step to the right would result in falling hundreds of feet into a creek full of smooth rocks. The other side was a shear wall of weathered grey-colored granite that offered little, if any, foot or hand hold. "Whatcha think, Dan'l?" said Samuel while nodding first to Catherine and then the ledge.

"Seems to be safe enough, Samuel. I'll go first to make sure there are no surprises," said Daniel as he stepped off toward the ledge.

"Let's fall in behind him, Catherine. Don't want to lose sight of him," said Samuel.

Ohhh no! Let's stay here a little longer. I'm so tired, she thought as she put one foot in front of the other with slow methodical but painful steps that soon dissolved into a hypnotic state of walking when she realized she had crossed the ledge and was standing next to Daniel at the edge of a large field. Her dad joined them.

The field was on top of a high smooth crested mountain. The vivid blue sky around the mountain's crest drew their eyes to look over countless mountaintops holding their heads above a blanket of heavy fog. "We are just starting to get to know what huge lands are below those clouds that need to be hunted and farmed," said Samuel. He then changed his tone of voice to one of contempt, "Should we step over the line? Do you see any Tory or English soldier guarding the place?"

"Nope, don't see a soul or anything to keep us from crossing it," said Daniel.

Catherine looked around her and over the field and said, "What line are y'all talking about? Who would put a line way up here anyway?"

Yona and Dragging Canoe gave each other a questioning look as they knelt behind a thicket of dense rhododendrons and young hemlock trees. "Why are they here? What are they looking for? Why is a young girl with them?" asked Dragging Canoe between tight lips. *They are our enemy*

"Good points, my friend. We could be here all day asking such questions. Let's go ask them," said Yona pointing to the group as he stood up, cradled his muzzle loader across his chest and walked into the open field. Dragging Canoe's look was of stunned disbelief. He recovered enough to exclaim in a loud whisper, "You wish to die?" He leveled his rifle toward the group.

Yona said, "Do not fire. If you see me start to defend myself then shoot the one with the black hat. I will get the other one."

Samuel saw a movement to his left and turned his head to determine what, if anything, was still in sight. His reaction was like Dragging Canoe's—stunned disbelief followed by a startled "good grief!" Daniel's reaction was one of silence. Catherine's reaction was a rapid intake of breath, widening eyes followed by the thought, *He means no harm.*

Samuel said in a low voice, "I'll drop him." He started raising his rifle to firing position. Daniel slowly put his hand on Samuel's rifle and held it down with meaningful force and said, "Not now!" He continued looking at Yona.

Yona, on seeing Samuel's reaction, started bringing his rifle into firing position and was about to tell Dragging Canoe to shoot. He stopped both reactions when he saw the other man, who wore the black hat, stop the other man from raising his rifle.

Catherine, for some unknown reason to her, started walking toward Yona with a slow purposeful steps never taking her eyes off his eyes. She had not even thought what she was going to say until she stopped about ten steps from him. She then said, "Hi, my name is Catherine Sherrill. What's yours?"

Yona watched the young girl as she walked toward him. He lowered his rifle to show the others he would not do harm to them. His black eyes never wavered from the girl's blue eyes. He saw in her eyes a look of "I am not afraid." Yona knew Dragging Canoe must be thinking all sorts of things and hoped he would not do anything rash due to his hatred of the white man.

Yona's reaction to Catherine's talk was one of respect and thoughts of, *Is her mind all right? Does she have special power? Is she on her way to becoming a revered woman among her people?* He said in his language, "I am Yona of the Cherokee. Why are you and the others here?"

Samuel could hardly contain himself. He looked at Daniel and said, "If he breathes wrong, I am going to kill him!" He then started walking toward Yona and Catherine. Daniel said, "Go no further, Samuel! You go off half-cocked here and no telling what will happen. I'll go fetch Catherine." Samuel stopped in his tracks and looked back to Daniel who gave him a look of "don't mess with me on this." Samuel knew he should agree with Daniel.

Daniel started walking toward Yona and Catherine. As he approached them, they turned their eyes on him. Daniel saw no fear in either set of eyes, but did see a look of cautious concern in Yona's eyes. At that moment, Dragging Canoe stood up from his position and aimed his rifle at Daniel. Daniel's reaction was one of slight widening of his eyes that focused on the man holding the rifle. The man's narrowing eyes showed an unwavering boldness that impressed Daniel while wondering if the smallpox had caused his pockmarked face. He heard Yona say something in their language which, if Daniel knew the language, meant for Dragging Canoe to put his weapon down as no harm is to come to these people. He slowly lowered the rifle, but his deep dark eyes spoke of killing all of the hated white men.

Catherine looked at Daniel and said, "I think I've made a friend," and turned to Yona with a smile on her face. Yona was taken aback by this young girl's manner which he was slowly appreciating due to the honesty of her apparent feelings toward him. He did not see any reason to smile back but nodded once to her. Catherine said, "I would like you to meet my father." She turned to Samuel and said, "Please come meet my new friend."

Samuel wasn't liking the situation but was not about to let his daughter down. And anyway, her take-charge attitude seemed to be dissolving some barriers between the two cultures. As he carefully strode up to Catherine, she turned to Yona and said, "This is my father, Samuel Sherrill." Yona looked at Samuel from head to toe while giving special note to his rifle and long knife. He did not utter one word or do anything to indicate he understood Catherine. She then held out her hand to her father who took it in his and gave her a gentle smile. This told Yona that family must be important to this white man and wondered if all white men had the same feelings. Yona's culture revered family, too.

Catherine turned to Daniel and said with the same smile, "And this in Mr. Daniel Boone. He is a friend of my pa's and me."

The reaction on Yona when he heard Catherine's introduction was one of wide-eyed surprise while slowly turning his head to Daniel. Dragging Canoe rapidly walked up on the group and said to Yona, "Did she say Boone?" Everyone recognized the word

"Boone" in his question. Daniel looked around in a worried surprised manner to Samuel and said, "Sure looks like they know my name. Wonder why and how?"

"He is the one we have been told that enters our land to hunt our bear and deer," hissed Dragging Canoe. "He must not be allowed to leave here!"

Turning to look directly into Dragging Canoe's eyes, Yona said in an even-toned manner, "No harm is to come to these people. We need to know them better and to find out why they are here." He turned back to Catherine and the two men. His surprise was evident in the way he drew back his head while looking at Elizabeth's outstretched hand.

"What are you doing?" exclaimed Samuel in a sharp-edged voice of concern.

Yona looked at Samuel noting that he was upset. He looked back to Catherine whose hand remained out to him. Yona's reaction brought an increasing smile to her face, and a heavy intake of breath from Dragging Canoe, when Yona slowly raised his hand and grasped her hand. He felt the firm squeeze of her small hand and knew that this girl was a chosen one.

Yona said, "I welcome you to my land," in a manner which showed no animosity, only one of cautious peace.

Catherine knew the large calloused hand holding hers was meant to be friendly. "Thank you for being my friend. Do you have any horses?"

Daniel said, "Horses? I can't believe what I'm hearing."

Yona finally released his grip and looked at Samuel. He gave a slight nod of his head and held out his hands palm up, hoping they would show he wanted to maintain the feeling of peace.

Three people whose culture was born in England and two men whose culture was born on the land they were standing looked at each other in silence. The only word they all knew was "Boone." Little did they know they were standing on the King's Proclamation Line, but even if they knew, they wouldn't have given it a second thought. There were more pressing things at hand to manage.

Catherine broke the silence, "Maybe they would like a biscuit. Whatcha think, Pa?"

Samuel looked at Catherine, turned his head to Daniel with a questioning look. "Seems like a good idea. No harm in trying." He started to reach into his pouch.

Yona and Dragging Canoe took a step back and pointed their rifles at Samuel. "What is he going to do?" asked Yona. "Not sure, but we must be ready to kill them," said Dragging Canoe.

Samuel stopped reaching for the pouch and wondered, *What do I do now?* when he saw Daniel slowly bend over and put his weapon on the ground and backed up two steps. He looked at Samuel and then the ground signifying he was to do the same. Samuel understood the silent message and copied Daniel's reaction hoping the two Indians would see they meant peace.

Dragging Canoe said in a low voice, "Shall we kill the men and take the girl back to our village? I do not trust them."

Yona looked at Dragging Canoe and turned back to look at Catherine. He saw the confidence in her eyes and knew that all would be all right if he responded to the peace overture shown by the two men. He then laid his rifle on the ground, backed up two steps and nodded to Samuel while glancing to Samuel's pouch. Samuel took this to mean there would be no problem with him reaching into his pouch.

Samuel withdrew the biscuits and passed two to Catherine and one to Daniel and said, "Kate, give one to each of them." She held them out to Yona and Dragging Canoe who looked at each other. "You aren't going to take that are you?" said Dragging Canoe. "They have given us much sickness in the past. See what they have done to my face! I will not trust them again!"

Yona could not refute Dragging Canoe's feelings and thought, *He has a right to be angry. Guess I would also. But I know it is right to do this.* He reached out and took one biscuit from Catherine's hand.

Daniel said, "Take a bite out of the other one, Catherine. You must show them there is nothing wrong with it." Catherine looked at her father who nodded his head in agreement with Daniel. She then looked at Daniel and smiled as she turned back to Yona and took a big bite out of the biscuit. *Mom can make the best biscuits! These are good!*

Yona thought, *She is truly a special person* and took a bite out of his biscuit. His response to the taste of the biscuit was noted by Dragging Canoe when Yona's look of satisfaction crept across his face. Yona took another bite. Dragging Canoe was hungry, but he wasn't about to eat the white man's food. *I'll starve before I do that.*

Samuel noted Yona's reaction with a feeling of relief. "Should I give him some of Mary's jam to put on it?"

"Heck no!" said Daniel. "I want that myself. But considering what is happening, I think it's a good idea."

Samuel looked at Yona and Dragging Canoe and slowly put his hand back in his pouch. The two men's attention focused on the pouch and the two white men could see the note of concern, especially from Dragging Canoe's reaction. Samuel slowly pulled a small powder horn out of his pouch and pulled a cap off of the large end. Mary had packed sweets in this manner many times for Samuel that he used on his hunting trips. She knew Samuel had a sweet tooth unmatched anywhere and she wanted to show him her love by packing these things for him. He handed the horn to Catherine and said, "Spread some on this on your other biscuit and give it to him. Guess the other one isn't hungry."

Catherine reached down to the top of her boot and withdrew a small knife. Yona's outward reaction did not change, but he inwardly thought, *This special one has many tricks,* as he filed away in his mind a girl's hiding place for a knife. She cut the biscuit in half then dipped the knife into the mixture made of cornbread, honey, and blackberries and spread it on the biscuit. She then handed it to Yona. Dragging Canoe said, "Don't eat that. It will make you sick and die!" Yona shook his head in agreement and handed it back to Catherine.

"Take a bite out of it, Catherine. They need to know we aren't trying to poison them," said Daniel.

Catherine looked at Yona and bit into the biscuit. As she was eating, she kept thinking, *This is good!* She then handed the remaining portion to Yona who took it while not taking his eyes off her eyes. He could tell there was no reason to suspect this young girl of doing harm to him. He bit into the biscuit.

Everyone watched Yona who could not suppress his smile as the sweet taste made itself known to his taste buds. He slowly nodded his head up and down as he took another bite. Dragging Canoe said, "That must be good. Let me finish it." Yona put the last portion in his mouth and said in a mocking voice, "It might kill you." Dragging Canoe was not pleased and it showed on his face.

Catherine then dipped her knife in the jam, covered the other half biscuit, and handed it to Dragging Canoe. His reaction to the treat was one of wide-eyed surprise. He slowly extended his hand toward the biscuit. Catherine placed it in his hand and then looked into his eyes and smiled. Dragging Canoe almost smiled back but thought that would be a sign of weakness. He raised the biscuit to his mouth and took a small bite. Everyone could see he was surprised and pleased as he took another bite to finish it and smacked his lips and said, "Let's take her with us and leave the others for the crows to pick over."

"We will not do that! We must try to see if we can make peace with these people no matter who they are," said Yona as he turned to Catherine. "I would like to have that powder horn of your father's."

All three knew Yona was wanting something by the way he kept pointing to Samuel's horn of Mary's jam. "I think he wants the whole thing, Dan'l. Whatcha think we oughta do?"

"As much as I don't like it, I think you should give it to Catherine and let her give it to him," said Daniel. "Hope it shows we want to get along with each other."

Samuel handed the horn to Catherine while watching Yona's eager eyes. "Give this to him. It might make for better things for us," said Samuel in a low tone to Catherine.

She looked at the horn for a long time noticing the name "Sherrill" carved on it. She slowly held it out to Yona whose surprise at being offered the horn and everything in it was evident to everyone. He took the horn and while turning it over in his hand saw the strange markings on it. *Wonder what those markings mean. Must be their name.* He pointed at the markings while showing a questioning face to Catherine. She looked at Samuel who said "Sherrill" in answer to his silent question. By gestures, Yona asked for the word again and again.

Samuel pointed to Dan'l and said, "Boone," then pointed to himself and Catherine and said, "Sherrill." Yona and Dragging Canoe questioning looks at each other showed they were still confused when Catherine took four more steps closer to Yona and pointed to herself and said, "Sherrill." She repeated the name many times. Dragging Canoe said, "Make her stop! Say what she is saying while turning to Catherine and said 'Sherrill.'"

Catherine was overjoyed at hearing her name. She clapped her hands and turned around two times saying, "Yes, yes, yes!" Dragging Canoe took this as some sort of dance and looked at Yona saying, "Let's do this also." He then clapped his hands and danced in a circle twice saying, "Yes, yes, yes."

A stranger just happening on the scene would have thought the sight of two men and one little girl clapping hands, hollering "yes, yes, yes" while dancing in circles was truly an unbelievable story to tell back home.

They finally stopped their dancing. Catherine pointed to Yona and with questioning gestures asked him for his name. Yona understood and said, "Yona." Catherine repeated the name until Yona shook his head up and down in a "yes" manner. Catherine then pointed to Dragging Canoe. He raised himself to maximum height with a stern look and said, "Dragging Canoe." Catherine looked at her father who then looked at Daniel. Daniel's narrowing eyes told everyone that his mood and manner had quickly changed to one of caution. He had heard rumors that this Cherokee had little regard for the white man, but at the same time, he wondered if the rumors were true since he had not done anything to hurt or threaten them.

Yona hung the jam horn on his shoulder and thought he should give Catherine something of his to her. *What do I have that a chosen one would need or want?* "You have anything I can give her?" he asked of Dragging Canoe who knew what he was thinking and why.

"Give her your other moccasins. You might not need them on our way back to the village," said Dragging Canoe.

Yona thought a moment about giving up his moccasins as they required a lot of work to make. *They are valuable to me which means they will know I am giving her something that is always a need to me.* He then reached into his pouch and took out the moccasins. He looked at them, then looked at Dragging Canoe who signified yes by the nod of his head. Yona then gradually extended his hand holding the moccasins to Catherine.

Catherine's drew back her head as her eyes widened in wonder at being offered something that was always a necessity especially while in the forest. She turned to her father and Daniel with a questioning look and saw that both of them approved. She then turned back to Yona and extended her hands toward him. Yona took her hands in one of his and held them for a moment and gently placed his new moccasins in her hand. He shook his head once and said, "Good," in his language. He noticed tears welling up in Catherine's eyes and then knew he had made the right decision. *This chosen one will always remember this moment.*

The two natives of the land looked at each other then bent down picking up their rifles. The two white men did not move. Catherine did not move as she caressed her gift. Daniel softly said, "These are honorable men."

Samuel said, "Why is it we can't all get along like this?"

Catherine said, "The Bible says to do unto others as you would have them do to you. I think that worked here."

Yona looked at Dragging Canoe and the unspoken message was to leave. They turned and started back toward their village a few days away. Yona looked back for a moment at the three white people and said, "Why can't each and everyone make peace like we just did. They didn't even want to give us their words on their paper. I think our bond is strong. They are not like the two scalp hunters Yanisa and Tawadi killed."

Dragging Canoe said, "My thoughts are that we must always be on guard with these white people especially the one they call Boone."

His eyes observed the drama of the five people unfolding before him. He felt the warmth of the sun as it started to dissipate the fog which allowed him to bring the far off valleys into focus. He spotted the river, where he had fished many times, flashing the sun's brilliance back toward the sky as if sending it back to its origins. The massive white clouds held firm against the deep blue sky. He then saw a movement and focused his eyes on a squirrel running along the ground in efforts to get to a chosen tree and then he knew what he had to do for his offspring. He folded his wings to his body and his white-colored head feathers identified him as he dove with lighting speed toward the unsuspecting squirrel. The squirrel was running and when he jumped to gain the safety of the tree, he was caught by the eagle's talons.

Samuel and Daniel sat on the ground looking in the direction the two Cherokees had taken. Catherine stood while looking in their direction and turned saying, "I hope to see them again. The one who gave me his moccasins is nice, but the other one is not."

"I can't believe they knew my name!" Daniel said with a puzzled look on his face.

"Just think, ol' friend, you might be famous one of these days. If they know you then it won't be long that folks back in our area will know you as…well, what would they know you by? He who gives sweets to the Cherokee?" said Samuel with a grin.

Daniel said with a look of mischief on his face, "Don't mess with me you two! You know I've hunted a lot in my short life and it was three or four years ago that I hunted on the other side of these mountains. It was cold up here. Winter hadn't given up by then this high up."

Catherine said with a tone of awe, "I don't believe I held his hand!" Just then the two Cherokee men looked back to the group and saw Catherine waving at them.

"My friend, I must admit they are good people. Maybe there is hope after all for us to get along with these people who take our land," said Dragging Canoe.

Yona looked at his friend. "That is the first time I have heard you say something that may be good about the white men. We can hope, can't we?" *We will remember those three, especially the chosen one.*

Catherine said, "Let's go toward the sun. I want to see as much of this as I can today. Just look around us! Is this the way it's supposed to be?"

Two men on a mission to prove to themselves, and others, that an order from across an ocean to not cross an imaginary line on top of these mountains was not going to be tolerated. A girl who wanted to live her young life to its fullest was lost in her thoughts of wanting to know more about these mountains and its people was with her father and friend. Samuel thought as he looked at the far off mountaintops receding in the distance, *Will I be able to make a difference? When I rise up to glory, will I have left behind a better place for my family?*

The three watched the sun slowly signal the end of the day. The sun's rays painted dusky red and orange colors on the high clouds, the sky was growing from deep blue to purple, an elk called its high-pitched sound, a wolf called its chilling call, and an eagle and his mate observed their chicks starting to snuggle down for the night after a full meal. All felt at peace. Samuel said, "This is truly a wonder of God!" Another wolf call broke the reverie. Daniel said, "We best make camp."

"Yeah, you're right, Dan'l. Let's find a good spot where we can wake up in the morning and see these mountains in morning's new light. And then we'll go back home knowing this line is nothing to us. That will allow us to work on this new Sugar Tax problem," said Samuel with an "I'm not gonna pay much attention to it either" voice.

Catherine didn't pay much attention to all the political talk as she wondered, *Sure would like to ride Betsy up here. Bet she would love it, too.* She let her eyes wander over the darkening horizon where the green was yielding to the velvet blackness of night. Venus was brilliant in the sky, and as she watched it, observed the stars as they slowly turned their lights on for their nightly performance.

"Best get some sleep, Catherine. Tomorrow will be a long walking day for us," said Samuel.

"Yes, Papa, I'm on the way. Good night, Mr. Boone," she said as she slowly closed her eyes as the carpet of stars in the Milky Way kept adding their blinking lights to its glory.

12

The next morning was just beginning to make itself felt when Mary sat in the shade of the cabin looking over the fields of corn stalks. Some were showing cobs full of yellow kernels and thought, *All is well with the crop. Wonder how much Samuel will use to make my lineament this year.* She well knew they needed the corn-based medicine for sterilizing cuts and used sometimes in her cooking but wasn't happy when the menfolk gathered for their "discussion groups" at the still and became somewhat boisterous in their arguments. The Proclamation Line was a hot topic but as far as she knew no one had been arrested for violating the act.

Samuel and his brothers William, Uriah, Adam, Aquilla who preferred to be called Quil, Isaac, Jacob, Moses, and his sons, Samuel Jr. and Uriah, who was named for his uncle, were harvesting the corn crop. All the Sherrill boys banded together to participate in the harvesting of each other's crops. This gave them time to review each other's thoughts about the current state of politics, crops, rifles, and making whiskey. The families had finished their yearly reunion five weeks before where they discussed the same items. Only this time, each had given each subject more thought and this was the way to help develop a better plan for the coming year.

Susan and Catherine were driving the full wagons back to the corn shed where Samuel Jr. and his brother Uriah unloaded them into the shed.

The month of October was approaching and the glorious colors of fall were beginning to show throughout the forest. The forest's horizon was draped with an unusually deep blue sky accompanied by seemingly motionless wisps of clouds. Samuel said, as he looked over the fields, "Isn't this a fine thing we can enjoy?" He motioned with his hand wanting everyone to enjoy nature's gift to them.

Uriah said in a mocking tone of voice, "Seems to me we could be finished a lot quicker if some weren't daydreaming about where he is. Sure wish it wouldn't take so long for us to get this corn. Seems to be sticking to the stalk closer this year. It sure is—" He was interrupted by a shout.

"Lo' the field! It's Sheriff Clark. Say something so I can get to you."

Samuel raised his rifle, which was never far from him while outside his cabin, and shouted, "We're over here Clark." He then turned to his brothers and said, "Wonder what kind of news he has for us now. Must be something new from those idiots in England."

Quil said, "Best keep that kind of talk to us and not him. He's just hunting for something to put on us so he can take us to the stocks."

"Howdy, boys. Man, am I lucky to get all y'all in one spot. Sure will save me some time," said Sheriff Clark as he reached into his saddlebag. He pulled out what looked like a letter. "Looks like you boys are getting your crops in on time this year. Getting a good yield?"

"Doing right tolerable, Sheriff. What brings you way out here to see us? Last time you told us about the line and I bet you have some..." Samuel cut his comments short knowing further talk would get him in trouble.

Sheriff Clark looked at Samuel and then the others saying, "Best keep that brother of yours in line. He's gonna git in trouble one day." He unfolded the letter and took a long time looking at it. He was savoring the moment of knowing something the others didn't know. Made him feel he was better than the rest. "Well, here goes! This here document comes to me all the way from London. What do y'all think 'bout thet?" He looked at each man.

Samuel shifted his feet while stifling the urge to say what he was thinking, *Here we go again!* Each brother's face reflected the same thought as they looked at the others.

It was plain to Sheriff Clark that he was going to tell them something they would find objectionable as he watched them with a creeping unease in his stomach. *Well, here goes nothing!* "Now hear this good. I'm not going to leave this paper with you this time. I was told to bring it back to the commander after I read it to everyone around here. Now listen to this and I'll read it real slow." Mode thought, *That's the only way you can read anyway.* "There is no standard money value common to all of the colonies. The British merchant-creditors do not favor this system because it is too complex to accurately determine the value of a particular note. The existing system does not take into account depreciation of notes due to the constant rise and fall off the colonial economy. Therefore, on April 19, 1764, Parliament has enacted the Currency Act. This gives control of the colonial currency system to Parliament. The act prohibits the issue of any new bills and the reissue of existing currency. Parliament wants a system based on the pound sterling. They are not inclined to regulate the existing colonial bills and, therefore, as of this date, they are abolished."

Each man met the unbelieving eyes of his brothers with most of them not believing what they had just heard. "Good grief, Clark! This means what little money we have is no good! Right?" exclaimed Samuel.

"That's the way I make it out to be unless it is the pound and I'm not even sure of that right now," said Sheriff Clark whose mood and manner was not its usual "I am better than you" smug look.

Adam said, "Clark, I think you need to turn your horse around and leave us to figure this out."

"You threatening me? Better think twice before you go too far. I am your sheriff and you had better not forget it. And, anyway, I've got the same money problems you have now!" said a nervous Clark. "I'm outta here! If you want a copy of this act then come to my office."

Eight brothers watched the sheriff of their region ride down the road until he disappeared over a rise descending to a small creek. Each was thinking how this new law affected them individually and as a whole.

"What's going on? Why don't they finish the corn?" said Catherine. "I bet that sheriff brought some bad news. I think I'll ride up there and see what's going on."

Susan with an "I know better than you" voice said, "That's none of your concern. Why is it you always have to know everything that is going on? I think you have enough other stuff to worry about than what is going on with Pa and our uncles."

"I dearly love you, my sister, but don't tell me what I can and can't do in my mind. Anyway, they need an empty wagon," said Catherine.

A pair of eyes inside the wood line watched the men and noticed a young girl driving a wagon toward them. He knew it was harvest time and reasoned why the young girl was driving the wagon. *I've got to find out just where I am. Wonder if'n they'll be mean to me. I just can't keep running if'n I don't know where I is.* He made his decision. He got up from his prone position behind a dense bush and started a slow hesitant walk toward the men. His eyes never left the figure of Samuel.

Catherine drove up to the group. She hesitated for a moment before getting down from the wagon seat and looked around the field of corn. It was a shock to her senses when she saw a man walking out of the forest toward them. "Pa, look yonder!" She pointed toward the figure. "That is…no, it can't be. But, that's a dark skin man, isn't it?"

"What! What are you talking about, Catherine?" exclaimed Uriah as he and his brothers turned to where she was pointing. It was then that everyone saw the man walking slowly toward them.

"Great day in the morning! Where did he come from? Is he armed?" said Mode in a cautious voice as he bent down to pick up his rifle. This was a signal for the rest to pick up their rifles also.

He saw the men picking up their rifles, and for a brief moment, took even slower steps toward the group. *Too late to turn back now. I'd be done in for sure if 'n I did.*

Samuel said in a level voice, "Just take it easy everyone! I don't see that he has any weapons other than that knife in his belt."

No one moved a muscle. Catherine's eyes were both cautious and inquisitive, but she did not make any move to get down from the wagon. The man stopped about twenty feet from them and after looking at each one said, "I be awfully hongry. Got some leftovers? My name is Boudroe. Where am I?"

Isaac said in a low voice, "Knows what he wants, doesn't he?"

Samuel said, "Say your name is Boudroe?"

Boudroe shook his head up and down and said, "Yas suh, that be it."

Samuel looked around at his brothers and could determine they were going to let him be their leader of this situation. *Well, I guess he is not harmful and needs help.* "Well, Boudroe, I think we can find you a bite to eat," as he motioned for him to come closer to the group. "Catherine, see if you can find another biscuit and meat in Mom's basket."

Catherine sat down on the wagon seat and reached under it to pull out the basket that contained lunch. She knew there was enough for everyone except Boudroe. *Guess I'll give him mine.* "Here is one, Pa." She handed it to Adam. "The rest of it is for y'all."

Adam started to give the biscuit to Samuel. "Go ahead and hand it to him, Adam. No use passing it around," said Samuel as he kept his eyes on Boudroe and gave him a slight nod. "Adam, on the other hand, give it to Catherine and let her give it to Boudroe."

Catherine hurried to get down from the wagon and walked over to her uncle and held out her hand for the food. She then turned to Boudroe and walked in a confident manner to him stopping an arm's length away. She slowly extended her arm. Boudroe's eyes never left the biscuit. He could almost taste it. He extended his hand to Catherine's with his palm up ready to accept the offering and nodded slightly in an "I thank you" manner. Catherine held out the biscuit in her palm wanting Boudroe to pick it up and was surprised when his left hand gently took her hand. Samuel had a quick intake of breath thinking *What if he grabs her* but held his ground.

"Thanky, ma'am. Thet's awful nice of you to help out a hongry man." His right hand took the food. While still holding her hand and looking into her eyes, he took a bite from the biscuit and slowly chewed the best thing he thought he had ever tasted. He closed his eyes while concentrating on the life-giving food. Catherine did not try to remove her hand and thought, *His hand feels like any other grown man's hand. Kinda like that Indian's and Pa's. Different colors tho'.*

Samuel watched Catherine and Boudroe and thought, *Food seems to be the trick with people we don't know.* "Best come on back, Catherine, and let Boudroe eat. Anybody got any water for him?" *Wonder what his story is?*

As everybody watched, Boudroe finished half of what had been his satisfying food in weeks. He said, "I'm really thanking y'all. Sure would be much owing ya if'n you could tell me where I am." He stuffed the rest of his biscuit in his pants pocket.

Quil said, "This is North Carolina. Polk's place is back over yonder." He indicated the general direction with a wave of his arm. "Where you going?"

Boudroe said, "Trying to get to a place where there ain't no slaves. I ran away from Devil's Track back yonder in South Carolina. Name fits. Thet overseer is hard."

"Slaves! You mean that is what you are?" exclaimed Adam. "Brothers, we gotta talk about this! We could get ourselves in a lot of trouble if somebody like Clark thinks we are hiding him."

"Speaking of Clark. Here he comes again!" Mode half-shouted to his brothers.

Samuel said is a hurried voice, "Hide him in the wagon bottom. Put some sacks and some of your coats over him! Be quick!" while motioning for Boudroe to keep low while getting into the wagon. "Catherine, drive back to the cabin. Don't try to be in much of a hurry."

Boudroe followed Samuel's orders without question and did his best to slide into the wagon without being seen by the sheriff.

Catherine was getting ready to leave when she said, "Won't it look strange to the sheriff that I'm going back empty?"

"Good thinking! Just sit tight. Boudroe, don't you even think about taking a deep breath!" Samuel said in a loud whisper and then thought, *How is it a twelve-year-old girl thinks like that.*

Clark rode up to the group and saw they were almost in the same position as when he left it. *Something's don't look right here.* "What's the matter, boys? You think thet corn is gonna lay itself up or are you having problems figuring out if your money is any good now? Well, no matter, I forgot to bring something up a while ago." He got down from his horse and walked over to Samuel.

"What's the other something you forgot to tell us. I think that new law about our money is enough work for one day," said Samuel.

Clark leaned close to Samuel and looked into his eyes as he said, "What's this I hear 'bout you and Dan'l crossing the line?"

Samuel looked back at Clark rapidly thinking what to say. He made his up his mind to tell the truth. "Well, Sheriff, I got to admit that I took Catherine to see the line and you'll never believe it, but she met and made friends with two Cherokees who were crossing the line coming our way."

Clark stared at Samuel for a long moment not knowing if he was being made the fool or that the truth was being told. He finally said, "Samuel Sherrill, I ought to run you in for lying to me. You really expect me to believe that cock and bull about little Catherine making friends with savages! And, to top it all, I hear Boone was with you."

"Yes, sir, Mr. Clark! What my pa is telling you is the truth! I'll take you there to see where I talked with them. It'll take us three, may four days at most," said Catherine as she got down from the wagon and walked over to where the sheriff stood.

Clark kept looking first at Samuel then Catherine, trying to determine how to get out of this mess. He looked at the other men whose countenance's spoke volumes about their feelings of his being made to look like a man who has lost control of a situation. "Well, boys, I guess that makes a case about rumors being made up. Ain't nobody gonna believe a little girl did what Catherine is saying she did plus being backed up by her pa. I'm outta here! But everyone of you better play things pretty close 'cause I'm watching y'all like a hawk."

Once again, the group watched the sheriff disappear over the hill; only this time, he was galloping away from an uncomfortable scene.

Samuel said with a small laugh in his voice, "Even telling him the truth is hard for him to understand. And, Catherine, even though you did real well in not letting him get close to the wagon, you have to watch what you say to him."

Isaac said, "That's all well and good, brother, but how did that information get around to him."

"Be darned if I know," said Samuel with a slight smile. "Guess one of us must have said something to somebody who told it to somebody else and on and on. I can hear it now…with enough telling it'll come back to us that because what Catherine did with those Indians, she became a great first lady of the land. Whatcha think about that, my daughter?"

Catherine knew he father was not making fun of her and said, "Awww, c'mon, Pa. You're just funning my uncles." She then thought, *I'm gonna be somebody. Yes, I will!*

Quil said as he motioned to the wagon, "I think the funning is over and the sheriff is gone. So don't y'all think we best be minding what we are gonna do about Boudroe?"

Samuel said, "I know one thing for sure. We best get back to putting up my corn and then we'll figure out what to do about him. Wanna help us with this corn, Boudroe?"

"I'm not used to be asked if I want to do something. Don't feel right," said Boudroe in a thoughtful manner.

"Well, then Boudroe, hop outta that wagon and help us pick this corn," said a smiling Uriah. Boudroe climbed out of the wagon, walked into the corn field, and started harvesting the ears of corn.

"Might need this gunny sack," said Catherine as she handed it to him. "Want another biscuit?"

"Yas, ma'am. Shore would like that," said Boudroe with a shy smile.

Catherine walked over to her father, "Why is he saying ma'am to me? I'm not his mama."

"Not a problem, my daughter. He's just being nice and polite plus he wants to find out where he is so he can make it to where he wants to go," Samuel said with a "that's 'bout the way of all things" thought in his mind. "Looks like the wagon is ready to go back. Give Boudroe my biscuit and head on back to tell your Ma that we've one more for supper."

"Kinda strange, isn't it, Pa, that I've held the hand of a Cherokee and a slave this year. What is going to be next?" said a thoughtful Catherine.

"Well, my daughter, you've done very well both times. I don't know how you came by that special talent of meeting people, but I'm glad I was with you when both of them happened," said Samuel.

Mary was busy preparing the evening supper when Catherine ran into the cabin. "Ma, Pa wanted me to let you know to set another place at the table."

"Is that so? And just who is this that is going to join us?" said Mary.

Catherine said as she studied her reflection in her mother's hand mirror, "Man by the name of Boudroe. New to these parts. Really likes your cooking. He's running from some place south of here."

"What's his last name. Might be from around the Waxhaws. Just might know Isaac," said Mary.

"He didn't give his last name," said Catherine while looking out the door. "Here they come now."

Mary was busy stirring various pots of venison and vegetables when she heard the others walking into the cabin. Samuel walked up behind her and motioned Boudroe over to his side. Mary sensed Samuel was going to play a trick on her and rapidly turned raising her spoon as if ready to strike Samuel. She stopped with the spoon held head high, getting ready to playfully strike her husband and looked at Boudroe with a "what in the world is going on" look.

Samuel said in a formal manner, "Mary, please say hello to Boudroe. He came to us this afternoon hungry, lost and tired. Boudroe, this is wife Mary." He was clearly enjoying Mary's reaction.

Mary held out her hand and said, "Good evening, Mr. Boudroe. Welcome to my kitchen." She then looked at Samuel and saw he did not expect this kind of greeting. *Serves him right for thinking he was going to scare me!* "Won't you please have a seat," pointing to Samuel's place at the table.

"Now, Mary, just wait a minute 'cause—"

"This is the seat of honor and I'm honored to have Mr. Boudroe with us," said an inwardly smiling Mary.

Boudroe was looking at all the venison, vegetables, and cornbread on the table and looked at Mary with a smile and sat down in Samuel's chair. *Ummm ummm, just look at all this,* as he started to reach for a plate.

Very quickly, Mary said, "Mr. Boudroe, we give thanks to God before we eat our meals."

"Yas, ma'am, I'm sure glad you do. I would think it nice if you would allow me to say the blessing," said Boudroe while folding his hands together in prayer. The others sat down at the long table, bowed their heads, and listened to a hungry man give Thanks to God for the people he was fortunate enough to run into today.

Just as they were finishing their apple cobbler dessert, Mary said, "Deep dark tan you got there, Mr. Boudroe. Mind telling us where you're from and where you are going. We don't get too many traveling though these parts and anything is news to us." *I sure hope he doesn't have a story like Isaac's, but being a slave, he might have been badly treated.*

Boudroe said with a small laugh, "Deep dark tan. Nevah ever been hearing that one befo'. Y'all have to know I am a slave, and was born across the ocean." He waved his arm toward the east. "I been at Devil's Track ever since I got here 'bout ten years ago."

Samuel didn't want to know the answer to the question, but had to ask, "Did they set you free or did you run away?"

"I be runnin' away! Got to pickin' cotton a few weeks back. Got to the end of the row at the wood line." After a brief pause, he then looked up at Samuel and then Mary and said in a long almost whisper, "An'...I...just...kept on goin'! Wot's gonna happ'n to Boudroe now?"

Samuel said, "You're gonna stay here until I can get this sorted out with my pa and brothers. You can sleep in the hayloft of the barn or where ever you choose, but just stay close."

"Well, if'n you don't care, I would feel better back in them woods. You know, just in case someone comes askin' 'bout me and you kin tell 'em that nobody like thet is at yore place."

Mary looked at Samuel with a questioning look on her face. Samuel didn't need to hear her concern since it was his also. *What if Clark gets wind of this?* ran around the back of his mind. He didn't want to say the answer, but he knew most of what would happen to him. The stocks for sure or worse.

"Why sure, Boudroe, just be careful out in those woods. Never know what's about," said Mary.

"Sure nuff I will. You be minding if I take some of that meat and biscuit to tide me over 'til morning?" said Buodroe.

"Gracious me, Boudroe, please forgive me for not asking if you wanted seconds. Here, now, take what you want," said Mary as she passed the ham and biscuits to Boudroe. She saw that he took two biscuits and enough ham to fill each of them. "Hope you get some good rest."

"Yas, ma'am. I think I will be able to do that alright," said Boudroe as he got up from the table and left the cabin.

13

The sun was barely casting shadows when Adam and his sons hitched their horses to the rail outside their church. A little bragging, some talk about the corn yield and the ever present topic of weather were being cussed and discussed.

"Gonna be a good crop this year," said Jacob. "Looks to be twenty bushels to me."

"Sounds good, Jacob. From what I saw your tobacco is looking good," said Isaac.

Adam said while pointing at the church door, "C'mon, boys. We've got some figuring to do." With that command, everyone entered the church, and after settling down, looked to their father to start the meeting. "We've got four things to cover today. The first three being what the devil's own lackeys in England are doing to us. And the first stupidity being that line proclamation, the second being the Sugar Act, and now this Currency Act that isn't even fit for the hogs and fourth, and probably the most important, is what to do about Boudroe."

Much talk, heated word references to British mentality and an overall feeling of unease permeated the group until Adam held up his hand and said, "What's with you, boys? Nothing I've heard yet makes any sense. Let's face it, the British and Tory's are making us their subjects just like they have done our ancestors for centuries. The difference this time is that this is a new land and the people living here just want to be left alone to do things that make us our own."

Quil said, "Left alone? Why? If we didn't have them looking over our shoulder, then it would be somebody else like the French or maybe even the Indians. Nobody is gonna leave us alone. There is too much here for the taking."

Samuel said, "Quil's right! And the only way we can keep what we have sweated blood for is to find a way to protect it!"

Moses said, "Then my brothers"—he paused to look at each one—"why don't we write a letter to the boys in England and tell them we are going our own way."

Silence fell over the room. Everyone sat back and lost themselves in thinking about what Mode had proposed.

Adam stood up, walked over to the window. *Wonderful country out there. Mode is right* and said, "I think Mode has hit on something we need to give a lot of thought to doing. You well know we can't take this on by ourselves. We will need help to get this right. And…if we start down this road then we will most assuredly be putting ourselves and our families in danger. Are each of you ready for that?" He looked in the eyes of each of his sons and was satisfied they would act appropriately and not give in to the passions of the moment. *We just might be having something here.*

"But, Pa, just how are we going to make this work for us? Let's think about those men around here who think the British have to be our leaders. When we figure that out then we'll have knowing to build us a plan," said William.

Samuel stood up, looked around at his brothers and waited for everyone to get quiet and said, "When I was last at Polk's place before going up to the line, I heard of a man by the name of Husband who, I was told by the smithy, has some of the same thinking we've been talking about today. I think he is trying to get men like us to pull together and try to get those who are loyal to the Crown and have been appointed sheriffs and judges to see our side of the things."

Moses jumped up and exclaimed, "Then let's go find him and get him to tell us what he is going to do! We'll just join up with him and run those Crown loyalists back to England!"

All sorts of talk, loud voices wanting to be heard, and stomping of feet on the church floor finally got the best of Adam who yelled, "Quiet! And…I mean it…right now!"

Once again, the vacuum of silence filled the room. Adam then said with a low commanding voice, "Samuel, you and Mode get on over to Polk's and find out what is going on. When you get back, we'll talk some more about what we are going to do. Anybody got a problem with that?" Not one son disputed or argued their father's points.

Adam stopped at the church door and looked at his sons as they got on their horses and started to their homes. *Adam, ol' boy, you are getting too old for this sort of stuff.*

14

The store owner, James Polk, looked up from his inventory book and recognized the two men entering the door. "Howdy, to the Sherrill folks. Anything I can do fer ya?"

Samuel said, "Might be. Just might be. We need to get some horse shoes and nails. Hope you have the same shoes I got last spring."

"Yep, sure do. Never change my shoes. How many sets you be needin' today?"

"Near as I can figure I think eight of 'em ought to do it. And don't let me forget to get some salt," said Samuel.

"Fresh out of salt," said James. "I might have some next couple of weeks. Everybody wants it this time of year and I just didn't stock up."

"Guess we'll have to make do," said Samuel. *Mary isn't going to like this news.*

As their purchase was being tallied, Samuel said, "Place sure is growing around here. Seems like four or five new houses and stores have been built along the road coming in here."

"Yes, sir. This place is growing by leaps and bounds. Seem people are coming from all over to be here. Never seen the like before. Makes me wonder how they find out about this place," said James.

Mode couldn't stand listening to what he considered idle chit-chat and said, "You know a man by the name of Husband around here?"

Samuel winced at the question. Polk ever so briefly paused his writing and then continued until he was finished figuring the bill. He turned the bill to Samuel who looked to see the final bill. There was no number. The owner had written "Not now."

While looking at the note, Samuel pulled out his coin purse making it seem he was getting ready to pay the bill. "Same price, eh? Never know these days what a price will be." He then called Mode over. "Mode, just look at that price and remember to tell Pa and our brothers." Moses read the note and realized what was happening. "Yep, sure nuff. Guess we'll have to pay it."

The owner said, "Uhhh ohhhh! Looks like I misfigured the amount. I forgot that I had to figure things according to the new Currency Act." He tore up the note and started writing another bill.

"Yeah and I tell you that new law is about as stupid as the others," said Mode.

Samuel casually turned to Mode and said in an even voice coupled with a meaningful stare into Modes eyes, "Why, little brother, you know the king knows what he is doing for us, don't you?"

Moses caught the rarely used Samuel stare and said, "Ahhh… guess you got a point there, brother."

As James was writing, he looked up and said, "Well, hello, judge. Didn't see you back there. Find what you needed?"

Samuel looked up from the counter to see the judge staring at him. "Howdy, name's Sherrill. I take it you're a judge around here." He held out his hand to shake the judge's hand.

Judge Alan Cannon took a long time to shake Samuel's hand. "Glad to meet you. Did I catch your Sherrill name correct?"

Moses held out his hand saying, "I'm a Sherrill also. Good to meet you."

"Oh, I see. Sherrill is your last name. Yeah, I've heard of you, boys. Especially, Adam. He yore pa?"

"Yes, sir! Eight sons and two daughters. Seems Mom put a halt to more when Quil came along," said Moses. "And we're all farming over across the Catawba."

"Ohh, yeah! Now I recall why I remember your names well. A man by the name of Taylor was brought before the bench awhile back. Seems he had murdered two boys and burned a cabin down on them. Y'all helped capture him," said the judge.

"He in jail now?" asked Mode.

"Nope. Sentenced him to hang. Sentence carried out the next day. Gotta give quick justice to those who break the king's laws. You agree?" He looked from Samuel to Moses searching for a hint of defiance to his statement.

Samuel put his hand tight on Moses shoulder and said, "Yep, quick justice is the best. C'mon, Mode, let's get over to the smithy. We need to get hinges. Wish we could stay and chat some more, but we seem to always be a little short of time. Come see us when you can." *Glad we've got a reason to leave that judge. He's worrisome to me. And I make my own hinges anyway.*

Judge Cannon said to Polk, "They get here much? How would they know Husband? You keep an eye on them and let me know if they do anything suspicious. Ya hear me now?"

"Gotcha, judge," said Polk as he was getting Samuel's order wrapped up. He thought, *The day hadn't been made when I tell you anything going on.*

The smithy was fitting a horseshoe when Samuel and Moses walked up. "Be with you, boys, in a minute," he said.

"Takes some kinda talent to talk when you have a mouthful of shoe nails," said Moses with a small laugh.

The smithy continued with his work until the shoe was properly fitted and filed down. He said, "Well, I'll tell ya' boys, when most of your business is conducted with a mouth full of nails, you learn real well how to talk plain. I seen you boys around here a few months ago." He held out his blackened calloused hand. Samuel and Mode shook it without thinking of the grime on his hand. "What can I do fer ya?"

"Looking for some iron to make some hinges that I can take back to the farm. Wish you lived close by our place so I could get you to make our hinge needs," said Samuel.

"Yeah, I've been thinking about that problem. What would you say if'n I traveled around, kinda like a preacher, fixing everybody's shoes, wheels, and such," said the smithy.

"Now, sir, that's a great idea. I know my brothers could sure use your help and like now," said Mode. "Gotta figure out how to pay you now that we've got new laws about what to use and what not to use. Ridiculous!"

The smithy said, "My name is Arnold Husband."

Samuel and Mode looked at him with surprised faces. "No kidding!" said Mode.

"No kidding," said Arnold.

"Well, then why don't you come over to our place and speak to our brothers 'bout what you are proposing. I know they'll be almighty interested in what you have to say," said Samuel with an I-think-you-get-my-thinking look. "And added to that we need to talk about..." and quit talking when he saw the judge.

"Hey, boys! Where's yore hinge iron?" said Judge Cannon as he walked up the the group.

"They don't have it, yet. I'm going over to their place on a visit to all the farms around there. That will give me more business," said Arnold. "Don't you think that is a good idea?"

The judge, being a suspicious man, said, "Makes some sense of the surface. Guess that means you don't have any reason to get all of the farmers together at one place to do any smithing. Right?"

Arnold purposely thought a minute and said, "Don't see any reason to get 'em all together. They'll soon find out about my taking my business to them and not the other way round. Why you askin' judge?"

Judge Cannon thought, *This has gone on long enough*, and said, "Well, you asked me if I thought it was a good idea. And it appears to me to be a good way to grow your business. I wish you luck." He turned to go back across the street. *Gotta keep an eye on those gents.*

"Dark clouds back over toward our place," said Mode with a motion of his hand to the western sky, "looks to be one of those gully washers. Wow! Didja see that lightning! Worrisome stuff... can really put the hurting on anything it hits."

Thoughts of the time almost thirty years ago when a storm dropped vast amounts of rain on the land flashed through Samuel's mind. The Catawba River had so much trees and brush that it formed a dam at a sharp curve in the river. When it finally broke loose, everything downstream was destroyed in its wake to the point of watching one of their horses being swept downstream never to be seen again.

"Yeah. We gotta get back to our homes. Hope this storm is passed by that time," said Samuel as he stepped into their wagon.

Arnold said, "Hope y'all aren't getting me mixed up with one of my relatives, especially the one named Herman. He's messin' in things that's gonna get him in deep trouble with the likes of Cannon."

Samuel said, "Hey, no problem. If you see him, tell him he's welcome to drop by our place if he's ever over our way. Might be riding with you to help out your smithing."

"Hmmm...not a bad idea. Haven't seen him in over a year. Just hear all sorts of talk about him. Wonder if it is fact? Well, hope to see you soon with your hinge iron," said Arnold.

Mode said with a dubious look, "Playing it close, isn't he?"

"Yep, I would too. Never know who you are talking to these days. Not knowing a man like Arnold very well and saying too much about how bad you think the English are treating us... well, it could land you in jail," said Samuel. *And I'm getting sick and tired of always having to be careful about what I say. Gotta be another way.*

"Hey! Hold up there," said Judge Cannon as he ran into the street to stop the wagon.

"Anything wrong?" said Samuel.

"Not that I know of with you two. But I have a letter from a sheriff in South Carolina who says there may be an escaped slave heading in our direction. Haven't seen or heard such have you?" said the judge while paying close attention to Samuel and Mode's reaction.

"Did I hear you say slave? Here? Why would such want to come here?" said Samuel with a look of innocence.

"What about you?" said the judge while pointing at Mode.

"No, sir, sure haven't. Any reward being given for his return?" said Mode.

There was a brief pause as the judge looked hard into Mode's eyes and said, "Who said anything about a man?"

"Just figured that would be the case. But I guess it could be a woman as well," said Mode. "I just don't know much about slaves 'cepting it's not right."

"Well, there are those who don't share your thinking. But anyway, if you hear of them or see them, just let me know," said the judge.

As the judge was walking away, Mode said under his breath, "Them? I say my brother, there's more to Boudroe than he's letting on."

"Got a point there, Mode. Let's get on home and get this figured out with ol' Boudroe. He might not have told us everything," said Samuel as he flicked the horse reins to get them moving to home.

Mary's mood and manner were one of caution as she poured the ashes into the ash hopper because at times there were hot coals lurking in the fireplace ashes. "Can't let hot coals get on me or start a fire in the hopper late tonight. Need these to get my lye to make our soap," she said to anyone who happened to be in listening range.

"Yes, ma'am, please don't get burned. Can I help?" said Catherine.

"Yes, matter of fact, you can. How about getting a bucket of water for me to use just in case something goes wrong," said Mary. She poured the remainder of the ashes into the hopper and saw there were no hot coals. "Looks like everything is doing fine. We can start making our soap after the hog butchering this fall."

Catherine had witnessed the hog killing and butchering every year and wasn't too keen on watching it another time. "Mom, is the only way to make soap done by killing our hogs?"

"It's the only way I know since we get the lard from the fat of the hog and cook it down all day. The next morning, the good lard is on top and that is what we use with the lye to make our soap," said Mary. "You'll be doing this for your home one of these days."

No way I'm going to make soap. "I don't know, Mother. I just won't make any since it is smelly and messy. What good is it anyway?" said Catherine.

Mary looked at her daughter and said with a wry smile, "Sure would be mighty dirty around the house if we didn't have that soap we make. And, your clothes would not be as clean either and I know you love clean clothes."

Catherine twirled around swishing her dress out from her sides. "Yes, ma'am, I will always be clean, but I don't have to make the soap, do I? Ohhh, here comes Pa."

"Hello, everybody! We're back! But, I guess you can see that," said a smiling Samuel as he stepped down from the buggy.

"Good to see y'all back safe and sound. Did ya get the iron and salt? And what's with this fantastic stuff? You courtin' me again?" said Mary with a coy smile. She could tell by the look on Samuel's face that he had forgotten something and she hoped it wasn't the salt.

Samuel said with a messed-up look, "Sorry Mary, but I had to order it. How needful are you for it?"

"I swear. You well know that we need it for making sure the meat doesn't spoil on us. And I was figuring on using some of it to make some hard soap," said Mary.

"Making hard soap? What's wrong with what we've always used?" said Samuel. "Salt is too expensive and hard to get to be using making soap."

Mode said with a thoughtful look, "Didn't one of those guys who came by here last year, you know, the one who helped build that road across yonder in Virginia back in '60, say something about a place where there is a lot of salt?"

"Yeah, now that you brought it up, I remember that guy talking about the salt place. Sounds mighty far away. I think maybe we could find a place closer that is trading salt. Let's ask around," said Samuel. *Might give me a chance to go over there.*

⌒

While Mary and Samuel were talking soapmaking, Yona was standing by a field full of corn and squash thinking, *the women have a good growing this year*, while turning to his wife, Awiusdi, and said, "You have done a great thing for the people. The corn will be plentiful for us this winter."

"Yes, my warrior husband. Just like you getting meat for us through the winter. Did you find more salt? We are needful of it."

"No, I haven't found any and I know the village needs it. But I do know the place off of our path up the valley has plenty of it and I'll start on my walk there tomorrow," said Yona. "I need four others to go with me to help bring it back."

"I don't know if you should do that since our people are no longer there," said Awiusdi. "The white man will not like seeing you there."

"Yes, I know. But we will find a way to get it. I hear of a man living on the Hogoheegee that has some for trade. We go there first," said Yona.

15

1767

Catherine looked up from pulling weeds in the bean and squash garden when she saw Daniel Boone and his ten-year-old son, James, riding their horses toward the house.

"Hey there, Catherine. How you doing these days? Seen any other strangers? And I do declare, I just can't believe how fast you are growing. Your pa letting you use his rifle these days? By the way, is your pa around?" said Daniel as he got down from his horse.

James seemed to be somewhat reluctant about getting off his horse when he saw Catherine smiling at him. "I'll just wait on you here, Pa."

"Awww, Mr. Boone, you just funning me. Aren't you? "C'mon, James, get down and help me with this weeding. Sooner I get done is the sooner I can saddle Betsy and we could ride over to the creek."

James looked at his pa whose countenance was one of "you just gonna sit there or get down and help out." At least he was letting James make the decision.

"Guess I'll get down and help. Long as you take me to the river and we can fish for our supper," said James thinking that *no way is Catherine gonna touch a fish.*

"Well, James, if that's the way it is then I'll just have to show you how to catch the biggest trout in that river," said Catherine while barely tilting her head to look James in the eyes.

James then knew his abilities were being questioned and said, "I don't think so 'cause the day ain't been made yet that I can't beat a girl at fishing."

"Kinda pretty, isn't she?" said Mary in a low voice to Daniel. "Susan is growing, too. Just the other day I saw how they continue to fill out toward being a woman." *Why must they grow up so soon?* I guess you're looking for Samuel I suppose. He's running some spirits for all the Sherrills over yonder in the still house." She casually waved her hand toward the little building.

"Don't sound too pleased with him making it," said Daniel. "It's kinda like salt in that we need it to put on our cuts to make them heal better."

"Salt doesn't do that," said Mary. "It preserves what we need to keep from going rotten. Well, great day in the morning, I'm preaching to the choir. You know all that."

Daniel smiled and said, "Well, Mary, never hurts to hear what the women folk have to say 'bout things. Tends to make the men folk a little smarter wouldn't you say?"

"Get on outta here, Daniel. And, anyway, we all know Becky is the smartest in your family," said Mary with a smile and a touch of smugness on her face.

"I'm getting on to finding Samuel before I get in way too deep for my mind," said Daniel as he turned toward the still house.

"Hey, the still. I'm coming in!" called out Daniel. "Smells awfully ripe around here."

"Bring it on in and hold these buckets for me," said Samuel as he stoked the fire underneath the heated pot of sour mash.

As Daniel held a bucket under the spigot, he said, "Looks mighty clear to me. Is it any good?" He ran his finger through the dripping stream. "Way to go Samuel, that stuff is smooth! You sure it's got healing power for cuts?"

"Yep, you can tell it's good by the way it's beading up," said Samuel as he pointed to the brew in the bucket. "What brings you this far? Since y'all moved over on the Yadkin, I thought we'd never see you much anymore."

"Yeah, it's a far piece all right, but I didn't come all this way just to watch you make whiskey. I've got to tell you what I'm getting ready to do and I want you to do it with me," said Daniel as he looked up from the bucket into Samuel's eyes.

Unhhhh ohhh. He's got traveling on his mind. "Well, my good friend, put it to me. Whatcha got on your mind?" said Samuel.

Daniel slowly looked around the small room as if trying to get his thoughts straight in his mind, took another finger taste test of the brew and said, "I'm going across the line and take another look around further into those woods and valleys."

"Good grief, Dan'l. You went to Florida most on two years ago and came back in a few months. I thought you had had enough of traveling," said Samuel with a questioning look.

"Well, yeah, I did, but things continue to get more and more controlled around here. I hear those British boys are getting ready to pass another tax on tea and some other stuff. Don't mean much to me, but you know how those English are with their tea. Think it's a reason to stop working for a while during the day," said Daniel.

"Well, great day, Dan'l. Those guys are always passing some bird-brain act or law whatever. Naww, I take that back 'cause it's an insult to birds. Let's see now 'bout four years ago, they did the line thinking we'd not cross over it. Just how stupid they think we are?" said Samuel.

"Yeah, then came the Sugar and Currency Acts the year after that. Those idiots don't know anything about here, but they think just the fact they say it that we'll just hop to whatever," said Daniel with a look of digust.

"Yeah, you're right. And what was it they did last year? Something about stamps, wasn't it?" said Samuel. "That was it!

It was called the Stamp Act. I'm tired of having someone that barely knows how things are here trying to tell us how we are to act, spend our money, travel where we want to go or, heaven help us, they may try to make us all one religion."

"Naww, they aren't gonna mess with anybody's religion, just ain't gonna happen," said Daniel. "But the other stuff will continue and now you know why I'm up to leaving this place and finding some room where they won't find me for awhile. And, anyway, it'll give me some idea of where I can move Becky and James, Israel and Susannah."

"When you figuring on leaving?" said Samuel.

"I hope it isn't me. I hope it's us," Daniel said with a look into Samuel's eyes in attempts to try and determine what he hopes will be an affirmative answer.

16

Mary sat in her favorite chair and bent her wispy frame forward, narrowed her eyes, and said, "I don't believe what I just heard. Mind repeating that to me once more."

Samuel had long ago became aware of the meaning of Mary's narrowed eyes when he brought up a sensitive subject. The last time was when he said he was going to take Catherine into the mountains. He said with a diminishing voice, "Ahhhh, uhhh, well...I said that I was...going to go on a...uhhhh...trip with Dan'l."

Mary held up her hand and said, "Stop! Don't mention another word." She then got up, walked to the door, and called out for Susan and Catherine to join her in the cabin.

Their daughters came running into the cabin and with breathless voices, looked at their parents and quickly figured out that this was not the best of times. "Yes, ma'am," said Catherine. "Is everything all right?"

Susan said, "Nobody is hurt, right?"

Mary, while looking at Samuel, motioned the girls to sit down. As soon as this was done, she said with an intense stare, "Now, my husband, say again what you said in the first place."

"Well, as long as we're going to talk about something, we'd might as well get the boys in here, too," said Samuel.

"Can't do that. They're scattered over around Mode and Quil's place. So you just go on with what you were gonna say," said Mary.

Samuel could see what was going to happen and decided to fight fire with fire. He looked evenly at each one and settled his eyes on Mary and said, "I said I am going across the mountains with Dan'l and nobody is—"

Catherine jumped up from her seat interrupting her father, which, until this very moment, was a definite no-no, and said, "Can I go with you again? Ohh, Mama, please tell him to let me go!"

Susan fixed her sister with a look of "you can't be serious" and started to say that when she looked at her mother and held off saying anything.

Both Mary and Samuel were looking at each other with Samuel's look of "Is she serious?" while Mary's eyes narrowed even further and her posture became almost threatening toward Samuel. "Now…just what are you going to do about that, my husband?"

Samuel stood up and without a word walked out of the cabin door. *Good grief and hades fire! Just what was that all about!* He saw Budroe walking toward the edge of the corn field, *think I'll have a talk with ol' Budroe. Might help me clear my mind of this mess.* He followed Budroe into the wood line.

"Ohh, Mama, won't that be just great! I get to go back on the mountain and this time I'll take Betsy! Wonder if I'll get to see that Indian man who gave me his moccasins? Sure hope so. He was so nice to me. Bet he is a king or something with his people."

Mary said, "I think you best not get your hopes too high." *No way will that happen even if Samuel goes with Dan'l.* "You and Susan go on about your chores and come help me fix supper."

"Awwww, Mother…" said Susan.

"Don't awwww mother me, young lady. You just do as you are told, ya hear me!" said a frustrated Mary.

At that moment, Samuel arrived at the edge of the field and started looking where Boudroe had gone into the woods. *Might have decided to strike out on his own again in hopes of getting to the place where he felt he would be free.*

After Boudroe had walked, he glanced back to make sure he wasn't being followed. *Uhhhh ohhh! Here comes Samuel. What's he up to?* He moved deeper into the forest and knelt down behind a large chestnut tree waiting to see if Samuel had seen him and was following him into the woods. He pulled his knife from the scabbard tied to his leg and, while hardly breathing, entered into an uneasy wait.

Samuel's sixth sense told him things were not as they should be. The usual noise of the woods was gone. He knew Boudroe could not have gone too far into these woods and wondered, *Why is he acting this way? Something wrong?* He knelt down behind a large pine tree and decided to wait out the moment.

Boudroe heard the throaty hiss and turned to see a bobcat staring at him while its tail slowly swished back and forth. The cat slowly crouched down into an attack position. Its beady eyes, laid back ears, and frothy mouth told Boudroe that this cat must be rabid. These cats do not usually hunt during this time of day. It took all the willpower he ever had to keep from jumping up and running away, but he also knew the cat would soon attack. Sweat started dripping into his eyes, but he didn't move a muscle. He couldn't get enough of a proper grip on his knife to make a cutting swipe if the cat attacked him.

Samuel's skills in the forest were at their peak as he silently crept to the area where he felt Boudroe was hidden. His ears barely caught the hissing sound of the cat and knew two things—got a cat that's crazy and Boudroe's in trouble. He carefully placed his next steps on a carpet of pine needles which gave further silence to his steps and could hear the cat increasing its growling and hissing. *It's getting ready to attack.* He knelt down while looking in the direction of the sound and then saw the cat not over ten feet from Boudroe. Samuel slowly raised his rifle, and while taking aim, saw the cat jump straight up, letting forth with a vicious, high-pitched snarl and when it landed, it started running in circles snapping at its left rear leg. That's when he saw the long-feathered tip dart sticking into the cat's leg. Then there was a second dart hitting the cat in the throat. Samuel stared at the cat in morbid fascination as it stopped its fury, turned to Boudroe, switched its head to one side and with what looked like a questioning look died before it settled onto the pine needles.

Samuel saw that Boudroe was shaking like a wind-blown leaf and just as he started to get up and say something to him, he was shocked to see a tall stately looking full-of-confidence woman step into the small clearing intent of getting to Boudroe. She held a blowgun in her hand and it was clear to Samuel that she was the one shooting the lances at the cat. She knelt down to see if Boudroe was wounded and on finding him in good condition other than his mental state said, "You can come out now, white man."

Samuel almost looked around to see if there was any other person beside himself hiding in the bushes and then he realized she was talking to him. He made doubly certain that her blowgun was not ready to use and thought, *Here goes nothin'*, as he stepped into the clearing. "Well, Boudroe, mind telling me what's going on?"

Boudroe said, "I tell you now, Samuel, I was…" when he saw Samuel lifting his hand signaling him to stop.

"Don't you think you need to introduce me to the woman who just saved your hide," said Samuel.

Boudroe looked from Samuel to the woman and said, "Samuel, this is Emma. She is my wife. Emma, thank you for saving me and I'm mighty sorry I forgot my manners."

Samuel's mouth dropped and his eyes widened in a surprised look as he stared back and forth from Emma to Boudroe. Emma stepped forward and held out her hand saying, "It is nice to finally meet you. I've heard so much about you from…Boudroe, get up! You aren't hurt! Sorry 'bout that, Mr. Sherrill, he needs tending to now and then. But, I guess you know that by now."

Samuel then smiled and said, "Guess this proves that skin color doesn't change the way a wife treats her husband." He shook Emma's hand. Emma smiled back and both sensed there was no need to pursue that line of conversation. *She certainly is a mighty handsome woman. Why is it the ugly men get the best looking women...then that makes me the ugliest man in these parts.* "Well, Boudroe, it looks like we've got a lot to talk about. Now Mary will know why you always put your seconds at dinner in your pockets. Late night snack seemed kinda lame to us."

"So, my man thought he was foolin' y'all, eh? I want to say that I really appreciate your kindness to him and now me. We ran off together and are trying to get to a free state," said Emma.

Samuel said, "No problem with the Sherrills around here about your wanting to be get to wherever you want to go. Let's head on to the cabin. I want you to meet my wife, Mary and my girls and boys. And, by the way, just how is it that you know how to use a blowgun? How did you make those darts? Are they poison?"

Emma's reaction to the rapid fire questions was one of "slow down a bit" and said, "Fairly simple, Mr. Sherrill. There are a lot of canebreaks around these parts and finding one that is just right for a blowgun isn't too hard. Hard part is making the darts and their wings. I'll show you how. Poison on the darts? No, I don't do that, but sounds like a good idea."

Samuel was impressed. *Now, I've found another way to hunt like the Indians. Sure would save on powder and lead.*

17

At the moment Samuel, Boudroe, and Emma were walking toward the cabin, Pattie Ferguson said, "Lord Pitford, I humbly beseech thee for another glass of your port. I must admit you are clever in keeping it hidden from your lovely wife."

"Ahh, Mr. Ferguson, I would be most honored if you would assist me in disposing the final drops in the bottom of this decanter. Perhaps my lovely wife would never know of this unique alliance between us," said Lord Pitford as he drained the last of the port into Pattie's cut crystal glass.

"Once again, I beseech thee in keeping this subject between us only and not reveal it to your lovely wife," said Pattie while observing how the sunlight streaming into the library created many hues of red and blue as it reflected off the port. *Must be the prisms in the body of the glass.*

Lord Pitford drew himself to his maximum height and said with an ominous tone punctuated by a steely stare, "Once again, sir. I must remind you of the precarious position you are placing yourself under with proposing such a profound change in our local governing body."

"Very well, my Lord, you leave me no choice." Patrick walked to the hallway entrance into the room and said in a modestly loud voice, "Mother, would you please come in here and show this impertinent judge the error of his ways!"

Pattie's ,mother, Anne, walked into the room, stopped and looked at each man with equal dignity and said, "What hath my husband and son created now?"

James Ferguson, known as Lord Pitford, and Pattie burst out laughing at their repartee. Anne had yet to even give the slightest hint of even smiling at her family. "And just what is it that you two are doing? Trying to hide some port from me I wager." At that moment all three were laughing until their sides hurt.

After all had resumed a quiet moment, Pattie said, "I think I will be going back to France for a nice visit in Nice."

James said, "And why is that trip necessary. I think you should cloister yourself and think about what you want to do and where do you want to be in ten years. You aren't getting any younger, my son."

"Yes, my father, I have been thinking long and hard about my future. I've decided to rejoin the British Dragoons. The military is where my interest lies and if things continue to decline for England in America, my country will need me to help bring them back into line."

"Pattie, I'm not about to dissuade you from your decision even though I think you are better suited for other pursuits. I am sure you could be a lawyer or a chancellor in a few years. Maybe follow in my footsteps…hmmmm?" said James with a look of "take the advice of an older man."

"Thank you, Father. But you know one must do what one must do. And, as you well know, to obtain higher ranks in government, I will need a successful military career to add to my qualifications. Where else could I attain that except in service in the colonies," said Pattie.

"Well said and painfully true, my son. But I just don't like the thought of you going off to some country that seems to be at odds with us all the time. They continually argue with us and fight against our Indian allies. I think they want their own government. Imagine that! A bunch of people who couldn't get along here and think they can make it on their own. Poppycock!" said James with an "I give up" arm motion.

Patrick said, "I feel sure that we, the most powerful nation in the world, can make them see the error of their ways either through peaceful negotiations or through the strength of our military."

"Another good point. Basically, what you are saying, is to use our superior force to mold them into a people who are loyal to the crown. They will thank us for that in the future," said James. *At least I hope so.*

~~

Boudroe said, "Well, Mizz Mary, I just want to say that we…"

"Boudroe, there you go again…why is it you keep calling me Mizz this and Mizz that? I've got a first name and it isn't Mizz! I don't believe I've heard you say Mizz, Emma," said Mary in a somewhat exasperated manner.

Emma, after meeting Mary, was made to feel at home and had been asked by Mary to share her story. Mary was interested in why she felt compelled to hide in the woods. "Well, Mizz… uhhhhhh, Mrs. Sherrill." She could see that Mary was not too happy with that salutation either. Uncomfortable as it was, she said, "Mary, we were just plain in fear for our safety and had agreed that one of us had to stay in hiding to help the other if he was captured or whatever."

"That makes sense. But didn't Boudroe tell you we were trying to help him?" said Samuel. "On the other hand, I can see why y'all felt you must be careful in the extreme."

Mary said with a wide-eyed look at her husband, "Careful in the extreme…Wow! Well-chosen words, my husband. You been reading something behind my back to gain that kind of talk?" Try as she may, she could not hold back a smile. "Since you two are at a point where you need to make some decisions, I am sure you

need time to figure things out. Just want you to be sure that you are most welcomed here," said Mary.

"I am most appreciative of your offer, but we can't stay here," said Emma. "You've got things that you need to do besides caring for us until we make up our mind."

Mary said, "Ohhh, we won't be, as you say, caring for you. Some things you will need to do. You will do some chores just like everyone else around here. Have you read from the Good Book?"

"We know a little about it, but I don't think nearly enough," said Emma.

"Well, Emma, you and Boudroe need to decide if you want to learn more about it, and from it, you will find out how we try to live. We'll start with Genesis and when we, I mean you, get to Deuteronomy, you will be well on your way in the Old Testament. Just remember, when you read the Good Book, remember to think what the word is when you take an "o" out of good," said Mary in a purpose-filled voice.

Boudroe said, "I can't spell."

"I can," said Emma. "Let's see, I take an *o* out of good…ohhhh, I see! It spells God! Ohhhh glory be! The Good Book would then be God's Book!"

A smiling Mary said, "What happens to the *o* you took out?" Everyone looked at each other and started saying words that began with the letter *o*.

Mary, after watching and listening to their efforts finally said, "To me, the *o* stands for 'our'. To me, that means God's Book is ours. So it all boils down to starting with the Good Book, then going to God's Book and then to 'our' book. Our God's Book. Simple, yet so meaningful!"

Samuel turned to a smiling Mary and said, "You never cease to amaze me, Mrs. Sherrill! I'm so glad I'm so ugly that I was able to marry such a beautiful woman and to also find that she is so very smart."

"You? Ugly? Where do you come up with that?" said Emma.

Samuel said, with a slight smile, "Us menfolk always say that the ugly guys get the prettiest girls which means that I'm ugly enough to run off a mad wild pig. Whatcha think about that ugly Boudroe?"

As Mary looked into Emma's eyes, she said, "You do have a certain manner of speech and way about you that doesn't belong out here. Where are you from?"

"I was a slave in the big house for the owner's daughters. They were decent and did what they could do to teach me some of what they had been taught. But their father was a wild man. Boudroe and I had jumped the broom and had decided to get as far away from Devils as soon as possible and as soon as we could figure out a safe way."

Samuel said, "I'm going to see Pa and find out what he thinks needs to be done. He's got a good way of figuring things out. Y'all need to figure out where you will want to stay over at night. You are welcome here, as you well know, but you have to stay out of sight as much as possible. Mode and I have already heard there is a reward out for you."

The knocking on the door sounded like the loud rumbling of a thunderstorm. Startled looks were passed around the room. Boudroe was approaching a state of panic. Emma's eyes showed a look of dread. After a pause, the knocking started again.

"Say something, Samuel. They know we're in here," said Mary.

Shaking his head up and down, Samuel said, "Be there in a minute." He walked toward the door and pulled the leather latch string. The cross bar lifted up, and he pulled the door open and saw Frank Travis who said, "Good grief, Samuel, you look like you have just seen a ghost. What in the world is the matter with you?"

Samuel stepped out of the door and shut it. "I guess I interrupted something mighty important. I'll head on over to Mode's," said Frank.

Mary's concern subsided when she heard Frank's voice and turned to Boudroe and Emma, "He's a friend. We're going to be all right."

"You'll do no such thing!" said Samuel. He looked deep into Frank's eyes that let Frank know what he was about to hear was very important. "Just listen to what I have to say. I want your honest thinking on it."

Frank's somewhat-puzzled look followed by a small smile said, "Well, great day, Samuel! You know I'll be as frank as a Frank can be."

"Blast it, Frank. I'm serious!" said Samuel as he leaned closer to bore his eyes into Frank's eyes.

He ain't funnin' one bit. "C'mon, Samuel! Give me a break! I'll be tight with you," said Frank.

"I'm going to tell you something. Just let me finish before you ask any questions. Can you do that?" said Samuel. Frank shook his head in an up and down affirmative motion.

Samuel proceeded to tell Frank the story of Boudroe from the beginning in the corn patch to the point of Frank knocking on the door. After he finished, Frank just stared at him not quite knowing what to say. Finally, he said, "Slaves? Escaped slaves? Y'all could be in for a lot of misery, my friend. What kind of reward would they bring?"

"What do ya mean when you say reward? You planning on turning them in?" said a narrowing eyed Samuel.

"I can't believe you'd think I think like that! My worry is all the people that will be out looking for 'em. We gotta find them a safe place. I know my mom will more than understand their problem. Being an Indian isn't the easiest thing in the world around here and she's been through a lot!" said Frank as his thinned lips and slow shaking head showed he had many sad thoughts about his mom's past since the white man showed up. "You gonna let me meet 'em?"

"My gosh, Frank! I'm not being too mannerly. C'mon in." He opened the door. Frank stepped in and saw his favorite part of Mary Sherrill's cooking ready to be eaten. He didn't know whether to eat the cornbread and butter first or meet the two strangers.

As he looked at the two strangers, he said, "Hi, Mary. Hope you got enough for the rest of you," He turned to Boudroe and said, "My name is Frank Travis." He held out his hand. While Boudroe was shaking his hand, Frank asked, "You going to introduce me to your daughter?" He looked at Emma.

The brief silence after Frank's remark was followed by hearty laughs all around the cabin. "What's so funny?" said Frank who was enjoying, playing the part of one who doesn't understand what is happening.

After calm was restored, Boudroe turned to Frank and said, "Mr. Travis, please let me introduce my wife, Emma Boudroe, to you."

Frank said, "Is nice to meet you, Mizz Boudroe,"

Samuel said, "Well, good people, we've got some figuring to do. Who wants to get this started or should Frank and I go on over to Pa's and get his ideas on what to do."

No one offered any ideas as the talk was about how to keep them safe. "Well, that does it. We'll go on over to Pa's," said Samuel.

"Not until you and I finish our little discussion over your going over the mountain with Dan'l," said Mary as she barely tilted her head, bore her eyes into Samuel's as she spoke.

"Uhhhh, yeah, that's right," said Samuel who knew what had to be said. "There is no way I'm going over there with this problem staring me in the face." *You weren't going anyway, my husband.* The look on Mary's face spoke volumes to Samuel plus the rest of the people in the cabin.

Samuel and Frank were on their way to Adam Sherrill's cabin and they had been talking about the best way to handle the problem with Boudroe and Emma when Frank said, "Going with Boone over the mountains, eh? My friend, judging by your wife's feelings, I think you best keep close and let Dan'l do his thing. What the heck, there will be plenty of time in the next year or two to go gallivanting round that country."

Adam was enjoying his rocking chair on the front porch. *Fine day to go fishing. Sure would like to see Santee again. Just might head out over there one of these days.* Seeing Samuel and Frank riding up the path broke his concentration. *Wonder what's up now*, as he waved to them.

After he was told about Boudroe and Emma, he sat for a long time not saying a word and looked around the farm, looked down at his feet, pursed his lips, looked at Samuel and Frank and then looked out toward the forest seeing nothing in particular. Samuel and Frank knew, from these actions they had seen before, that Adam was giving the subject a lot of thought. No one would say a word until Adam spoke, and when he did, it was usually final.

"I'm taking this to Santee. We solved a lot of problems together. I think he will find a way out of this problem that will rest well with everyone. You game to go with me?" He looked at each man.

Samuel said, "Well, Pa, uhhhh…I just don't know about leaving right now. Mary wasn't too keen on my leaving for awhile with Dan'l to go over yonder." He pointed toward the western mountains chain.

"I heard that. Can't say I blame her either. But that's talk for another time," said Adam. "What do you think about going with me, Frank?"

"Don't know, Mr. Sherrill. Let me ponder on it a little," said Frank.

"Well, boys, you best make up your minds 'cause Elizabeth sure isn't going to let me go by myself. Then this problem doesn't get solved, does it? Whatcha gonna do now Samuel?" said Adam with a slight wave of his hands.

"Well, hang fire, Pa! What's so important about talking with Santee? He doesn't know a thing about the mess I'm in! You act like he's got some special gift of knowing things," said a frustrated-looking Samuel.

Adam looked into his son's eyes and slowly got up from his rocking chair and took the two steps from the porch to the ground where Samuel and Frank were standing. Adam slowly pointed his index finger toward Samuel's chest and pushed hard until Samuel lost ground. "Let me tell you one thing, my son. Don't ever think or say anything or question me about what I may say about Santee. If it wasn't for him, your ma, my wife, would not be alive and I know you know that cause I've told you about that many times!"

"Uhhhh, yes, sir! I didn't mean any disrespect about him. I guess when we talk with him, he will see our problem from a different way," said Samuel.

"Do I take that to mean you're going to go with me?" said Adam.

"Yes, sir. Just as soon as I tell Mary about the trip. How long you expect it to take?" said Samuel.

Frank said, "If y'all are going then count me in. Not sure how my mom is going to take this, but—"

Samuel told Mary about his talk with his father and the decisions that had been made. Mary was not too happy about it but could see the wisdom of maybe solving the problem.

"Guess Samuel Jr., Susan, and Catherine can do some extra work while you are gone. Maybe Mode, Quil and the others will keep check on us,' said Mary.

"You know how it is with us Sherrills," said Samuel. "We take care of our own. So don't worry about the crops or such. We've gotta solve the Boudroe and Emma problem quick."

"And you will tell Dan'l that you won't be going with him, right?" said Mary eyeing Samuel with a "you had better not leave with him" look.

"Yeah, I'll make sure he knows. Maybe send Samuel over to tell him. I just wish I could yell it out and he would hear me. I betcha that that will happen one of these days," said Samuel.

Mary looked at him and said, "I'm beginning to think you have been sampling your still's medicine. Hmmmph, yelling over many miles so somebody can hear you. You're just like your pa thinking about what might be."

18

Santee could not believe his eyes! He stood up, rubbed his eyes, looked hard at the three men walking up to his home. "Adam, is that you? How great it is to see you!" He grabbed Adam in a hug that almost took the wind out of Adam's lungs.

"Good grief, Santee! This old sixty-seven-year-old body can't take the punishment it did when you and I were in these mountains," Adam said while pretending to be in pain.

"Samuel, Frank, it is good to see you both again. How are your mothers doing?" said Santee.

The sun was the color of rusty orange as it slowly slipped behind the high ridge to the west of Santee's village. The fading sunlight allowed lengthening shadows to creep into the small valleys while the sun's light could be seen through the trees growing on the ridges. A far off cry of a wolf added a certain serenity to the scene laid out before them. "Each day I come here to watch it end and wonder at the majesty of it all," said Santee.

Samuel with a long look at the disappearing sun said, "Sure does make all that we do seem awfully small."

"My Indian blood becomes restless knowing that this land is changing so fast that one day, we will not recognize it," said Frank as he let his eyes sweep the grand spectacle of nature.

Adam said, "My friend, once again you have helped solve a problem for us. I think it is a brilliant idea to bring Boudroe and Emma up here to stay with y'all. Who knows, they may find they like it so much that they'll want to stay here."

"I, too, find it an answer to a prayer. Not only does it give them a safe place, but it takes care of the problem of keeping them hid. I live in dread that the sheriff, or his English loving friends, will discover them. Then I've had it!" said Samuel.

Santee said, "All I know is if one of you is in trouble then all the rest will come to his or her rescue. That's the Sherrill way and I know I wouldn't want to have all of you after me. Wouldn't have a chance."

Samuel said, with some reluctance, "Pa, we better get on back. Much as I like it here we need to finish what we started."

The wolf howled again and was answered by another wolf. Santee said, "Just look at Venus and the way she shines on us. Remarkable, isn't it?"

Adam said while looking around the sky, "Yes it is, and we'll soon see the stars coming out for the night. Wow! Talk about feeling small. I hear tell there are more stars out there than people on earth. I hear tell of people who study the stars and planets through spy glasses."

Santee said with a small smile, "There you go thinking again. I remember when we were looking across a valley and you said something about having a boat that would float on the air to the other side. Seen one yet? Now you are into the heavens. Guess you think you're some kind of Galileo, eh?"

"Darn right and I think he will have his name on one of those boats when someone shoots it into the heavens," said Samuel.

"I must say, Samuel, you are some kind of dreamer," said Santee.

The men sat on the edge of the rock shelf with legs dangling over it and fell silent as the darkening purple of night crept over them.

"I hope he isn't up to doing some kind of mischief on us," said Santee as he looked into the darkness.

"What do you mean by that?" said Adam.

"Someone out there is watching us. I haven't seen him. I haven't heard him. I feel his eyes searching us," said Santee in a low voice.

Adam, Samuel, and Frank exchanged looks and then looked in the direction pointed out by Santee. They didn't see anything either.

⌒

Yona had watched the four for a long time when he recognized that one of them was the father of the little girl, the chosen one, he had met on the ridgeline last year. *Is the chosen one with them?* flashed through his mind. *Does she wear the moccasins I gave her?*

Twadi said, "We have seen what is needed by our chief. Let's get back to our camp for the night and get up before the sun starts another day. I know the one called Santee. Wonder who the other three are with him."

Yona said, "I have met one of them on what the English call the Line. The man named Boone was with them."

Chief Attacullaculla raised his hand for silence among members of the tribal council. He looked at Yona and gave a slight nod of his head signifying Yona was to speak.

"It is as it should be at the place where Santee lives. We have been at peace with them for a very long time, but we also saw two men, not of the village, with him. One who stayed there many years ago and you know him from your meeting at the Peace Island. The other was new to the place of Santee, but I have met him at the Line the English put on top of the mountains. And I think Santee knew we were watching him."

Attacullaculla said while nodding his head in an affirmative way, "It is good that you keep watch over Santee and his people. They are our friends. You must find out why these men was there. I know the man called Boone is not with them. He has been seen in the gap close to the white cliffs."

Yona said with a surprised look told Attacullaculla, "That man must be watched at all times."

Attacullaculla nodded his head and said, "You will do that," and with a slight wave of his hand indicated all were to leave his lodge. The meeting was over.

19

1771

The early morning sky has the deep blue splendor of October. The air is cool. The ground fog is slowly retreating into the woods. The leaves are showing their tinge of autumn color. The silence is deafening.

The six Tory militia, sitting on their saddled horses, displayed feigned indifference to the show of loathing coupled with fear in front of them. Their leader places his hand on his sword, tightens his fingers around the hilt, and starts to pull the sword out of its scabbard. Everyone hears the faint click of one, then two, rifle hammers being pulled back into firing position. The silence becomes increasingly deafening.

Moses's eyes changed in an instant from concern mixed with fear to a narrowing look of knowing, that in a split second of time, his enemies mood had changed from one of confidence to one of extreme caution. He continued to look deep into the eyes of Hank Hoffman while ignoring his five companions.

Hank is noted in the region for his sympathy to the British objective of putting down the increasing Regulator uprising in the region. His unbridled desire is to own the land permanently settled over twenty-five years ago by Adam and Elizabeth Sherrill and their eight sons that has become known as Sherrill's Ford. He knew he would own this land as he had been told by British officials in General Cornwallis's staff that the deeds would be handed over to him when the Regulator insurrection had been defeated by the British and their Tory allies. This, in Hank's mind, meant that he had full authority to make sure either the Sherrills were eliminated or driven from their productive farmlands.

"Whatcha waitin' on, Hank. One rifle ain't gonna git us all," said Bill Cooper who reached for his pistol tucked inside his belt. The unmistakable sound of a third hammer click from the opposite direction made Cooper slowly hold up his hands in the surrender while cautiously looking in the direction of the click. He did not see the person holding the rifle. The other Tories quickly glanced at each other as their mood and manner abruptly changed from caution to the thoughts of "I could be killed here."

"One bullet will get Hank. The other will get Bill. I wonder who will be the third to get hit and which will get hit first," said Moses while not taking his eyes off of Hank.

Moses and Hank continued to look at each other until Hank said, "You got us this time, Mode, but I'm a warning you to clear out or change your ways. We ain't puttin' up with yore rebel ways." He took his hand off the sword's hilt, grabbed the reins, turned his horse around, and was followed by the others as they started to leave the barnyard.

"Hold on, Hank!" shouted Moses. "Just to let you and your so-called friends know that if you come back here again, you'll have all of us to mess with."

Everyone knew that "all of us" meant all the Sherrill men. It was common knowledge in the region that when one of their kin was in danger, or in need, then the rest were going to stop what they were doing to help them out.

Hank knew he would be walking on thin ice when he decided to confront Moses; but his desire for the land overrode what little was left of his common sense.

"We'll go on to them Moore's and get them straightened out and come back here and burn this place down," mumbled Hank to his men as he turned to get another look at Moses. He was astonished to see a woman carrying a rifle emerging from the barn and a young boy walking out of the woods carrying another rifle. To add to his surprise, he saw a young pretty girl move from the back of the cabin holding a rifle in firing position. He knew the Sherrill men were expert marksmen, but never knew about the Sherrill women being able to even hold a rifle. *Gotta remember that gal*, he thought as he and his band of Tories disappeared around the bend of the road.

"Maybe I shoulda let him draw that sword on you and then shot him," said Sarah, who was watching to see if the men would return.

"Great day, Sarah! In all our married life, I never thought I'd hear that from you," exclaimed Moses while looking at her with an astonished smile on his face.

"Guess not. Sorta surprised myself for saying that. But it was you or him. Wasn't hard for me to figure out what to do at the time," Sarah said, "Plus you didn't have anything to defend yourself with. Glad I came across your rifle in the barn."

"Kinda helped out, didn't I?" said John the nephew and son of Samuel as he looked at his aunt and uncle wanting them to say he had been very helpful and brave.

"Yes, siree John, you really helped put the scare into them. There aren't too many nine-year-old boys who will take on a job like you just did. You helped save your uncle's life!" said Moses as he hugged him.

Then Moses put his arm around Catherine's shoulders and said, "And I'm mighty glad that my niece decided to stay overnight with us rather than going back to your cabin when it was almost dark. Hearing that hammer being pulled back got those guys attention real quick."

"Well, if Aunt Sarah was going to shoot then I was too!" said a stern-faced Catherine. "And I was aiming low like you and Pa always told me to do."

"We best be tellin' my brothers about this 'cause it sure looks like Hank and his boys intend to steal our land," said Moses. "I'm beginning to wish we had crossed those mountains with Samuel to take a look at what's over there for a hardworking family. I think I'd rather fight Indians than those redcoats and their Tory buddies. I swear, I just don't understand those men who don't want to be free of England."

"Uncle Mode, didn't you and that Hank guy used to hunt together?" said Catherine.

"Yeah, that's true. Kinda sad that one day someone is your friend and the next day he is your enemy. Never quite figured out why he thinks England is going to help him out. The way those redcoats are, they'll just up and leave one of these days and leave their so-called friends out in the cold," said Moses.

"Okay, John, how 'bout you telling your uncles Jacob, Uriah, and William that we need to meet here in two days. I'll ride over and tell Quillar, Adam, and Isaac the same thing," said Moses. *I sure wish Samuel hadn't taken off across those mountains*, he thought. *He's our best marksman.*

"Ohhhh, no you don't!" exclaimed Sarah. "You're acting just like your father. Always going off and leaving your mother all alone and fending for herself. Somebody is going to stay here and help me and the rest of the boys while that Hank is wandering around." Sarah was clearly upset and by the look in her green eyes she meant every word.

Moses, after looking at Sarah for a few seconds, and seeing a fear in her eyes set off by a set chin and tight mouth, said, "Yeah, you are right. Maybe John can stay with you and I'll get Ute to let Joseph help us out while we are gone."

"Well, that might work just so long as Mary and Judith aren't left alone," said Sarah. "You Sherrill boys are always leaving your wives. Mary's Samuel, Judith's Ute, and me. What's with y'all anyway? Can't you just settle down and not keep looking for someplace else to live? With as many Sherrills as y'all are around here you could make your own colony."

Moses said with a thoughtful look, "You just might have something there my smart wife. How come it is that you are always one step ahead of everybody else in thinking of good ideas?" Sarah just smiled which told Moses "well, what did you expect?"

"I'll be around," said a very confident sounding Catherine. "And I am a good shot. Not too good at reloading, but when it is done I usually hit my target."

Mode said, "Yes, Catherine, you are a good shooter and I proud you are. Maybe you can give Mary some help with her rifle."

Catherine didn't say anything. Her smile was enough.

20

Six brothers sat around the fire outside of Moses cabin. It had taken two days to get all of them together and Moses had been concerned that the Hoffman gang would return to try again to drive him from his land whether by English law or force.

Much talk was going on about the usual topics of weather, crops, bragging about their hunting skills and their families. They were purposely avoiding talk about possible war with England as each knew this was another reason, beyond helping Moses, for getting together today.

Aquilla said, "I gotta tell y'all about hunting a bear that hurt one of my two cows so bad that I had to put her our of her misery. I vowed to hunt that murderin' skunk and put him down if it was the last thing I was going to do."

"Ohhhhh, boy! Here we go again! Quillar's gotta tell us, again I might say, that he's the best hunter in this pack," said Jacob while the twinkle in his eyes and smile on his face.

After Aquilla told them of the harrowing story of finally getting the bear he added, "Ran across a family, name of Jackson as best I recall, from down around the Waxhaw's, and got to talking to him about the Regulators fighting the British and their Tory buddies."

All of a sudden, the mood of the group changed from one of general talk to one of a serious issue. They were interested in any of the latest news since word of mouth from people passing through the region was one of the major news sources available to them.

"Well, what did they say?" asked Uriah. "Just how close are the Redcoats to us now? Last I knew, they were over around Charlotte's town and that ain't too far from here. Speaking of Charlotte's town, I wonder whatever happened to ol' Polk?" He really didn't expect an answer.

"Well, Ute, they said they'd been told of a lot of fighting in the low country around Charleston and such and that some Redcoat colonel, name of Tarlton or Tartun or something sounding like that, was burning, beating and hanging some of the settlers in the back county," said Aquilla.

Mode said, "Seems all they want to do is hang people. It hasn't been over a couple months or so that Carolina's so-called Governor Tryon led a bunch of his soldiers against some of the Regulators and hung six of our guys down at Hillsborough! That's just not right!"

"Hanging?" exclaimed Uriah. "I can't believe someone would hang a body and just stand back and watch him die. Ain't natural. Just shows the British or their so-called friends think they can do anything with us they want to do."

"Think that's bad, huh. What about taking one of us out of our cabins and shooting us while making our families watch?" exclaimed Isaac with a look of scorn and an increasingly loud voice. "I say we gotta get to them 'fore they get to us. An eye for an eye like the good book says!"

"What do y'all think about hurting our boys and girls? The Jacksons have a couple of boys who were made to shine boots for the English soldiers and seems one of the officers didn't like the way his were being shined. He pulled out his sword and hit one of the boys with the broad side of it, but it still cut his arm," said Aquilla.

"Jackson's introduced me to the boy and showed me the scar from that cut. Andrew is his name, 'bout ten years old. He's a feisty one all right. Told me that when he is growed up he is gonna go after and get rid of that officer who cut him."

"Sounds kinda like John," said Moses. "He had a bead on one of Hank's buddies the other day. If Sarah had shot then John would have shot one of them too. And to beat all, Catherine had her rifle aimed at one of them ready to let go at 'em."

"A rifle is kind of heavy for a young boy, Mode," said William. "Bet he had it in a notch of a tree or on some kind of support."

"Yep, sure did. Just like Samuel taught him. Dang man, that rifle is about as tall as John, but he's gaining fast on it. But when he sights a target, you can count it gone," Moses said with a look of "you can bet your bottom shilling on that."

The smack of a lead ball hitting the log Ute and Quillar were sitting on was immediately followed by the sound of the rifle that fired it. Everyone scattered like a rising covey of scared quail seeking a safer place. Another shot ricocheted off the rock Moses had been sitting on leaving its telltale high pitched whine as it tumbled through the air. Each knew that a torn and ragged edged richocheted ball could do more damage to a body than the ball alone.

Quil said, "There's two of 'em. I think both of 'em are close together."

Hank Hoffman said with a tight-lipped look, "Just about got him!"

"Yeah, ya did, but this ain't horseshoes," said Bill Cooper as he started pouring gun powder into the muzzle. "Only thing I got was a broken off rock."

Hank and Bill had decided they could not take on all the Sherrills all at once. They decided to use ambush tactics much the same as the Indians use so successfully with whatever target they choose to use.

They both finished reloading and started peeking over the log underneath honeysuckle encased bushes. Harry heard a dull smack followed by the sound of a rifle firing. Bill Cooper didn't have time to say a word or hardly feel the pain caused by the ball tearing through his brain. The last thing he saw was bark on the pine log.

Harry's surprised look was followed by the shock of seeing the hole in his best friend's forehead and that he died so suddenly. His next thought was for his own safety followed by fear of not knowing how close the Sherrills were to him. Each thought their hiding place was undetectable. All he could murmur was "One shot only...I gotta get outta here." *I'll come back later to get Bill.*

"Think you got one of 'em, Jacob? I never saw anything," said Isaac.

Mode said, "I barely caught the sight of two guys. Right over yonder in those bushes between that chestnut and oak. Hadn't seen any other moving going on."

William said, "Let's everybody spread out and start sneaking up on 'em. Just be sure to stay far enough apart that we'll see a head moving back and forth trying to see us. One of us can get a bead on him."

Each brother instinctively knew what the others would do as they started forward to find the attackers. First one would move and then another as they did not want to show more than one target at a time. Of course, the attackers would not know where the next target might be either.

Hank had moved to what he thought to be a safe distance from the log and Bill's body. The scrub oak and pine sapling growth made what he thought was a great hiding place. He decided to wait until full dark before he would escape. He hoped that some animal wouldn't try to make a dinner out of Bill's body. His nerves were approaching a raw edge, his eyes stung from the sweat dripping down from his forehead and slowly became aware of a silent forest. Being a hunter and backwoodsman, he knew the signs and signals of a forest. The signal of silence was starting to make him paranoid. *Gotta calm down. I'll put my hat on a stick, raise it up and if nothing happens I can get outta here.* He put his hat on a stick and slowly raised it. Nothing happened. No shot. No shout. No nothing.

Mode saw the hat slowly being raised above a thick line of oak saplings. He looked over to Quillar who shook his head signifying he had seen the hat. Mode's held up four fingers which was a signal the brothers had worked out a long time ago. Each number meant they were to say "one thousand one, one thousand two, one thousand three, one thousand four" before whatever action was to be taken.

Hank started to lower his hat. *Guess I can make it out of here.* His hat flew off the stick and the stick shattered just below the hat. This sound of two rifles almost seemed to be one as their lead bullets found their mark. Hank tried to become part of the ground. *That was much too close. Why in the world did I try such a stupid trick? I've gotta get outta here!*

"That was some shootin', Mode. Which one of us got the hat?" said Quillar.

"I think you did. I shot the stick. It was a tougher target," said Mode while trying to suppress a smile.

"C'mon, Mode! Get serious! We gotta get this boy," Quillar said with an exasperated look on his face.

They finished reloading their rifles and turned back to see if there were anymore targets. They saw the flash of reflected sunlight from Jacob's knife, and then another flash from Isaac's knife. A quail gave its unique call and another close-by quail gave an answering call. "Now we know where Adam and William are. Danged if they don't sound just like them birds," said Mode.

Hank heard the quail call and knew enough to know there wouldn't be any such calls by the real birds after a firing of rifles. *Those two are almost behind me. I'll crawl on outta here to my right. If I can make that big chestnut, then I can put it between me and them.* He started crawling on his hands and knees toward the big tree. *I'm gonna make it for sure!* as he got to the tree. After getting to the other side, he stood up, adjusted his gear and rifle, and looked at the hole in his hat. He put the hat on his head and turned to creep further into the forest keeping the tree between him and where he felt the shooters and quail callers to be. As he looked back to check his position, he almost fainted when he felt the edge of a knife on his neck.

"Going somewhere, Hank?" said Jacob in a no-nonsense "don't mess with me" manner.

Hank said in a false confidence voice, "You'd…better not try anything to hurt me. I'll…I'll get the others down on you if you do."

Jacob called out to the others who seemed to appear out of thin air. Their looks at Hank were stern and unyielding. "I declare, Hank! What has gotten into you? We have been friends for a long time, that is, until you took up with the Brits. And the knowing of you and Cooper trying to kill us is just too much! Whatta we gonna do with this Tory, my brothers?"

Quiller said as he leaned into Hank's face locking his eyes on his, "Let's just shoot him and go 'bout our business. Save us all a lot of future trouble."

No one said a word as they locked their eyes on Hank whose fear for his life was running rampant through his mind. *Those guys are gonna kill me.*

William pointed his rifle at Hank's chest and with a look of utter indifference pulled the hammer back. Hank's eyes grew larger when he saw the muzzle pointing at his heart. "Listen, guys, I'll do anything…anything you want! Just let me live. Don't kill me. Let's pretend this day hasn't happened!"

The lead ball shattered Hank's arm joint at the shoulder. The rifle sound followed. Hank hollered in pain while the Sherrills, once again, reacted like a covey of quail.

Frank Moore kept his eyes on where Hank had been standing and tamped down the next lead ball in his rifle barrel. "Burn down my barn, you snake, your soul will burn in hell, but I'm gonna make it miserable for you before you git there," he murmured to himself.

After a few minutes, Frank realized the Sherrill boys may be trying to find him. He slowly backed away from the log, slid into a dry creek bed and started jogging away. *I'll get the other shoulder before the week is out.*

"Anybody got an idea where that shot came from?" said Mode while getting up off the ground.

William said, "Happened quick. I thought my rifle had fired."

Hank was starting to come out of his shock of being hit by a lead ball. He started crying out, "Help me! Help, I'm gonna die...Ohhhh, it hurts!" He tried to stop the bleeding. "What didya shoot me for? Ohhhhh, it hurts like I've never hurt before. Anybody got any whiskey?"

Jacob said with a fierceness in his voice, "Far as I'm concerned, he can stay here and tend his own self. Ain't worth saving anyway. Did you shoot him, William?"

"Naww, my rifle is still loaded. I didn't pull my trigger. Wanted to though. Somebody else beat me to it," said William with somewhat of a matter-of-fact voice and shrug of his shoulders. "Jacob is right. Let's get on back home and let him be."

Mode said, "Listen to y'all! You think Pa would agree with you? What we're gonna do is take him back to my place and we'll see what to do with him from there."

All the brothers reluctantly agreed with looks of grim resignation. Jacob said while helping Hank up said, "Sure would be easier to go ahead and shot him now."

Hank said through clinched teeth, "You gotta get Bill. He's dead. His family will need to know...ohhhhh, it hurts bad!"

The brothers' "what are we gonna do now" look to each other was met with silence. No one wanted to take Bill Cooper's body back. Jacob said, "I say we just shoot Hank right now and forget about both of 'em. Buzzards or bobcats will finish 'em off."

Five brothers looked at Jacob with an "I don't believe what I just heard" look in their eyes. "Whatcha lookin' at? At least it's got you to thinking how we're going to handle this," said Jacob.

A collective intake of breath and sigh of relief by Jacob's brothers got them talking at the same time trying to solve the problem. Mode said, "Well, let's go find him, bury him and then let Hank tell his family, and the judge, what happened and where he is buried."

"Ahhh, my brother, you are a smart one. Sounds like a winner to me," said Quiller. "What do the rest of y'all say?"

They half-carried, half-dragged a moaning and groaning Hank to Mode's cabin.

⌒

"Don't like to see you go so soon. Josh and Ashdon will go with you to bring Boudroe and Emma back here. I wish I could go with you, but maybe another time," Santee said. *Just hope there will be another time.*

"You better believe it, my friend! Elizabeth would love to see you again, and I'm sure, Frank's mom feels the same way. After all, if it wasn't for you and Saka then I may have lost Elizabeth. If that had happened I think I would have just wandered off somewhere," said Adam as he clasped both of his hands around Santee's.

Both nodded their heads to each other and Adam turned to Samuel and Frank and motioned with his hand that they were to move on out to go home. Samuel and Frank knew that Santee knew they were much obliged to him without a word being spoken. Santee said something to Josh and Ashdon who followed Adam and the others.

The five men walked along faint paths toward the east climbing steadily higher toward the high ridge leading to a small gap in the mountain chain. They finally broke out of the wood line onto a treeless expanse covered with rhododendron bushes and patches of grass. "I never ceased to be amazed at these places around here. Why don't trees take hold here?" asked Adam almost to himself.

They set up camp for the night only far enough into a thicket in the woods so their fire would not be seen. The call of a wolf floated up to them from the depths of a nearby valley. Another wolf answered, then another until the call of a pack of wolves caused each man to look around the perimeter of their campsite and at each other. Samuel said in an almost whisper, "We gotta keep a sharp eye and ear tonight." The unique, high-pitched call of an elk close to their right made Adam say, "These calls remind me of what Mary calls the natural beauty of a place, but beauty is closely followed by danger. Josh, Ashdon, you have it made and probably don't know it."

Josh said, "I agree. We are very fortunate. But with all the moving in by people like yourselves, it's starting to change things for us. We've just got to adjust…somehow. That about all we can do."

After supper, they walked out to the open field, found some rocks to sit on and watched as the stars slowly twinkled into existence for the night. "Just look at all this!" exclaimed Samuel as he waved his arm across the sky. "I'll never get over the feeling of being so small when I look into God's heavens and see his work. What's he do with all of it?"

Adam said with a low voice, "Your mom says it is because we don't have the brains to figure it out. And what if you did, what good would it do ya?" He pointed toward the southeastern horizon and said, "There's my Orion. I think that is the most powerful constellation in the sky."

They remained silent for a long time trying to take in all the stars and constellations. Samuel said, "How in the world did Santee's kin know which stars to guide their ships by? There are so many."

Frank said, "I don't know about all of that and don't think about it much, but I do know one thing for sure—we are being watched by someone or something."

Adam and Samuel knew enough to know that Frank's instincts were not to be ignored. "How close you think they are, Frank. Ashdon, do you feel the same thing? How about you, Josh?"

Yona turned to Twadi and whispered, "They are staying in camp tonight. I see no need for us to get any closer. Let's get back to our camp."

"I agree. What good would it do anyway to kill them now?" said Twadi.

"That is the last thing we will do. Attacullaculla told us we were only to do what is necessary to find out what they are doing and that is all," said Yona.

They crept back from their hiding place behind a large rock near the edge of the wood line and reached their camp site located in a stand of majestic hemlocks. They made a small fire to cook their venison. "They go back to their village, but somehow I feel they will be back with more people. Those whites are like the floods that happen after the snows. They just keep coming and coming with no end in sight," said Yona.

Twadi said, "I hear from others visiting our village that the ones who wear the red coats are always making treaty's with the people who are building cabins on our land. Does that mean they will treat those people like they treat us with their worthless words on paper and then force them back across the big water?"

Yona said with a hard-eyed look to the horizon, "Who knows what or how the white man thinks. All I know is they have brought ever more people and that sickness they call pox which is the killer of the Indian. We cannot fight what we cannot see."

Twadi said, "That is true. Dragging Canoe's face tells the story of his pox sickness."

"I will be the first guard," said Yona. "I will wake you when the moon is the highest."

21

Mary kept kneading the bread dough and said, "Catherine, you must be more thoughtful about how boys your age want to talk to you and be seen with you. After all, you are seventeen and maybe the right man will come along and ask your pa for your hand."

"Hmmmpphh, I've got a lot more to do than pretend to be something I'm not around a bunch of boys who can't even ride as good as me. And I think I'm a lot smarter than most of them. Some can't even read very well," said Catherine with a determined look in her eyes.

"That kind of thinking will make the boys look elsewhere for a wife," said Mary.

"Wife! The very idea, Mother! I've got way too much to do than settle down with some boy who wants me to do what you do for, Pa," said Catherine. She immediately knew she had said the wrong thing to her mother. "Ohh, Mom, I so sorry! I didn't mean it the way it sounded."

Mary kept kneading the dough although a little bit harder and didn't take her eyes from Catherine's almost tearful eyes. After what seemed like an eternity to Catherine, her mother said, "Come over here and sit by me. We have a lot to talk about how a woman gets by in a man's world."

"Why is it always a man's world. We're the ones who clean, cook, have babies, take care of the children, and hoe the corn while the man gets to go hunting for weeks at a time, make whiskey, and sit around talking about the English," said a frustrated Catherine.

"What you say is very true most of the time. But it depends on the man and more dependent on how a man and wife start their lives together. One of these days, you will meet a man and think he is the best thing on this earth and you would do almost anything to make him yours for life," said Mary.

"Well, I haven't met such a man yet. Seems all the men or boys I am around, all they do is look me over like I am something to buy or play with. I've heard of those girls who just live to make a boy want to do whatever with them," said Catherine with a "that isn't going to happen to me" look.

The rattle of the door lock being pulled up by the latch string interrupted the conversation. Samuel pushed the door open and said, "Well, hello, pretty lady. Do you have any idea how much I have missed you?" He swept Mary in his arms and gently pressed his lips on hers. He then turned to Catherine saying, "It is no wonder why you are so pretty. You take after your mother."

Catherine said with a big smile, "Ohh go on, Pa. You always funning me about me." *Now, if I could find a man like Pa then maybe...*

"Where's Susan and the boys?" said Samuel.

After learning all his family was safe and sound, Samuel started telling them about his meeting with Santee when Adam stepped in the cabin. "I must admit it is with much relief that I'm back home among my children and their families. How are you doing Mary? And you Catherine?"

After all the talk of what had happened since they were gone and the condition of the farms, Adam said, "We need to get the boys together at the church to go over what needs to be done about Boudroe and Emma. Samuel, best get Samuel Jr. and one of the other boys to alert the family. I'm heading to my Elizabeth. Josh and Ashdon staying here tonight, right?"

"Pa, please let me take Betsy and make the rounds of my uncles' places," said Catherine. "When do you want them to meet you?"

Mary said with a questioning look at Samuel, "Might not be good for a young lady be out riding by herself."

Catherine said with an exasperated look, "Ohhh, Ma, I'll be just fine. And anyway, if something or somebody comes after me Betsy will leave 'em in her dust."

Adam said, "Well, son, you've got some decisions to make. I'm on the way. Oh, by the way, let's make our meeting after church service this Sunday." He closed the door behind him.

Catherine had passed the meeting information to her Uncle William and Jacob and was on the way to Uriah's cabin. She had to pass through part of the forest that contained immense oak and chestnut trees. She stopped to admire one particularly huge Chestnut tree and thought *how beautiful this tree is. It's got to be hundreds of years old. Nothing, except a man's axe, will destroy such beauty.* The feeling was followed by the thought *I'm not alone!* clicked to life in her mind. At first her eyes widened in fear then a calmness settled over her body and mind. To anyone watching her eyes showed no fear as they became calm. Her sense of hearing became focused.

"Hi there pretty little lady," said a man's voice from in front of her.

"Yeah…I agree…a pretty woman! And all alone in these woods. Imagine that!" said a man's voice behind her.

Catherine did not move a muscle. Her mind was calm yet rapidly thinking of how to get out of this situation. Judging by the voices, it didn't take a lot of smarts to figure what was on their minds. Her only defense was a never used leather whip, wrapped around her left wrist, that was made to urge horses faster. It had a tight knot with leather thongs hanging free on its end. She slowly tightened her grip on the whip and waited for their next move. *Pa has always said surprise is the best defense.*

The two men slowly rode from opposite sides of the tree. She couldn't go right because of the tree and couldn't go forward or backward due to the two men blocking her escape route. Only to her left was any hope of escape. She recognized the one in front as being Sheriff Clark's son, Tim. It had taken her a long time to realize he seemed to be always around her when she was at a church social or, on that rare occasion, at Polk's store with her pa. With the poise of a queen she said, "Hello, Tim. What brings you and that other guy behind me out here? Hunting or following me?"

Catherine could tell by Tim's reaction that he was surprised at her question and manner of asking it. He shifted uneasily in the saddle and said, "Ahhhhhh, well, ahhhh, me and Mike saw you riding out from your uncle's place into these woods. We thought you might need some company on the way."

Yeah, uhhh huhhh, need some company. They think I'm stupid. "And who is this Mike who won't show himself to me?" Catherine said.

Tim was growing unsure of how things were going and said, "That's Mike Conroy. He'll help you. C'mon, Mike, get down from there and help Catherine down from her horse. She must be tired. And, Catherine, you do know that my pa is the sheriff around these parts, don't you?" The implication was not lost on Catherine.

Catherine heard Mike getting off his horse and his walking to her. He appeared at her side with a repulsive wolfish smile showing tobacco stained teeth. *He sure is ugly.* She saw him getting ready to lunge at her to drag her off of Betsy. Just as he started forward, she brought the whip up and lashed out with all the force she could muster at Mike's face. The crack of the whip sounded like the sizzle of a lighting bolt as it struck a tree. The thudding sound on Mike's face staggered him back two, then three, then four steps while nearly losing his balance. The momentary delay in pain signals to his brain from the knot hitting him in his eye finally made itself felt. He yelled in great pain and rubbed his eye only to find that the eye was hanging from its socket. The shock of his eyeball hanging from its socket brought him to his knees, cupping his hands over his face. His wailing sounded like a wounded panther.

Tim's reaction was one of shocked surprise at seeing Catherine's attack and its outcome. He took his eyes off of Mike to look at Catherine. Another surprise awaited him as Betsy, at the urging of Catherine, was well on her way to running into him and his horse. Tim's horse was knocked back losing its balance. Tim hit the ground and barely had time to look up and see his mount falling on him. The horse hit Tim with a muted thud and stepped on Tim two or three times in the process of regaining its balance. Tim did not move.

Betsy was ready to enter into more combat and pranced around the two men and their horses. Catherine was having a hard time calming her down and all she was thinking was to quickly leave the scene. Betsy finally calmed down which allowed Catherine to regain her composure. She quickly looked from one to the other. Mike was up and whimpering as he struggled to comprehend what had just happened to him while holding his eyeball as close to the empty socket as possible. Tim had not moved.

Maybe I should help them. But why? It doesn't take much thinking to know what they would have done to me. She pressed her knees against Betsy's side. Betsy slowly walked out of the area and before disappearing behind the large trees, Catherine looked back to see Mike staggering around while Tim was still on the ground. She flicked the reins and Betsy started a faster trot through the forest toward Uncle Uriah's cabin. *I'm going home. I have to tell Ma about this and figure out what to do!*

Mary heard the pounding of hooves and immediately went to the door. *Something has happened. Hope no one is hurt.* She saw Catherine bring Betsy to a stop and jumped off to run into her mothers protective arms. "Ohhhhh, Mama, something terrible has happened! I may be in a lot of trouble!"

"Are you all right, my child?" said a very concerned Mary as she looked Catherine from head to foot but did not see any outward problem. "Now, Catherine, you have got to calm down!"

"Ohhhhh, Mama, it was terrible! I'm in trouble!" said Catherine in a louder voice.

"Kate! Listen to me! Sit down here and calm down!" said Mary while guiding Catherine to a chair. "I'm calling Samuel to come in here."

Samuel looked at Mary and she knew he was raging inside, "I'm going to go out there and if he is still on the ground, he will soon be hanging from the nearest tree limb! No man or boy is ever going to touch one of my daughters or wife without having to go through me first! No, siree, they ain't!"

Catherine's wringing hands and tears on her cheeks said in an almost whisper, "Ohhh, Pa, I'm so sorry this happened! I should have listened to Ma and not gone out by myself! What's wrong with those boys?" She then started crying and tears cascaded down her cheeks.

Mary moved closer to Samuel and gently said as she laid her hand on his knee, "Do not, I repeat, do not leave this house at this time. We must give Catherine support. She needs both of us here to feel safe and know that she is loved and we support her decision today. We must be like Samuel's Hannah and trust in God's timing for us."

"Samuel? Hannah? Who is she? Is Samuel Jr. mixed up in some…ohhh, that Samuel," said Samuel as he started to reach a calm state of mind.

Mary and Samuel sat by the fire. Not a word was spoken. Each was thinking what needs to be the next step in this situation. Catherine knew better than to say anything. At the same time, she was a mass of conflicting emotions inside her mind. *Will I have to go to jail? Is this going to cost Pa some money? What if we are driven out of here. The others will stand by us.*

Mary said, "Samuel, you have got to get your brothers together to figure out what to do as well as Boudroe and Emma, so get to it."

Samuel slowly sat back in his chair and kept looking into the fireplace. He then turned to look at Catherine and turned to look at his wife. "That makes good sense. How is it you are so smart and pretty at the same time." He pushed himself up from his chair. "Catherine, you will stay here with your mother. I'll start out to Uriah's and when Samuel and William get here send them to get the others. We will assemble tomorrow at noon." With that, he turned to pick up his rifle and hat and walked out the door.

"Ohh, Ma, I got us in a lot of trouble today and it wasn't my fault!" Catherine said as she sat down by her mother and put her head in her lap.

"Don't worry about things you have no control over, my child. *And she is rapidly growing toward being a woman,* said Mary as she pulled a comb through her daughter's hair.

22

Adam and all his sons, except Samuel, were sitting on the rough hewn bench in their church. The talking started out with the usual embellishments about their corn crops and farm animal breeding until Jacob said, "And what continues to make me madder every time I think about it is what those Redcoats did to the people in Boston last March. And what I've been told is they just plain murdered those people on the town square. Who do those Redcoats think they are anyway?"

"You hit the nail on the head with that, Jacob," said William. "Every time you turn around someone is raising some kinda holy terror in the streets and the Redcoats are killing someone else. Y'all remember when that peddler told us about what went on in New York. Having battles no less with people like us. Next thing you know, that English scum will be shooting at us just for having this meeting."

Everyone heard the horse outside and the footsteps on the church step and became silent as they watch the door. Samuel stepped in, looked at each of his brothers and then his pa. Adam motioned him to come up front and said, "Okay, boys, let's get down to some serious business once again. We got three things to figure out. One being the problem Catherine ran into, what to do about Boudroe and Emma and finally, what to do about the problem with Hank and Bill Cooper."

Moses said, "The way I see it, Pa, we have another problem also." Everyone looked at Mode and waited for their Pa to make the next move.

"That's what we are here for to make sure we have covered all the family problems. But how much more can we handle? Not much, I tell you!" said Adam.

"I don't think this is a family problem like we usually talk about, Pa," said Mode. He had everyone's attention now and they looked to him to speak up.

"Well, my pa and brothers—" said Mode as he was interrupted by Quil, Jacob, and Uriah saying in so many words to get on with it. "Just give me half a chance. Y'all help me with this review of ol' George in London telling us what we can and can't do. He wants us to be like what he rules over in England."

"Well, who around here would want to be like them over there?" said Uriah.

"That's just it. George wants us to be like him by telling us 'This is how you are to make America like England.' That boy is crazy," said William. "I bet if someone told him to go knock some bark off a tree he wouldn't know what to do."

Everyone looked at each other and then broke out in hilarious laughter and knee slapping. Mode said, "Good ol' George can't knock bark of a tree…just ain't got the power." That brought on more stomach aching laughter. The melee finally died down.

"Now, my brothers, I believe they call what he has is delusional," said Quil.

All heads with questioning looks on their faces turned to Quil. It was obvious they wanted to hear the meaning of delusional. "Well, from what I've been told is it means his thinking about making laws and orders are based on his own figuring despite what he is being told. He could be told good things about us, but he figures we are all bad regardless. Does that make sense to y'all?"

They all looked at each other with the general feeling that what Quil says has got to be thought about in more detail.

Mode said, "Well, that tells me he really is losing it. Let's go over what he had done to us. First thing I recall about eight years ago is his Proclamation Line Act in these mountains, then the Sugar Act, followed by his Currency Act, then that is followed by his Stamp Act. All these acts are nothing but ways to get our money and make us bend to his rules. And no telling what he is cooking up for us now. I ain't gonna stand for much more of it either!"

They all heard the galloping hoofbeats of a number of horses stopping in the churchyard. No one said a word while they watched the door. It was thrown open with a sharp slap against the wall. Sheriff Clark stalked in the door, pulled back his coat revealing two holstered pistols, and stood there glaring down at each brother as if trying to make up his mind which one to shoot.

"I'm only gonna say this once 'cause if I have to repeat it my pistols will do the saying. Now, boys, which one allowed that Catherine Sherrill to kill my Tim? She sure couldn't have done it by herself plus blind his buddy in one eye. One of you had to help her. Now who is it!" as he put his right hand on one of his pistols. Two of Clark's men walked in and took positions in the back of the room in opposite corners. They also pulled their coats back to reveal their pistols.

The room was as quite as a tomb. No one stirred and hardly breathed. The brothers knew they were in a tight place but not one was going to do anything to help a man who held his office by the fact he was loyal to the British. Seconds ticked by when Adam stood up and calmly walked to stand almost nose to nose with Clark. "Now, Sheriff, you are not going to do anything in this church to profane its existence. If you want to continue your discussion then you and I will step outside. Have I made myself clear?" He held Clark's eyes with a steely penetrating unblinking stare and slowly inched forward.

Clark couldn't stand Adam's look and backed up a step saying, "You are in a poor position to bargain with me, Adam. I am the law and my son is dead because of you Sherrills."

"I beg to differ. You are not the law in this church! And I'm sorry and really feel bad about your son. Do you know all, and I repeat, all of the particulars about how he died?" said Adam.

Sheriff Clark said with a rising voice, "Yes, I do. Mike Conroy, Tim's buddy, he's the one that got his eye put out in the fight, told me all about how they were attacked by Catherine Sherrill and one of you boys. So, which one of you was it and can tell me I'm not right!"

"I can!" Every head turned toward the speaker. Catherine had been hiding at the side of the church wanting to hear how her grandfather, father, and uncles were going to handle the problem with Tim Clark. She could not tolerate that fact that the truth was not being told here and decided to make it known. She looked around the room and settled her "Sherrill" gaze on Sheriff Clark and with a calmness and clarity of voice said, "You ready to listen to the truth?"

The sheriff's head snapped back as if he had been hit and then tried to regain his composure. Samuel quickly took his place beside his daughter's side and said, "Whether you like what she says or not, she stays with the family. After you have heard her story and think you need someone to be captured by you then you will take me."

"No, Pa, that won't happen. Sheriff Clark's badge says he is a fair and honorable man and when he hears the truth he will know what to do. Right, Sheriff Clark?" said a composed Catherine as she looked deep into the sheriff's eyes.

Mode was not alone in his thoughts of *what will she be when she is full grown.*

Sheriff Clark who realized he had no way to answer except to say, "Yes, you are right." He didn't want to look anyone in the eye and pretended to study the planks in the floor. Everyone knew there was only one way to answer Catherine's question. "All right then, young lady! Tell us your story!"

The only person in the room that knew the total story was Samuel and he didn't have time to tell the others before Clark burst through the door. Catherine took a deep breath and slowly told the facts of the story from the time she had stopped at the chestnut tree. When she finished there was a quietness in the room. Many thoughts were in everyone's mind, but the most prevalent one was, *How did a young girl do all that?* Samuel thought, *Sure am glad she didn't tell the reason she was riding.*

As if reading Samuel's mind, Sheriff Clark asked, "And just why was it that a young woman goes riding by herself in these woods when she full knows what dangers there are from animals and no telling what." He could have kicked himself for saying that part.

Catherine said, "I've traveled that way many times with Pa and my brother. You know, going from Uncle Jacob's cabin to Uncle Uriah's cabin. I was telling them Grandpa wanted to have a family meeting."

"And what was this meeting about, Adam?" said Clark.

"I was going to help them plan their next season's planting. You know, such things as how much corn to plant, how many acres of tobacco and such," said Adam. He saw no reason to cover the total agenda.

Clark had to give some indication of his control even though he knew her story sounded reasonable. He, like the others, had a difficult time with the fact she was alone and had caused such havoc. He walked up to Catherine and said, "Knocked his eye out with your whip, eh? Mind showing me how."

"Wait here and I'll get it and show you," said Catherine. When she returned, she asked, "You ready?" She didn't wait for an answer as she quickly raised her arm and cracked the whip close to Clark. The quickness of her move and the sound left a stunned look on Clark's face and knew the force of that whip could have cut a splinter out of a plank.

"Ahhhhh, well, all right. I can see that you know how to handle a whip. I'm leaving now, but I'm gonna give a whole lot of thought to what you have said here today. I will tell Mike to restate his story. I will be back to see each of you! And there's the matter of what got Hank shot plus no one has seen Bill Cooper for a long time. Musta left the country," said the sheriff as he tried his best to show everyone he was in charge. He didn't charge out the door like he did when he came in; he just calmly walked out. But everyone knew he was in a mood to get even.

Samuel was thinking all sorts of things. *No way he can prove Catherine wrong. The time between now and when he gets back…we can use to get Boudroe and Emma to Santee's place.*

Catherine looked around the room and then seemed to wilt into a chair. All the brothers crowded around her to make sure she was going to be all right. Almost as a chorus, they said, "You did very well, Catherine. We are proud of you." She smiled and placed her hands in her lap as Mary had often showed her how young ladies were supposed to act.

Adam said, "Well, boys, we now know the whole story about our Catherine. She will not, I repeat, will not, have to stand trial. Not as long as I'm breathing." His sons echoed the same sentiment.

❧

Mary said in an incredulous voice to Catherine, "You did what? Tell me it isn't so! Just what gives you the right to go off without telling me where you are going and what you are going to do! Seems like once should be enough for anyone in two days!"

Samuel looked at Mary and said, "Now, now Mary. Just let Catherine tell what happened at the church with Clark. She did the right thing."

"Samuel Sherrill! I declare! You know only too well that two wrongs don't make a right! Just what do you say we do about this?" said a still upset Mary.

"Ma, just let me explain and I think you'll see what Pa is trying to get across. And Ma, I'm most grateful you are my ma. The Good Lord blessed me when he let me have you for a mother. And if it hadn't been for your showing and telling me the ways to stand up for myself, I would still be bound here to this cabin. There's a wonderful world out there, Ma! I want to be a part of it. No, I will be a part of it!" said Catherine.

Samuel looked at Mary with a tilted head that signified she's got a point. "Well, Mary, you have to admit she got her smarts from you. Thou reapest what thou sowest."

Mary shifted her stance and softened her features to the point of starting a smile and said, "I don't know what I'm going to do with you two. I think y'all planned this whole discourse just for my benefit."

Catherine looked at her father and said, "What's a discourse, Pa?"

Hang fire if I know. "I think the smartest member of our family can answer that better'n me," said Samuel while pointing to Mary.

Mary knew exactly what he was doing. *Smartest one, who's he think he is kidding.* "Well, Catherine, that means you and your father had an in-depth discussion about what you were going to tell me about your being at the church. Doesn't that about sum it up, my husband?"

23

Josh and Ashdon were sitting on the cabin porch with Samuel. They were eager to get going back to their village. Josh said, "Both of us want to get going back. Boudroe and Emma are getting their things together ready to go with us."

Samuel said, "I really thank y'all for taking your time to do this for us and them. It sure does solve a lot of problems."

Samuel, Mary, and their children were standing next to the cabin when Ashdon, Josh, Boudroe, and Emma joined them. Mary said, "Emma, Boudroe, I sure am going to miss you two. Seems like we were just getting started to know each other better and now this," as she casually waved her hand toward the mountain.

"Mary, you have been almighty good to us. We won't forget it. Who knows, maybe we'll see each other one of these days. That is, if we don't make it to New York."

The Sherrills watched two Melungeons and two Negroes slowly disappear into the forest heading west over the mountains. *Wish I was going with them*, thought Samuel and Catherine. As if by command, they turned and looked at each other. Catherine said, "Pa, I think we're thinking the same thing." Samuel smiled at his daughter and slowly shook his head with an "I agree" look.

Mary said, "Somehow or other, I feel we will be seeing all of them sometime soon. Why? I don't know, but I do think it will happen."

24

Judge Cannon read the case docket his clerk had made up for hearings today. He half-mumbled to himself, "What is going on with the Sherrills. Hank Hoffman problems with the brothers, Tim Clark's death, and Mike Conroy's losing one eye both due to being attacked by Catherine. What is this world coming to? Women attacking men…hmmmphh." He got up and put on his judge's robe and opened the door to the court room. *Good grief! All the Sherrills are here! Talk about protecting their own.*

"How do you plead? Guilty or not guilty," said Judge Cannon as he peered over his glasses to Hank Hoffman.

"Mind telling me again just what it is I'm charged with," mumbled Hank who had a pronounced uneasy look in his eyes. "I didn't do nothing to nobody." *And I'm not going to spill the beans on what I'm using the Tory thing for anyway.*

Alan Cannon knew why Hoffman was appearing before him, but he also knew that he had to rule in favor of England. "Nobody said you did anything to anybody except your claim you were fired upon by the Sherrills while you were out hunting deer. Is that your story?"

"Yes, Alan…uhhh…Judge Cannon. That is the truth. All them Sherrills fired on me. In fact, one wanted to shoot me down on the spot after they surrounded me."

Mode leaned over from where he was sitting on a long bench, looked down the line of his brothers, and said loud enough for all to hear, "Hunting deer! That's a lie!"

Judge Cannon banged his gavel, leaned over the table, and gave Mode a hard look and said, "Any more comments like that and you'll be in the stocks! Now keep quiet unless I call on you!"

As if by a signal all the brothers signified their assent by nodding their heads once. It almost looked like they had practiced the maneuver many times.

Alan Cannon knew Hoffman and Cooper had many times in last year made life difficult for people who were not doing what the English proclamations and acts demanded of the colonies. They were doing these things under the guise of working for the crown. That was not the case with these two. If he gave them a proper sentence, he knew his position would be given to someone else the next time appointments were made for official offices.

"Then Mr. Hoffman, would you tell the court where Mr. Cooper is located. Has he skipped the area knowing that both of you may be guilty of a crime against these Sherrills? And which one shot you? Point him out to me," said a stern-voiced Judge Cannon.

Hoffman looked at the brothers and saw to his discomfort that all were giving him the icy Sherrill stare. The stare was menacing to behold and it gave the clear signal that the receiver of that stare that their future would be one of constant worry. *Them Sherrills are a clannish lot. Hurt one and you hurt 'em all.* "Tell you the truth, Judge, I can't say for sure which one it was. Seems like the sound of the rifle was behind all of us, but I really don't recall since I was the one shot."

The judge banged his gavel down on the table and said, "Case dismissed for lack of proof. Now onto the Catherine Sherrill case. Where is the defendant?"

Samuel got up and walked to the door and said, "It's time, Catherine." He led his daughter into the room. She was not about to show a submissive attitude to anyone in the room except maybe her pa and uncles. Not saying a word, she sat down next to Samuel.

The judge said, "And who is the plaintiff?"

"Right here, Judge Cannon," said Sheriff Clark. "But before we get too far into this I have to admit that for a girl to do what Mike Conroy said she did…well, I been thinking about it. And it just don't add up. I say she had the help of one of her uncles or even her pa!"

Judge Cannon saw that the brothers were not reacting to Clark's testimony. *They know he is wrong. I know he is wrong. He's just trying to make it look like he is not to be questioned.* "Got any proof of your claim? How do you know they were not at their cabins or fields or even out hunting?"

"Great day in the morning, Judge! No way I can find all that out about those boys. No one is going to say anything bad about them. They might burn you out if'n you did something to one of theirs," said Sheriff Clark who clearly understood he did not have a good case to present to the judge.

The comment about burning someone's property was not sitting well with the brothers and Judge Cannon could see their "I've about had it with this" look.

Samuel knew Mode and Quil were the first ones to react to comments about their honesty and especially as heinous crime as burning someone's property. He looked at each one. The two brothers sat back in their seats, crossed their arms across their chests, and stared at the sheriff who became increasingly uncomfortable being the center of this kind of attention.

"Let me review your facts, Sheriff. You say a girl, namely Catherine Sherrill, could not have committed the beating on Mike Conroy and, God rest his soul, your son, Tim. You say she had to have help yet you do not have proof of such. Is that correct?"

Sheriff Clark pursed his lips, looked down at the floor, and mumbled a barely audible comment.

"Speak up, Sheriff! I can't hear you!" said the Judge.

"I said that is the way it appears, but you know just as much as I do that Catherine Sherrill and her pa are guilty as charged. My stocks and jail are waiting," said Clark.

Judge Cannon locked his eyes onto Clark's and held them until Clark looked back down at the floor. He certainly wasn't going to look at the Sherrills. "Don't you ever bring such a half-baked case into this, the King's Court, again. Case dismissed."

Clark's surprised look told everyone what they needed to know. They knew he was sure his case would be accepted and Cannon would rule in favor of his testimony. The Sherrills stood up, nodded their heads to Judge Cannon, and turned to leave.

"You boys know I'm going to be like a hawk watching your chickens. So don't think this is going to change anything. For that matter, I bet you know something about that slave," said Sheriff Clark.

Judge Cannon looked at the sheriff and then at the backs of the men leaving his court room. *I wonder if they really know anything. Maybe I ought to get into this a little more.*

As the brothers were leaving the court, four people could feel the increasing upward slope of the mountains they were climbing as they headed west. They stopped for a much needed rest by a clear stream silently moving around smooth rocks tinged a tawny green by lichens and moss. The cloudless sky was a stark blue, a barely felt wind whispered through stately hemlocks. "How can one not know God in a place like this," whispered Emma to all around her as she let her eyes wander over the majestic scenes around her.

Boudroe said, "I'm ah getting colder by the minute. I think… ahhhh, did I say sumthin not right?" He caught Emma's look into this eyes. *Uhhh ohhhh, I'm in trouble now.*

Josh quickly jumped into quelling a possible argument by saying, "Why don't we build a small fire, catch some fish, and have us a good supper."

Boudroe said, "How yo' goin' to catch fish. Nobody got no fishing pole and even if you did, you ain't go no hook."

Emma leaned close to her husband and said, "Husband of mine, you'll never learn! Let these men do what they know how to do. Who knows, even you might learn something." She smiled at Boudroe who knew he was being "funned" with.

Ashdon tied the string around his rifle's ramrod and reached into his game bag to find a hook. Josh used a stick to unearth a few grubs. Ashdon impaled one of the grubs on his hook, broke off a piece of hemlock bark, put the hooked bait on the bark, and gently placed it in the water. Everyone watched as he let the bark slowly float by one of the rocks until it got to a position Ashdon knew would most likely get the attention of a fish. Ashdon then slid the grub off the bark. It floated in the water and started wigglying back and forth. The water exploded as the fish cleared its surface. Ashdon pulled back on the rod and set the hook in the trout's mouth. Boudroe's mouth was hanging open in surprise at seeing how the fish was caught and he turned to look at Emma. She gave him a gentle smile and a look that said "learn something?"

During the meal that was cooked over the small fire, all Boudroe could do was talk fishing with Ashdon. He forget his being cold as he reviewed over and over watching the trout breaking the water and seeing the colors on its body flashing in the daylight.

Everyone started settling down for the night with Josh volunteering for the first watch with Ashdon and Boudroe following at four hour intervals. Josh moved enough distance from the camp to let his eyes adjust to the complete darkness. Tuning his senses to the sounds around him, he was able to settle in his mind that no danger was present. The howls of the wolves and far off bleating of elk made him feel at home as his eyes drifted to the sky and its magnificent display of countless stars. *Good grief, what was that? And there's another one and...I don't believe this...another one!* He rushed back to camp and awakened everyone with a "You have got to see this! Come on now!"

Everyone followed Josh to his lookout position at the edge of a large clearing and stopped as if on command by Josh. Everyone saw what Josh was so excited about as they followed his gaze into the night sky. The sky was full of streaking lights and bright spots of light that vanished almost as suddenly as they appeared in the black sky. Everyone was awestruck at the celestial fireworks show and many comments of "Look at that one! Didya see that long streak? Where are all those things going? Hope we don't get hit by one of them!"

Emma said, "Back in Carolina, we were always told to make a wish when you saw one of these lights and the wish would come true. Can you imagine the amount of wishes I am wishing right now?"

The four people sat close together lost in their own thoughts and three men made a wish of their own.

◦⌒◦

Patrick stood on the beach listening to the waves as they rolled and crashed on the beach and felt the ever-present wind as he watched a glorious sunset slowly signal the ending of another day. The sun's orange orb was huge and he kept looking directly at it as is hypnotized by the way the sun's light faded. He turned to the east and saw stars slowly signal their presence. One red star captured his attention. *Mars is really showing off tonight.* The sun blinked out and it became dark. *Wow! Look at those meteors! The sky is full of them!* He watched the sky and gave up counting the many meteor trails as he sat down on the beach and enjoyed the show. *God is letting us know in a beautiful way just what power he has for us.* He thought as he watched the sky, *This makes me think of home with Father watching meteors over the years. I've made up my mind! I'm going back to Scotland.* He rubbed his leg in hopes the ever present pain would go away. *I wish I knew what it was I caught in Germany that has caused this.*

"Major Ferguson, sir! At last I've found you," said Captain Alexander Chesney.

"Is there a problem, Captain?" said Patrick.

"Ohh, no, sir, no problem at all! In fact, it is something you will be very interested in hearing and reflecting on the rest of the night. It truly is—" said the captain as he was interrupted.

"Good grief, Captain! What is it you are carrying on so about? Are the slaves staging a revolt? Are we being attacked? Out with it man!" said an increasingly frustsrated Patrick.

"You are going home, sir! You are going home! I was told to bring you the news. You, sir, are a difficult man to find when you do not want to be found."

Patrick turned his eyes from the captain to continue his watch of the meteors. "Aren't those heavenly bodies a sight to behold? Where do they come from? I'm glad they don't hit us with their fire."

"Yes, sir! I, too, am much amazed at those fireballs. Wonder why they wait until night to show themselves?" said Captain. He quickly realized the error of his statement and said, "Of course, the sun will block out those lights."

"You had me worried for a moment, Captain. I thought you were beginning to lose your senses," said a half-smiling Patrick.

"You know something, sir. Speaking of losing senses, why is it the people living in and moving to America are resisting England's proven way of living and government? Most of them lived in England and know that our way of living and our laws are the best in the world. There's no way they can make it on their own," said a frustrated Alexander.

"Well, Alexander, I see that you really do have your senses about you. Your analysis is correct and the one way they don't know anything about is how to organize and equip a military to fight for their cause. I bet some of them don't know what cause to defend and, even if they did, they would not know who the leaders should be or how to get them to lead. They've got so many factions that oppose each other that they'll never find any way to organize themselves for a common cause. That is where they will always need our help. And, in my way of thinking, their rag tag bunch of rebels will have to be eliminated before the rest of them realize England's way is best," said a determined voiced Patrick.

At that moment, a meteor made a bright path on the horizon. The two men watched it disappear over the horizon. Alexander said, "I'm beginning to see that our military might, both land and sea, will have to be in America for a long time. Maybe years and years."

Patrick said, "You are right, Captain. And, for that matter, our blokes will be dying not knowing exactly what it is, or who it is, they are fighting and why. Just following orders. Lining up shoulder to shoulder to get killed, but our armies will prevail over there."

Sure hope the major knows what he is talkin' about, thought Alexander. "Well, sir, it's time to be getting back to get you packed for your sailing back home."

⌒

Samuel and Mary sat on the log bench with Samuel Jr., Catherine, Susan, Uriah, Adam, William, John, and Mary Jane either lying or sitting on the ground around their parents. There was complete silence, except for an occasional "ohhhh and ahhhh," among them as they watched meteors streak through the sky. Catherine said to no one in particular, "I wonder if my true love is watching these heavenly fires, too."

Mary knew that her sons and daughters faces were now turned toward Catherine and each had the "did I hear what I thought I heard" look. Mary said very casually, "Well, now my daughter, you want to share something with the rest of us? I don't recall any suitors coming around here."

"They'd better not be doin' such a thing unless I'm asked about it first!" said a clearly upset Samuel. He wasn't aware that she had had any suitors calling on her. "Anything goin' on that I ought to know about?" as he turned to Mary.

"Well, I must say!" said an equally clearly upset Mary, but it wasn't at Catherine. It was at Samuel. "Just mind your manners,

Mr. Sherrill. If anything was going on with suitors, do you really believe I would not tell you? That almost makes me want to light up like those lights in the sky! Great day, Samuel, she is seventeen years old and you well know she is what boys would call a pleasing-looking girl. She's not going to be around us forever," said Mary with a little catch in her throat.

"Just look at Susan. She is twenty years old and that Leroy Taylor boy is getting mighty serious about her," said Samuel with a matching catch in his throat. "In fact, he is thinking about crossing the mountains to settle down."

"Ohhh, Pa, you don't expect Catherine and me to be here as a bunch of old maids do you? We have a life to take on like you and Ma," said Susan.

Samuel said, "I know my children, but…"

Catherine and Susan at the same time said, "Pa, we are not children! We are young ladies!"

Mary said, "All right, everybody, let's just settle down and talk about those lights in the sky."

Samuel Jr. leaned over to Uriah and whispered, "Our sisters think they're ladies. Just what makes a lady?"

"Danged if I know," said Uriah.

"What's that, boys? You don't know what?" said their mother in a suspicious tone.

"Oh, nothing much, Ma. We're just shootin' the breeze."

Samuel said, "Speaking of shooting. I just can't seem to get over the way those British soldiers killed, no murdered, innocent people in the middle of Boston last year. I hear all they were doing was making a fuss about the taxes and such that ol' Georgey boy in London makes us do. I tell you now I am getting fed up with all that is going on with those…well, you know those guys who think they know what they are talking about when it comes to us and what we want and how we should live. Bunch of idiots!"

"That's not what we want in America! I'm sick and tired of some people across the ocean telling me what to do, how to eat, and most likely, they'll be checking out the fish we catch and tax us on that, too!" said a frustrated Uriah. "It's gonna lead to more shootin' and killing if we and they don't watch out."

Mary said, "Can't y'all talk about anything else besides shooting, killing and maybe war. I just do declare that isn't the only thing we have to be worried about. The crops need tending and harvesting so's you best do some talking about those things. And, Susan and Catherine needs have to be looked after since they are being courted."

"Just what is it about this Leroy Taylor, Susan. He hasn't spoken to me about anything except to ask to see you. I know he comes from good stock and is one of the best farmers I know of…besides me and my brothers, of course," said a half-serious Samuel.

"Great day, Pa! He's hardly touched me…" said Susan.

"And he had best not bother you because he knows what is in store for him if he does. And that goes for you, too, Catherine. Which, by the way, who is this that is seeing you. I'm upset that maybe something is going on that we should know about. Now what is it, Catherine," said a concerned Samuel.

"Ohhh, c'mon, Ma and Pa. All I said was that I guess my true love is watching the same star show as we are tonight. I'm just figuring that, whoever he is, must be watching the same sky tonight. I was thinking that both of us, who will meet one of these days, are out tonight. Nothing is going on that you wouldn't know about. That is a promise!" said Catherine with a look into her parent's eyes that told them all they wanted to know.

"Ma, we must have done something right in raising our family. We are just plain lucky. We are safe here with our friends and family all around us. Thank goodness we aren't living somewhere like Boston. Let's go back to looking at all those night lights," said Samuel. *With what's going on up there and the pesky Tories around here is growing into a big problem. Things are just not right. I just hope the next night lights we see aren't homes being burned by those guys.*

Mary broke Samuel's thoughts by asking, "Think we are just plain lucky, eh? In my way of thinking, I feel God is leading us and all we have to do is just let him use us for his plan." The room grew quite as everyone was turning Mary's comments over and over in their mind. Speaking of plans, have you heard anything about Dan'l? I've been having him on my mind a lot lately. I just don't see how Becky makes do without him."

"You're right, Mary. Let's go over to their place tomorrow. We'll take them some beans and corn from our crops. Bet she would like that," said Samuel. "I'm looking forward to seeing ol' Dan'l again to hear what he has seen over those mountains." Mary winced at the constant thought that was always in Samuel's mind—moving across those mountains. *Just wonder what he thinks he'll find over there.*

⌒

Samuel shouted, "Hello, the cabin!"

The door slowly opened. A rifle barrel appeared pointing to the ground by the wagon. Mary's gasp was barely audible as her hand slowly came to rest on her chest. Samuel hopped down from the wagon and with purposeful strides walked toward the cabin. Mary's eyes were wide with terror as she saw Samuel put his hand on the rifle and push it toward the ground. He broke out in a cold sweat when nothing was said by the person holding the rifle. At that moment from the corner of the cabin, he heard Daniel say, "Well, I'll be! Samuel Sherrill! How in blue blazes are you doing? Israel, just back off with that rifle. We've got friends here."

"Dan'l Boone! If you ever allow that to happen to us again, I'll skin you alive!" said a much relieved Mary. "You had me mighty worried there for a minute." After a moment of calming down by smoothing out her dress, adjusting her shawl, and touching her hair, she was able to calmly say, "Boys, you just get on down from here and see what you can to do help around here. Where's Becca?"

"Well, c'mon down from there, dear lady, and we'll go huntin' for her. I set a trap next to the hearth and I betcha she's in it," said Daniel.

Samuel with a mildly concerned voice said, "Mind tellin' us why you set a trap at your hearth?"

At that point, Rebecca stepped into the doorway saying, "I'm so glad to see you Mary, Samuel Jr., Susan, Catherine, Adam, Uriah, John, and William! My, my…what a great-looking family. Everybody is growing up so fast these days!"

Uriah said, "Mrs. Boone, how'd you get outta that trap?"

"Trap? What trap?" said Rebecca.

Adam said, "Mr. Boone said he laid a trap out for you on the hearth! That's not right!

"Ohh, he just thinks it is a trap to make me cook his favorite meal. I'll tell you for sure that the only time he ever trapped me was when I said 'I do' to the preacher," said a smiling Rebecca as she tousled Daniel's hair. "Y'all got to be worn out. C'mon in and rest up."

After all the talk about crops, hunting, and weather, Dan'l said, "I'm mighty pleased y'all came over to see us, but, if I know you Samuel, you got something else on your mind besides a visit. Where'd you spent the night?"

Samuel said as he casually pointed toward the direction they had traveled, "Came up Pa's path toward Wachovia and where we split off to get here is where we set up camp for the night."

"Yeah, that Sherrill's Path is a good one. I hear a lot of wagons going south to Salisbury are using what they are calling the Wagon Road. Heard some call it The Great Wagon Road," said Daniel.

"That suits me. Keeps them from coming to our place and trying to settle down. That means crowding in on us Sherrills. 'Specially me. But if it starts, then I'm moving," said a determined-voiced Samuel.

Daniel sensing what Samuel was wanting to discuss said, "You shoulda gone with me. Course it took longer than I had planned.

Two years matter of fact and Becca didn't like it one bit. But I'm getting ready to move, lock, stock, and barrel across those mountains to the prettiest land you ever saw. Full of buffalo, elk, deer, bear, and land that's just waitin' for a plow."

"Sounds kinda like it was around here when Pa set foot across the Catawba. Things sure have changed since then," said Samuel. "When you figurin' on leaving and how you gonna get all your stuff across those mountains?"

Daniel looked deep into Samuel's eyes and saw a spirit wanting to join him in his move, but at the same time, holding back for fear of the unknown. "Well, Samuel my friend, you just gather up just the stuff you feel you need and come here. We can then go together and be safer that way for all of us. I know the way, but it won't be easy to get a wagon across them without some serious scouting. Facts be known, to my way of thinking, there just isn't a way for a wagon the way I found."

Samuel looked down at his hands, pursed his lips and said, "Will Mary have to leave a lot of her kitchen and sewing stuff? She has a lot of feelings about such." He looked at Daniel and said, "She's not interested in moving 'cause she feels it is safe here. Maybe I best keep to a safe way to go. Might take more time. I'll just go up there and find that wagon road and take it to a place we can meet."

"Safe? You know as well as I do that the Tories are getting worse than ever with wanting to take over anything they can get their hands on. You and I'd call it stealing and such. But the worst of it is the English will let them do it! Guess you heard what went on down at Hillsborough?" said Daniel with a sharp tone. Daniel extended his arm and made a sweeping move toward the mountains. "Over there, the only problems are from the Indians, but I think they will allow us to live there if we go about letting them know we aren't going to make any trouble for them and will stay off their hunting grounds."

"When you leaving?" said Samuel.

"Most likely soon. Want to get over before the winter weather makes it impossible to travel up high," said Daniel as he, again, casually swung his arm back toward the west. "If'n I do leave will you put up my corn an such?"

"Not a problem," said Samuel. And after a moment of thought, "But why put it up to just rot? Why not let me sell it for you and I'll pass the money on to you the next time we meet?"

"Seems fair enough. You take a tithing of ten percent. No arguing with me on that, ol' boy," said Daniel as his finger repeatedly punched Samuel's shoulder to emphasize his point.

Samuel Jr., Israel, and Catherine joined the group and talked about the trip long into the evening when Samuel said, "Know something, Dan'l. I'll just do that loading up the wagon and head up to the Wagon Road and catch the road down to a place, that I just remembered, called Chiswell. And you well know there was a road built from there to the place Pa went a few years ago on what I hear is the Holston River."

Catherine said with a voice that got everyone's attention, "Pa! You really mean it! We're going across the mountains? I can't wait! I just might see the man who gave me his moccasins."

Mary, as she and Rebecca walked up, heard Catherine's comments. *Why is she wanting to leave here? I thought she was satisfied here.* "Samuel, Dan'l…mind letting us join your talk. Near as I can figure out you are talking about land over there." She slowly pointed toward the mountains.

After all the good and bad points about moving their prized possessions, each family settled down for the night. Mary stood up and slowly walked to the well to draw a bucket of water and whispered to Catherine to follow her. Mary wound the rope around the wooden cylinder until the bucket cleared the well's top and Catherine pulled it to the side. "What's troubling you my child?" said a worried looking Mary.

"That's just it, Mother! I'm nineteen years old and not a child anymore! And ever since Tim Clark and that Mike character tried to take me hardly any boy will pay me much attention. Act like they're afraid of me. Nineteen, Ma, and no prospects of any boy, or man, asking me to marry them! I think my chances would be much better if we were to move. I wish we were over there now!"

At that same moment, Sheriff Clark was developing a way to take his revenge, legally, out on the Samuel Sherrill family. *No gal is gonna make a fool of my family. I'm gonna make it so tough on them that they'll pack up and leave. And I've got to keep this to myself cause if Cannon finds out then I'm outta job. He's a Tory, but he still keeps the law as best he can. I know what I'll do! I'll make it look like they are part of the Regulators.* A satisfied feeling settled in his mind as he thought of his next move.

25

Mode rode up to Samuel's cabin, and after looking around at the cabin and barn, walked with purpose-filled stride to the cabin's door. "Samuel, we've got to talk!" as he knocked on the door and pulled on the heavy leather latch cord and entered the room.

"Great day in the morning, Mode! What in the ever loving is up? You seem as tight as bark on a tree," said Samuel.

"I'm here to tell you right now that your brothers and our pa have been talking about your pulling up stakes and leaving this place! And we don't think that's right."

"Not sure I'm following you, Mode. Are you saying I've got to stay here because my brothers and Pa think it isn't right for me to live somewhere else?" Samuel said with a questioning look.

Mode's emphasis wasn't lost on Samuel, "You've got that right! With all that is going on around here with those red-coated Brits and their Tory friends, we feel we all have to stick together. You well know that a single stick can be broken, but a lot of sticks bundled together is a lot harder thing to break. That's the way all of us see it."

Samuel stood up, walked to the fireplace, and took down his favorite rifle. He looked at it as if inspecting it for the first time, rubbed his fingers over the front and rear sights and thought, *Mode is right. We have to stick together.* "Well, Mode, let's get the family together and talk this out. Regardless of who does what, we've got to work through these things and come up with something we all can live with."

"I'll round them up and meet at the church tomorrow 'bout noon," said Mode.

At least he's willing to hear us out.

"I sure hope you are bringing some of Sarah's ham and biscuits for lunch," said a smiling Samuel.

Next day, when the sun was at its height in the sky, all the Sherrill brothers and their father were, once again, sitting on the hard oak benches in their church. Adam stood up, looked each son in the eye and did not find any wavering or blinking from his penetrating stare. Adam knew each man was intent on keeping the well-known fact of "You mess with one Sherrill, you mess with them all."

"Can I give the blessing, Pa?" asked Jacob.

Adam was very grateful that Jacob volunteered for the prayer. Everyone well knew that Quil was always available to give the prayer, but they also knew he would ask God to bless every twig, leaf, blade of grass, cow, goat, and nearly every other thing under the sun, but thanks to Jacob, he would not have that chance.

After Jacob's prayer, Adam described the reason for the meeting. "Boys, we have got to make sure that each of us knows, at all times, what the other is thinking especially about pulling up stakes and leaving this area. And we all know that Samuel continues to talk about moving across these mountains to find another place to settle down. Now, do any of you others feel the same way or have somethin' to say 'bout his pulling up stakes and crossing them mountains?"

Samuel felt the stares of his brothers and well knew he was the only one giving thought to doing what his pa had just described. No one said a word. A gentle breeze moved from one window to the other, carrying with it the tangy smell of pine trees. Finally, Samuel stood up and said, "Well, listen to me, my brothers. Maybe I'm right, maybe I'm wrong in my thinking. But I have to at least explore as many ways as possible for the welfare of my family both from their safety and providing for them. And yes, it is true that I am giving a lot of thought to moving over around a place around the Nolichucky River."

The whole room erupted in questions of when and why was Samuel so moved to leave them. Some of the comments were "Has any one of them created this desire to leave? Is it because of Catherine's problem or Susan's choice not pleasing to him?" Just what was it that was causing the problem.

Mode said, "Is it because of what Boone is telling you? Have you got the 'Boone itch' to tromp around this world trying to find who knows what?"

Isaac said in a sullen voice, "Looks to me like a way to get out of working the farm." Samuel gave him a look that said "just don't go there," brother.

Adam could see that this was starting to get emotional and no telling what might be said that would create more problems for the family. He stood up and waited until each son was quiet. He looked at each one and, with his hands clasped behind his back, slowly walked over to the open window. *This needs to go another direction. No use can come of everyone getting his britches in a wad.* He turned around and said, "Has anyone of you heard more about the fighting over at Alamance? Seems Tryon is hell-bent on making it look like all of us are a bunch of problem makers for ol' crazy George."

Once again, the room erupted with louder comments about King George, England, the Tories and the killing of some of their friends at Alamance a six weeks ago.

Quil shouted, "They started this killing. This will lead to war and I'm joining with the Regulators or whatever army we can put together to drive them from this land!"

Uriah thumped his fists on the hard seat and outshouted Quil, "And that devil Tryon started it all! He is just as afraid to get his hands dirty as that king of his in England. Yeah! He thinks that you boys go out and fight and get killed while I sit back here enjoying great company and good food and no telling what else in his palace on the river."

Adam let the uproar slowly subside. *Glad they got off their problems of Samuel thinking about moving out.* He raised his hands to settle his sons down to some semblance of restrained composure. He said in a clear steady voice, "Does this mean we have the beginning of a new plan for us Sherrills? Are we going to allow Tryon and his English Parliament to continue their ways with us? Are we going to take more of crazy George's edicts and acts like the Line, Sugar, Currency, and all the others in the last few years? Do we stand here and protect our name, our land, our families, and our chosen way of life?" And with increasing volume to the point of almost shouting and shaking his fists above his head said, "By the grace of God, we will make our stand, like David did when he was up against Goliath. We will work our plan for this land and our country! God will lead the way!"

Adam's sons were stunned into jaw dropping, not a muscle moving, silence as they watched and heard their father, who was usually even tempered and slow to anger, bring their plan to a finite point. All at once, as if on command, they all jumped up, shouting that no one or no army could make them bow down and pounding each other's backs with an uncharacteristic enthusiasm seldom seen of the Sherrills in these parts. Adam watched with a proud feeling of his son's embracing the fact of remaining together. *I hope I'm not sinning for feeling this way.*

A lot of talk about getting the clan better organized and with emphasis on communicating in a timely manner with each other. It was decided that the eldest son would be the messenger for his family and when the others saw them approaching they were to immediately go to him for his reason for the visit.

Samuel said with an "I'm not sure we need to be talking in this manner." Does this mean we let it be known that we are openly committing to the Regulators? And if we do, will Tryon try to bring down his troops on us around the ford?"

Much discussion followed about the Regulator movement with the final decision being to not officially join them, but at the same time, let the leaders know of the Sherrill availability. Quil said, "That's a fine line we're drawing on the Regulators. For me, I just as soon as let it be known that we will fight for our rights. But majority rules here and I can go along with it."

26

Yona leaned against a large hemlock tree growing on the edge of a clear stream and was lost in thinking how peaceful the stream made him feel, especially when it mirrored the colors of the changing leaves this time of the seasons. His thoughts were suddenly broken as a fish with streaks of colors broke the surface in a successful effort to catch a small moth hovering over the water. *Are my people to be treated like the moth and be swallowed by the white man? Why can't they live in peace with us? Why is it they think they need more land than they can possibly use? We have been here forever and know how to live with the land. Why won't they learn from us?*

Twadi and Yanisa were standing motionless in the water, holding high their hickory spears, ready to impale a fish for their meal. Yona watched and thought, *Even the white man doesn't know how to get fish like we do even though we have shown them how to do it.* Suddenly, Twadi, with a snap if his wrist, shot the spear into the water. The spear rocked back and forth as the dying fish tried to escape its fate. Twadi casually waded to the fish and on pulling it out noticed it was big enough for all of them to eat a satisfying meal. He handed the spear and fish to Yona and then climbed onto the bank and turned to watch Yanisa. With a like snap of the wrist, Yanisa also had a fish for their meal. "We eat well before the night covers us," said Twadi.

"Nice fish," said Yona. There was no need for any congratulations for catching the fish as the sharing of food was an accepted way of life for them.

Ashdon had crawled to what he thought was no more than a spear's throw from the three men around their campfire. He knew them all but wanted to make sure they were a hunting rather than a war party. Having satisfied his ever-present awareness of his surroundings, he gave the call of a whipporwill. Yona looked across their campfire to Twadi as a whisper of a grin built on his face. He said, "What is it my friend Ashdon wants?"

Twadi and Yanisa looked at each other with a questioning manner while a surprised Ashdon was gathering his wits at Yona's greeting.

"Come to the fire, my friend," said Yona as he looked directly at the place Ashdon was hiding even though Ashdon thought his place was perfect. Ashdon got up and walked into the fire's light and said, "How is it that you always know I am around? I have never been able to sneak up on you."

Twadi, after gathering his composure from not knowing a possible enemy was in a position to do harm, said, "Good whipporwill sound you make. Think about next time you use that call. Use another bird's call. The whipporwill stays away from us."

Yona looked at Ashdon with a "gotcha again my friend" look and motioned him to sit down. Ashdon said with a feigned frown, "Just when I thought I knew everything I find out that I'm just a beginner. It is good to see all of you."

After much talk about squash in their gardens and fields full of corn, Yona changed the subject when he said, "Does my friend want to tell me about the other people of another color you have in your village?"

Ashdon said, "My friend Yona seems to know all things about us and we don't know much about you. Why is that?"

"We are always seeing what is different on our land so that we can be ready to protect it," said Yona.

The implication was not lost on Ashdon. "You make a very good point. I guess we best start sending scouts out to find you and figure out just what you are about to do. But I need to tell you about Emma and Boudroe."

All three Cherokees listened intently to Ashdon's story about the darker color man and woman. At times, they would turn to look at each other to make sure they each understood what Ashdon was saying. Twadi asked, "They have war clubs and rifles?"

Ashdon said, "We gave them a rifle and some knives. They are helping us supply our meat needs and such. Emma is a woman who can heal the sick. Boudroe is good with planting."

Yanisa said, "Planting is done by our women. Does this Boudroe man know our ways?"

"Not nearly as well as he should. But, he is not afraid to defend what is his," said Ashdon as the pointing of his finger emphasized.

"That is what we are doing now and have been doing ever since your like entered our land!" exclaimed Yona in a loud voice.

"But what is needed is for all of us to be like you and me and learn how to live with each other," said Ashdon.

"I'll say one more time. We want to live in peace with your kind. We want to be sure the people of a different color know your ways with us," said Yona as he abruptly stood up which signaled the end of the conversation. "We meet again. No whippor-will call this time."

Ashdon watched the three natives of this land disappear into the forest as silently as a deer. *I agree with Samuel. They continue to be confused about their future. What the heck, I'm confused about my own when having to tangle with them Tories. Sure don't want to tangle with the Indians and Tories at the same time. One in front and the other in the back. Not good.* He took another look at the way Yona and his friends had taken, shrugged his shoulders, and started toward home. The three natives watched him go, then turned toward their village.

27

1774

Catherine stood by Betsy at the barnyard fence brushing its mane and was thinking about her future. *Here I am, nineteen years old, and the only man not afraid to be seen with me, or court me, is Wayne. He says he loves me and wants to ask Pa if he could ask me to marry him. I guess it's now or never.* She continued a rhythmic brushing while still thinking about her future, or lack of it. *But I like Wayne, but loving him is another matter entirely.*

The look of concern for her daughter was on Mary's face as she gently moved the rocker back and forth. *Something is bothering Kate and I think I know what it is.* She got up and walked down the steps heading toward Catherine. Along the way, she noticed her flower and herb garden thinking how it suddenly perked up after the rain last night. *Squash and beans wrapping around the corn are looking good. Rain done 'em good.* "Look like you're doing some deep thinking, Catherine. Anything you want to talk about with your mother?" as she reached out touching Catherine's arm.

"Ma," said Catherine as tears glistened in her eyes, "I'm getting old. I don't have a husband. I don't have children! I don't know what is going to happen to me." She stopped brushing her horse and took a handkerchief from her apron pocket and wiped her eyes. She looked past her mother toward the ridgeline behind the cabin trying to find answers in her mind.

Mary watched and could almost feel Catherine's painful thoughts. She knew the other women around the area were saying they felt sorry for Catherine not being married while, at the same time, thinking, *Sure glad my daughter isn't facing what Catherine is doing now*. She knew those comments were starting to bother Catherine's usual "like me as I am or not at all" regard for herself. As she reached out to touch Catherine's arm, she said, "Well, my child—"

"Ma, I am not a child! When will you realize that? I am a full grown woman whose past actions, especially when protecting myself from those boys in the woods, has kept menfolk from coming around to see me," exclaimed Catherine in a emphatic manner. "I'm beginning to wonder just how ugly I am."

"I'm not trying to treat you as a child and you certainly are far from being ugly! That time is long gone when we treat you as a child! All I want for you is for you to be happy! And my daughter, you are not happy and it concerns me," said Mary with an equally sounding emphatic manner.

"Great day, Ma, I don't mean to take out my being sorry for myself on you. I think I'll go for a ride and think things through. You know that Wayne wants to talk with Pa about me, but I'm not sure I want him to do that," said Catherine as she started saddling Betsy.

"I don't think your going off on a ride is a good idea. You know, the Tories are out trying to round up some known Regulators. Never know what those Tories will do if they see someone, especially a woman, riding around out there," said Mary as she waved her hand back toward the forest. "And they feel sure Pa is a Regulator, but can't prove that he has done anything with them. That puts all of us on a edge of deciding about staying here or moving over those mountains to that Nolichucky area."

"What do you mean move? Just when I might be asked to become Mrs. Wayne Tallston! No, you can't mean that we are leaving here…no way!" Catherine jumped on her horse and rode at full gallop across the pasture toward the wood line thinking, *Nolichucky? I don't want any part of it!*

She's right, but we have to think of the whole family. Hope she settles down after her ride, thought Mary.

"Just what the heck is…ahhh, is happening…out there?" said Sheriff Clark as he slowly turned his eyes from watching Mary and Catherine to Wayne Tallston. Tallston shrugged his shoulders while not taking his eyes off Catherine. *Sure is a pretty and mighty feisty thing.*

Clark said in a low menacing tone, "I'm paying you to keep me told about what they are doing and especially about what her pa is doing. Is he one of them Regulators or what?"

Tallston understood the menacing tone and said while slowly backing away from their hiding place behind the pasture's split rail fence, "I've told you everything that I have seen or heard around Catherine's place and if that isn't good enough, then get someone else to do your dirty work."

"Dirty work? You think knowing as much about your enemy as you can is dirty work? You need to make up your mind, boy!" Clark said with his low menacing voice, "You got to be for the king or for yourself. Now which is it?"

Go along with this mudman. "All right, all right…don't go getting so uptight, Sheriff. I'm gonna do what I told you I was going to do," said Tallston. *This guy is crazy to get even with them Sherrills.* The "getting even" thought about the Sherrills was a troubling thought to Wayne. *Tangle with one and you tangle with all of 'em.* "I'm off to see Catherine." He put his foot in the stirrup, swung his leg over the saddle, and turned his horse to catch up with Catherine.

Catherine guided her horse by the press of her knees to turn toward the left or right. Betsy felt the nudge of her left side and turned down the path toward the cornfields that ran up against the forest. Catherine remembered her father talking about the clearing of this land and that he meant for it to be kept in the family. She was thinking about the possible move when she heard Wayne's horse galloping across the harvested field. *Why is he coming from that direction? Nothing is there except a couple of dove hunting blinds.*

Wayne slowed his horse to a walk as he guided it toward Catherine and said, "Catherine! Catherine! It is Wayne."

Catherine looked over her shoulder with a look of "why are you here" while slowing stopping Betsy beside the fields split rail fence. While looking at the fence, she thought of how much time and effort that had been put into chopping down the trees, splitting them into rails, and then building the fence. *Pa will have to do this all over again when we move.* Her thoughts were interrupted by Wayne stopping his horse on the other side of the fence.

As if reading her thoughts, Wayne said, "Mighty fine fence. Bet it took forever to get it in place." His eyes followed the rails to the end of the field. "Lots of trees needed to make this." He slowly turned his head toward Catherine and waited for a response from her.

After a long silence, Catherine said with a hint of a smile, "I hope you didn't come out here to look at Pa's fences."

"Nope. I was on my way to your door when I saw you riding and I thought 'what the heck, I can see her now' and not have to bother the rest of your family," said Wayne.

Catherine said, "Kinda sudden about you being here, isn't it? We hadn't planned on you visiting me when we last saw each other. Something on your mind?"

Wayne started feeling like he was putting himself in a corner, but didn't want to give Catherine any idea of his real reason for being close to her house. After another lengthy pause, he said, "I was just out looking to get a deer for the folks." By the look in Catherine's eyes, he knew that was a lame excuse for being in the area.

"No deer around your place?" said Catherine and with a flip of her wrist said, "You out here spying on me?" She noticed a brief narrowing of his eyes, *What's that all about?*

Wayne gave a slight smile and said in a manner designed to make his statement sound like a joke, "Yeah, I've gotta admit I'm out here spying on you. What man wouldn't want to sneak a peek of a pretty lady out riding along this cornfield?"

Catherine recalled the last time a man, or men, talked the way Wayne was starting to do in their conversation. She let a tough as nails confidence settle in her mind and looked at Wayne with the Sherrill "don't mess with me" level tight-lipped gaze. "Wayne, I do not like your lack of manners and would appreciate your taking your leave now." She locked her eyes on his until he blinked and looked away.

"If that is what you want, then I'll be on my way. Not sure when I'll be back either," he said in a low-toned manner. He wheeled his horse around and galloped down the path thinking she knows something isn't right. He looked around and was met with the same gaze and as he continued his riding, he thought, *Sure would hate to come home to supper with her around.*

Catherine sat back in her saddle. *He is wanting something and I feel it isn't me. Will I ever find a man!* Tears were on the verge of running down her cheeks as she thought about the plight, not to mention future disgrace, of her spinsterhood. *Am I that difficult to get along with? People say I'm pretty, but is that the truth? What is to become of me?*

∽

Samuel said, "Go with you where?"

With a tilt of his head to the west, Daniel said, "Over yonder to that place called around Caswell and some others call it Watauga. Ya know that's the one I've been talking about ever since I got back from that Kaintuck ground in '71."

"I sure remember that time. Becky was not too happy with you being gone for most of two years," said Samuel. "And knowing that you must still be hurting from the Cherokees and their friends' doing in your son last October must be a worrisome thing."

"No matter. What's done is done. Can I help it if I'm a man who keeps some of his thinking to himself and then wondering what is beyond the next mountain? Well, I'm obliged for your concern about us losing James. You'd better believe we are hurting over it, but that is something we've got to bear up amongst ourselves. Now, I'm asking ya again if you want to go with me on this trip?" said Daniel. "Been a number of folks pulling up stakes and going over there."

"How long you think it'll take to make it?" said a worried sounding Samuel. "Don't want to miss planting season."

Daniel bent down, picked up a stick, and sighted down its length, and his knife appeared in his hand as if by magic. "Yep, this'll do." He started peeling off the bark. "Might take four or five weeks each way. Might as well stay a week or two to get used to the goings on. Looks like ten maybe even twelve weeks." He continued the work on his stick.

"Dangnation, Dan'l, that's three months out of the plowing and planting times. Hardly see how it can be done," said Samuel.

"Got them boys of yours, don't ya? Seems to me they can do what's needed while we're gone. I don't see the problem," said Daniel.

"Well, what's to do when we get there?" said Samuel.

"Got a visit back from John Finley who traveled around those parts. He told me about some gaps over there that can be used to get people through those mountains. I saw some of 'em real good back in '67 and know how they might be used to make better trails for wagons and livestock than the Indians have made from those old buffalo trails. All I see that we need to do is find the places where we are going to stake our claim. Much like we have done here," said Daniel.

Samuel looked at Daniel for a long moment lost in thoughts. Should he take the risk of moving to a better place for a better life? *Can I really leave my brothers here? And will we be safer from the English who slowly takes away a man's freedom?* Daniel could tell what Samuel was thinking and continued whittling and not saying anything to disturb Samuel. He made one last cut on the stick, inspected and felt the knife's edge and slowly put it in his scabbard and said, "Tell you what, Samuel, why don't you give it a day or two to think about something that will change your life, good or bad, forever." The implication was to discuss it with Mary, but he didn't want to make Samuel appear that he couldn't make the decision on his own.

"Know something, Dan'l? I'm going over there with you, but I'm going to take you up on your offer and be back in a couple of days." Both men knew that he was going to get Mary's agreement to move, and after that, the decision to go with Dan'l would be easy to make and a necessary part of the plans.

"Done!" said Daniel. "Let's plan to leave as soon as you get here."

Samuel said, "I'll be back in two days. Let's make out a list of what we're gonna need for the trip." He put his foot in the stirrup and swung his leg over his horse's back.

"Not to worry 'bout what to take. Just get back here," said Daniel as he slapped the horse's rump.

As he trotted off, he wondered about his decision, *Just what the heck am I doing this for? Is it really that bad around here that I'll leave all this behind and start over? I'll go see Pa tomorrow and get his feelings.* He slowed to a trot and slowly looked over his fields of corn that had taken a lot of hard work behind the plow. *Just don't know I'm gonna do it, just don't know* played through his mind.

Adam and Elizabeth sat on their cabin porch that Adam and some of his grandsons built last summer. Elizabeth had always wanted a porch where she could card wool, sew, churn milk, and other chores while watching the change of the seasons.

"Looks like Samuel's got something on his mind." She pointed toward Samuel who had just cleared the edge of the forest on the road that led straight from the cabin. Nothing else was said as they watched him approach and Adam thought, *Seen him walk this way before when he's troubled.*

After talk of family and crops, Samuel looked into the eyes of first his pa and then Mom and said, "Got something I need to tell y'all about."

Adam said with an unwavering eye-to-eye contact while slighty moving his head up and down "Figured as much."

Samuel did not break eye contact with his pa and said, "I'm leaving for the Watauga area next week, most likely Thursday."

Elizabeth said, "Why at this time? Seems like a poor time to be leaving the crops."

"Ma, you didn't hear me! Me, Mary, and the kids are leaving here and moving over to that valley!" said Samuel.

Elizabeth slowly looked from Samuel to Adam. Adam slowly shook his head up and down saying, "Guess it had to happen to one of 'em at some time."

Elizabeth sat back in her chair, took in a long breath while looking at her second born son and slowly shook her head up and down. *Now I know how my Ma felt.*

Adam got up, walked down the two steps off the porch, and put a hand on each of Samuel's shoulders, looked deep into his eyes and with a slight smile, said, "I wish you a safe journey and I want you to seek God's help for such. Gather up the families after church Sunday. We've got to let them all know about this."

The following Sunday, all the families were present at the churchyard and were combining their abundant prepared foods on the oak slab tables underneath a large elm tree. Inside the church, Adam stood up, which brought an immediate silence to his boys and said, "I've asked you boys here for listening to what Samuel has to say." He turned to Samuel with an extended hand.

Samuel stood up and slowly looked at each of his brothers and finally his pa. It suddenly hit him that all the women should hear this at the same time and said, "Let's go outside so I can talk to everyone at the same time."

Mode said, "Why do that? You making this sound like something bad like you're moving," which he suddenly knew he was right.

Everyone let what Mode said penetrate their minds and almost as one started questioning Samuel who got up and walked out between his talking and gesturing brothers. After getting outside, Samuel climbed on top of a table and in a loud voice, said, "Let's all get around me. What I've got to say will be this time only." He looked around for Mary and motioned her to join him.

"Everyone, listen up!" Samuel motioned for everyone to get a little closer. When he was satisfied with the result, he said in a raised voice, "I, along with Mary, want to let you know that we are moving over the mountains to the place around the Nolichucky." A brief silence followed with everyone looking at Samuel and Mary with an unbelieving look of "I don't believe I heard what you just said!"

"Sherriff's gonna be mighty interested in what's going to happen next Thursday," mumbled Wayne Tallston who continued to lay well hidden and within hearing range underneath some low-growing bushes close by the Sherrills. His attention turned to Catherine and while looking intently at her started thinking of their times together.

Catherine, who knew what her pa was going to say, drifted from the group and started busy work, arranging some fried turkey and venison next to some fried squash grown in their garden. She suddenly felt a slight sensation in her mind that made her look up and slowly let her eyes drift the wood line. She passed at a place that appeared to be overgrown vines and brush from land that was cleared a couple of years ago. Some unknown force pulled her attention back to the vine-covered brush. *Something is in there looking at me! and I'm gonna find out what it is!* She started walking toward the spot while keeping an intense stare on it.

Wayne's staring at Catherine ended and started focusing his attention on Samuel's actions. A movement caught his attention and he suddenly realized Catherine was fast approaching his hiding place, *Hell fire! It's Catherine. No way can she see me. I've got to get out of here!* He started backing out of the tangled growth of vines and bushes.

Catherine could see the vine-covered bush moving plus noticed two cardinals flying from it and then became wary of what she might run into such as some animal hunting for food. She picked up a sturdy oak branch, tested its strength by hitting it on ground, and finding it to her liking turned her attention back to the brush.

It didn't take Wayne long to realize he was not going to escape being caught by, of all people, Catherine. Snap judgment led to his using a moderate-toned voice, "Catherine, help me get outta here!"

Catherine had no intention of helping Wayne and said, "Help yourself Wayne Tallston! I wouldn't even help one of my brothers out of there if they were spying on me like you're doing!"

Wayne, being no fool, even though he certainly felt like it now, said as he struggled out of his hiding place, "Can't say I blame you, but I wasn't invited to this shindig, so I thought this was the best way to see you without causing a fuss or whatever."

With a stern look, Catherine said in an even low voice "I don't believe you. Why didn't you just ride on up to our church meeting and picnic instead of peeking at us through these bushes?" She started slapping the oak branch in her hand. Wayne could see, and hear, the branch being easily handled by Catherine, *Gotta be real careful here.*

Samuel and Mode were talking about the pending move and both had noticed Catherine walking toward the woods and Mode said, "Seems something is fretting her. We need to make sure there is nothing…" His comment was cut short when he saw Wayne step out to meet Catherine. "Looks like we'd better go over there.

Wayne saw the two men coming toward him and started thinking, *I've gotta get outta here.* He backed up from Catherine and turned to go back into the woods and with a slight wave, said, "Gotta get on back. I see your pa coming up to us, so tell him 'Hi' for me."

Catherine looked back to see her Pa and Mode rapidly walking toward them and grabbed Wayne's shirt sleeve and said, "No way you gonna leave now. You tell Pa 'Hi' yourself."

As Samuel and Mode got closer, they saw the man was Wayne Tallston and when getting close enough, offered a handshake greeting with Samuel saying, "Good to see you, Wayne. Gotta admit you kinda got a different way to enter a group. Could get yourself hurt. You be all right, Catherine?"

"Yes and No!" said Catherine. "I got that feeling that someone was staring at me from these bushes and came over here. I've got the notion that Wayne was almost spying on us! But that makes no sense."

Wayne noticed an immediate tightening of the men's eyes and the start of the Sherrill look. "Aw, c'mon, Catherine! Why in heaven's name would I do such a thing! Makes no sense."

Is this the smoke before the fire bit? Mode said, "Wayne, seems a number of people know that you are sometimes seen talking with the sheriff. You keepin' him posted on us or, could it be, you are taking up with ol' George?"

Wayne was well aware of the Sherrill's feelings toward the Tories, but also knew they weren't part of the Regulators even though there was talk about them leaning toward that group. "Mr. Sherrill, you've got to know my feelin's for Catherine and I know she knows my feelings for her. All I was wanting to do was trying to find a way I could see and talk to here alone without having to go through what I'm going through right now."

Is he close to asking for her hand? Mary couldn't take that right now! "Well, I guess those feelin's you're talking about does have a way of making guys do strange things, but I think you best go on your way and tell your pa we all said 'Hi,'" said Samuel. *But I can't help but feel he is in cahoots with Clark.*

Wayne moved toward Catherine and held out his hand, but she did not respond and looked at him as though seeing him for the first time. Wayne dropped his hand, gave her a brief smile, and started walking toward his horse. As he was stepping into the stirrup, he looked back to the group and nodded his head once then swung his leg over the horse settling into the saddle. With a slight wave, he said, "Hope to see y'all soon." He turned his horse toward home.

"Pa, you don't trust him do you?" said Catherine.

"Can't rightly say one way or the other. That boy has some strange ways," said Samuel. And while absently rubbing his chin said, "Just don't know 'bout him."

Mode said, "Well, heck, let's get on back to why we are here and find out if you have some serious second thoughts about leaving your kin."

As they walked toward the others, Samuel said, "Mode, don't you believe for one second that I am abandoning my kin! No way! And I want you to help me get that across to the others," said Samuel. "All I'm doing is trying to make things better for me, Mary and our kids. That plus the fact that we can get away from the English and their Tories. I stay awake a lot thinking about them and what they want to do to us."

Samuel decided it was time to tell all the others about the plan to move and when it would happen. He continued to worry about how Mary really felt about the move even though they had discussed it many times in the past two months. As he walked toward the group, a hush settled over his kin. They watched him walk over to Mary. He whispered, "You still feel that we are making the right decision? If so, I want to make it known one more time to everyone here and now."

Mary looked at her husband with a loving look and a peaceful feeling of trust in him, smiled, and gave him her approval with a slight nod of her head.

Catherine saw her parents' reactions to each other, and in an instant, knew what had transpired. She also had a sudden realization that her husband will have to be like her father. She also knew Wayne was not anything like her father. *I'll find that special man over there.*

"Everyone, listen up for one last time!" said Samuel as he stepped on a bench. All talking stopped as they turned their attention to him. "I have to tell y'all what I think you already know. We have done a lot of talking, thinking, and praying about our decision to move over the mountains to the Fort Caswell, or as some call it the Watauga area. We will be moving within the next few weeks."

No one said anything. His brothers looked at each other with the knowing they were expected to support each other's decisions and be ready to assist each other in any way they could. The women gathered around Mary offering to help while the men gathered around Samuel offering their help with harvesting his crops, selling his cabin and land, and tending livestock. Samuel said, "Why don't we agree my keeping the land and y'all farming it anyway you choose. All I would like in return is y'all keep the place the way you keep yours. Pa taught us if we take care of our things, then they would take care of us." All agreed to Samuel's plan.

Samuel Jr., Susan, Uriah, Adam, and William slowly walked over to Catherine. Their voices were low as they talked about what their futures and what things would be like at their new home.

At the same time, Sheriff Clark was riding his buck board when he saw Wayne riding across a clearing and yelled, "Hold up there, Tallston!"

Wayne's first reaction was one of mild surprise at seeing the sheriff. *I can't ever lose this guy.* "What can I do for you, Sheriff? You making sure everything is peaceable?"

"You know darned well what you can do for me! What's this I hear about the Sherrills gathering over at the church. Samuel leaving?" asked Clark.

Wayne's mixed emotions came into play when he said, "I hid in the bushes close to their meeting place. Lotsa talk about crops, hunting, and the goings-on yonder over the mountains."

"Anything about Samuel, you fool! Whatcha think I hired you to do? Sure wasn't to find out about their crops! I want to know about Samuel's family picking up and movin' outta here," said Clark in a rising voice.

"Well, Sheriff, anything might be possible that they will be doing just that...maybe before the next planting," said Wayne. *No use in telling him all the stuff. He's scary.*

❧

Samuel and Isaac leaned on the split rail fence and watched the early morning clouds build up over the mountains, and in an off and on fashion, talked about how the farm could be maintained after Samuel moved to his new place. "Looks like some wet weather coming our way today and...what ever is he up to riding like that? Uriah riding his horse like a bunch of panthers are after him. What in the world..." said Isaac as he waved his hand at Uriah.

They watched with questioning looks as Uriah came to a sudden stop and jumped off the hard ridden lathered up horse, and said, "Got some bad news. Pa is bad off. He wants all of us at his place like now. Y'all the last ones I've seen. Been riding way before sunup. Lend me one of your horses, Samuel, and we can get going!"

Samuel's cabin was located further from his father's house, what was known as the "main house" than his brothers' cabins.

"Take your pick and let's go," Samuel said as he threw a blanket and then a saddle on Betsy's back and rode out of the barn not looking back to see if Isaac or Uriah were following him. Catherine and Susan were just leaving the cabin when they saw their father and uncles riding as fast as they could toward Grandpa's home. Susan said, "What's going on? Looks like they're racing and just look at Pa riding Betsy. Did you know that?"

"No, I didn't," Catherine said with a worried look as she shielded her eyes toward the riders as they disappeared over a small hill.

The brothers jumped off their horses and not tethering them to anything ran between the other horses standing at the front of the Main house and ran through the dogtrot to their parents' bedroom. At that moment, Elizabeth came out the door, saw her other three sons, and hugged each with a long hug. No words were spoken until Uriah said, "Ma, how's Pa? Can we see him?"

Elizabeth stepped to the door and pushed it open and the last three joined their brothers. All eight sons, William, Samuel, Uriah, Adam Jr., Aquilla, Isaac, Jacob, and Moses stood around their father's bed. Adam's eyes were closed, his breathing was very shallow, and his face never belied the look of pain. He slowly opened his eyes and looked at each of his sons as a small smile formed on his lips.

"My, my, just look at my boys. Me and Elizabeth...are surely blessed by God to have such fine...and I do mean, fine boys," said Adam in a slow-paced manner. "Y'all know to remember that we are ready to help the other one out. Isn't that right, Elizabeth?"

Through eyes misting over with tears and a slightly choking voice, Elizabeth said, "That's right, Adam. I think you and I have done a good think raising such great men who know what is right and know what is wrong."

Adam slowly closed his eyes and just as slowly reopened them and said, "Any grandchil'uns here? I want to see them."

Elizabeth called to the three standing in the dogtrot to come into the bedroom. Catherine, Susan, and Samuel Jr. had just arrived, and Catherine led the way and her uncles stepped back to let them get closer to their grandfather. Adam reached out his hands to touch his grandchildren's hands and said with a small smile, "Guess the room isn't big enough for all of 'em."

Catherine quietly said as she gently squeezed Adam's hand, "Grandpa, I know you will be getting better and we can go riding together again up the Sherrill Path. Who knows, we may find some of our Indian friends."

Adam, in a hesitant low voice, said, "Boys, I want you to always keep your Sherrill name in the highest honor. It is a name that only a few have, so make sure you protect it." He slowly pointed to each son. He then looked at Elizabeth, who was holding his hand and tightly as she dared and with a look of everlasting love said in a whispered voice as he looked at Elizabeth, "I will be with you always." He paused a moment as he continued to look at her and with a steady voice said, "Let's cross the river and find our place." Adam then breathed his last and slowly closed his eyes. Elizabeth held his hand for a long moment then gave out a high voiced gasp and sat down on the bed next to her Adam. Each son had a look of deep felt sadness and all had tears slowly making their way down their cheeks. Catherine and Susan went to their grandmother and hugged her for many moments. They both were softly crying and turned to go out of the room.

The last shovel of earth was put on Adam's grave by the oldest son and said, "I just don't believe that Pa is gone. But he is now at the place looking over the river that he always said would be his final resting place."

William and Samuel talked a long time about how their Pa had raised them to manhood and how he made sure they were ones who could depend on each other no matter what. "Wonder what Pa meant when he told Ma to cross the river with him?" said Samuel.

"Thought 'bout that a lot with Ma. And the only thing I can come up with is that's what he said to her when they got to that river bank and saw across it the place to put down roots," said William as he casually waved his hand toward the river flowing a stone's throw from them.

"Yep," said Samuel as he bent over and gently smoothed the dirt on his fathers grave, "he loved that river and this place on it. Ya know, that's why he gave this land for the church and final resting place."

The two brothers stood for another long moment by their father's grave then walked away without looking back. The May weather was doing its best to reflect the remembrance of Adam by showing new leaves, profuse dogwood blossoms making their trees look like they were covered in a thick blanket of snow and a refreshing warmth in the air. Adam was at peace.

28

Samuel and Jacob leaned on the split rail fence and were close to finishing their talk about the looks of the corn and tobacco plants stretching out in long rows before them. "Made some mighty straight rows there, Samuel."

"Yep, takes a lot of plowing to learn how to do such," said Samuel. "Pa was darn good at doing that and I guess I learned it from him."

"Yeah, I recall him telling me how to plow, but it didn't take on me like it did on you," said Jacob.

"Talk 'bout taking, have you heard any more news about what the English and the Tories are doing and did you hear about the British killing some guys in Boston?" asked Samuel as he looked down a row of corn to where it ended by the fence. *Sure took a long time to build that fence.* The next instance, he couldn't believe his eyes when he saw a man, whose brown skin melded with the the surrounding field, emerge from the forest. "Uhhhh ohhhh, that might be trouble coming this way." He half-pointed and nodded his head in the direction of the man.

"Hope he's not a runaway," whispered Jacob. "Never know what might be going on with those slaves. And we'll talk about that Boston thing later."

The two men stepped apart, as their Pa had always told them to do whenever something came up that looked like possible trouble and kept their attention on the stranger. They both looked to the right and left attempting to determine if others were with him. They did not see others yet the man was walking toward them with no fear showing in his movements. He raised his hand in greeting and said, "Samuel, it is good to see you!" Samuel looked at Jacob with a puzzled furrowed brow look and turned his look back to the visitor. In a flash of recogniton, he said with a broadening smile, "Boudroe! Is that you?"

"Sho'nuff is, Samuel. Been a mighty long time since we've seen each other. Too long, if'n you asked me," said Boudroe. "And, let's see now, this here is one of your brothers, right?"

"Yep, sure is. Betcha you don't recall his name, do ya," said Samuel with a nod of his head toward Jacob.

"Ummm, let's see now. There was Uriah, Quil, Adam... unhhhh, I bet this is Jacob." Boudroe was all smiles as he pointed his finger at an unbelieving Jacob who said, "I recall barely meeting you some years ago yet you remember me. How in the everloving world can you know everyone you have met?"

"Well, Jacob, to tell you the truth, I don't rightly know. It has always been with me as far back as I can remember. Carl and others think it is a God given thing and you well know, you don't question anything like that."

Samuel said, "What's bringing you over this way? I'm sure it isn't hunting deer or some such cause you got pretty good pickings around your home place."

Boudroe hesitated a few moments, took in a deep breath, and said, "I'm here asking for help again. Goodness knows that if it wasn't for y'all my Emma and me would probably be dead."

Unhhh ohhh. Gotta be careful on this one. Samuel bent down and picked up a small oak twig and started peeling back its bark and then said, "You in some kind of trouble at your place?" He gave Jacob a sideways look and said, "Got any questions?"

"None that comes to mind right now,"

Boudroe said with a matter-of-fact tone of voice, "I need help finding a place for some of my kind. You know, the ones who have escaped. I thought my coming over here might get y'all to help me out. Kinda like y'all did back then for me and Emma."

"Speaking of Emma, how is she?" asked Samuel.

"Doing just fine, just fine. We got three chilun's now. Two boys and a girl. We have been blessed," said Boudroe.

"C'mon, Boudroe, let's get a bite to eat and figure out what you need. Whatcha think?," said Samuel. *Give me some time to figure a way out of this mess.*

After Samuel and Jacob shared their food with Boudroe, during which they discussed ways to help, they developed a plan that everyone knew might work.

"Let's see now, Boudroe, Jacob will ask our brothers if they can use some of your people. But the biggest problem with that is there are no papers saying they are their property. I don't think they will agree that it is a good idea," said Samuel.

Jacob said, "There's no way I would do it and I'll say so to the others."

Boudroe said, "I'm thanking y'all for at least trying it out. If'n it don't work then we go to the next step where's I take 'em to my place and see wot happens after that."

"One other idea, Boudroe, is when I get over the mountains, I will need some help with getting my land ready for planting and such. I would like to get some help from the people you have if they are willing to work for me," said Samuel.

"Ohhh yes! And you want them to be your slaves. Right?" said Boudroe.

"Not at my place, they won't be slaves. They'll have to earn their keep and take care of themselves just like I have to do. And at any rate, I wouldn't have any sale papers showing they were my property. That makes it look like I'm going to the stocks, or worse, for stealing someone else's property. Uhh, uhh, no way," said Samuel in a purpose-filled voice.

With a look of "what am I going to do now," Boudroe said, "Why is it that we all could live in a land where all people are free to do what they wanna do. Just not right. I guess I'll have to figure out a way to get my kind to some place that will allow us to be free."

"Boudroe, I'm feeling for you. You have got a lot on your shoulders, but you have made the best of hard times in your past and I know you will figure out a way to make where you are now a better thing," said Samuel with an "I know you can do it" look.

"Yeah, guess I can. Just had to have someone tell me I can do things that I set my mind to do. I'm being thankful for that from you," said Boudroe in a wistful manner. "Well, enough of my troubles, what about y'all? Whatcha gonna be doing?"

"You're not going to believe this, but Samuel is thinking about pulling of here and we're hoping he will change his mind," said Jacob.

Boudroe looked at Jacob in a questioning manner and then looked at Samuel and said, "Pulling outta here? Why? And where? I just heard you say you were going over them mountains. I figured that was just a wishing saying from you."

Samuel said in a low somewhat terse manner, "Just thinking hard about it at this point. But if it happens, it will be over there around the Fort Caswell and"—Boudroe interrupted saying—"that's not too far from where we live! And when you get there you gotta have some help getting things going. What about some of my people staying with you to help you out?"

Samuel looked at his corn growing in straight lines, *What am I doing? Is this right? What if I got some guys to help me?* He bent down and picked up a small stick and then looked at Boudroe with a slight nod of his head and said, "Not a bad idea. If I go, I'll get word to you and maybe we can set up a way to work it out."

Jacob said, "Sounds like y'all have some kind of plan, but I think we better plan to drift apart and quick. No telling who might come up and…Well, you know what might happen."

Boudroe's head jerked back at the reality of Jacob's comment and said, "You be right!" He shook Samuel and Jacob's hand, and with a smile, turned and jogged down the corn rows to the wood line. They watched his disappear into the woods and almost at the same time heard horses coming their way.

The brothers glanced at each other in a questioning manner as they watched the three riders slow their horses as they got closer. It became evident that the riders were well armed with rifles and pistols.

"Howdy men, name's Roy and these are my boys." He quickly stepped down from his saddle and held out his hand. Samuel and Jacob briefly glanced at each other then shook Roy's hand. They could tell by the feel of his hand that he was not into farming where calloused hands were the norm. "What can we do for you?" said Samuel. *Do hope this is not some of those English lovers.*

"Ahhh, I like a man who gets right to the point. What we are doing in these parts is trying to find some people called Sherrills," said Roy. "Wouldn't know any of 'em would ya?"

Samuel and Jacob didn't look at each other, but each knew what the other was thinking. *This doesn't sound good. Gotta be careful with this one.*

Jacob said, "And what would y'all be wanting with them? And who might these others be?

"Y'all must be related as both y'all get right to the point. Like that, no use wasting time these days. Never know what may happen. Well, them two are my sons and we're from the Waxhaws," said Roy. "Last name is Logan."

Samuel looked at Roy with a furrowed brow, *Logan, he was the one at the cabin awhile back* and said, "Wouldn't be related to Isaac Logan would ya?"

All the Logan's reacted to the name and started talking at the same time. Roy said, "Sure would, he's my brother! Are you one of them Sherrills? Isaac sets a whole lot by y'all and asked me to look y'all up while in these parts."

"Well, Mr. Logan, please tell Isaac that you found us and that we are glad to know that he is doing all right for himself. That man had been through some tough times when we first met him.

I've thought about him a lot and wondered if he was able to get back his health," said Samuel.

After much talk about Isaac and the general feeling of how the English were always making things worse by taxing anything they choose to tax plus allowing those people who expressed loyalty to the Crown certain rank and privileges and then there are the problems that happened at Boston. After a lull in the conversation, Roy casually asked, "Hadn't seen any stray slaves, have ya?"

"Stray slaves? We know some families around here who own some, but I haven't heard of any problems with them," said Samuel. *Sure hope he didn't see Budroe.*

"Well, I guess we best be getting on with our stuff. Wish we could stay around, but we got things to do. Just wanted to pass on Isaac's words and to say thanks for saving his life. He feels he owes ya," said Roy.

"We'd be much obliged for your telling him we are glad he is doing all right. Never can tell when we might be close to the Waxhaw's one of these days and look y'all up," said Samuel.

They watched the three men take the path going north. Jacob said, "Strangest thing isn't it that they just happened to find us out here. Just doesn't feel right to me."

"Kinda feel the same way," said Samuel with a musing look on his face. "And he didn't even tell us his boys' names. Guess we best be a little bit on guard about Isaac's kin."

29

1775

Moses was deep in thought as he kept the plow in a straight line. Hank, his mule, plodded along pulling the plow as he had done countless times. The weather was showing signs of an early fall; but he thought as he plowed. *He was going to move in a few months. Before the meeting was out, he said it would take more time. Here it is '75 and he's still here. Maybe they won't move at all. Hope he had a change of mind.*

"Hello, Mode, my man!" yelled Daniel as he walked out of the dense spruce and scrub oak tickets rubbing his hands together for warmth. "Hold ol' Hank up there! He needs the rest anyway."

Mode dropped the reins, ground hitched Hank, and rapidly walked toward Daniel saying, "You be a sight for sore eyes, Dan'l, it's great to see you! Where ya been and whatcha seen beside a bunch of elk and buffalo. Seen some new land?" Mode was always interested in hearing about new lands that were explored and ready to be settled.

"Been over Long Island way and Kaintuck again. And what continues to surprise me is a bunch of settlers are needing a road to get over to Kaintuck. You really ought to see that land! Thought I best get back here to see if any of you Sherrills and maybe some others will go back over there with me," said Daniel. "I know y'all are knowing that my family is living over close to Martin's place in Virginia."

"Yeah, we know that y'all are over there and been wondering how y'all are doing. By the way, you seen Samuel yet?" asked Mode.

"Nope. Hoping you would tell me where he is. I'm guessing he is still stuck in his cabin," said Daniel with a sly smile. "By the way, you been jumping in some creeks lately? That time beat all and you thinking I was goin' to put some hurt on y'all."

"Yep, I recall that real well and especially things that happened after that time in the creek," said Moses as he unhitched Hank, and leaving his plow in the field, they walked toward Samuel's cabin. They talked about the work that Daniel had been doing and some of his ideas about what to do with the new land. Daniel talked about the two main gaps, above Long Island, in the mountains that allowed settlers to make a less weary and dangerous trip to the "Kaintuck" lands.

As they walked into the cabin's yard, Samuel came out the door and grabbed Daniel's hand and about shook it off and said, "Mighty good to see you, Dan'l. How's Becky and the chilun's?"

As Daniel was rubbing his hand, he said, "They're fine as frog hair. Becky's been asking for a long time if she would ever see Mary again."

"Let's see now...best I figure y'all have been gone about a year, right?"

"Yeah, reckon so. Hard to believe the time that gets away. Seems like yesterday that we started farming here."

"Coming over to stay awhile or just visiting your friends and old neighbors?"

"Some of both. One thing I wanted was to get you off this little river and head on over these mountains with me. Becky loves it over there and the land is ripe and ready for your plow."

"Dan'l, he's gotta stay here and that's all there is to it!" exclaimed Mode. "He is much needed here to help make sure we keep our land from the Tories and their English crowd."

"Mode, Samuel, I am going back tomorrow early. Let me know if you are going with me. No use kicking this around anymore," said Daniel in a determined voice. "Now let's see what's for supper." He clapped his hands together.

Just as the sun's morning light crept over the land, Samuel and Mary watched Daniel as he settled in his saddle. Mary handed him a worn-out shot bag full of biscuits and salt cured ham. "Be careful, Dan'l. Becky needs you by her side."

Samuel said with a smile that did not convey his feelings, "Hold tight that shot bag, Dan'l. Took me long enough to make it out of that bear hide."

Daniel said, "Y'all are making a mistake…"

Catherine ran out of the cabin and took hold of the horse's reins and said, "The very idea! Not even saying 'good-bye' to the rest of us!" Then a small smile appeared on her face. "I think I'll have to go over there to find me someone who wants me for his wife."

"Catherine, watch what you say!" exclaimed Mary. "That's nothin' Dan'l is interested in. Shame on you!"

It was only a few seconds, but the silence seemed to go on forever. Daniel said, "Not to worry, Bonnie Kate, the man you'll find will be very special because you are very special in your own way."

Samuel, Mary, and Catherine looked at Daniel as though not believing what they just heard. Daniel smiled at them, touched his heels to his horse, and with a wave exclaimed, "Be seeing you on the other side!"

They continued waving to Daniel as he rode down the wagon trail finally losing sight of him as he rode over a small hill by the river. "Sure you don't want to go?" asked Mary.

Samuel said with a look toward the mountains as he turned toward the barn, "Nope, not now."

30

"Hey there, Samuel. Got a minute?" said Judge Cannon. "Didya hear about the goings-on in Boston and Philadelphia?"

"Boston, yeah. But not anything about Philadelphia," said Samuel as wrapped his horse's reins around the hitching rail. *Hope I haven't done something that's gonna get me in trouble with him.*

"C'mon, sit down. Let's talk," said the judge as he sat down on the store bench. "I've read a letter that said the boys making up that Continental Congress will be meeting in Philly again."

"Didn't they meet about a year ago and came up with a plan to stop letting England push us around? Not sure if anything came of that or not. Sure can't tell around here if anything happened to help us out."

"Good grief, Samuel, you are behind times!" exclaimed the judge. "The Redcoats shot eight of our men dead a couple of weeks ago in Boston."

"From what you are telling me, we are at war with those Redcoats, right?" Samuel said with a frown and questioning look at the judge. *I knew about Boston. But why tell everything you know.*

The judge searched his pockets and finally found the knife he wanted to sharpen on the whetstone that the store owner had tied with a leather strap to the side of the bench. Not a word was spoken as both men gave thought to what the future would be for them and their families. Then judge said in a hesitating manner, "Yeah, Samuel...I'd say we are at war with England. The killing of men on each side in that battle is the start of a long row to hoe for both sides."

Samuel leaned forward and stared at the mountains and thought of all the things that Boone had told him about the new territory over there. *Might be something to give a lot more thought, especially now.* While turning to the judge, he said, "You hear anything about why George's parliament keep putting a tax on just about everything we do? Why is it they need all that money from us? And have you seen anything going on from our so-called Tory friends? They may think they can bring the war here."

Judge waited a few moments thinking of his answer then said, "Probably give some of them an excuse to do no telling what. You know that most of them don't have much between their ears. But from what I've heard from some of my judge friends up north is that the French and Indian war back in the 1760's cost England a lot of pounds sterling. They can hardly pay their debt, even during these times, on the pounds they borrowed back then. Guess having so many soldiers around the world is really draining their treasury. Ya know something, if you can't afford it then don't do it!"

"Yep, ain't it the truth. I can't run my farm like that. Hang fire, Judge, you'd have to put me in debtor's prison if I tried to borrow everything to feed my family. But I don't think we're going to put up with all their taxing this and taxing that to pay off their debt," said Samuel.

"Well, my friend, it's apparent to me they think that what they say we are going to do will be something we will do just because they said so," said Cannon.

"That's for sure! Just like that time when Clark said that boy named George over there put a line on the tops of those mountains and we couldn't cross it. As you well know, some of us went up there to find that line, and you know what, we haven't seen it yet! They'd have to have all the soldiers in the world keeping guard on it to make it work," said Samuel with a disgusted look toward the ridges of the mountains.

Judge Cannon waited a out a long silence and said in a low tone, "You still thinking about loading your wagons and going over them hills?"

Samuel didn't move a muscle. *Is he fishing for himself or someone else?* Once again, he turned toward the judge and said, "You know as well as I do that we have to keep all possibilities up in the air. Never know when you'll reach out and catch one."

"My aching back, Samuel, you're talking in riddles. Y'all going or not?" the judge said with a look of feigned disgust and turned back to the whetstone and his knife blade. *Bet he thinks I'm up to no good.*

Samuel slowly stood up while brushing a small amount of dust from his shirt sleeve and said while gesturing toward the hills, "I promise you one thing, Judge. You will be among the first to know if I ever decide to do anything like that and, if I did decide to go over that way, you have my permission to put me in the stocks until I get my thinking straight again. Guess I better get over to Nick and pick up the shoes for my mule and Betsy here."

"Whatever I hear about the goings-on in the north country, I'll let ya know," said the judge.

"Yeah, do that. Be seein' ya," said Samuel as he stepped off the porch toward the blacksmith's shop.

Samuel said, "How's things, Nick?" He walked to where Nick was pushing the fire pit bellows making the iron glow with the color of a golden sunset. Samuel always admired how Nick could take metal and make useful things out of it. *Gotta be born with that way.*

"Howdy, Samuel. Long time no see. What's going on out your way?" said Nick while brushing his hands on his horsehide apron and then shook hands with Samuel.

Samuel said, "Something is always going on with a farm. Sure keeps one busy. Boone dropped by a few days ago, but other than that, we are keeping busy. Just dropped by to get my shoes."

"Got 'em right here," said Nick as he turned to go into the building and in a startled voice yelled, "Whoa up there, Clark! Whattha devil you doin' back in there?"

Sheriff Clark slowly walked out into the light, "C'mon, Nick, I didn't mean to scare you none. Right touchy, ain't ya? You know what they say about people who have something to hide are the ones who are so skittish." He let his eyes drift over to Samuel's.

He's fishin' again. "Seems you are always at two places at once, Clark. How you do that?" With a slight "I'm not going to tell you anything" smile, Samuel said, "Guess I best get my things, Nick, since it looks like you and Clark have got some business to talk about. Guess y'all heard about the English killing some of our guys up around Boston."

"Whatcha mean…our guys? You starting to sound like one of them Regulators!" exclaimed the sheriff eyeing Samuel with a hard stare.

Samuel looked at Nick then looked at his forge, then the anvil and slowly let his eyes focus on Clark's eyes and thought while giving him the Sherrill stare, *You idiot. You're bent on taking me down. You have a long way to go before that happens.* Then, without a word, took the horseshoes from Nick, nodded his head at him and mounted his horse. From the saddle, he looked at Clark and said, "Your just like a dog with a bone—never finishing fretting over it." He turned the horse to the road and rode back to his cabin.

At that same moment, Catherine knelt down and reached under her bed and pulled out her muzzleloader rifle. She inspected all the moving parts and made sure everything was in working order. She stood up and started for the door of the cabin when her mother entered the room. "What's going on, Catherine?" she said.

"Nothing much, Ma. Just going to ride a bit up the river. I need some time to do some thinking and can do it best when out," Catherine said with a small smile as she stepped out the door.

"I know that put-on smile. Care to tell me what's bothering you?" said Mary.

"No, ma'am. Just needing some thinking time about where I am and what I want for myself," said Catherine. "Ma, am I so terrible looking? Why is it I can't find a man who will take me for what I am?"

Mary said. "Kate, your time for a man will come when you least expect it. You are a pretty girl who has no problem attracting the menfolk."

"Yes, ma'am, and when they seem to want to start talking to me, it doesn't take them long to be needing to do something else. Figuring out men is a waste of time. Guess they want someone who is all flirty and acting like the man they talking to is so smart. I'm just as good as them and better in a lot of ways!" Catherine said with a firm look in her eyes.

That's just the problem "Tell you what, Kate, just take your ride, find a place you can feel safe, and sit down and think about what you just said. Ask God, in a prayer, to help you," said Mary with a knowing look.

"Yes, ma'am. I'll do it. Reckon I'll be back soon enough to help with supper. What we havin' anyway? Naw, don't tell me, let me guess," said Catherine with a small smile and sparking eyes.

She slowly rode up the river bank thinking things through and what she wanted to do with her life. *Here I am twenty-one years old and not married. Susan is twenty-three years old and has a baby. What's wrong with me that I'm not attracted to any men? They seem to be attracted to me until they get to know me. People say I am pretty, but that doesn't mean much these days, I guess. Hmmm...this looks like a good place to get down and make plans of what to do for the rest of my life.* She stepped out of her stirrups while holding her rifle as if she had been born with it.

Catherine leaned back on a huge chestnut tree with its soaring arching height. The sun's rays were warm and soothing as they filtered through the leaves. She watched the clear water slide over smooth rocks and occasionally noticed the short flash of reflected light off the sides of fish in the stream. The far off bellow of an elk, a woodpecker's occasional rattling sound while searching the tree bark for grubs and the gentle murmur of the breeze in the treetops caused her senses to develop a peace that she rarely felt, especially since her mom and dad started talking about moving over the mountains. Her head slowly tilted forward as her eyelids slowly closed and drifted into a relaxed sleep.

Yona and Tawadi slowly turned their eyes to each other silently acknowledging Catherine's presence across the creek. For two days of their hunt for elk, they knew they were getting too close to the land of the white man, but they were willing to take the risks. They slowly backed out of the thicket and when they were safely out of hearing range of Catherine, they stopped and sat down on the pine straw left by tall pines.

"White girl alone in these woods...not wise," said Tawadi. "She will live with us."

Yona caught the meaning that Twadi was implying which was to capture and take her to their village where she would be treated as a slave. "No, my brother, I remember seeing her for the first time, a long time ago, on the mountain with her father and the man named Boone."

"Boone! Do you know what he has done on our land around the Hogoheegee? You should have killed him."

"Stop it, Tawadi. You're hurting my thinking."

"Hurting your thinking? What's there to think about? Let's take her and go back to the village. At least we will have something cause we don't have the elk," exclaimed Tawadi with a wave of his hands back in the direction of their village.

Yona said with a level voice, "We will not take her captive! She has special power. And what would our people say when we bring in a captive women rather than some elk meat. And you well know, we can't do both of them."

"Well spoken. Then let's surprise her and leave her."

"Good! Shows we are wanting peace," said Yona as he found a dim path back to the stream. "Let's not wake her. We'll stand close by where she is and when she wakes up…talk about a surprise!"

They slowly and silently approached Catherine making sure she wasn't aware of their presence. Yona thought, *The water falling over the rocks will hide our sounds.*

Some unknown instinct slowly, but carefully, awakened Catherine. She did not make any move except allowing her eyelids to open just enough to see in front of her. At that moment, she saw two Indians slowly approaching her. *I'll shoot the one on the left and club the second.* They stopped and stood very still as they watched for any movement from her. No one moved for a long time until Tawadi slowly turned his head to Yona who responded in like fashion. They shrugged their shoulders at each other which showed they were wondering when, and if, she would awaken.

Catherine saw the chance she was waiting on and deftly picked up her rifle and pulled the hammer back. The sound was deafening to Yona and Tawadi. They quickly turned their surprised attention to Catherine and especially the rifle that was pointed at them. Not a word was spoken. The men stared into Catherine's eyes that were filled with a sense of wonder mixed with a special hardness.

I've met him before…but where? thought Catherine as her finger slowly released it's pressure on the trigger. It was becoming apparent the men were not planning to harm her. *They coulda done some kind of bad to me.*

Yona's stern look slowly dissolved into one of a hint of smile. Tawadi noticed Yona relaxing his posture and took his eyes off Catherine. *What is he up to now?*

The relaxed look of one of the men slowly released a memory of a past meeting with him on the mountain years ago. The name "Yona" surfaced in her mind along with the memory of the moccasins he had given her. She pointed with her left hand index finger while keeping the finger of her right hand on the trigger and said in a mild voice, "You are Yona."

Tawadi's reaction was a jolt of wide eyed wonder at first Catherine and then to Yona, "She knows your name!" Any thoughts of capturing her vanished.

Yona was somewhat surprised, but was able to hold his emotion in check, and said in hand signs and a few words, "Yes…I am…Yona."

The surrounding forest was almost soundless as if waiting for some important statement or action from these three people. Catherine said, "I mean you no harm." She placed the rifle on the ground, stood up, took three steps toward the two men and stopped with held out her hand to Yona.

Yona turned to Tawadi, "I will hold her hand. You well know they do this type of greeting to each other."

"Seems like she wants to make sure you do not have a knife. All whites want to hold our hands," said Tawadi with a small shrug.

With gestures, well-known hand signs, and a few English words, Yona hoped Catherine knew he wanted her to know she was in no danger. Catherine wanted to make them realize that she wanted them to be her friend.

Yona and Catherine stood looking at each other with unwavering eye contact. Each was lost in that moment that transcends all emotions. Yona thought, *This cannot be. We could not last.* At that moment, Tawadi said, "You will not do what I think you are wanting to do!"

Catherine caught the meaning of Tawadi's words, but could not break the spell of knowing this man was somehow connected to her inner being. Her hand remained open for a handshake and Yona clasped it with a cautious firmness. They continued looking into each other's eyes until Catherine slowly removed her hand and with a smile said, "Thank you for your trust." She looked at Tawadi and nodded slightly to him and held out her hand.

Tawadi ignored her hand and said, "We go, Yona! Now!" with a strong swing of his arm with his finger pointed toward the mountains.

Yona slowly moved his head to Tawadi, "This woman has the courage of a warrior. She will be with a leader. I hope the leader is not against us. Her eyes tell all." He then turned back to Catherine and with a quick smile turned to his right and started walking along the creek toward the mountain peaks. Tawadi followed him. Catherine noted how silently they walked along the creek bank.

"You were thinking about taking her into your lodge," said Tawadi. "You had me concerned about your mind."

"One must study one's possible enemies for a long time. What is learned may not be valuable now, but it will be in some distant day," said Yona. And with a punch to Tawadi's shoulder said, "If I were to take another into my lodge, especially a white, I would want you to tie me to a rock where the trees don't grow and leave me for the bears and wolves." They both laughed at the thought. "Now, let's go find the elk."

She is a woman who, I am sure, will be a revered woman to her people, thought Yona.

Catherine stood for a long time looking at the two men melt into the forest and said in a whisper, "I believe I would have gone with him if he had asked." She looked at her rifle and noticed the hammer was still in firing position. *Never have I ever done that!* She picked the rifle up, and after making it safe, looked once more toward the place she last saw the two men. She let out a deep breath, turned and walked slowly to her horse.

Yona and Twadi saw her get on her horse and start toward her home. They looked at each other and turned to go toward their village. "We are different, yet somehow the same," said Yona.

They kept close to the small river knowing the elk would return to the same places to drink each evening. The task was finding those places as they kept their eyes on the banks hoping to find elk and deer tracks. They stopped to examine a number of animal signs and talked about whether or not to follow a recently made hoof print.

"This is elk," said Tawadi as he knelt down to examine the print more closely. Yona nodded and said, "We'll find them."

As they started following the prints, rain started falling in slow steady almost silent drops. Yona stopped and knelt down while holding out his hand to stop Tawadi. He felt a presence that had the coldness of danger in it.

Wayne sighted down the barrel of his rifle and placed the sights on the Indians he saw with Catherine. *No blasted Indian is going to mess with my woman!* He placed his sight on the one who had held Catherine's hands and slowly pulled the hammer until it clicked into position. The sound was not lost on either men as both dropped to the ground just as the ball of lead hit the tree with a dull thud next to them followed by the sound of the fired rifle. Both men reacted as if they had practiced their movements many times as each crawled off in opposite directions. They knew what the other was doing and thinking as they slowly and silently moved toward the place they had heard the rifle shot. Nothing moved in the forest and nothing made a sound except that of Wayne as he reloaded his rifle. He looked down the sight of his rifle again hoping to see some movement from one of the men. He didn't recognize the silence of the forest as being one that meant danger. There was a brief moment of no rain as if waiting for the rapidly darkening, lightning-filled clouds to enter on the scene. Sudden bursts of wind bent tree limbs while streaks of lightning followed by thunder made the forest change its silent mood to one of aggressive behavior.

The storm made Wayne wary due to not being able to hear if anything would be close to his position. He had no idea the location of the two Indians. *I've got to get out of here!* flashed through his mind. He took his eyes off his surroundings to check if his priming powder was dry. When he looked up his startled look was not lost on Yona, who was standing to his left and Tawadi was on his right. Wayne's eyes locked on the muzzle of Tawadi's rifle as he was sighting down its barrel. Wayne knew he was in his last moments of life as he watched Tawadi pull back the hammer and pulled the trigger. A bolt of lightning flashed and was followed by an immediate clap of thunder. Wayne didn't know what hit him when Yona's rifle butt knocked him out. "The Creator is with this white man. He has much luck, our powder is wet," said Tawadi. "We will take his hair." He took out his knife while kneeling by Wayne's side. He reached down, grabbed a hank of hair, and readied his knife to cut Wayne's scalp.

"No! Do not take his scalp," said Yona.

The silence of the forest seemed to wait on Tawadi's reaction as he looked into Yona's eyes. Never had he been stopped killing his enemy. "Why?"

"He can be used to help bring the peace. Killing him will make his kind angry. I will go to the woman and bring her back to take this man to her people. This will show them we are peace people," said Yona.

Tawadi looked off in the distance for a moment and said as he turned to look into Yona's eyes, "I will go get the woman. You stay here!" he said in a steady "not to be reckoned with" voice.

He thinks I want to take that woman back with us. "Good. Now go! I wait here for you."

Tawadi located Wayne's horse, jumped into the saddle, and took off after Catherine. The horse seemed to have a sense of his own as he galloped around and between trees, dense barriers, and rock outcroppings. They ran into a clearing where the horse picked up even more speed. A covey of quail jumped up and flew off with the sound of their rapidly beating wings. Under normal circumstances, the sound would have been startled the man on the horse.

Catherine was letting Betsy pick her own way with a leisurely pace and was thinking how nice the weather was for this time of year despite the sudden storms. She looked into a field of yellow and blue flowers and thought, *How wonderful!* At that point, she felt a presence and looked to her left, then to her right. The sight started her into a speechless wide-eyed look as she saw Tawadi blocking her path. She looked into Tawadi's eyes and saw nothing except an expressionless face. *Is he going to rape me, kill me or what? A* calmness came over her as she tightened her hold on her rifle. Then she noticed that he was riding Wayne's horse.

Tawadi noticed the slight widening of her eyes and the tightening hold on her rifle and motioned her to turn around saying in hesitant voice "Go…back." He didn't give her a chance to say anything as he rode to her while keeping his eyes locked on hers. He reached over and gently took the reins out of her hand and started leading Betsy, who somehow sensed Catherine's unafraid acceptance of the situation, back to find Yona. She had no idea what she would be facing, but somehow knew that she would be seeing the man's friend. She observed her surroundings as if seeing it for the first time. Her gaze at Tawadi's back with the rippling muscles of his shoulders made her wonder how much strength could be called up at any time. He did not look back one time as he led her along old paths that she would have never seen. *Maybe Pa might see these. I wonder what made this path.*

She was led into a small clearing surrounded with large oak and even larger chestnut trees. In one smooth motion, Tawadi swung from the saddle and said, "The woman is here!"

Catherine's right hand fingers involuntarily jumped to her mouth accompanied by a wide-eyed stare at Yona thinking, *What a handsome man.* Yona walked over to her and held out his hands to help her dismount. Catherine didn't move. Yona moved his eyes over her body and stopped with a "you will not disobey me" stare into her eyes. As almost hypnotized Catherine moved out of her saddle and felt Yona's hands holding her waist and gently lowering her to the ground. Yona stared into her eyes. Neither moved to break the spell. Tawadi saw what was going on and said, "Yona, you aren't thinking right."

Yona slowly turned to Tawadi and as if coming out of a trance said, "You are so very right! Get the man!"

For the second time since entering the clearing, Catherine was startled when she saw Wayne being half dragged into the clearing from behind a large chestnut tree. Tawadi released his hold letting Wayne hit the ground. Wayne was slowly regaining consciousness and tried to get up but could not get beyond having to be on his hands and knees on the ground. Tawadi said in a disgusting manner, "He has the look of a sick dog."

Catherine's first thought was to help Wayne, but an immediate second thought was, *why is he here?* stopped her from going to him. Wayne finally mustered enough strength to look up to Catherine and said, "Help me. Help me. They want to kill me."

Yona and Tawadi look to each other left no doubt they were puzzled by the fact the man and woman knew each other. Yona said as he turned to Catherine with a questioning hard-eyed frown, and at the same time, asked Tawadi, "Did she know he was here and that he was trying to kill us?"

"One never knows about the white man. But somehow I think she is surprised to see this man. I'm sure they know each other back in their village," said Tawadi.

Catherine had not moved and said to Yona "You know English?" He nodded and held up his thumb and forefinger barely touching and said in a hesitating voice, "This...much." Catherine's small smile puzzled Yona, but he thought it was a good sign.

"Was he trying to hurt you?" she slowly said to Yona.

Yona thought he recognized the word "hurt" and figured she wanted to know if Wayne had tried to kill them. He pointed to Wayne and said in English, "He shoot me...Tawadi."

Elizabeth immediately reacted and said, "You...hurt?"

Yona looked at Tawadi and shrugged his shoulders saying, "What does she mean?"

"By her looks, she thinks you are hurt."

Yona then looked at Elizabeth and by gestures showed that he was not hurt.

Elizabeth inwardly breathed a sigh of relief and said, "Let me take him home."

Yona caught the meaning of her word "home" and said to Tawadi, "It will be a sign of peace to give her this man."

Tawadi gave Yona a look of disgust and shrugged his shoulders in acceptance.

Yona then pointed to Elizabeth, then to Wayne, and said, "Take!" while pointing toward their way home.

Catherine bent down over Wayne and said, "Get up!" while picking up his rifle saw powder in the flash pan and blew it off. The two Indians looked at each other and knew the woman was not afraid and because of that was to be respected. She walked back to her horse, pulled her water canteen from her saddle, opened it and let drops drip down on Wayne's head. He slowly stood up with a dazed unsteady condition. In a hesitant voice, he said, "What…happened?"

"Get up, Wayne! "She thought as she watched him struggle to get up and keep his balance. *Just why was he here? Following me?*

Wayne slowly regained his thinking and steadiness skills and started walking toward Catherine. "Do ya think we can get outta here?"

While looking at Yona and Twadi, she said, "We can leave. You are going to walk back behind me"

Wayne said, "Walk? You're crazy! I'm riding with you!" He started walking toward Betsy.

"You touch Betsy and I'm leaving you here with these two!" While pointing toward Yona and Twadi.

Wayne couldn't believe his ears and said in an unbelieving tone, "You mean I've got to walk all the way back home?"

Catherine looked at Yona with a look of respect, tinged with feeling of wanting, *he's a mighty fine-looking man.* And in a flash of recognition, thought, *He's old enough to be my pa!* She then touched Betsy's side and turned her toward home. She didn't even look back to see if Wayne was following.

Wayne looked at his captors while slowly walking after Catherine. When he knew he was being released, he started a more rapid pace to try and keep Catherine in sight. *Stupid woman…Leaving me and making me walk! Just who does she think she is…some high and mighty whatever.*

She let Betsy take her own pace and did not look back, *If he makes it, then that is up to him. He's got some answerin' to do to me! Just why was he following me? He's mighty lucky to still be breathin.*

As Catherine was brushing down Betsy after their ride, Wayne came straggling into the barn's shadow and sat down on a tree stump that is used for splitting wood. "Been thinking 'bout how you been treating me and its not good! But I guess I ought to thank you for helping me get out of a bad thing back there."

"What do you mean 'thank you'? If I hadn't shown up, you would be meat for the forest critters! And I don't blame those men for wanting to send you to your Maker!" exclaimed Catherine as she glared at Wayne.

He had never seen her in such a manner and said, "You'd better watch what you say to me! I've got friends who can make it mighty tough on your pa."

Catherine stared a long time at Wayne with a lot of things going through her mind with the last thought being *I'm leavin' this place.* She turned her back to Wayne and walked toward the cabin. Her action was perfectly clear to Wayne that she was wanting him to leave. He finally stood up and gave fleeting thought to taking Betsy to take him home. After a few seconds thought, he turned and started walking to his cabin hoping he could make it before nightfall. *Guess I've got some explaining to do to Pa and that sheriff.*

Just as he was getting ready to leave, Catherine came walking back to him with a purpose-filled look and said, "You breathe a word of this to anyone, anyone I say, then I will tell how much of a coward you were with them and that I alone saved you! Got that?" She turned and left him standing with a speechless look.

31

They each sat in a favorite cane woven chair brought out from their cabin to sit under a huge oak tree. They were looking at each other absorbed in the decision they had just made for their future and change in a lifestyle that offered some deep unknowns and opportunities,

Samuel let his eyes drift from Mary's to the tops of the mountains they would soon be going over, or around, to their new home. He sat forward, found a small twig, took out his pocket knife, and started lightly shaving the bark exposing the white wood. This was a favorite way for him to give himself some time to think about serious decisions. Sarah knew what he was doing and left him to his thinking time. She looked at their cabin, barn and fields, and gave into the feeling of "are we sure we want to do this?" Samuel folded the blade of his knife back into the handle, brushed the small shavings off his pants and shoes, looked back at the mountains for a long minute and looked back into Mary's eyes and, after another minute, said, "Guess we best be packing up and moving on. We'll leave here next Monday. That'll give us six days to get ready." *Why are the things that you know are the right thing to do are so hard to do?*

"All of us, especially Catherine, will follow you wherever you think best. I must admit, again, that I don't want to go through the work of packing up and taking untold days to get to where we are going. Who knows, it might take over a month," said Mary as her voice became almost a whisper. Then, in a matter-of-fact voice said, "We best get the family together and give them the news."

Samuel looked at Mary with a deep respect for her intelligent thinking, *She's always coming up with good ways of doing things*, and said, "Ya know something? We'd best be getting Ma, Pa, and my brothers and sisters together and tell them of our plans. Right thing to do!"

The next morning after making their plans, Samuel hitched his horse and walked up to the porch steps of his parents' house. *This is not going to be easy.*

It was her usual habit to sit on the porch after breakfast, and on this morning, Elizabeth saw their second son riding toward them. *He's got something really eating at him. I don't think I want to hear what he has to say. Hope nobody is sick.*

"Howdy, Ma. How y'all getting on this morning?" said Samuel as he pulled up a chair and sat down next to his mother. "Need to talk with ya 'bout something."

The silence was uncomfortable to each one of them. Then it hit her in a flash of understanding and in a matter-of-fact tone said, "When y'all moving?"

Samuel knew there was nothing to be gained by trying to soften the fact, "Yes, ma'am, Mary and I have decided to move across the mountains. We want to settle in the area around Fort Watauga."

Elizabeth looked at her flexing fingers and then to Samuel, "Mind telling me why?" She felt she knew the answer since she and Adam had been at this point in their life before moving to where she was now.

Samuel had rehearsed the answer to this question many times and said, "Ma, I've prayed about this for a long time, Mary and I have talked about it a lot and what we want for our family. With all the problems we are having with England and their people, like the sheriff and the Tories, telling us what we can and can't do will only get worse before it gets better. These things helped us make up our minds to move from here." *There now it is out in the open.*

Elizabeth's tightening lips was all the emotion she allowed herself to show and said, "Mind telling me more about where?"

"No, ma'am, sure don't. Like I said, we'll be moving to that area around Fort Watauga."

"You've never been there. How ya know it is better than here?" said Elizabeth. "I know your pa was over there a long time ago and he said it is a country, kinda like around here. Not many people either." *No use beating this to death* while getting up, said, "When?"

"Most likely within the next few weeks," said Samuel in a quite voice.

With a firm voice, Elizabeth said, "You will again tell the rest of the family about this and then, make up your mind when you'll be leaving." *Hope the others don't get the idea to follow him.*

⌒

The church was filled with the Sherrills. They knew why they were assembled and knew this was always Pa's way of making sure everyone was hearing the same thing at the same time. "Listen up, everybody," said William. The room that had sounded like a hive of upset bees suddenly became very quiet.

Elizabeth looked around the room, and as always, wondered why God had blessed her so richly with such a large family. *What have I done to deserve this?* "Am mighty grateful that all of us can get together. Let's give thanks to God. Quil will lead us in prayer."

As always, when the family got together like this, Pa asked one of his sons to lead them in prayer and it was always something the brothers tried to figure out beforehand. Long ago, they had decided there was no way to figure out who would be the next one picked to pray. Mode smiled as he looked at Quil who had the look on his face of "I did it last time, why me?"

As their Pa had usually done in long winded prayers, Elizabeth said at a brief pause in Quil's prayer, "Amen! Now, you all know what we are gathered here for, so I want to make sure that all your questions are answered. Maybe you can come up with something Samuel and Mary have not thought about for themselves."

Samuel stood up and said, "Each of us has gone over and over a lot of things about our moving, and I don't want to get into rehashing what's already been talked about. But just to make sure, I'll go over some of what we think are the most important things to us. Rehash? Maybe, but at least it'll be in front of all of us. So here goes."

Everyone leaned forward wanting to make sure they didn't miss any comment. Isaac said, "It's like Pa has always told us. What we hear in our meetings in this church stays in this place when we leave. Sure don't need the problems that would be on us if the sheriff, or his like, find out that we said something about those George-loving boys." Nodding heads giving the acceptance look and comments of "Amen" were said throughout the church.

As was usually the case during these meetings, Catherine listened intently to what her pa had said when he told the family about moving across the mountains. She didn't want to miss out on anything that would help her with the positive feeling that the move was the best thing for her and the rest of the family.

Samuel said, "As y'all know, we are moving over to the place around a new fort called Watauga. Pa had seen that land and we talked about how the land lies and what can be grown on it. That is important to me, but the other things are just as important. I just want to be left alone to make up my mind what is best for my family. Which one of us wouldn't think and do the same thing."

Uriah said, "Tell us again what you mean by 'left alone.' I just want to make sure that we aren't the ones who got you to that wanting-to-be-left-alone feeling."

Samuel said in a rising voice and punching his hand with his fist, "Being left alone by ol' George's people is what I mean. He and his new taxes and saying we can't go over that Proclamation Line plus his Tory friends are acting like we gotta do what they tell us. And if we don't, they get the feeling we can be made to do it or put in the stocks if we don't. And I just not gonna take that kind of getting along with them. Next thing you know is Georgy telling us what to plant and give it to him. No way!"

"You got that right! If I were a betting man I'd bet my last ear of corn that he will wake up one morning and decide to put a tax on our stills! Just let him try that and see what mess he gets into!" said Quil while shaking his fists in the air.

The thought of taxing their stills created more shaking fists, red faces, and loud talk when Isaac shouted, "He'll have a war on his hands for sure! No one is going to tell me what I can, or can't, do with my still!" That comment created increased loud talk. Susan and Catherine looked at each other with a shrug and small smile because they knew how important the alcohol based liquid was to each family and they also knew that some people could not drink it without becoming drunk and rowdy. They also knew it was an absolute necessity for cleaning and treating wounds and other ailments like insect and animal bites.

The uproar was getting out of hand when William stood up and with upraised arms shouted, "Quiet! Stop all this infernal shouting and carrying on!"

"What Isaac says about a war with that king just may be on the way to all of us! Samuel, you tell us about what the judge told you about the fighting and killing, that we already knew about, somewhere in Massachusetts a few weeks ago between men like us and the English soldiers. Next thing you know, that sort of stuff will be here in this part of North Carolina," said Quil.

Moses said, "You are right about that, Quil. We got to be sure of things like that so we can best be prepared for people like Clark and his Tory friends. We got to lay low until we know for sure what's going on and then we'll make our plans. Got that, everybody?"

All talk and movement stopped at the same time. All heads turned to Elizabeth. She looked at each son with a look that all knew, almost from the moment of their birth, meant full attention and respect was to be given to their parents.

"Samuel, you have shared with the family the reasons why you are taking your family across the mountains. Some of us may not agree with your leaving the family and—"

Samuel jumped up interrupting his mother and emphatically said, "I am not leaving the family! I am just going to be a few days away from you rather than a few hours! Don't y'all see what I'm talking about? Don't you see that I am a Sherrill and will always be ready to defend and help my family wherever they happen to be and I know each of my brothers and sisters feel the same way about me and Mary. Right?" He looked at each brother who each nodded his head in agreement. He then turned to his mother in hopes that she would also agree with him.

Elizabeth looked at her son with a look of pride, *He makes a lot of sense*, and said, "Well said, Samuel, You are right. You aren't leaving your family. You are just expanding the Sherrills across this land and I understand your reasons. Your grandpa and grandma left their Devonshire kin behind and came to this country and look what it has done for the growing family." She then looked to the others and said, "Let's all give Samuel and Mary three cheers for their move! Only thing different is it'll take a little more time to go see 'em."

There was a moment of no sound as each thought about one of their families leaving them. Samuel looked at his Ma who looked into her son's eyes and realized how much he needed the support of his brothers and sisters. The step she took seemed to bring everyone out of their own reverie and at the same time the family erupted in loud cheering, pats on the backs, smiles and laughter at the release of the tension that was so evident at the start of the meeting.

"One last question. How you going to get over there?" asked Isaac.

Samuel said, "Been doing a right smart thinking about that. Talked with Dan'l about what he knows about the best way to go and then to some others who have come down the Wagon Road. So we're going to take the path, you know, Sherrill's Path, to the Carolina Road and go north to the Big Lick settlement. From there we'll meet up with some others who are going to the same place and start down the Wagon Road. I hear that some call it Frontier Road. As we get closer to a place called Black's Fort, we'll find out how to get over to Fort Watauga. I've been told that Fort Womack is another place to go on the way to Watauga."

"Now listen up, boys! "said Elizabeth, "Want y'all to lend a hand to getting them loaded up and help decide how to keep their farm going for them. Samuel, you tell us when you want us at your place and we'll do what we can." *Never can tell, he might decide to come back here.*

Samuel looked at Mary whose small smile let him know that all was good with her and she was ready to get things going to their new home. "Guess we'd best be getting on with this, my husband."

The final days of spring weather were slowly giving way to the start of the start of summer as Samuel opened the cabin door. The morning breeze carried the pleasant smell of pines mixed with honeysuckle. The sun was starting its climb in the sky casting its first rays on the tops of the mountains. He bent down and picked a suitable stick for whittling and started slowly shaving the bark off. *Sure don't like leaving this place.* As he walked toward the barn, he saw Aquilla riding up the road and waited for him. *Guess he is getting here to help with the moving.*

"Glad I got here before the others," said Quil. "Seems Clark is coming around to each of us to tell us about some of the same thinking men as us getting together again in Philadelphia. He wants to make sure we aren't with them."

"You know what? We'd best be not getting our stuff together until he gets by here. I don't want him doing what he can to stop me from moving," said Samuel. "If he does…well, let's say he might run up against a half mad bear in the woods. Wouldn't that be a stroke of luck for us."

32

At the same time, Samuel and Quil were talking to each other Patrick Ferguson mumbled to himself, "I wonder if the idea would really work." While still recovering from the illness he had gotten in Germany and France, he had told his parents that he was going to attend Light Infantry camp in Salisbury sometime this year. There was much talk about his leaving with his parents and their efforts to get him to give himself more time to heal. The real reason was they didn't want him to leave at all.

After his arrival at Salisbury, he found that the training exercises took a lot of time and effort in close order drill, bayonet practice, and marksmanship with pistols and muzzle-loading muskets. The process of loading and firing muskets in the order of battle was a growing concern to him. He kept thinking of ways to improve the tactics used by the men on the firing line during the many battle training drills. The process of loading gun powder, wadding and ball in a gun and then picking a target, aiming and firing to only repeat the process over and over was especially inefficient in his way of thinking. He knew a soldier could go through the firing process only three times per minute at best. He had discussed this problem many times with his fellow officers, and almost to a man, they said comments of "Well, Patrick, that's just the way it is." This problem had always been on his mind and especially while he was in what was called the "Fever Islands."

He picked up the commonly used Brown Bess muzzle loader musket and studied its design, especially concentrating on how to improve the loading and firing process. *This musket is heavy making it hard to hold and aim plus it isn't worth even trying to hit a target over half a rugby field.*

After studying the efforts of the French and English weapon developers, he decided the best of them was a way to load the powder and ball at the back of the barrel rather than the muzzle. *I'll just take the best of all of these and put them together and make a better gun.*

"I say, Patrick, you are spending a lot of time fretting over these muskets," said one of the other officers in training named Charles Byrd. "Even if you get a good idea, you will have to get the money to get it made."

"I realize that, Charles, but I do know that I'll need to get a patent for it for obvious reasons," said Patrick. *And you better not try to steal this idea from me.*

"Well, more importantly, what do you think about the bayonet training guide we are getting now?" said Charles.

Just then a bugle sounded meaning that all the officers were to assemble for more training. Patrick followed Charles out of his room and locked the door. *I'll be glad when this if over with and can get on with my plan.*

33

Once again, Elizabeth watched Samuel walk up to the porch and after a moment that they all knew was coming, "Ma, it looks like we are ready to go." He bent down and gave his mother a long heartfelt hug. Elizabeth wiped a tear from her eye and said, "The Lord be with you, my son. Just don't forget that we are always here for you, no matter what." Samuel kissed her cheek.

"Ma, like Pa always said, I'll make sure our Sherrill name remains one of honor. You have made sure that all of us don't forget it." They faced each other looking deep into each other's eyes when Elizabeth said, "I know you will, my son. God is with you and I know you'll never forget that." They gave each other a tight hug. Samuel took a step back and looked at her with a small smile and turned to walk down the path to the wagon.

"Ma, I've gotta tell her good-bye one more time." Catherine jumped down from the wagon seat and ran to her grandmother and without a word gave each a tight hug and then, while waving, ran back to the wagon.

Mary Jane and her brothers and sister waved to Elizabeth. Mary also waved one last time, *I don't like good-byes. Takes too much out of me.*

Samuel stepped up on the wagon wheel and into the seat as he looked back to see his first son, Adam, holding the reins of horses

pulling the second wagon. He picked up the reins, gave them a swinging motion, "Let's go to our new home." The horses tugged at their halters, the wagons started rolling, Elizabeth stood up and watched them roll out of sight. "Well, I'll be whatever, it looks like we have started another chapter in our book," she whispered to the slight breeze thinking she would have said the same to Adam. Then out loud she said, "It is a beautiful day today." She looked at the last place where she saw the wagons disappear down the road. The clouds looked especially bright this morning and the sun was starting to share its light to the new day that would soon usher in a new season.

◡◠◡

Yona and Tawadi were talking with Attacullaculla and Dragging Canoe in a camp next to Fort Watauga. The rippling sound of the river gently rolling over the water polished rocks in the shoals sounded promising to Yona that warmer weather would soon be here. He said, "What is it that you are going to do? This Henderson man is here to get a lot of our and the Mohican land."

Dragging Canoe poked at the fire with a long stick and gazed at the energy given off by the wood. It was always a mystery to him how the Creator made something that didn't use fire to grow yet it gave off fire when it was used for such purposes. He finally looked up from the fire to Attacullaculla, Yona, and Tawadi saying, "That white man doesn't know anything about our land and thinks that offering us something he thinks is valuable will make us agree to his plan. That man thinks we are mixed up in our heads and is not telling us his true feelings and he thinks like a slow turtle."

Yona said to Tawadi, "You can be known as the best marksman here." He waved his arms over the camps of many Cherokee people at Sycamore Shoals. "It has been a long time since I have seen so many of us at one place."

As he was cleaning his muzzle-loading rifle, Tawadi said, "There are many of us and few of them. Why don't we just kill them and keep our hunting grounds the way they are now."

"That's the way Dragging Canoe wants it. I asked him what was the latest he could give me on talking with their man Henderson and he said that Oconostosta and Attacullaculla are wanting to sell much of our land to him," said Yona with a look of not understanding why this was a good idea.

"Attacullaculla thinks he must be part English since he got back from their main village and talking with that king 'whatever' over there," said Tawadi as he sighted down the barrel of his rifle. "I think he needs to think about this for a moon or two."

"You might be right. Dragging Canoe told me they want to give us ten thousand pounds of something called British sterling. What do we need with that stuff since we are already joining them against the Henderson kind of people," Yona said while looking over the camp and the partially built fort. "See how they keep to themselves. I feel they think they are better than us," said Yona with a perplexed look at the white man. And I was told our chiefs and their man named Henderson will talk tomorrow."

Tawadi said as he looked down the sights of his unloaded rifle at a white man and suddenly recognized him. "Yona! That white man is the one they call Boone! What is he doing here?" said Tawadi with a menacing tone in his voice.

Yona said, "You have sharp eyes. Yes, that is the man called Boone. I remember him when we met his friend Sherrill who had his daughter with him. She was a special girl then, and as we now know, a special woman."

"Keep up such talk and thinking about her, like you did when we were hunting around where they live, and we all might not like what her future holds for us," said Tawadi while still looking through his sights following Boone as he walked toward the fort walls. *I could kill him now.* "What's with that fort? They building it to keep us out or keep us in?".

"We must talk with Oconostota. He can tell us what will be happening to our land. I am not in all agreement with what this Henderson man says. He is a white man and we know they do not speak in truth to us," said Yona. "What good can come out of their sterling they will give us? Nothing is my feeling," said Yona in a tight-lipped manner.

Dragging Canoe said "That white man doesn't know anything about our land and thinks that offering us something he thinks is valuable will make us agree to his plan. That man thinks we are mixed up in our heads and is not telling us his true feelings and he thinks like a slow turtle."

After a lengthy thinking time, Dragging Canoe stated, "We must keep what is ours. Henderson doesn't know the land as well as we do. All he wants to do is sell parts of it to his own kind. There are too many of them now!"

"Yes, that is his plan. He will ask that man called Boone to make a trail from our peace island to the path through the mountain gaps into the land they are buying," said Attacullaculla.

"We are helping the English country led by their chief called George. And even he told us when you, Attacullaculla, were at his village, that they will help us keep his kind off our land. He showed us that even his words are not kept. He can't even make these white men stay on their side of the line he made across the tops of our mountains. But we have to keep trying to make our living together one of peace," Oconostota said in a matter-of-fact voice.

More silence followed which was broken by Dragging Canoe saying with a fierceness in this voice, "I will tell Henderson and his people that the land he wants will become a dark and bloody ground. They cannot keep what is written on that paper they call a treaty. I say they keep their sterling and we keep what has been ours. It has been ours for longer than our elders can remember. And the Mochican's have always said part of that is theirs. We don't need to have them fighting against us, too."

The sky was starting to show the first streaks of red on high clouds, the river continued its silent flow and the lengthening shadows of the trees made the scene one of peace. The men remained silent and each knew the other was giving serious thought to what they were doing and the impact their decisions will have on their people.

34

Catherine and Samuel Jr. walked beside the heavily laden wagons being driven by their Pa and brother, Adam. The others were also walking since there was no use riding all the time making the load heavier for the horses and mules, "Pa, are we still on the road that Grandpa made when he came here?" said Samuel Jr.

"We sure are, Sam. And even though this was close to the way Pa used to get around this land, he wasn't the only one to make what started out as a path. Others coming in here kept using it until it got to how it is now," said Samuel.

The next few days were taken up with listening to the methodical hoof beats of the horses and mules leaning into their harnesses pulling the wagons. The slope of the land was becoming a gentle rise with each day and Samuel had to make more frequent stops to rest the animals and his family. On one of the stops, they were approached by another wagon going in the opposite direction being led by a young man and his wife.

"Hello, the wagons," he said as the driver of his wagon held up his hand in greeting.

"Hello, back to you. How's it going for y'all?" asked Samuel.

As they stopped their wagons, they looked at each other forming first impressions of peace or danger. Samuel saw no weapons close by the stranger, but he was aware of his musket's visibility leaning on the wagon seat. "Where 'bouts you headin'?" asked Samuel.

"Didn't catch your name, Mister. But since you asked, we're headin' off to Georgia to settle down," said the man. "By the way, name's Jubal and this here's my wife, Nancy."

While quickly tipping his hat, "Name's Samuel. And I gotta tell you this isn't the road to Georgia. You musta taken the wrong turn. That is, if you were coming down the Carolina Road."

The downtrodden look of disbelief on Jubal and Nancy's faces made Samuel feel somewhat sorry for them. "Yeah, we came down that road from Big Lick about a week ago. Got tied up a couple days with a broked wheel and the others just kept on going and leavin' us to our own figuring."

"Sorry 'bout that. But you gotta look on the bright side. At least you ran into us to help you get back on the right road. C'mon, follow along with us til we get to the Carolina Road where we'll go our own ways," said Samuel.

During the nights stop, they built a fire for warmth and cooking and settled down to an easy time of getting to know each other. Samuel asked," Got anything on the goings-on of the English up your way?" *Gotta go slow, never know which side he's on.*

"You like King George?" said Jubal as he locked in on Samuel's eyes. Samuel could see that he wasn't going to beat around the bush to get an answer.

"Well, Jubal, one has to be a little careful these days in answering such a question. But I must tell you that the way he and his parliament try to make it tough on us doesn't sit too well with me," said Samuel.

"You ain't one of them Tories, are you?" asked Jubal.

"Jubal, you gotta go slow with such talk. You're lucky I'm not one who finds favor with what is going on now; but I sure don't tell anyone I've just met how I feel. Never know when it might come back and take a bite outta me," said Samuel. *He's gotta learn to mind his words to strangers.*

The next morning sky was showing its splendor with hues of red colors bouncing off the high clouds. A slight breeze was stirring in the tops of the tall oak and chestnut trees as Catherine slowly opened her eyes from a deep sleep. *God is doing some of his glorious painting* a she smelled the smoke of the camp fire. *Guess I best get up and help get breakfast.* She stretched and rubbed the sleep from her eyes and was startled when Adam came close to her saying, "Gonna be a rain today. Best get ready for it."

"Adam, you scared me! Let me know when you are close! And what do you mean about rain today?" exclaimed Catherine.

"Just as Grandpa told me many times. Red sky in the morning means rain later in the day and, you know what, that is almost the way it is," said Adam.

That afternoon the two family's wagons came to the junction of the Carolina Road and Sherrill's Path, and they could see tall, billowing, angry-looking clouds building in the western sky. Samuel stopped his wagons and jumped down to walk back to Jubal's and Nancy's wagon. "Well, this looks like where we go our separate ways," as he held out his hand to Jubal. As they shook hands in parting, they heard the deep rumble of far off thunder and looked to see streaks of lightning jumping from cloud to cloud. The darkening sky gave the unmistakable look that left no question as to its power.

"We gotta be quick and find some kind of shelter from what's coming! Try to stay away from the tallest trees!" shouted Samuel as he raced back to his wagon. He turned back to Jubal and shouted, "Maybe we'll see you some other time!" He snapped the reins and the horses and mules knew they had to find some shelter as they moved to the place directed by Samuel. Mary saw what looked like steep wall of exposed rock on their left. "That rock will give us some protection and is big enough for our two wagons," she shouted to Samuel, who, without a word, directed the horses to the wall. He looked back and waving to John, who was driving the team of the second wagon, to drive his wagon to the wall.

"Where's Jubal?" shouted Mary. "They've got to find some place to stop!" As if on cue, the rapidly darkening sky ushered in howling winds, bending trees to their breaking point while shredded green leaves were being blown like a winter snowstorm. There was no doubt that torrents of rain would soon follow. The blots of lightning were so close that their cracking sound caused every living creature close enough to hear it to cower in fear of being hit and split open by the blinding light. A powerful hissing jagged streak turned a large chestnut tree into a frenzied monster full of a momentary destructive energy followed by a loud cracking noise. The tree stood its ground as if defying the power of the storm.

Samuel crawled under a wagon after making sure his family was as safe as he could make them in the storm. He glanced through the spokes of one of the wheels and was startled to see a man standing facing his wagons. The rain cascaded from his hat adding to his already soaked clothing. A hissing bolt of lightning lit up the scene. The loud explosive report made Samuel wince, but the stranger did not appear startled in the least. The brief light was all Samuel needed to recognize Sheriff Clark. *What in the ever loving world is he doing out here?*

Sheriff Clark had finally reached the wagons after being told two days ago that Samuel and his family were on the way across the mountains. After finally catching up with Samuel, his hard feelings for him made him oblivious to the elements swirling around him. *Thought he was going to escape from me! He's going back if it's the last thing I do. My rifle will make them go back!* It was then he realized the rain was making his gun powder useless and the only weapon he had was his knife which almost futile in this situation. Clark took one more look at the wagons, but didn't realize Samuel had recognized him and turned to retrace his steps into the forest. *I'll wait out this storm and then take 'em on.*

Just as quickly as the storm arrived, it passed on leaving everything dripping wet. Mary Jane and Catherine were huddled in middle of the wagon thinking they would be hit by the lightning or something worse when the storms noise became one of water dripping off the wagon and the leaves of the trees. Catherine said in a low, almost breathless, voice, "I've never been so scared in my life. I thought we were all goners for sure. "C'mon, Mary Jane, let's see how everyone is doing." They both stepped out of the wagon and turned to see if the other wagon had made it through the storm with no problems when seemingly out of nowhere a voice behind them said, "Catherine, Mary Jane, be real quiet and follow me." They turned to see Sheriff Clark and thinking something was wrong did what he asked even though Mary Jane had a sharp intake of breath.

No sooner than they had started following Clark, Adam asked, "What y'all doing?"

Clark in a low menacing voice said, "Don't bother us!" with a look that told Adam that he needed to protect his sisters. He shouted as he started running toward where he last saw Samuel, "Pa, Pa. Catherine and Mary Jane need help!"

Clark then drew his pistol and pointed it at the girls saying, "Move and I mean now!"

Samuel ran up to the scene when he saw Clark pull his pistol. "What is it you're trying to do?" he said with a look that belonged only to the Sherrills. "Have you lost your mind? Those are my daughters! Let them go and now!" as he reached out to them.

"I'm wet, I'm mad and you are not leaving my territory without my consent which you don't have," said Clark without looking Samuel in the eye.

"You don't have the authority to tell me where I can or can't live," Samuel said in an even tone of voice accompanied with his continuing icy glare. "Now just put your pistol back where you keep it and leave us before someone gets hurt."

"No way are you going to tell me what to do! You come with me back to my place and I'll see what my people have to say about you," as he slowly turned his pistol toward Samuel. Catherine and Mary Jane looked to their Pa who, with a slight motion of his head and eyes, caught his meaning and slowly moved away from Clark.

Samuel saw a silently walking Jubal, who carried his musket, moving to get behind Clark. "Just what do you say I do with my family when you take me back to see your Tory friends? And do you really think they'll agree with me?" said Samuel in order to keep Clark's from realizing someone was creeping up behind him.

"I don't care what you do with your family," as he looked at Catherine and Mary Jane. He saw Mary Jane glance behind him with widening eyes and the experience of years being sheriff made him develop a need to know what was going on around him at all times. "On your knees and now!" Clark said with emphasis to Samuel. "Whoever is behind me, better show himself now or I just might pull this trigger. On your knees, Samuel."

Catherine knew she had to somehow distract Clark. *I've got to do something*. It suddenly occurred to her to scream, which she did with all the strength of her voice. The scream seemed to shock even the leaves on the trees and the animals in the forest, but more importantly, the people around her. Clark, who was looking at Samuel, heard Catherine's high-pitched scream and reacted with a jerk of his arms. The jerk caused his hand that held the pistol to swing up which, in turn, caused him to pull the trigger. Catherine's continued screaming covered up the click of the pistol's hammer. The flint did not spark the powder in the pistol's pan. A misfire! By this time, Mary Jane, who almost fainted when Catherine screamed, also started screaming at the top of her voice.

Samuel jumped up and ran to Clark when he realized the pistol misfired and clapped his hands hard on Clark's ears. The pain caused Clark to take a few wobbly steps backwards as he drew his knife. He was starting to attack Samuel when Jubal hit him a glancing blow on the head with his musket. Clark staggered forward trying to keep his balance and, as he lost consciousness, fell face down at Samuel's feet. Everyone heard him emit a muffled grunt when he hit the ground.

No one moved or said a word as each tried to get back to some semblance of normalcy. A very relieved Samuel, who had been looking down the barrel of Clark's pistol, said, "That was close. Thanks, Kate, for your scream. It even shook me up. Thanks, Jubal, I sure am glad you were here. You put the hurting on him." He bent down to see if Clark was beginning to come around from being knocked out. Clark had not moved, Samuel rolled him over on his back and saw the knife that Clark had been holding sticking in his midsection close to his stomach.

"Uhhhh, Ohhh," said Samuel, "this doesn't look good. He fell on his knife" as he put his hand on Clark's chest feeling for a heartbeat. "Out here in the middle of nowhere not even close to a doctor. We gotta try to fix him up!"

"Let me see him," said Mary. She then cut Clark's shirt from around the wound and saw that there was not too much blood. *That's a good thing.* "Mary Jane, Catherine, get me some clean rags and Pa's still stuff and be quick about it. Samuel, get ready to pull that knife outta him when I say so."

Everything was in readiness when Mary looked at Samuel and gave him a nod of her head. Samuel took a deep breath, took hold of the knife's handle and pulled on it. "That's in pretty tight. I'll get a better hold." He then held the handle tightly, and with a quick jerk, pulled the knife out. Clark's wound started bleeding slowly at first then building in volume. Mary poured the alcohol-based liquid on the wound which caused Clark to stir from his knocked out state. "Hold him down!" said Mary to Samuel and Jubal, who had stood transfixed at the happening before him. Mary applied the bandages to the wound and told the men to help hold Clark upright enough so she could wrap the bandage around his body to keep it compressed on the wound.

"Looks like you got him fixed up," said Jubal.

Clark slowly regained his senses to the point of realizing what had happened to him. He murmured words that no one understood and started to fall back into an unconscious state. Mary said, "Don't let him get back to where he was! He might not come out of it."

Samuel used one of the wagon wheels to prop Clark on and kept talking to him to keep him awake. Clark's senses finally came to life when he coarsely whispered, "You going back with me. All you Sherrills are going back to where you belong. Y'all ain't leaving me! And who is this guy anyway," as he pointed to Jubal.

Samuel ignored the sheriff's comments about going back, but did say, "This man is named Jubal. He is going to take you back to Polk's place to see a doctor about your cutting yourself."

Jubal said, "What do you mean I'm going to take him to Polk's place? We hadn't talked about that and anyway, where is this place you're taking about?'

"It's on your way a bit down the road yonder. You know, the one I showed y'all to take to get on to Georgia. Kinda works out for all of us, doesn't it?" said Samuel with somewhat of a level gaze at Jubal.

Jubal caught Samuel's meaning and thought, *Guess he feels that is the least I can do for him getting me back on the right road.* "Yep, guess that does make sense. Help me get him in the wagon and we'll be on our way."

Clark, in a hesitant low voice, said, "I'll get back on my own and take everyone with me," as he tried to stand up. It soon became apparent that he wasn't able to stand for more than a few seconds.

"Guess you need to make a decision. Either go with Jubal or stay here and fend for yourself," said Samuel. "We are finishing our move, and even though I can't believe I'm saying this, I hope you recover from your knifing yourself."

"You move on and you'll always regret it! I'll find you no matter what!" said Clark as he tried, in vain, to stand up. "Help me up into this wagon."

"Jubal, I will pray for you to have a safe journey. Here's a note signed by Mary and me as to what happened here. Keep it on your person as you may need it on down the line. If you need more help get word to one of my brothers. All you need to do is say you know me and want to talk with one of the Sherrills," said Samuel as he shook Jubal's hand. He then climbed up to the wagon seat and taking hold of the reins shook them signaling the horses to start pulling the wagon.

The increasing incline of the land slowed their daily travel. After getting through Maggoty Gap, the land leveled out toward Salem and Big Lick. "Pa, I wish we had waited a few weeks before leaving. It's colder here and the tree buds are just now getting a little green on them," said Mary Jane.

"Samuel said as he looked over to Mary Jane sitting beside him on the wagon seat, "Yeah, I agree that it is colder which I expected. But we should be at our new place in a few weeks which will give us time to get settled down and start planting our crops. Does that make sense, my youngest daughter?"

Mary Jane said as she nodded her head, "I never thought about that part of it. I just hope it isn't as cold there as here."

Samuel and Mary sat by the early morning fire and watched the sun's rays light up the clear sky. "It's going to be a beautiful day," said Mary in a whispered voice tinged with wonder at the scene unfolding in front of her.

Samuel said, "You always look on the bright side of things and I thank you for sharing your thoughts with me." At that moment, the sun's first rays appeared above the eastern hills.

They continued to watch the sun rise until its brightness became too much to for their eyes. Samuel said, "We best get going. I think we will make the Wagon Road today. I just hope we can find others going the same way."

The road wound back and forth that led to the top of a ridge where they stopped to absorb the view. Catherine said to Adam and Samuel Jr., "This looks like the place Pa wanted to get to today. I hope he can find some other people who are going our way." *Who knows there just may be some man, who isn't married, going to the same place we are.* She smiled at the thought.

Samuel and the boys inspected the horses and mules to make sure they were in good shape. And after making sure all were all up to their tasks, they inspected the wagons to make sure the wheels, axles, brakes, and bolts were safe to continue down the steep road as it zigzagged to what appeared to be a gathering spot for a number of other wagons. Mary looked over to Samuel and said, "Looks like a lot of wagons getting ready to go somewhere. Let's hope they are headed down our way."

The descent was slow and required a lot of pulling back on the brake bar to slow the wagons when they finally rolled onto level ground. They drove up to the place they had seen earlier containing seven wagons and hitched teams. Samuel said, "Looks like they're getting ready to move out. Maybe there's someone who runs this outfit and can tell us about what's going on."

Samuel and Samuel Jr. started toward the nearest wagon hoping to find out who was leading them or if they were just gathering on their own to go to the same place. "Hello, the wagon," said Samuel.

"Hello to you," said a man kneeling beside a fire pouring a cup of coffee. "Come sit a spell. What can I do for ya?"

"Samuel Sherrill is my name and this is my son, Samuel Jr. We're looking to head down to the Holston River country," said Samuel. "We just wanted to find out if we might join some others going the same way."

"Well, Samuel, you have come to the right place at the right time. This whole passel of wagons is headed that way today. That is, just as soon as I finish this coffee. Mike Stone is my handle."

"Are you the wagon master or whatever the leader is called?" asked Samuel.

"Hey, that's a good handle. Wagon master. I like it. Yes, I am that guy and we can always use another set of hands in trips like these," said Mike.

Samuel said in a hesitant manner, "Trips like these? Does that mean there are some major problems along the way?"

"Well, none other than some upset Indians, some guys bent on robbing, and of course, the road isn't the best in the world. Put all that together with having to cross a river or two on ferries makes for some possible trouble at times," said Mike.

"See what you mean and the more wagons and families the better off all of us will be," said Samuel in a matter-of-fact tone. "Well, Mike, I guess we best be getting back to the wagons. Where in the line do you want us to be? And what do you call the road we going to use? We just came up the Carolina Road."

Mike said with a wave toward the Southwest, "Ohh, I'm not sure one way or the other, but I've heard a number of guys call it the Frontier Road. But for me, I'm just calling it the Valley Road. In the next few days, you'll soon see why I call it that. The way I look at it is you can call it anything you want just so long as it gets you to where you want to go."

Catherine looked over the wagons with their owners checking and rechecking their equipment to make sure all was in order. *A lot of people are heading our direction. Just hope those English and their Tory friends aren't over there. Who knows maybe I'll find someone who I want to marry and he wants to marry me.* She moved closer to her pa and Mike to get some idea of what they were planning. Samuel said when Catherine approached them, "Mike, this is one of my daughters. Catherine, this is Mike who is the wagon master,"

Mike said as he stood up and removed his hat, "Pleased to meet ya." *Not bad looking.* You just let me know if there is anything I can do for you or your family while we are on our way down yonder. And just call me Mike if you don't mind. And I'll call you, Catherine."

"Much obliged, Mike. I'll keep that in mind. Is your family with you?" asked Catherine.

"Naww, Ma doesn't want to make this trip again. Our place is here in Salem for right now and she keeps the place going while I do the wagon master thing. Ya, know, Samuel, I really like that handle," Mike said with a half smile. "Guess I'd best be getting all these people together so I can tell them what we need to do while on the trail. Such things as what to do if we get attacked by Indians or guys trying to rob us."

Samuel said, with a questioning look, "Indians? Has that happened to you before now on the trail we are taking?"

"Not yet, but I've seen signs of them on the last trip I made last fall. Only thing I want everyone to know is to be on the alert at all times and the reasons why," said Mike.

"Yeah, I think you are on target with that thought. I hadn't given a lot of thought to being attacked on this trip. Darn glad you are leading us," said a pensive sounding Samuel.

The wagons, pulled by horses, mules and oxen, kept up a steady rhythm of hoof beats that almost lulled Catherine into a trance. This was broken when Mike called for them to stop and rest. He came riding back along the caravan telling the wagon drivers that he will go on ahead and make sure the ferry across the river is still working.

Catherine said to Mike, "I've never seen a wagon on a ferry. How safe are such things on something this big?"

"Not to worry. The fellows operating the ferry know what they are doing plus I wouldn't be going this way unless I thought it safe for us," said Mike as he pulled on the reins of his horse and headed toward the ferry. *Not going to tell them this is the only place to cross this river.*

"Samuel, when we get to the ferry I want you and Catherine to drive the second wagon and Mom and I will drive the first one. We have got to learn from the others that cross before us. Let's keep a watch on our teams. I'm not sure how they will act on the ferry," said Samuel with a worried look as he pointed to the teams. *Sure hope they don't get skittish on the way over. Wonder if we should take their harnesses off.*

The early morning sky showed high wispy clouds tinted with various colors of red painted on a backdrop of light grey color as the sun continued its path through the heavens. Catherine sat on the wagon seat looking at the sky with thoughts of questioning wonder. *I thank God for allowing me to be here. I can't begin to get my mind around how and why he made all of this.*

Mike rode by each wagon telling the drivers that the ferry pilots were ready to start and for each wagon to pull forward to ready position after the wagon being taken across was safely on the other side. He reminded everyone to do their best in keeping the animals calm on the way over the river. The ferrymen had told him the river was running higher than normal due to yesterday's storm in the mountains upstream. He saw no reason to tell everyone that news since they had enough to take care of without having to worry about higher than normal water level.

Samuel and Samuel Jr. stood on the river bank observing how the ferrymen and wagon drivers handled the way their wagons rolled onto the ferry, and more importantly, keeping the animals calm. After talking with the ferrymen, Mike made sure the person that the animals trusted was at the head of the team holding onto the bridle while guiding them onto the wooden plank floor. Mike mumbled a worried comment to himself, "Never had a team of ox's before."

"Wonder if we oughta unhitch the team when we get on the ferry?" questioned Samuel. "If the wagon started to roll off it would pull the team in with it. I hate to think of what might happen if the team got out of control on that thing."

Due to the storm, the rivers flow was much faster than normal, but the ferrymen did not seem to be worried about it as they went about their business. The first family and their wagon moved forward to the tip of the ferry. The horses were hesitant to step onto the ferry floor and the driver and one of the ferrymen got them calmed enough to drive them forward until the wagon was safely on the ferry. The men placed rocks on the back and front of each wagon wheel to keep them from rolling. When all was ready, the three ferrymen tightened their grip of the rope and started pulling the ferry toward the far side. The fast-flowing water pushed hard against the flat side of the ferry which made the men on the rope work harder to get to the other side. The horses started stamping their hooves on the floor making a hollow drumming sound. This, along with their neighing and the grunts of the men pulling on the ferry rope, made a lot of noise. The other teams waiting to go forward became skittish due to the team on the ferry. Mike gave a worried looked from the ferry to the waiting teams, *I gotta get them back to a place where they can't see the ferry.*

"Cover their eyes! Do what you can to make 'em quiet!" said Mike as he rode up to each wagon's driver. The ox team appeared calm.

After what seemed a forever time frame, the ferry docked on the other side and a relieved family followed their wagon off the ferry onto hard ground and gave a loud cheer to their success as the ferrymen started back to get another wagon.

Catherine and Uriah sat on a large lichen covered rock and watched as each wagon was taken across the river. "You know something, my brother? All the belongings we have are in our wagons. Just like everyone else with us. I hate to think of what we would do if we lost our wagons."

Uriah kept his eyes on the last team starting across and said, "Yep, it sure would be bad. Unhh, oohh, that team is starting to get riled up. He'd better get them calmed down and now!"

The horses that Finn Stewart was trying to keep calm were rapidly overcoming his yanking on the bridle and bit while desperately trying to avoid the flaying hoofs. The wagon wheels being pushed against the heavy rocks, placed against them to prevent rolling, were starting a rocking motion that moved the rocks and which caused one back wheel to roll on top of the rock. Finn's wife was pulling hard on the reins and his four children were giving it everything they had in pulling on the ropes attached to the wagon axle trying to prevent the wagon from moving. The ferrymen were pulling on the guide rope as fast as they could to get to the other side. The scene was one of maximum desperate effort to make things right especially since all had gone so well as evidenced by the other wagons waiting on the other side.

Catherine looked up the river and with a gasp, "Ohhh, nooooo!" as he pointed to the river. Samuel and Uriah turned their attention to where she was pointing but didn't immediately see the problem. The large tree was almost underwater with its roots projecting above the water line like periscopes. It was headed toward the ferry while riding up and down in the swirling water. Samuel finally saw the tree and immediately realized the disaster if it struck the ferry. He started running toward the docking area shouting to Mike to bring as many men as he could to the bank to help the Stewarts get their wagon safely to shore.

Mike jumped off his horse before it fully stopped and ran to the bank. Samuel told him as he pointed upstream, "That tree is going to hit the ferry! We need to get some ropes out to the ferry and pull it in!"

Mike started shouting orders to the gathering men to try and get ropes to the ferry. Finn's horses seemed to know they were in increasing danger and started straining the reins almost to the breaking point. Mike yelled to Finn to unhitch the horses. Without hesitation, Finn started trying to take the bridles and reins off the horses and realized that it was not going to work with all their scared movements. He took out his large knife and started cutting the leather straps that attached the horses to the wagon tongue. He then ran to the back of the wagon to tell his boys to grab hold of a board, rail or anything to keep them from falling off into the cold river when the tree hit the ferry. His wife handed the newborn daughter to him and climbed down to the floor of the ferry taking the baby back in her arms. Finn looked to the men on the far bank and realized their efforts to get ropes to him were not working as the distance was too great. He shouted to the boys to grab the ferry rope to help speed it to the bank, hopefully letting the tree pass by without hitting them.

With one wagon wheel sitting precariously on top the rock and the wagon free from being tied to the horses coupled with action of the occasional water waves of the fast-flowing river started it moving toward the back of the ferry.

All the people gathered on the bank saw the tree floating straight to the ferry as if guided by some unseen force. They were shouting to the Stewarts to watch out for the tree. Finn and the ferrymen saw the tree with its roots looking like spears used by the devil's army coming fast toward the ferry. He shouted to his family to hold tight to the boat and not the wagon. Everyone held their breath when they saw the tree hit the ferry. The ferry guide rope was pushed to its limit, the ferrymen quickly got back up from being knocked down and started pulling on the rope. The wagon's front wheels struck a chock, making them turn and causing the tongue to swing out over the water. The wagon tilted to one side, and in what seemed to be slow motion, fell on its side. The tongue followed the steering wheels as they moved back into a straight position. Finn's oldest son, Terry, saw the tongue swing up and then fall toward the ferry floor. It struck one of the horses knocking it into the river. Terry had grabbed the bridle bindings in effort to steady the horse and was pulled into the river with the horse. The rapid current pulled both around the ferry. Finn saw Terry hit the water and ran to the back of the ferry to grab him when he floated by, but the rapid current had pulled Terry too far out. Finn started pulling his boots off to dive into the water and rescue his son. Finn's wife screamed, "No, no, don't do it!" She realized that both might be lost in the water.

Samuel and others stood motionless on the bank as they watched the unbelievable action on the ferry. When Terry hit the water, they knew what they had to do and started running downstream to rescue him and the horse. Samuel held up his arms in effort to stop the men stating, "Three of us can save the boy," while pointing to two other men. Mike shouted to the others to get ropes to the ferry to save the wagon.

Terry was desperately trying to keep his head above the cold water and could feel his strength slowly leaving him when he saw the tree that had hit the ferry coming straight toward him. He grabbed one of the roots and slowly pulled himself onto the tree trunk. He could see the horse trying to swim to the bank and then saw men trying to keep up along the bank to rescue him. Ropes were thrown out toward him, but he was too far out for them to reach him. The current was strong and carried him rapidly downstream to the point that the rescuers could not keep up. They watched as Terry on the tree log disappeared around a sharp bend in the river. The men stopped and looked at each other as if trying to come to a plan.

Mike said, "We cannot keep up with the river. We don't have boats and the banks at this part of the river are steep. We'll need two men to ride on down the river to see if they can find him. The rest of us will go back to help with saving their wagon."

Finn mounted his horse and yelled while riding off, "I'm going after my boy! If someone wants to come along then so be it."

The Stewart wagon was finally pulled off the ferry on its side. The men attached ropes to it and gradually let it down as two horses pulled it over on its wheels. Finn's wife, Martha, was almost sick with worry about Terry plus the problems of losing some of their worldly goods in the river. She did a quick inventory and found that salt, sugar, and salted pork were missing.

Mary Sherrill quickly came to her saying, "I'm sure your son will be all right and found soon. Now, let us help you get your wagon ready to ride on down the road." Other women of the group started offering help to Martha with many saying they are praying for her son's safe return to her.

Terry held onto the tree roots as it rode the rapid river current. It was getting toward dusk and had not seen any sight of men trying to rescue him. *Hope I can find a place where I can get off this thing.* As he looked around, he spotted a burned out tree canoe headed in his direction. *Great! Maybe this is someone who can help me!* As he watched the approaching canoe, he realized the two men paddling it were Indians. They were really pulling hard on the paddles trying their best to intercept the tree. *I'm in trouble but I have no where to go or hide.*

The two men were almost to the tree and one leaned over and grabbed one of the roots while the other swung the canoe around so that it was side by side with the tree. The one in the rear gave quick hand signals for Terry to get in the canoe. Terry had no option and slid down the trunk of the tree and gradually lowered himself into the canoe. The men looked at each other and with a slight nod of the head pushed away from the tree and headed the canoe toward the riverbank.

Terry got out of the canoe grateful to be on dry land. He was scared for his life, but tried not to show it to what he thought were his captors. "Thanks for saving me," he said with as much a positive attitude as possible. The Indians looked at each other shrugging their shoulders and started talking in their own language. One said in his language, "Let us take him to his people and tell them we want a rifle for him." The other said, "Will make a good trade. Want to let him know we know a lot of his tongue?"

"No, we keep him confused. Let's feed him and go to his people," said the other man as he took hold of Terry's arm to guide him to their camp.

Ohhh no! I'm in for some hurt! I've got to get out of this! He tried to keep calm as he constantly searched for ways to escape.

In their language, the Indians made plans since seeing the white boy on the tree. "We did well in that river. Now we have this white boy, what do we do to get rid of him?" said Shafah to Koeetah. There was a moment of silence as they thought about the question and some alternatives to answer it. Terry did not understand their language, but could determine he was being talked about.

Koeetah said, "We need a rifle. As we have just said, we will trade him to the wagons for a rifle."

"That is good. Let's go!" said Shafah as he turned to Terry pointing the direction he was to start walking. *Going back upstream. Maybe they are taking me to Ma and Pa.*

Catherine and three other girls were out gathering firewood when one looked up to see two Indians holding Terry by his arms walking toward the encampment. The girl let out a scream that startled every one. The Indians stopped while the men of the encampment recovered their initial surprise and grabbed a rifle or other weapon to defend the wagons.

Shafah said, "We put our weapons on the ground. They must know we are not attacking them."

Both put their weapons on the ground. Samuel saw their action and shouted to everyone to remain calm as he started walking toward Shafah, Kooetah, and Terry. Finn joined him and said, "If they hurt him, I'll kill both of them!"

Samuel said in an even tone of voice, "We will put our rifles on the ground when we get to them. They show they do not want a fight. We will do the same thing."

Finn looked at Samuel who, in turn, looked at Finn with the Sherrill look. Finn then realized he had better follow Samuel's lead and get his boy back.

Samuel stopped in front of the Indians and Terry. He then laid his rifle on the ground and looked at Finn to make sure he was doing the same action and then looked at Shafah and Kooetah with a steady gaze and then looked at Terry. "You all right?" he said to Terry.

Finn said, "My son!" as he stepped forward to touch him. Shafah stepped in front of Terry and by the shaking of his head and hands showed that Terry was still their captive. Shafah then pointed at Samuel's rifle and then Terry and kept the doing the same hand action until it occurred to Samuel the meaning of the hand gestures.

"They want to trade Terry for a rifle," said Samuel. He then made hand movements from his mouth to Terry indicating that he wanted to speak to Terry. Kooetah said, "He wants to talk with this boy. That is good." He shook his head up and down approving the proposal. "The one who is the father is ready to fight us. Be careful of him."

Shafah pointed to his mouth and then to Samuel and Terry signifying approval to talk with each other. He said to Kooetah, "We step back from the boy and let them talk." He then nodded to Samuel and with hand gestures made it known they could talk with each other.

Samuel said, "Are you hurt?"

Terry said with a hesitant voice, "No, I'm not hurt, but I don't mind telling you that I am scared of what they might do to me. Pa, is Ma all right?"

"Everything is good. Ma and the rest of us are getting the wagon ready to roll again. Got kinda scary there for a little bit especially when you floated off down the river."

Shafah stepped back up next to Terry showing hand gestures to stop talking and said to Kooetah. "Let us get a rifle and be gone."

"I think that is good. The faster the better for us," said Kooetah as he shook his head up and down. He then pointed to Terry and to one of the rifles.

Finn said, "I think you are right that they want a rifle for Terry. That is a trade I'll do any day of the week. My boy is alive and well. Thanks be to God." He then reached down to pick up his rifle to hand it over to one of the Indians.

Shafah jumped back and yanked Terry back with him. "He means to kill us!" Kooetah didn't move and looked in Finn's eyes and then to Samuel. Samuel had the steady gaze that showed neither fear or superiority. He said to Finn, "They think you are making ready to shoot them. Do not pick up your musket!"

The four men stood still and looked at each other waiting for some action or gesture indicating intent. Finally, Samuel thought that having himself and Finn step back far enough that would show the Indians that there was no intent to start any misunderstood action. He said, "Finn, let's take four steps back from our rifles." Finn nodded his head in understanding and they both stepped back.

Shafah and Kooetah looked at each other, nodded their head once to each other in understanding what the two white men wanted them to know. "You pick the father's rifle and make sure it works. If it looks good to you, bring it back here and we'll let the boy go to his father," said Shafah.

Kooetah looked at Samuel and Finn and seeing nothing to indicate a problem stepped up and while keeping his eyes on the two men, picked up Finn's rifle. He slowly turned it over two times checking for any broken or missing parts, sighted down the barrel and noticed there was no powder in the pan which, if it had been ready to fire, had spilled out when it was laid on the ground. He pulled the firing hammer back and slowly let it down on the pan. Once again, he sighted down the barrel while slowly swinging it to the point he was aiming at Samuel. Samuel clasped his hands together, raised them to his chest, and in his way, gave the Sherrill gaze to him. Kooetah said, "This one is a warrior," while slowly dropping his aim and took steps back to Shafeh and Terry. He nodded to Shafeh who then let go of Terry and stepped back to Kooetah. Terry jumped forward and ran to his father. The two Indians looked at each other, nodded their heads, and turned back toward the woods.

Finn grabbed Terry and gave him a tight hug and said to the two Indians, "Thanks for bringing my boy back!" Kooetah and Shafah looked back to Finn and then to each other, shrugged their shoulders and looked at Samuel. He raised his arm and opened his hand hoping this would show a peaceful gesture. *I think this is what he told me to do*, referring to a conversation with one of his Catawba Indian neighbors. The two Indians gave the same motion and turned to go back into the protection of the forest.

"To go out hunting for deer and come back to the village with a rifle and a deer will make for much talk," said Shafah.

Kooetah looked back toward the wagons, "White man has a lot of things with them. We get more of us and go back and take what we want."

"No use in making the white man hate us. We have to keep peace with them. They are like the seeds in our corn. They keep increasing their numbers. They already have more than we do," said Shafah. Kooetah gave Shafah a thoughtful look and shook his head in agreement and continued their walk in silence.

Samuel watched the two Indians as they melted into the forest. *If the rest of them are like those two, then we can learn a lot from them.* He watched a while longer then picked up his rifle and walked back to the wagon train, giving more thought as to what the next few weeks would give them.

35

Mary and Catherine sat on the wagon seat while Samuel Jr. drove the team. Not much was being talked about, and Mary kept glancing at Catherine who seemed to be in some trance-like state as she let her eyes wander over the horizon to the left and right. *Those mountains go on forever. I could never get tired of looking at them.*

"Ma, just look at those mountains. Aren't they beautiful. And look at the snow on the highest mountains ending down into what looks like a straight line across all of them," Catherine said in a low, wondering voice.

"Yes and don't you know it is cold up there. Makes me wonder how the Indians and occasional white man live on them," said Mary. "I guess it is all in what you get used to doing."

Catherine continued to let her mind wander as they continued on what was called a road. She wondered when a path became a road in the thinking of the times such as now. Her brother, John, climbed onto the wagon seat and followed his sister's searching look. After a few minutes, he said, "Makes ya wonder what it was like before the two-legged beast got here, doesn't it?"

Catherine continued her searching look especially at the tree leaves that were showing the coming of the spring season. She let her gaze, once again, come to rest on the peaks of the mountain range off to left of the wagon train. After a few minutes, she turned to John and answered his question with a smile followed by "That's a good thought. Shows you've been doing a lot of thinking about this land. Makes you wonder how long ago that the elk, deer, bears, and whatever ruled this land." They both fell back into silence of letting their eyes roam over the small rolling hills and noticing how they gradually rose up to the base of the mountains. *I think I will learn to love this land*, thought Catherine.

The southwestern sky was slowly giving up the light from a rapidly descending huge globe of orange-colored sun as Mike, Samuel, and three other men sat around a glowing fire used for preparing supper, discussing plans, and the timing estimates of getting to various forts and stations along the way. Mike said, "We'll make Fincastle in a few days, and then about a week or so later, we'll make Wolf Hills where Black's fort is located. Once there, we can decide which way everyone wants to go or divide up."

Samuel said with an emphatic voice, "I've been told a number of times that the Watauga and Nolichucky area are becoming a place where a man and his family has the freedom to make his own decisions without asking someone else for approval. And there are no taxes or levies on what we make. I can use my still all day long. And I can walk in the woods without having to be on the lookout for some Tory telling me that I've crossed a line that ol' Georgy boy sez we can't go over."

One of the men said, "I guess you know we left that line a long time ago. In fact, that line runs along the tops of them mountains up yonder," while waving his hand toward them. "And I want y'all to know thet I'm a' going to Kaintucky and stake my claim."

Samuel Jr. approached the fire saying, "Pa, there's a man on his horse about a rock's throw from here just looking at us. Seems to be by himself," as he pointed in the direction of the stranger.

Samuel and Mike got up and, without a word, walked toward the area pointed out by Samuel Jr. About half way, Mike said, "You go around the front of that wagon and I'll go around the rear. Check your powder." They both looked at their priming pans and readied the rifle to go into firing position quickly if needed. "I'll do the talkin' to him."

The man didn't move a muscle except his eyes as he did not want to make any suspicious action. He saw two men coming from the front and rear of a wagon headed in his direction. *Smart. Keeping a distance between each other.* At that point, he slowly raised both arms with hand extended open.

Samuel said, "Looks like he is alone. Why not invite him to come in at the fire."

At that point, the stranger said in a loud voice, "Hello, the wagons and you two gents."

Mike glanced at Samuel who kept his eyes on the stranger, "I'll call him in." Samuel nodded in agreement.

"Come on in, but make it slow," said Mike in a commanding voice while pointing out the way with his rifle.

The rider said, "Mind if I get down from here and lead him to where you want me to go?"

"Keep your body in sight at all times and come on in," said Mike.

The rider did as instructed and with little wasted motion got down. *Mighty uptight bunch* and said as he walked closer to Mike and Samuel, "Name is Thomas, or Tom for short. Am headed to a place called Bean Station. Ever hear of it?"

"Just come on inside the wagon round up. Want a cup of coffee?" said Samuel.

"That's the best offer I've had since Jefferson's place. I'll get my cup." He dug around in his saddle bag, pulled out his cup, and turned around to see Samuel's rifle pointed at him. "Whoa there!" as he raised his arms while looking in Samuel's eyes. "What's goin' on?"

Samuel lowered his rifle and said, "A body never knows what may be pulled out of a bag by a stranger. Just wanted to be sure that you weren't going to pull a pistol on us. Don't want it said that we aren't ready for the worse."

Mike said, "Now all that's over with come on and get your coffee. Been on the ride long?"

A visibility shaken Tom walked to the fire pit, "Not used to being surprised like that." *Gotta keep an eye on this Samuel. He means business.* He picked up the pot and poured his cup to the brim of the hot steaming coffee. "Looks like this will float a horseshoe which means its good for a tired body.

Samuel said, "Got any news from back yonder?"

Tom looked into the fire and after a few moments said, "I just came from Jefferson's place a week or so ago and he told me that Patrick Henry had made one of his speech's where he said something like "Give me liberty or give me death" before giving up his freedom to the English.

Other men had joined the talk around the fire and many started asking questions about what is going on and how it might affect them.

Someone asked, "Where was he when he made that speech?"

Tom said, "Jefferson said he was in Richmond at a meeting. I think he said the House of Burgess meeting or something like that. At any rate, I bet he got everyone all riled up to throw them English boys In the sea and tell 'em to swim home." Everyone laughed at the mental picture of a bunch of men swimming across the Atlantic.

Samuel said, "Been hearing about Henry off and on. Bet he is going to be a man to be reckoned with by Georgy boy over there. Just want all to know that I am with him all the way!"

Others around the fire murmured their approval of Samuel's feelings. Mike asked Tom, "Jefferson's place, you say. I hear tell it's on a hill way out of Charlottesville and he sells lots of stuff made and grown there."

"Yep, you're right about being way out from nowhere, but I guess that's the way he wants it. He's a right, nice man. At least he was to me. He asked if I would want to buy some nails if he had any to sell, said Tom.

"Nails?" said Samuel. "What would you be wanting nails for now? You plan on building a shed or something close by? Seems like hauling those things around would be more than you would want to put up with."

Mike said, "Knowing where to get 'em is a good thing. That is, once you get to where you are going to settle down."

Tom said, "You're right. And I'm sure I can get nails and whatever else I need once I get to Jacob Brown's and get me a place to put down roots."

"Who is Jacob Brown and where does he live?" said a much interested Samuel.

"Near as I can make out. He came from South Carolina and bought some land from the Cherokee. He is farming some of the bottomland and trying to sell parts of it to settlers like us," said Tom.

"Got any idea where it is?" asked Samuel.

"Down close to a river called Chucky, or something that sounds like that, and a little piece west of Watauga. All I know... it sounds darn good enough to check it out. I gotta settle down," exclaimed Tom.

Later on in the evening, Samuel and Mary discussed the latest information he learned from Tom and agreed to a plan of meeting Jacob Brown. "We need to tell the rest of the family," said Mary.

The next ten days were marked by a steady walk and ride heading southwesterly to get to the Watauga and Jacob Brown region. During an evening talk around the fire, Mike said, "We most likely will be getting to Black's fort tomorrow if we don't run into any trouble."

"Trouble? What kind of trouble? You know something we all need to know so we can best be on the lookout for anything?" said Samuel. "Anything I don't like is surprises."

"Naww, I don't know of any problems except for some wolves around here that may try to get at the dogs," said Mike. "Don't think the Indians are up to anything since Dunmore's war. By the way, that war is why the fort was built about a year ago by a man named Joe Black."

Samuel said, "Wolves you say. I recall Boone telling me about a place where his dogs got in a fight with some wolves. I'm not wanting to run up against a pack of wolves. I hear they are good at getting their next meal to be by itself. I'm not wanting that to happen to me or mine."

Catherine had been listening to the men and made a mental note of how easy it would be to get caught in such a problem regardless of animal or man. *Guess I'd better be more aware of what's around me in these parts. I think it best that I talk with Pa about this.*

Catherine said, "Pa, I have heard some the comments from Mike and the other guys around the fire about the wolves being a problem, and I've been thinking that there seemed to be a lot of forts around here. Do we still have the same problems with the Tories like we had back home?"

"Yeah, I wondered when you would figure out about these forts and wonder why they are here so much," said Samuel. *She is always thinking and doing some good thinking at that.* "You can see one thing clearly and that is we are more into the Indian lands than we have ever been before and that coupled with the problem with King George's proclamation line, makes us needing to be constantly on the lookout for problems."

"I sure hope all the others are knowing what you just said. Makes me feel like we could get into a lot of trouble. Shouldn't we have a family meeting on this thing is my question," said Catherine.

"That's a good thought, Kate. Thanks for bringing it up," said Samuel.

36

After a two-day stay at Fort Black, the Sherrill family were relieved that they would be out of the place where wolves roamed the area.

"Well, Samuel, where are we headed to now?" said Mary. "Catherine was talking about other forts that we will be going to and I was wondering why we had to do that. Why don't we just go on to our destination and find the man named Jacob Brown. I'm ready to start settling down to our final place."

At that moment, Catherine and Adam walked up to the wagon and started listening to what their Ma and Pa were talking about when Samuel said, "Mike told me that we will be going to Fort Womack next and it is probably going to take all day or maybe a day and a half to get there. Going over or around some of these steep hills is not the easiest thing in the world. We just have to make sure that we do not get too anxious and make a mistake." *Gotta keep an eye on these wheels and rims. Would hate to have a problem out here with one of them.*

As the wagons rode around the various sized and sometimes steep hills, and next to a few clear cold streams, the pioneers' eyes and ears were constantly aware of their surroundings. It didn't take too much imagination to realize what could possibly happen if they let their guard down for even one moment.

⟿

"Whata you mean we ain't gonna rob them wagons?" said Yance. "I'm getting low on things and gotta get stuff for my kin. They be starting to hurt fer thangs now!"

The four men were seated around a campfire about a mile from the Mike's wagon train. "How many wagons are in that train?" said Yance. "And for that matter, who is leading them?"

The other three men looked at each other and with a shrug of the shoulders indicated they did not know the answer to the question. And it was apparent that they were not about to try and find out.

"Bunch of no-count boys. You won't hit at a snake if it was making ready to bite ya. All you want is for somebody else to give you things to git ya by 'cause you sure ain't gonna do any work, that's fer shor'," said Yance. "I'm gonna head on over there and find out some things."

"Well, be sure you let us know how ya make out and just what is it you're gonna do," said one of the others.

"Yeah, and then if I get something, you think y'all are gonna git some of it fer doing nothing except sitting on your fat tails waiting fer a handout," said Yance with menace in his voice as he stood up from his log seat, picked up his rifle and headed toward the wagons.

Yance heard the creaking of wagons and the low hum of the animals and people talking before he saw them. As he looked out from a densely wooded laurel thickets, he saw what might be some easy pickings. He saw one of the wagons being pulled by a team of fine-looking horses. *Bet I can get a lot of pounds for them.* That team happened to belong to Samuel Sherrill. *Wonder what would happen if I just got up and walked down to them. Naww, I best ride on down. Might look strange for someone to be walking way out here.*

Tom, Samuel, and Mike were walking to the outside of Mike's wagon when they heard Catherine calling from the driver's seat

of Samuel's wagon. She said, "Pa, looks like we got some company." She pointed toward Yance, who was riding a mule barebacked down the hill toward them. She said as she pointed in his direction, "There he is right up there, see him?" The three men watched the stranger. Tom said, "You two really know how to welcome a stranger. Don't see many men on mules. Mind if I team up with you for this one?"

Mike said, "More the merrier. C'mon, let's see what this guy wants." The three men checked their rifle loads and pans, spread out, walked about twenty spaces from the wagon and stopped to wait for Yance. *These guys know what they are doing. I've got to be careful and play my cards right.* He kept riding toward the men and stopped enough distance away that he could keep all three in sight at the same time. "Howdy, boys, y'all be doing all right out here?"

Mike said, "Didn't catch your name."

"Didn't say it, but since you asked, my name be Yance. And might I ask what your name, that is, if you don't mind telling me."

"Don't mind at all. Name's Mike Stone. These other two guys are Samuel and Tom. Can we help you with anything?"

Yance said, "I reckon so, 'specially if you could tell me where we are now." *Mike Stone! I have heard of him. He is not one to be messed with.*

Samuel thought, *He sure is fidgety. Got shifty eyes. Something about him is not right.* Samuel half-whispered to Tom, "Man out here all by himself is just not right. Wonder if he's got any pals up there in those woods."

"Yeah, you're right," said Tom while keeping his eyes on Yance. "I'll keep watching him close and how 'bout you looking around the woods for anything that might look out of place."

Yance could see that he wasn't making much of an impression and asked if they could spare a cup of coffee. Mike said, "Sure enough, come on down to the fire ring. Before you do that, blow off your pan." Yance held the rifles pan up to his mouth and blew the powder away. "Not too trusting, eh. I like that." *I'll use better speaking with these people. No use acting the fool like with the boys.*

A number of other people gathered around the fire with Mike and Samuel eager to listen to Yance talk about what he knew about this new territory, at least new territory to them. Some of the women gave Yance some biscuits. Yance could not remember when he had been treated so nicely by other people. *I don't think it would be right to try to rob or hurt these people.*

Samuel got the feeling that Yance was doing some deep thinking and said, "You asked where we were headed. We are on our way to Fort Womack."

Yance said, "Womack, eh? I've been by there when it was being built. Never been inside it."

The cooking fires were started for the evening meal. John and Adam had gathered sticks and downed tree branches while Mary and Catherine prepared the food. Soon pleasant cooking odors were permeating the air. All was at peace. The men were inspecting their livestock and wagons and talking about getting started the next day to get to Womack. The creek they were camped by meandered its way from a saddle between two hills, and the three boys could see the occasional flash of fish in one of the deep pools.

"I'm gonna wet a line and catch me some of those fish. Bet they make good eating," said Adam as he looked around for a suitable stick to tie his line to make his fishing pole.

The men around the main campfire watched the boys fish and made comments about how good it was to see them making good use of their time. Yance kept watching comings and goings of the people and in large part appeared very contented with their adventure into new territory. This caused him to think that he would like to become a part of this settlement of new land.

Mary, Catherine, and Mary Jane were arranging things in the back of the wagon and talking about what they plan to do once they were at their final destination. Mary said, "From what I have seen of these people wanting to pick up and move to new territory like we are doing, I think they will make good neighbors."

Catherine said, "Yes, ma'am, I think you're right. But some of the new people that we have met on this move make me pause to wonder about them. Take that Yance for instance, I don't know what it is, but something makes me think that he is not what he wants us to believe."

Mary said, "Yes, Catherine, I think you are..." she stopped speaking when Yance appeared around the corner of the wagon. Catherine thought, *I sure hope he did not hear me talking about him.*

Mary Jane said, "Hello there, Mr. Yance, how you doing?"

"I'm doing all right, how you doing, little girl?" said Yance with a slight smile.

Mary Jane said with the noted Sherrill gaze, "I have you know I am eleven years old and not a little girl!"

Yance took two steps back, took his hat off, and bowed from the waist to Mary Jane and said, "I must humbly apologize for my behavior. I will be more careful when I speak to you from now on."

Mary Jane looked at her mother and her sister and then to Yance and said with a smile and curtsy, "Your apology is accepted."

Mary and Catherine gave each other an incredulous look of "where did that come from" then smiled and Catherine said to Mary Jane, "Well done, Mary Jane, I am sure Mr. Yance knows that he is talking to a young lady."

I really like these people, thought Yance. He said, "I have not heard anyone playing any music around here or even any singing going on. Is there something against that with this group?"

Mary said, "O gracious me...that is not the case at all. Matter of fact, no one said anything about music since we joined this wagon train."

Catherine thought for a moment, then turned and walked to some of the other wagons. She briefly stopped and spoke with the owners of three wagons and while at the fourth the owner, Jubal Lachlan, turned around on the wagon seat and disappeared into the wagon and momentarily came back out holding a violin and bow. Jubal said, "Can you play the violin, Catherine? If you can't, then I prefer you not try to play it." After a moment of what appeared to be a moment of inward reflection, "This was handed down to me by my grandfather who lived in Scotland and whoever handles it will have to do it with very careful hands."

Catherine said, "No, Mr. Lachlan, it is not for me. Yance had asked Ma and me if any of us ever get together to play music. I told them that none of us had played any music, but I would try to find out if anyone was interested in doing so."

"Let's go talk with Yance and see if he knows something about music. And maybe he could even play the violin," said Jubal.

Yance could scarcely believe his eyes when he saw Jubal carrying a violin toward him. *That's a fine-looking violin.* "That's a fine-looking violin, Mr. Lachlan. It's plain to see it is well cared for and well used by a knowing person."

Jubal said as he held the violin out to Yance, "It sure looks like you know something about a violin. By the way, how 'bout you just calling me Jubal. So let me know who can play the violin?"

"Well, Jubal, I thank you to play it for us, but if you want me to go ahead, I'll be happy to give her a try," said Yance.

Jubal glanced at his violin, then Catherine and then to Yance, and in a slow manner, handed it to Yance. He turned to Catherine and with a small smile said, "Looks like you started something here."

Most of the people were gathered around the main campfire, and as what usually developed after the supper meal and before turning in for the night, the sounds of idle conversation and children playing were heard. Yance looked at the violin and gently felt the shape and feel of the wood. He carefully examined the bow while slowly sliding his fingers getting the feel of its strings. With a slight easy smile, he slowly placed the violin in position to start playing. He placed the bow on the violin strings and slowly pulled it over them, generating a sound that he wanted to hear. He adjusted the tension on one of the strings to his liking then walked up to the campfire. He asked, "Does anybody have a favorite song that they would like to hear?" There was a lot of talk among the people. But no one came forth with a title.

Catherine, Adam, and Mary Jane were standing outside of the ring people around the campfire and each looked to the other when Mary Jane said, "Someone has to come up with a song!"

As if a sudden flash of inspiration hit her, Catherine said in a loud voice, "Can you play a song called "Londonderry Aire" or one called "Greensleeves?"

Yance asked in a quiet voice, "Do you know the words to 'Greensleeves?'"

"I read them at some time in the past. The only words I remember are 'Greensleeves, now farewell! adieu! God I pray to prosper thee.'"

Mary looked at Samuel, and with a surprised look on her face, mouthed the words to the obvious question "I don't know" silently as she held out her hands in a questioning manner.

Yance tucked the violin under his chin while telling everyone that he would play "Londonderry Aire" first. The music that came from the violin floated to the ears of the settlers whose life had been dramatically altered due to moving to a new land. It created a spellbinding awe from all who heard and felt the power of the music. After the last note sounded, no one said a word or attempted to get up. After a long pause, there was a single clap of hands followed by another and another until everyone was clapping and loudly saying they wanted more from Yance. There were other songs that Yance was asked to play and who tried to make everybody happy. After he decided that the last song was finished, he walked over to Jubal and said as he handed the violin to him, "You have no idea how grateful I am to you for allowing me to play such a fantastic violin."

Jubal said, "Fantastic is also the way you played it. I hope you will continue to play your music in the future for us. Music will be a way of life for them and give them a break, a much-needed break, in their daily routines."

Catherine said, "Will you be playing again tonight or tomorrow night? I sure hope so."

"I would be pleased to make music for everyone here on every night," said Yance with a small smile. *I gotta get back to the boys and call them off.*

The next morning, the sky was so clear it almost seemed unreal and the sun's first tinge of light had yet to appear on the horizon. Samuel looked at the western horizon and thought, *It never ceases to amaze me of God's work,* as he watched the few remaining stars gradually lose their light. *Be seeing you tonight,* he thought and turned around and was startled to see Catherine close to him. "Good morning, Kate. You're being mighty quiet this morning."

"Just wanted to be with you and saw you looking at the sky," said Catherine. "It makes me think of Psalm 19:1."

"And just what does that Psalm say..." as he saw Yance walking up to them.

"Morning, Lance. That was some good fiddlin' or violining or whatever you call it that you did last night," Samuel said with a small smile.

Yance said, "Thanks, I appreciate that. Wanted to let you know that I'm leaving for a couple of days and hope to catch up with y'all at Fort Womack."

Samuel said, "In case you do not meet us there, we will be going on to Fort Watauga as soon as we can. Could be that we will see you there. Godspeed." He extended his hand to Yance.

As Samuel watched Yance ride into the woods, Catherine, who was joined by Mary Jane, said, "Guess his leaving us is gonna make for no music for awhile."

"Guess so, but you never know who might start another round of playing for us. Got to be a talent somewhere with some of these settlers," said Samuel as he turned to walk back to the wagon.

37

Jacob Womack was standing at the gates of his fort when he heard the wagon train. He half-mumbled, "Looks like we're gonna have more visitors."

As the wagon train drew closer, he said, "Well, I'll be, it looks doggone sure like Mike Stone bringing another bunch of settlers to us again. He just never quits working."

Mike rode back to all the wagons announcing that they had arrived at Fort Womack. He then rode up to the fort and saw Jacob and said, "Jacob, it's been a long time since I've seen you."

"Yeah, I have heard that you are pushing more settlers into the west than any other man. You just never know when to quit work, do you?" said Jacob. "Ezra, open the doors wide and let them ride into the fort."

That evening, when they were sitting in Jacob's log cabin around a long table, talk was about where most of the settlers were going and the Indian problem. Some stated they would be settling in the Watauga region.

Jacob said, "Those of y'all headed further to the west need to get to a place called King's Mill. It's not a fort, but offers some protection at the least." Someone asked who runs it. "Man by the name of William King. Just built the mill about a year ago. Might take a couple days to get there from here."

Samuel said, "I never expected to see or hear of so many forts over here. Seems like every place I go, there is a fort or station springing up. If I was going further west, what other places would we find forts?" Others expressed the same interest by asking many questions about what they might find further west.

"Well, let's see 'bout that. Those going west should, or if I know Mike, will be going on from here to King's Mill then on to a recently built place called Anderson's Blockhouse and team up with more wagons...ya know, the more the safer thing. From there, ya gotta make up your mind on settling down around there in places like Carter's Settlement or I hear of another new place further west that some man, named Bean, is putting up a station.

Someone asked, "Are the roads from here as good as the one we came down the valley on?"

Jacob said, "Don't rightly know about those past Andersons, never seen 'em, but I've been told the trail looks to be a good one. All I know is Henderson got a man, can't rightly come up with his name, to blaze a trail from Long Island to the Gap about a month or so ago. That's when Henderson bought all that land in Kaintuck from them Cherokees. Haven't heard how far he has gotten the trail."

Catherine, who was listening outside of the firelight, came forward and asked, "That man who cut or as you said, blazed the trail wouldn't happen to be named Boone, would he?"

After a moment of silence, a surprised Jacob said, "Matter of fact, that's the name. You know him?"

Samuel, who was somewhat perturbed with Catherine's boldness, said, "Yes, we know him. In fact, he's a good friend of ours, and if it wasn't for him, we may not be here now. By the way, his full name is Daniel Boone and he's told me of the many times he has been around these parts."

There was more talk about who was going further west and who felt they had almost gotten to their destination around the Watauga and Nolichucky river area. Those going further west were anxious about not having much of a road, or any at all, to get to some place they could call home. Jacob said, "Who knows what will be happening, maybe Judge Henderson will start building a road along the trail Boone made."

Mike spoke up, "I tell you one thing and that is if you want the best and sweetest water you ever had, you best be getting it from that spring over there." He pointed to the spring water flowing from side of a hill close to the fort.

Catherine said, "Sure changed the road talk, didn't he?"

38

What was barely a road from Fort Womack to Fort Watauga wound through the never-ending forest, or so it seemed to the people, ever since they left Salt Lick. Catherine was in thought about the beauty of the trees with their budding leaves and some plants on the forest floor taking advantage of the sunlight before the tree leaves brought shade to the forest. *These trees have been here forever.* She turned to Mary and said, "There are enough trees and land here for the Indians and us. Why fight over it? Just doesn't seem right to me."

Mary, after a moment of thought, said, "I think you have to put yourself in their position. This is their forever home and they don't like us coming in and taking any of it. Can't say I blame them for those feelings."

Catherine said, "Yes, ma'am, that's a good thought, but I do hope…"She didn't finish her sentence when she saw Samuel ride up to them.

"Fort Watauga is right over that hill. We have to ford the river. Thank the good Lord for it not being high enough to float the wagons. We'll be across it before dark."

The wagons crossed the river one at a time and gathered around the fort. Mike came out from the double door gate and stepped on a high stump saying, "They have things here that we can use and other things you can buy, just like at the other forts. So, c'mon in and get to know the place."

After supper, Samuel was seated with others around a fire where talk about the weather and if the land in this area was suitable for farming. Everyone knew about the hunting being good enough to supply their food needs. No one brought up the fact that the people who have lived on this land forever may have major problems with the intruders who took land without asking or bargaining, in some manner, for it.

Mike introduced a few of the men who were managing the fort. Samuel asked one of them, "Do you know a man named Jacob Brown?"

"Sure do, matter of fact, he is standing over there next to the tree sharpening his knife," said one of the men while pointing to Jacob.

Samuel walked over to Jacob and said, "Got a minute or two?"

"Depends on what for," said Jacob while not looking up from his work.

Samuel said, "My name is Samuel Sherrill and I am looking for some land. I hear that you have some that you might be leasing or selling."

"Then you must be new to this area. Y'all just come in with that wagon train?" as he looked up from his work to Samuel.

Samuel held out his hand to shake hands with Jacob. Jacob closed his knife and put his whetstone and knife in his pocket and shook hands with Samuel and said, "Name's Jacob Brown. Yep, I got some land along the Nolichucky River that you might be interested in looking at. Guess that means you are interested in settling down in these parts."

"Yep, I would. *Land next to a river means good bottomland.* Just let me know when you got time to show it to me," said Samuel.

Jacob said, "It'll take the better part of a day to get there and back. That be okay with you? If it is, we can leave early in the morning and be back at dark."

"Sounds good to me. I'll tell Mary and the rest of my family," said Samuel and shook hands in parting. "We have those two wagons over there," while pointing to them.

Looks like he knows how to keep things up. "Okay, I'll see you in the morning at that room next to the woodshed. Sharing that with your wagon master Mike," said Jacob. *I'll tell him how I got the land on our way tomorrow.*

Jacob was a merchant who secured a lease from the Cherokees, for a large tract of land on both sides of the Nolachuckey and as far west as Big Limestone Creek. This lease was transferred into a purchase in 1775 when full authority was granted to Brown for the lands.

The next morning, as Samuel and Jacob were riding out from the fort, the sun was not yet showing over the eastern horizon, but there was enough light to see high wispy clouds rapidly moving from west to east. "Looks like we might have some wet weather later on today," said Jacob.

Samuel said, "Well, it won't be the first time I've been wet in a rainstorm. I hope it's not so bad that I won't be able to see your land."

Jacob said, "Are you interested in knowing how I got this land?"

"I don't care too much to pry into a man's business. But I am interested in knowing that you are the rightful owner of it."

"Well, Samuel, you get right to the heart of things in pretty short order. I like that," said Jacob while shaking his head up and down in small movements. *This man is pretty sharp.*

Samuel said with a hint of smile, "I guess my pa taught me that there's no use beating around the bush, especially in things having to do with business dealings."

The remainder of the trip was filled with much discussion about Jacob's acquiring the land on the Nolichucky from the Cherokees as well as his being one of the founding members of The Watauga Association three years ago.

Samuel asked, "What's the main reason for that association, and if I do get some land here, does that mean I should join it."

Further talk about the association gave Samuel a brief overview of the basis for it. "We saw the need to keep people out who broke laws somewhere else and were trying to run from it. We don't need that kind here. They're almost as bad as those Tories." With that statement, Jacob closely observed Samuel's reaction to the Tory word.

Kinda snuck that one in on me. Trying me out, "Yeah, where we came from over in Carolina, we had problems with those Tories and ol' George. Sure glad to find that I'm among people who think like me," said Samuel. "I hope to meet some more of your members."

Jacob visibly relaxed his concerns and decided to show Samuel his best land that would be close to his place. And he decided to tell him about the forming of the Washington District Committee of Safety and the Watauga Association.

After Samuel had some time to think about all this new information, he said, "Y'all are making sure that things are safe around here. Makes me glad that I might be a part of it. Hope I can meet some of the other members."

"Yeah, that we'll do. One of them is a neighbor who's got a place on Limestone Creek. Name's John Sevier. Moved here from Virginia a few years ago. He's to be trusted," said Jacob. "Kinda one of those natural born leaders, I'd say."

Yona and Tawadi were well hidden, while still on their horses, under a copse of hemlock trees as they watched the two men. Yona said, "We will talk with Brown to fix your rifle again. I think I have met the other man a long time ago on the other side of the mountain."

Tawadi said, while not taking his eyes off Jacob and Samuel, "That tells me they can be trusted. At least, I know Brown can be. Let us go to them."

Samuel was looking across the river seemingly lost in thought about making this area his family's home. Jacob said, "Don't jump or go for your gun or knife when I tell you this, but two Indians are coming toward us and I think I know them."

Samuel turned to the direction Jacob was pointing and saw the two Indians. "Yep, I see 'em. Think they are friendly or what?"

Yona and Tawadi rode up to Samuel and Jacob with the easy confidence of ability to take care of any situation.

That has got to be the man we met when Catherine, Boone, and I were in the mountains a lot of years ago. He locked eyes with Yona. Yona shifted his eyes to Jacob. Jacob gave a small smile and held up his hand in greeting which also showed no intent with a hidden weapon and said, "Welcome to Yona and his friend. I want you to meet my friend."

Yona looked back to Samuel and pointed to Tawadi saying, "This is Tawadi. He is the best in shooting a rifle. Is your *uwetsiageya* with you?"

Tawadi said with a harsh stare and punched the air with his fist, "What do you mean by asking him that? You would still like to carry her to the village. You don't think right!"

Samuel did not understand the language and turned to Jacob saying, "What did he say to get the other so upset?"

"Near as I can figure out, I think he asked about one on your children. Why in the world would he asking that?" said Jacob.

"Makes no sense to me!" said Samuel. "Are we getting in trouble here?"

"That would be a big surprise to me. I have made rifle barrels for the both of them and know them to be okay," said Jacob.

Then Yona looked at Tawadi with a hardening stare and said, "I want you to know that what I think is for me alone. Let us get the rifle fixed."

Tawadi said, "Good!" He then turned to Jacob while holding his rifle out to him. "Needs new trigger."

Jacob took the rifle and then looked at Samuel and said, "I think we are all right now." Samuel shook his head with a sigh of relief. *That was getting a little too close for me.*

Jacob said to Tawadi, "This will be ready tomorrow at my place."

Yona and Tawadi with emotionless eyes locked on Samuel, and after a long silence, Yona said, "We go." They turned their horses and started back into the forest.

Jacob thought, *Seems like Samuel knew these two. I'm not going to pry and maybe he will tell me what that was all about.* "Seems like we have had a lot going on today. Maybe we need to be getting you back to Watauga before dark."

"Sounds good to me. Do me a favor. Let's keep the meeting with those two to ourselves for right now. No use getting Mary and the children all riled up," said Samuel. Jacob nodded his head in agreement.

39

After Mary and Samuel talked, they decided it was time to tell the children they had decided on the place they would be settling down. Everyone seemed to accept the fact and Samuel answered a few questions about what exactly would have to be done to make a home. Catherine said, "Please tell me that we will not have a dirt floor like some of the places I have seen here at the fort or will we?"

Samuel looked at his family and thought, *I have got to be as truthful as I can with them.* "Settling down here, along the Nolichucky River, will not be easy and will require a lot of hard work for all of us. But I can tell you that we are with people of our own kind who think like us." Samuel looked at Catherine knowing full well that she would have justifiable concerns and said, "Kate, got any comments or questions. If so, we need to find them out right now."

Catherine said, "Only thing I want to do is to meet some of these people. I think we need to know who are the ones we can trust around here. I have learned, especially from political leaders, that there's not much trust for them by anybody. I just hope they can tell us how things really are rather than a lot of lies that we hear from that English king."

Samuel said, "Kate, you certainly do a lot of thinking about the political situations, don't you? And to the rest of my family,

I've asked Jacob to introduce us to some people around here who happen to be at the fort."

The sun was turning into a bright orange ball floating over the western horizon and the cool breezes were settling down for the night. Mary, Catherine, Mary Jane, Adam, and Samuel Jr. were getting the wagons ready to move out toward their new land when Samuel and Jacob plus two other men walked over to them. Samuel said as he turned to Jacob, "Let's gather 'round for a little bit. I've asked Jacob to introduce a couple of men to y'all."

"Thanks, Samuel. I'm sure you know by now that your pa and I went down to the Nolichucky River bottom land and your pa selected a very nice piece of land where you will be building your home. He was interested in meeting some of your soon-to-be neighbors. So as luck would have it, I saw these two men and now I want to introduce them to you. May I introduce Mr. John Sevier and Mr. John Carter." He then turned to the gathered family and then back to the two men saying, "Gentlemen, I present Samuel Sherrill and his family. They are from Sherrill's Ford, North Carolina. Have been on the Wilderness Road for a couple of months."

John Sevier said, "I'm glad that such a fine-looking family has decided to settle down close to me. A lot of our kind is moving in here on a regular basis and I feel we are of one accord in that we want to be free of a government telling us what we can and can't do and taxing us to death."

Mary leaned over to Samuel and said in a low whisper, "Doesn't leave much to the imagination about how he feels?" Samuel shook his head in agreement.

Jacob then turned to John Carter and said, "John, since you are a founding member of the Watauga Association, would you mind telling something about it?"

John said in a half chuckle while turning to John Sevier, "I certainly do not have the way with words Mr. Sevier has, but at least you know where he stands in his thinking. Let me tell you a couple of the basic points I think you need to know about our Watauga Association." Samuel, Mary, Catherine, and Samuel Jr. were paying close attention to his comments. "First thing we wanted to do was establish laws that everyone understood. We wanted to keep out the people who cheat, rob, and who can't seem to keep from breaking the laws of the land. And the other prime reason for this association is to establish a method for filing wills, deeds, and land transfers, and other things needing some legal help. I hope this gives you some basic idea of how we are trying to govern ourselves."

Catherine was trying very hard to make it appear that she was not looking at John Sevier with more than a casual interest. *He is a good-looking man in a rugged sort of way. Wonder if he is married? Bet I could beat him in a race with or without horses.*

Sevier caught Catherine's eyes looking at him more than once. He walked over to her and while taking off his hat bowed to her saying, "And you are...let me see...Catherine. It is my pleasure to make your acquaintance. My wish is that you will like this land as much as I do." *Haven't lost any of my Virginia manners.*

Catherine felt a blushing in her cheeks and, for once was at a loss of words. She looked at Mary whose beginning of a smile increased the color of Catherine's cheeks. She stood up, extended her hand to John. Their handshake seemed a fraction of a second longer than might be expected. Their eyes met and Catherine said, "I am positive I will love this land," and looked at John Carter and said, "Does your association have any races or shooting matches?

Carter's surprised look was followed by, "Matter of fact, we haven't had one for a long time and, as fate would have it, we're planning one next Saturday. Seems everyone wants to start this spring with a good celebration. By the way you asked your question, I think you would be interested in entering the contests. Am I right?"

Catherine said as she gave a hopeful look to Samuel, "You bet I'm interested. That is, if Pa has no problem with me shooting my rifle."

Samuel gave a small smile and said, "Nope, I won't mind but I'm not so sure the men will like getting beat by my daughter."

Samuel hardly finished his statement when a man galloped up to the group, jumped from his saddle, and rapidly walked to Carter and Sevier. He said in an anxious voice, "Cap'n Carter, Cap'n Sevier, some of our men have been killed at a place named Lexington. They tried to stop the British from taking over the town and that's when the shooting started."

Sevier said, "Where'd you hear this?"

"Heard it from some men camped around Black's Fort. Had some breakfast with 'em and all they talked about was Lexington. Thought y'all ought to know what's being said."

Carter said, "If we can get some more facts, then we need to call an association meeting to alert everyone. We gotta keep on guard especially now."

Samuel said, "I know I am new here, but shouldn't everyone around here be told this news? To me, if those men are right then when you add in what those British did at Boston a few years ago to this…well, I hate to think about it, but this could be the start of a war with England."

Carter and Sevier looked at each other and briefly nodded their heads showing agreement with Samuel. "He's right! Let's get everyone together at Watauga. It'll take the better part of a day to let all know about the meeting. So the meeting is to be noon the day after tomorrow. Let's get a move on!"

Sevier walked by Samuel and quietly said, "Good thinking, Sherrill."

The meeting was attended by over a hundred men who were most of the landowners in the Watauga and Nolichucky areas. John Carter was asked to lead the meeting.

Catherine stood as close to the assembled men as possible keeping in mind that women were not allowed to voice opinions or cast votes at these type of meetings. *They don't know that they need women to help make big decisions. I wouldn't be here if Ma hadn't agreed to pick up and move here.*

It was decided that the men should assemble outside the fort to prevent overcrowding and ease of movement. There was a lot of talking and some with raised voices noting concern over what was happening with the British. John Carter stepped up on the walkway along the top of the walls and shook his hands in effort to calm the men.

"Men, I'm here to tell you that we think we are at war with England," said John with a rising voice. There was a stunned silence for a moment. "But we have not been able to get much more information other than the fact the British killed some of our kind somewhere around or in Lexington."

The stunned silence was turned into the harsh sound of many men voicing their feelings about what England had done and was doing to the settlers. John tried settling the men down to tell them that he had sent a messenger to get more accurate and detailed information even if he had to go to Lexington. He motioned to one of the men to get him to pass his rifle up to him. He then shouted to the men asking them to quieten down, but too many were ignoring him. John raised the borrowed rifle and put the sights on one of the corner posts and looked at the men to see if they were quieting down. Only after they heard the rifle fire and saw the top of one of the logs splinter did they became quiet. John handed the rifle back to its owner and said, "Nice rifle. Accurate too." He then looked over the quietening crowd and said with increasing ferocity and loudness, "I am in complete agreement with nearly everyone here. You are right in your feelings toward King George and the fact he thinks the power of his army and navy can cripple us enough to make us accept him as our king and leader. I'm here and now say that we won't let any leader who has never served in an army, who has not even seen America, and who thinks that all he has to do to make things go his way is to tell his supporters what he wants because they will give it to him. No people anywhere need such a simpleminded leader!" All of the men shouted various comments almost at the same time about the British and those who were more Tory than anything else were closely watched by the Patriot neighbors.

Catherine was spellbound at the proceedings and became energized to the point of clapping her hands and yelling, "Down with the British cowards!" John Sevier observed her actions and thought, *Nothing is gonna make her do something she doesn't want to do.*

Mary was cooking the evening meal when Catherine walked into the room. "Ma, why is it there can't be peace with what could be our distant relatives over there in England? The men are really riled up about those men getting killed at Lexington."

Samuel, who had just walked in the house, said, "I heard part of what you were saying, Kate. The only comment I can give is the ones who think they know what is better for people like us are completely ignorant of even themselves. They exist in their own I-know-it-all space."

"And one other thing. It seems to me the British and their Tory friends are becoming our enemies worse than ever," said Catherine.

"That's not all of the picture. We're up against the British plus the Indians that are being stirred up by them. We've got enemies in the front and rear of us which means we have to keep cool heads about where we go and what we do and say," said Samuel.

40

1776

Dragging Canoe, Attacullacullah, Yona, Raven, and Old Abram sat on logs placed close to the doorway of Yona's hut. No one said a word much beyond greetings. All were looking at the glowing fire embers thinking about their future with the white man. The spell of watching the fire had created a sense of peace except for Dragging Canoe who broke the silence by saying in a low voice, "I still say that ground will be dark and bloody," while continuing to look at the embers.

No one said a word. After a long time had passed, Old Abram said, "They kill their own kind. That's like me going through one of our villages killing our own kind. These are strange people."

Every man nodded his head while glancing at each other then lapsed back into thought filled silence.

"After visiting their king and coming back home, I felt their people here would be following him. But that isn't what is happening. Some are for him while others are not thinking he is their chief," said Attacullaculla.

"Then we should become friends with their chief and help them like the Mohawks and Shawnees are doing in their land. The others, who do not like the king, do not have a chief," said Dragging Canoe.

Raven said, "We must give that point careful thought and develop a plan that we can use to drive these people from our land."

Even though Yona was not a chief, he had gained their trust due to his wisdom. "What Raven tells us is good. I think the plan must be made by Dragging Canoe."

They all agreed with Yona's comments. "So be it. You have until the next moon to bring us your plan," said Attacullaculla. Everyone nodded approval.

Dragging Canoe said, "I will make sure that the man named Stewart will keep his promise to bring us rifles, powder, and ball." He met eyes with Yona, "You will find this, Stewart. What he brings us is part of the plan. With those things, we cannot fail." As if on cue, a limb of firewood started popping due to expanding gases trapped in the bark. As they watched the flying sparks, Raven said, "This is a good sign. The Creator will approve our new plan."

ᝌ

Patrick was on his way to London to meet with Lord George Townshend about his rifle design that he knew had much potential for making the English soldier considerably more effective in battle. The early spring weather was making it easier on everyone's senses since the winter had been, at times, one of biting cold. *I hope to find his lordship in good spirits this morning.*

"And a grand and glorious morning to you, Ferguson. I trust you are feeling better these days. How is your leg getting along?" inquired Townshend. "Please sit down and have one of these delicious crumpets."

"Thank you, your lordship. I am honored," said Patrick.

"Let's abandon this lordship business. It makes for conversation much too long. Just call me George if you don't mind and I'll call you Pattie. And what is it that I can do for you this fine morning," said Townshend.

"My lord…uhhhhh, George, I am a career military officer, and as such, am always looking for ways to improve our king's army. To get right to the point, I have developed a rifle that will measurably improve the effectiveness of our soldiers," said Patrick in what he hoped was a convincing voice.

Further discussion about the rifle brought Townshend to the point of agreeing to the project and making plans to demonstrate the rifle to the officers selected by King George.

The next few weeks found Ferguson in London taking charge of producing and testing his invention and to make sure it would perform since he had to demonstrate it to the officers that it was effective. The demonstration was set for the first of June.

"This has got to work," said Patrick to the arsenal manager. "I am satisfied with our tests and about to show all these generals how good it is."

"Yes, sir, Captain Ferguson, your rifle is a great weapon. I feel you will make and sell thousands of these rifles. You will be a rich man. I trust I will be the one to oversee their manufacture," said the manager.

"Yes, and we may have to use them in what looks like a war that is heating up in the American colony. Their officers have been slowly building men against us and now it is in the open. We will march in and finish that business over there," said Patrick while looking down the barrel of one of his new rifles.

The demonstration of the new Ferguson Rifle was a success. An order to make a hundred of the rifles was given to an overjoyed Patrick. *This will help get me out of debt. Has cost a lot to get this rifle going. I will finalize getting the patent.*

41

Billowing clouds were gently changing their shapes against a deep blue sky. Peaceful breezes stirred the leaves of low growing bushes. Robins and chickadees were flitting from one tree branch to another searching for another seed or insect.

He lost himself in thoughts of how fortunate he was to be alive at this time and place. His eyes drifted to the horizon and followed the majestic slope of the mountain range in front of him. He let his eyes drift back and saw a hummingbird hovering over deep-throated flowers. *The Creator performs wonders...* His reverie was interrupted by three men, two of which he knew, while the third was a white man, approaching him. *Hope they have something good to say* and said, "Good to see Dragging Canoe and Yona. Who is this?" as he pointed his finger toward the white man.

Dragging Canoe said as he waved his hand and pointed to the north, "He comes from the land of Mohican. He is the Englishman named Stewart. We found him after seeing the smoke from his fire. The man is stupid. He doesn't know how to keep a fire that doesn't smoke."

It was obvious to Oconostota that Dragging Canoe was not at all satisfied with bringing this white man to see an important chief. Oconostota looked into Yona's eyes with an expression intended to get a response from him. Yona caught the look and said, "He comes in peace. He wants to make talk with you. He wants you to help his people."

Oconostota turned his unblinking eyes to the white man, and with no change in his expression, held the eyes of Henry Stuart trying to determine if some unspoken message would pass between them. While holding his gaze, he thought, *This man can't be trusted. He thinks he is better than us.*

He looked at Yona and asked, "What is it this man wants? Where did you find him? Does he know our words?"

Yona said in an even tone while letting his eyes drift from Oconostota's to Stuart's, "He tells of his people wanting to help us. He wanted to be found and must be very brave or very stupid in thinking we would not harm him. He does not know our words."

Oconostota intently watched Stuart's expression and satisfied himself that he understood Yona's words when the smallest narrowing of his eyes occurred when Yona said he did not understand their language. "This man is not to be trusted. Send him on his way or, better yet, cover his eyes and take him to the mountaintop where the mad She-Bear lives and turn him loose. If he makes it back here, we will talk." Oconostota let his eyes drift to Henry's eyes, and seeing no response, looked at Yona and Dragging Canoe. His slight nod toward the mountain told them to do as instructed with Henry. *If his knowing the ways of our land and gets back without harm, then I know the Creator is with him. He can then be trusted.*

It didn't take Henry long to realize he was in a lot of trouble and things were not going the way he was told they would go by his brother, John. He had not been present at the meeting with some Cherokees who came to St. Augustine to get rifles, ammunition, and other supplies. These supplies would help make war on the people who were taking their land. They were told by John that the requested supplies would be sent to Echota. Henry had become separated from the rest of the caravan during one day of driving rain. He was trying to find his way back when he finally determined that he was lost. He was relieved to be found, but now his plight seemed to be worse that being lost in these woods.

In an anxious voice, Henry said, "I have rifles!"

There was no sound from anyone. The Indians looked at each other trying to make sure that what they heard was "rifles." Henry, thinking they did not understand, started saying the same words over and over "I have rifles" until Yona's hand motions told him to stop talking.

Oconosstota said, "Yona, you go tell Raven and Old Abram that we will have rifles soon. Dragging Canoe, finish your plan of how we rid ourselves of these white men."

"It will be done. But can we trust these men who fight his own kind? The men they fight are true warriors. We must be ever alert to their fierceness. I go now to alert the others," said Dragging Canoe.

42

With tears welling up in her eyes and a quivering lip, Catherine said in a low voice, "Ma, do you realize I will be twenty-five years old this year? I wonder if I will ever be wanted by a man! Don't I act nice? Just what is it that I'm not doing right?"

Mary and Samuel had talked many times about Catherine and her not finding a man who would ask for her hand in marriage. They made the decision that it takes more time for some things to happen than generally accepted by their friends and neighbors. Samuel had said many times, "All things in God's good timing." They both knew that Catherine had some difficulties with that statement as she grew older.

Mary told Samuel that maybe Catherine should not display her horsemanship and ability with a rifle too much, especially in contests. Samuel agreed that defeating men at their own game was a way to make them avoid her even though she was pretty and had very nice curves in all the right places. "Might want to talk with her about those things. There is such a contest coming up next week at Watauga, and I know she wants to enter it."

Samuel pushed back his chair at the table and without saying another word left the cabin to get the boys and tend the cleared fields.

Mary decided to wait for Catherine to come back from her ride and talk with her about the upcoming event at Watauga.

It had been two weeks since Samuel and Mary had discussed Catherine's plight. Most of the family rode the wagon to Watauga to attend the much anticipated event. Mary had told Catherine that she wanted to see her before she entered any of the events. "Ma, is this a good time to talk about what you were wanting me to do while here?"

Mary pointed to a bench placed under the outspread branches of a large oak tree. "Have a seat. Let's talk about what I think you should consider doing while at this contest. Heaven knows, you are old enough to know what to do, but just listen to your mother here for a few moments."

Catherine said, "Does this have to do with finding a man for me?"

Mary said, "You have always been very perspective. Yes, this has to do with such. Just keep in mind this is your mother talking and it may not fit into what the younger folks are doing now."

"I'm more than willing to learn from you, Ma. Just what do you want me to do?"

"You've got to lose or, put another way, you cannot win any of the rifle or horse races," said Mary with a no-nonsense look into Catherine's eyes.

Catherine held the gaze of her mother for a moment. She then leaned back on the tree trunk looking at various things people were doing. After a long time, she said, "I see where you are going with that line of thinking, and I must admit, what I have done in the past at such things is to show up a lot of men. Now, at this new place for us is the time for me to change my ways. Thanks, Ma, I am thankful for you and your wonderful mind," said Catherine with a look of love for her mother.

Mary said, "Just be sure that the men don't figure out what you're doing."

"Kinda dishonest is my thinking," said Catherine.

"Not at all. You're just using your abilities to meet your goal. Can't say there is a rule of shooting a rifle that says you can't shoot anywhere you want. Just so long as it isn't the usual bullseye," said a smiling Mary with a tilt of her head and a twinkle in her eyes.

The rifle match was set up close to the fort gates. The targets were cut into the shape of a V nailed to another plank with a hole drilled at each end. This target was held in place by two posts with wooden pegs that held the target planks. The targets were placed at fifty, seventy-five, and a hundred yards. The winner would be the shooter placing their shot closed to the apex of the V without hitting the sides of the plank.

"All riflemen take a number from the hat on the table. That will be your place in line. Each man has one minute to load, aim, and fire. Is that understood?" said John Sevier. "Samuel and I will be the judges for this shoot. Any questions?

Catherine walked up to the gathering holding her rifle with both hands. She knew if she approached the event holding it with one hand that the other contestants would know she was familiar with the rifle. She did not want to be seen as some woman who knew how to handle a rifle. "I want to enter this contest if it's all right with the judges?"

Samuel had no idea what Catherine had in mind. He only knew she could probably outshoot any of these men. *Not a good idea, my daughter. Might chase 'em off again.* "John, I think you need to make the decision since she is my daughter."

Some of the men shouted comments that led everyone know they had no problem with women entering the match, even though it was unheard of in these parts.

John looked at Catherine for a long moment. *Pretty thing she is. I think she knows something. Guess we're gonna find out.* "Well, Samuel, why not? She may show us a thing or two about being in a match. Some of these boys are darn good shots." He quieted the contestants and said, "Let's start the match. Your turn will be the number you pick out of Samuel's hat. Let's see now, how many we got in this match?" He pointed at Samuel Jr. and said, "You're number one. The man on your left is two. So Samuel, start counting." The last man said twelve.

Samuel wrote the numbers down on separate pieces of paper and put them in his hat and shook them up. John said, "Ladies first." He motioned to Catherine to take a number. She reached in the hat and drew out the paper with twelve written on it. The others drew their number from the hat.

While standing on the fort's walkway, Samuel looked over the top of the wall and saw a man slowly leading a lame horse. *Wonder which one is worst off? Both are limping.* He then turned his attention back to the shooting contest. As John explained the target and rules, one of the men interrupted him saying, "Why don't we just have a bullseye target like every other time?"

"Ohh, c'mon now. You know as well as I that every man here can hit the bullseye. That's why we figured on the V target. Y'all gotta be dead on to get that one," said John. He could see that some agreed while others didn't.

"Can't please everybody, John. Let's get on with it," said Samuel. At that moment, he saw the limping man and horse enter the gates. *Something 'bout him makes me think I've seen him before.* He approached the men and asked in a hesitant manner if this was a shooting contest and if there was any money prize for the winner.

The men turned their attention to John. He leaned over to Samuel whispering, "We didn't figure on any prize. Whatcha think we oughta do?"

Samuel said, "Get each man to put one shilling into the hat. Winner take all."

John was in complete agreement. "C'mon, boys, let's everyone put a shilling into the hat and winner take all."

One man said, "Hard money's tough to come by, John. And it kinda takes the fun out of a shooting match is my take on it."

Some of the others murmured agreement, others shook their heads in agreement.

John, recognizing the problem, said, "Well, then why don't we forget the prize idea and get on with the match. Let the man who has number one start."

Catherine had been looking at the limping man when she, in a sudden moment of recognition, said in a low voice, "Yance, is that you?"

Yance slowly turned to Catherine and with a small smile said, "Sure is, Miss Catherine. It's great to see you again. How you been?"

"Been all right. We got a place down on the Nolichucky. That's Pa up there with John Sevier. He is a neighbor of ours," said Catherine. *Why did I tell him all that.* Looks like you have had some problems with your leg."

"Yeah, I got jumped by a bunch of no-gooders who were out to rob anyone they could find. They got to me after I left y'all back when y'all were close to getting to Womack. Thought they were gonna kill me," said Yance as he slowly looked around the fort.

"Guess being by yourself they must of thought you were easy pickin's. Tell you something. You help in this shooting match and you'll sit down at our supper table today," said Catherine with a small smile.

The match was close, but no one had put a shot in the V. There was lots of grumbling about the V being too little.

John called out, "Number twelve. Get ready."

Catherine had closely watched the various methods the men used in aiming and firing their rifles. Her plan was to let the men know she was not much a marksman. She knew she was being closely watched and her first attempt at loading the rifle was a planned clumsiness. She let more powder hit the ground then went down the rifle barrel. Gun powder was a precious commodity on the frontier since it offered a way to put food on the table and protection. Catherine repeated the loading procedure and loaded powder onto the pan. She looked closely at the target. *I can hit that with my eyes closed.* Since the shooting was in the standing position, she almost took a proper firing stance where the right leg and foot gave a steady position. She raised the rifle and put the barrel sights on the target. All eyes were upon her just waiting to see her mess up and probably not hit the target. Catherine knew what they were thinking and raised the barrel just enough to make her target the right corner of the board holding the target. She took a deep breath, sighted, and rapidly squeezed the trigger. She knew the proper procedure was to slowly apply pressure to the trigger and so did the men.

The corner of the board disappeared as her shot hit it as aimed. Not too much was said about her missing the target. Some thought it was a miracle that she even hit the board.

Others took their turn until it was decided that two men had to fire at the one hundred yard target. Catherine thought, *I could take that target any day of the week.*

Just as the shooters prepared to fire their rifles a rider raced his horse up to the fort. Everyone could tell the rider was very tired and his sweat-lathered horse was close to falling down. "Someone cool down my horse and get her some water and grain," said the rider as he slowly got down from the saddle and just as slowly walked to a log, turned and sat down. "I've gotta see Captain Carter! Is he here?"

"Mind telling us who you are," said Samuel.

"Ohh, yeah, guess it would be best to say so. But, I shore would be obliged if one of y'all would tend to my horse. She's a good 'un."

Samuel looked at Catherine with a "need your help" manner as she said, "I'll do it," and took the ground hitched reins and led the horse to the river for watering. She would find feed later. *Not sure why I am doing this. Felt like the right thing to do.*

The rider watched as Catherine took his horses reins and said, "Much obliged," and turned to look at Samuel. "Name's Isaac. Last name's Thomas. I've gotta see the captain." He slowly drooped over and appeared to fall asleep. He slowly looked up and said, "And tell him about the Cherokees getting ready to attack us.."

The Cherokee War had started and the plan was for Chief Old Abram to kill, burn, and destroy crops and forts along the

Nolichucky and Watauga river areas. Dragging Canoe would be raiding along the Hogohegee river and Eaton's Station while Raven would do the same in the Carter Valley area on his way to Wolf Hills. Some Tories had agreed to accompany the Cherokees in the raids in effort to rid the area of people who wanted to manage their own future rather than obey the orders of King George.

There was a stunned silence among the people. Sevier immediately recognized that any organized resistance was about to be lost due to people heading off into many directions to protect their property. He shouted, "Everyone gather up here!" as he jumped onto a wagon seat so he could be seen by everyone.

"Samuel, do your best to wake up Thomas and find out what he knows! You others start checking the fort to make sure it has everything needed to protect ourselves! Make sure the line of fire is open enough to hit your target from at least one hundred yards."

At that moment, he looked toward the Nolichucky thinking, *Sure hope we can get to all the people in time.* He then saw the first wagonloads of neighbors coming up the road.

"Here comes some people. Samuel, you've got to get him awake!" said John.

Samuel took a bucket of water and splashed it over Isaac. The response was fierce as he came awake, jumped up, and drew his knife ready to defend himself.

"Whoa, there, Isaac! You act like we gonna hurt ya. Just settle down!" said Samuel as he held up his hands in a surrender manner. He saw Isaac slowly settle down.

"Thought you were one of those murdering Indians. I'm good to go now."

"Mightily glad of that. But you gotta tell us what you know about any Indian attack around here," said Samuel.

"Nancy Ward told me and three other guys that her people were getting ready to wipe us out. She said we had to let all the whites know what is going on. They plan on killing all, burning everything and killing livestock," said Isaac.

John said, "Nancy Ward? Good grief, she is their Beloved Woman! Why would she tell y'all that tale? She must know this will make for serious setbacks for the Cherokees. But first, we gotta stop them now. At least we won't get ambushed."

"Aren't we wasting time talking about it? Let's get the word out to the other forts and stations to alert the families around them!" exclaimed Samuel.

"You're right! Let's get some guys to light a shuck for Womack, Beans Place, Eatons, and others!" said John. "Samuel, take the Nolichucky. I'll take the Long Island and Carters Valley. I'll find others to make out for the Wolf Hill area."

Isaac said, "I've already told those along the Nolichucky. Not sure if the other guys have gotten the word out to the other areas." Those wagons are from the Nolichucky, I bet."

Samuel questioned some of the last wagons and they said they saw some smoke coming from the area behind them. All agreed it was most likely the Cherokee burning their cabins and barns. He kept looking for Mary but in the fading light did not see her.

"Pa, you seen Ma?" said a worried Catherine.

"Nope, have not. I'm gonna go find her and the rest of our family. She said something about going back home, and I guess that is what has happened. She never has done anything like this before without telling me."

"I'm going with you!" said Catherine as she turned to find her horse. "Don't leave without me, Pa! I'm bringing my rifle."

Samuel knew there was no way to keep her from going with him. He also knew she could ride like the wind. "Let's go then!" as he saddled his horse.

Mary was worried that their home was being left unguarded and no telling what might happen if a bear or wolves decided to attack the chickens and livestock. She was relieved to find everything was in good shape. She knew Samuel and Catherine were still at the fort, and she had all the children in the wagon ready to go back to the fort. All except Adam. She knew he had gone hunting after breakfast and also knew he would not come home unless he had something to show for it. It was late morning when Isaac Thomas had ridden up to tell her that the Cherokees were on their way. She thought of firing a rifle hoping the sound would alert Adam to come home.

She fired the rifle and decided to wait one half hour after which she could not wait any longer to take the rest of the family to the fort.

Adam was anxiously watching a long line of Cherokee warriors. He was hiding in a laurel thicket next to an almost hidden deer trail. He had been patiently waiting for a deer to make its way down the path. The deer would provide needed meat and skin for his family. He watched a covey of quail scratching the ground for seeds and clucking to each other when each suddenly stopped their activity and looked in a direction to Adam's right. *Uh ooh, might be a deer.* He slowly started to put his rifle to a firing position. *Gotta make this perfect. Hope those quail don't rise,* knowing that the fluttering sound of each bird would blend into one startling sound which would alert any creature within hearing that something had scared the quail. Adam hardly breathed and slowly turned his head toward the direction the quail were looking. He saw the quail quickly leave in a single file. *Never saw that before. Heck, never heard of such either.*

The far-off sound of a rifle being fired let Adam know that whomever heard it was to quickly come to its location. *That was at the cabin!* He started to rise when he heard men rapidly talking in the language of the Cherokee. Adam hugged the ground and barely looked in the direction of the sound. Two of the Cherokees were starting to jog up the deer trail when another called out to them. They stopped within five yards of Adam and turned to listen to the other voice. Adam had no idea what was being said and was deciding what to do to defend himself since he could see they had the war colors vividly painted on their faces. He also had been told by his pa and Mr. Boone many times to not look at someone a long time for fear they would somehow feel the stare and turn to look in your direction.

The two Cherokees wanted to go in the direction of the rifle shot. Twadi said, "Old Abram knows the whites have been told of our coming. We must get to the fort before the whites get inside." He started along a faint path toward Fort Watauga. The two standing next to Adam shrugged and turned back to follow the others. Adam had hardly breathed and slowly backed out of his hiding place and silently stood up making sure of no sound. Satisfied that he could not be heard, he took off to his cabin knowing for sure they were wanting him to quickly get home.

Catherine galloped up to the wagon and saw everyone except Adam. She had also heard the shot. "Ma, everyone is heading to the fort. The Cherokees are heading toward us to drive us from our homes! Where's Adam?"

"We know about the Indians when Thomas came riding through telling everyone he saw to get to the fort. Adam is hunting and I shot the rifle to let him know he is needed," said Mary.

"Ma, take the others to the fort and I'll wait a little bit for Adam. I'm sure he will be here soon. He can ride with me. We'll catch up with you, but you've got to leave now. Pa will meet up with you. He is checking the stock."

Mary saw no more reason to talk about what to do and slapped the reins on the horses. They started at a fast walk seeming to know the need to get away quickly.

Catherine led Betsy to the well and pulled up a bucket full of clear cold water for herself and Betsy. As Betsy was drinking, Catherine looked toward the fields and forest for any sign of the Cherokees. Her eyes searched everything she thought would show signs of danger. At the same time, she became aware of the beauty of the tops of the mountains against a hazy blue sky, the shadows in the valleys nature had cut into the mountains, the placid water of the river and the complete silence that enveloped her. Her reverie was abruptly interrupted when the quiteness of her surroundings thought hit her like a reaction of spilling boiling water on the hands. She strained to hear anything beyond the desolate silence. Then she knew there was danger close by. *The Cherokees must be close. I've got to find Adam.* She slowly walked toward Betsy and climbed into the saddle and started toward where she thought Adam may have gone. She was alone and knew her survival skills must be at their best.

She let Betsy slowly walk toward the barn while placing her rifle across her lap. She leaned forward on Betsy's neck in order to see around the barn's corner. Betsy's ears bent forward. Catherine then tensed knowing some person or animal was close. The two Cherokees, painted in war colors, were more surprised to see Catherine than she was to see them. She pressed her knees to Betsy's side who started running at top speed on her second step. The two Cherokees were desperately trying to get out of Betsy's way when she ran over one knocking him to the ground. He grabbed his broken shoulder and limped toward the tree line. Catherine took care of the other just as he was raising his rifle and hit him in the head with the butt of her rifle. He crumpled to the ground without a groan. Catherine looked back to see the one hobbling to the tree line and the other prone on the ground. *Wish I had time to shoot 'em. Gotta find Adam and fast.*

Adam ran into the yard and saw Catherine running down the two Cherokees. He yelled to her. She turned Betsy toward him shouting, "Get on and let's get out of here!" Adam jumped on Betsy's back behind Catherine, and not needing further prodding, Betsy ran as fast as she could in the direction of the fort. The sound of a rifle being fired only served to let them know there were other Cherokees close by. Betsy continued a full run weaving around trees and rocks. Catherine let her pick her own way and was surprised and thankful at the way Betsy found old, barely recognizable animal trails through the woods.

Chief Old Abram and other men, including Yona and Tawadi, of the war party heard the shot and thought some white men had finally been found. The other cabins had been empty, and in their rush to do battle with the white man, they did not take the time to burn the empty cabins and barns. On arriving at the Sherrill homestead, Yona asked the injured men what had happened to them.

"A devil woman on a devil horse rode over me breaking my shoulder and she almost killed Running Deer," said the man sitting on a log next to the Sherrill home.

"Who fired the shot we all heard?"

"I did as best I could raise my rifle. Only thing I hit were a lot of tree leaves."

"Was the devil woman tall and knew how to ride the horse well?" asked Yona.

"She rode well, but I didn't have time to find out how tall she was. She sure knew how to swing the stock of a rifle," he said while rubbing his shoulder. "And, don't ask me her name either."

Yona said, "I think I may know who she is. *She must be the one I've seen many times over the last few years.* I think she is a Beloved Woman to the whites like our Nancy Ward is to us. I now must find Old Abram."

Catherine and Adam reached the gate of Fort Watauga and yelled to those inside to open the gate doors. It was almost dark when they arrived and the gate had been locked. A voice called out, "Who are you?"

"I am Catherine Sherrill with my brother Adam. My father is Samuel. We have got to see him," yelled Catherine.

The gate doors squeaked open just enough to let them through with Betsy. "Your pa is over there with Sevier," said the gatekeeper as he pointed toward where others were sitting and standing around the fire pit.

"Pa, we just got here. Is Ma and the others here?" said Catherine.

"They got here this afternoon. Did you run into any trouble? And I sure am glad to see you both are safe," said Samuel.

Catherine and Adam explained to Samuel, John and others, all that had happened to them. "The ones I saw are on foot, but I think some must be on horses," said Catherine.

John said, "That means they may get here late tomorrow. We've got to be on alert and double the guards on the fort walks."

"Yeah, I agree. Let's get enough men on the walls to make sure we aren't ambushed by those savages bent on killing us," said Samuel as he looked around at the rest of the men. "Let's make two-hour shifts so no one gets sloppy in keeping awake and alert."

Early the next morning, just before daybreak, Catherine climbed up on the wall walkways. The night had been warm with barely a breeze stirring. She had put her pallet outside the hut in an effort to avoid the heat. *Looks like it's gonna be another hot one*, as she looked over the fort walls. The sun's light was just starting to turn the dark into a hazy grey color. She could see some of the cows starting to move toward the fort in anticipation of being milked as was the case for them each morning.

"Looks like this is the start of a good day," said John Sevier who had silently walked up to her. "The guards are making sure we are safe."

"Yeah, I've noticed them and have seen a number of cardinals and dove flying and feeding. That tells me that we are safe," said Catherine.

"I like it when the womenfolk can read the forest," said John. "Makes for another pair of eyes and ears for a couple." He looked closely at Catherine.

Catherine became a little embarrassed at the way John was looking at her and thought he was trying to pay her a compliment. "I bet Sarah knows the ways of the forest better than most. Well, I've got to go with the others and milk those cows before they start bawling."

Catherine, Noah, Nell, Mary Ann, and Jess walked out the gate toward the herd of cattle. Noah said, "Sure wish we were back home. Why is it those Cherokees are so riled up against us?"

The guards were very alert when the women were out from the safety of the fort. Samuel thought as he surveyed the outer perimeter of the fort, *Things just don't feel right this morning.* As he walked, he kept close attention for any movements. He noticed a few birds rising above the tops of some trees back in the forest. He then knew the Cherokees were close by. "Hank, Joe, alert everyone! Those killer Cherokees are close by. Send someone out to the women now!"

Old Abram saw the birds fly up and knew their rising had alerted the enemy at the fort. "Make everyone ready to attack. I will give the first yell. Be sure and pick out your first targets. That will be the only time you have an easy shot. Make it count."

The Cherokees spread out in a line facing the north and west wall of the fort. Yona and Tawadi were facing the north wall and made ready to join in the attack. Old Abram had hoped to launch a surprise attack, but he was sure the birds had given an alert to the enemy. He noticed a man hurrying outside the gates toward a herd of cattle and closely watched him. *He has been sent out to get the cows inside the fort.* He saw a number of women rise from the herd and start back to the fort. He knew the time was right to launch the attack. His high-yipping yell pierced the air like a rifle shot. The whole tribe joined in the yelling and started firing toward their selected targets.

Immediately after they had been alerted to get to the fort, the women started running full speed toward the fort's gate. Some were still carrying their pails while others had thrown them aside as they hindered their running ability. Catherine was further out from the fort than the others due to her cow being the on the edge of the herd. She heard the man tell them to drop everything and get back to the fort. She stood up and rapidly started to the fort when she heard the yells of the Cherokees and the firing of their rifles. The women ahead of her were running and screaming toward the gates. Catherine looked at the pail half full of milk. *I should take that*, and on her second step was running full speed. *That bucket will still be there later.*

Being the best marksman in the tribe, Tawadi was carefully picking out targets and had already wounded one man on the fort walls. He was loading his rifle when he heard the screaming women running toward the fort. "Yona, I will shoot those women." He noticed the last one rapidly catching up with the others. He put his rifle sights on her and gave his aiming point enough lead so that his rifle ball would intersect her path killing her. He started slowly squeezing the trigger. At that moment, a hand pushed his rifle barrel toward the ground just as it fired. Yona, looking down at a puzzled and very upset Tawadi, said, "We don't kill a chosen woman."

Tawadi's said with a menacing tone, "You mean that is the woman, who was a child, you first met with her father and Boone. Plus she is the one we rescued from a white man. You've always had the thought that she would be in your hut!" He turned his attention to reloading his rifle and saw she was the last of the women. She was running toward the fort wall and had three Cherokees waving tomahawks trying to catch her. Yona watched the race and said, "They won't catch her. She is too fast."

Catherine heard the yells behind her and knew she couldn't take time to look over her shoulder. She was shocked to see the fort gates starting to close after the other women had gotten safely inside. *Why now?* Her next thought was, *I'll climb the walls*, and picked out a place she felt she could jump to and pull herself over the wall. She concentrated on one of the pointed logs and somehow increased her speed to it. The yells of the pursuing Cherokees were joined with the yells of the other Cherokees witnessing the race.

The men on the plank walks were firing their rifles as quick as they could be loaded at the enemy. John Sevier looked down the barrel of his rifle trying to pick out a target when he saw Catherine running toward the wall. He quickly looked at the gates and saw they were shut. The sound of rifle balls hitting the fort walls with a sickening thud were sending wood splinters in nearly every direction. That, coupled with the yells of the enemy, were enough to make any one drop down to safety. John shouted to the men closest to him, "Grab my belt and hold on!" He leaned over the fort wall and shouted to Catherine, "Over here, over here!" while frantically motioning for her to grab his hand.

Catherine saw John's frantic waves and with another burst of speed, she didn't know where it came from, jumped as high as she could and reached as high as possible with her outstretched arm. John grabbed for her hand and clasped his hand around her wrist. Catherine grabbed his arm with her other hand and felt herself being pulled up. John yelled to the men, "Pull me back!" as he rapidly pulled Catherine over the wall to safety. He then grabbed his rifle and leaned over the wall and shot one of the pursuers who was trying to jump up on the wall in the same place used by Catherine. The other men stood up and fired into the other Cherokees trying to catch Catherine. The Cherokees at the wood line had stopped firing at Catherine. They did not want to kill or wound any of their own men who were trying to catch the white woman.

Samuel and Mary ran to Catherine who was sitting with her back against the fort walls. Before any questions could be asked, she said in a halting almost breathless manner, "I'm…all right. If it hadn't been for John, I don't think I could have make it over the wall. God gave me the strength to run faster and jump. I was just about done for."

Mary yelled to John hoping he would hear her over the battle sounds, "Thank you, Thank you!" His only response was a quick look back at Mary with a nod of his head. He immediately turned back to finding Cherokees to target and kill. Samuel standing next to him was firing as rapidly as he could, especially at the enemy who tried to catch Catherine. He then patted John on his shoulder and shouted, "Thanks," and turned his attention to reloading his rifle.

The Cherokee's effort to capture the fort was not successful after laying siege for two weeks. Chief Abram stood just inside the wood line facing the fort. He had been told of Dragging Canoe's defeat around Long Island and that Dragging Canoe had been wounded in the leg and carried off the battlefield. That, in addition to many of the tribe having been killed or wounded, caused him to end his part of the raiding efforts. He said to some of the others gathered around him, "We go!" He turned and walked back to tell the other men that the raids were over.

Samuel and some other men were reviewing the attacks when one man said, "Didn't some rider come in and tell us that some men had signed what he called an Independence paper?"

"Yeah, you're right. Is he still here? Other than the Cherokees, we did talk about what the heck does that mean to us," said another.

Everyone in the fort heard the yells of the men on the fort walks. "Don't tell me this is another attack!" said Catherine as she turned from helping her Mom make biscuits. She and her brothers ran outside their cramped cabin and saw men on the walks yelling "They're gone! They're leaving!"

Catherine climbed the ladder to the walks and was joined by her father and John Sevier. John said, "Glad to see 'em go. We gotta be careful that Abram is really leaving and not planning an ambush. He's a crafty ol' fox."

Samuel said, "I still have a problem with the way they feel they have to kill and torture us like they did that Cooper boy. I still hear his screams as they tortured him."

Five men volunteered to scout out the land around and beyond the fort to make sure the Cherokees had gone back to their home. After a full day of scouting, the men came back with reports that it appeared to be safe enough for the families to go to their homes.

Mary told Samuel, "I'm dreading to see what's left of our place."

Samuel said, "I'll go check it out and then come back for you and the young'uns."

"No way will I do that…we all are going with you!"

After a full day of travel, they topped the rise that would allow them to see their homeplace or what was left of it. Everyone stood in a state of surprise when they saw the cabin and out buildings still standing. "Ohhh, Samuel, we are truly blessed," said Mary. "Our home still stands. Thanks be to God."

Catherine, Adam, and the rest of the children said, "Amen!"

43

Samuel, Adam, and Uriah were inspecting the crops and had stopped at a wood line next to the cornfield.

"Looks pretty darn good, Pa," said Uriah.

Samuel turned to Uriah and started to say something when he saw the startled look on Uriah' and Adam's face. They were looking behind him. He turned to see a Negro man with two boys with him coming out of the wood line toward them.

Unhhh ohh, what's going on here. Samuel slowly turned his rifle that would allow a quick shot if needed. "Let me handle this, boys. Don't say or do anything."

The man and boys stopped a few feet from Samuel and his boys. "Don't ya know me, Samuel?"

After Samuel's initial surprise and finally recognizing Boudroe, he saw Catherine as she rode up to the group and quickly slid out of her saddle. She then walked to Boudroe and said, "Boudroe, it is good to see you again. Been maybe nine or ten years ago that we saw you leave us." She held out her hand remembering the first time she met him.

"Wow! You're Miss Catherine?" said Boudroe with a startled look.

Samuel said, "That she is. Somewhat grown up I'd say. And Boudroe, it is good to see you again."

After much talking and finding out what had happened to them in the last few years, Uriah asked about the two boys with him.

"They be my sons. I'm looking to find them a place to settle down." He then turned to Samuel and said, "Could they stay here with you?"

Samuel was somewhat taken aback and said, "Uhhh, Boudroe, we barely have enough to get by as is and taking on two more boys is something I don't see how we could do."

"Well, let's see. You wouldn't need to pay 'em. Just a place to put their head and food for their always empty stomachs is all I ask."

Gotta think about this some more. "Well, let's see, Boudroe, give me til tomorrow noon to give you an answer." Samuel said with a concerned look.

Boudroe said in an almost whisper while looking at the ground "They would kinda be like your...slaves."

Samuel's quick and meaningful response, "Not around my place!"

Boudroe said, "I'm not liking it either, but what else can I do? They gotta get out on their own somehow. Being where we are is a living, but it ain't gonna help 'em enough to amount to anything. Sho' hope you'll let 'em stay here."

"As I said, I'll let you know tomorrow. Care to stay with us tonight?" said Samuel.

"Thanks, but the boys and I will camp out by that river and get us a mess of fish for supper," said a smiling Boudroe. "By the way, my boys are named Hank and Jumper. I'll tell you tomorrow 'bout how Jumper got his name.

44

Patrick was overjoyed that he had been awarded a patent for his rifle. The December 2 timing of the patent made it almost like a Christmas present from King George. *I know he was impressed. Maybe he made sure I would get my patent.* "I know this rifle is hard to make, but it could win the war over in America and I will be seeing Lord Townshend soon," Patrick commented to his rifle works manager.

Patrick knocked on Lord Townshend's door. The butler led him into the library. "Good to see you, Pattie. How is the patent holder of a new rifle doing these days?" said Townshend as he shook Patrick's hand.

"Well, my lord, uhhhhhhh, I mean George. All is well and production of the rifles is a little slow at first, but my manager says it should speed up."

"Ahhh, very good, Pattie. Have a seat and let's talk about your future."

Over port wine and roast beef sandwiches, the two men discussed Patrick's plans for his new rifle. "I say, Pattie, that fellow named John Montagu came up with the idea for the sandwich a few years ago. You know, he was Earl of Sandwich."

"Yes, I've met the Earl and he told me of his inventing the sandwich. Not quite a new weapon, but meets the need of a number of us."

While slowly twirling his wine glass, he said, "Well, Pattie, the sandwich and your rifle are recent inventions for the empire. Just what do you have in mind for your rifle."

"I want to form a company of riflemen who I will train in the use of the rifle. When the training is finished, I want to take them to America and show those rebels that we mean business. They are getting out of hand over there!" exclaimed Patrick and waved his hand with such vigor that the sandwich flew from his hand. "Ohh, sir, I apologize for such rude behavior." He started to get up and retrieve his sandwich.

"Think nothing of it. It will get cleaned up," George said with a flip of his hand. "On the other hand, maybe you could put it on the hearth. Now, let's go over your plan."

"I want you to know this rifle will cost more than the Brown Bess. But its superior firepower will be of major help in winning this war. That fact alone should overcome the increased expense," said Patrick. *At least, I hope so.*

The rest of the morning was taken up with developing a plan to present to the proper channels for approval.

45

Catherine was in a state of shock. John Sevier had just asked her pa for permission to court her. It had only been five months since Sarah died in February. And that coupled with the fact he now had ten children at home, the oldest being twelve, was a lot for Catherine to wrap around in her mind. These facts, plus the fact of her age, added additional challenges to her mind. Ever since being rescued by John from the fast pursuing Cherokees during their raid on Ft. Watauga four years ago, she had given fleeting thought as to how somewhat attractive he was, but the fact of having a certain authority about him was especially appealing to her. She never dreamed of marrying John, but that never stopped her admiration of him. Then the death of Sarah made her think about how devastating it must be for John especially when he had ten children to raise. She watched John mount his horse and trot toward his home.

Samuel asked Catherine to sit down with him and Mary. "Kate, I want you to tell you something you might be suspecting. John came by here to let me know his feelings for you."

"Yes, Pa, I heard y'all talking while I was in the loft. I think I heard something about his wanting to court me. Can that be?"

Mary said, "I know it must be a big surprise to you. I couldn't be happier for what might be in your future."

"Your ma is right. I'm happy for you and, if you say so, I will let John know that I approve of his courting you. No use for

me to go into what I feel for him 'cause I want this to be your total decision."

"That plus the fact that you have always wondered if there was some man for you in this world," said Mary. "John may be the man."

A long time later, Samuel and Mary thought it best for Catherine to make up her mind in the morning. "Yeah, Pa, I know you always say to 'sleep on it' before making a big decision."

Catherine was the first to awake before sunrise. She stepped out of the cabin door and walked to the smokehouse and sat down on a bench. The colors of the leaves and colors of many wild flowers gave her a feeling of deep thankfulness for her many blessings. The light from the early morning rays of the sun wove its magic paintbrush of burnished reds and oranges on the high clouds. *I know I must agree with Pa's plan to tell John.* She thought of many things as she looked at the nature before her. The thought that constantly caused her increasing concern surfaced. *I'm now twenty five years old. Could it be that I have found the man to love and live with.*

Samuel and Mary sat by the hearth watching the flames of the fire dancing against the chimney rocks. "Remember when all of us built this fireplace," said Samuel.

"Yes, I do. There's some skinned fingers in some of those rocks," said a slightly smiling Mary. "Now, Samuel, I know you want to talk about something other than this fireplace. So, out with it."

They both fell into silence and seemed to be mesmerized by the fire and the heat that the rocks radiated into the room. A loud pop followed by a small shower or burning splinters from one log brought them out of their reverie. Catherine walked into the room, "Heard that pop from the fireplace. Just had to see if everything is all right here."

"Am glad it brought you. I think we can use your thinking ways to help us solve a problem. That is after you tell us your decision about John," said Samuel.

"No use for me to go into a lot of words. Yes, I am ready for John to court me. I've thought about what might be and, even though there could be a lot of problems for us to solve, I feel it is the right decision."

Samuel said with a low voice, "Then that is the way it will be." He stood, reached out to Catherine and hugged her. "We'll always be here for you. Now let's tell the others what is going on." *I hope she's doing this for the right reasons.*

Samuel then described the situation with Boudroe. Mary was in complete agreement with him.

"The way I see it is we can do two things. Either tell him no or yes, but with them having to agree with the way to solve the problem," said Catherine.

They talked and planned the next steps. Mary said with a look of a proud mother, "Kate, I just don't see how you can be thinking of nothing but John. But here you are helping us work out a brand new thing for us. You beat all, my daughter."

∽

Boudroe watched his sons trying to catch fish for breakfast. He heard Samuel's approach and got up to welcome him to the camp. "Mighty fine morning we be havin'. Wouldn't you say?"

"Yep, sure would. What y'all eating for breakfast? Boudroe, we gotta talk."

"Want me to get the boys to hear this?"

"Nope, I think you have to agree with it and then you tell 'em and I'll jump in if needed. Here is the way I want to help y'all. We'll sell each five acres of our land which they will pay for in equal amounts for five years. We will help them build cabins and plow their first fields. That is, if they want to farm it. I will hold the deed until the final payment."

Boudroe said in wide-eyed half whisper, "You mean they own the land. What if they don't want to farm it, then what?"

Samuel said, "That is their decision. But they have to find a way to pay me each year. If they don't, then they lose it."

"Fair enough. I'll get the boys up here to tell them they can be land owners if they want it."

Boudroe explained the proposal. Hank was all smiles. Jumper got so excited the stood up and started some tip toe jumps. He finally settled down and with a simple question said, "What are we gonna do with the land?"

Hank looked at his brother, pursed his lips and said, "Jumper's right. Just what can we do?"

Boudroe was visibly surprised at his sons. "What in the ever lovin' is the matter with you two. Y'all farm the land, sell crops you don't need, and pay Samuel at the end of each year."

Samuel could see that the initial euphoria was being lost and felt this was the place to help Boudroe. "During the first year, the boys and I will teach you how to plow, how to plant, and show you what needs to be done to get better crops."

"You mean y'all will do all that for us the first year and then it is up to us to take over for the rest of our days," said Jumper.

"Yep, that's about it. Kinda reminds me of a story I heard that came out of China. Seems there was a man who said something like we could give you some corn or bean seeds. You could eat them and not be hungry for a day, but if you planted and tended them right and harvested their crops then you would never be hungry again," said Samuel.

Boudroe then said, "What he is telling you is that you gotta work and plan your life 'cause there sure ain't no high and mighty person or something like the Watauga Association to take care of you."

Hank said, "You mean that if it ever did work out that some high and mighty would be telling us what to do all the time instead of helping us like here at Samuel's…" After a moment of thinking, he said, "That is like making us slaves to them."

Boudroe said, "Good thinking, Hank. I was a slave once and that is not the way you want to live. Now, you boys give it some thought today and then sleep on it. You can then tell us in the morning what you're gonna do."

Samuel said, "Your pa is right. Anything real important needs to be thought about, and if you got the time, sleep on it overnight and then make up your mind. And it looks like we've got their minds working. Y'all gonna stay here for the night or come to our place. Course, you'll have to bed down in the barn."

"Naww, we'll stay here. Sure know that we'll be talking a lot way into the night," said Boudroe.

"Knowin' what you mean. I'll see ya in the morning," said Samuel as he started back to his cabin.

The morning's sunrise seemed to be more glorious than the previous one. The red and orange shades that seemed brushed on a deep blue sky were slowly giving way to the suns brightness. Samuel seemed lost in thought as he watched the skies majesty perform its morning ritual when Boudroe and his sons walked up. "Mornin', Samuel. The boys have something to tell you."

Hank and Jumper looked at each other and said, "We're gonna take you up on your offer."

They spent the next hour working out the details of the deal. When the plans were finalized, Boudroe said, "Samuel, I can't thank you enough for what you are doing for me and my boys. We'll be on our way and get everything ready to move over here."

"Boudroe, Jumper, Hank, let it be known that we know you will be the best farmers in this valley," said Samuel with a wide grin of satisfaction. They shook hands and Samuel watched them as they started back to their homeplace.

Samuel turned back toward the cabin. *Best be checking the barn* as he walked along the corn and bean plants. *Rows sure are straight. Gonna be a good harvest,* as he observed everything in the yard. *Boys are keeping things nice and neat. Gotta see John and tell him about courting Catherine.*

46

John and Catherine were together many times. It was the end of June and the weather was perfect for picnics and riding the trails that John considered to be safe from surprise attacks by the Cherokees. It wasn't until July 21 that John asked Catherine if he could kiss her. *I been wondering if he would ever ask.* "This kiss is to let each know of the love we have for each other. It is also a date that we first held hands. Do you know the date and where it was?"

Their first kiss was neither passionate nor timid. It was surprisingly gentle to Catherine and immediately told her of a side of John she had not detected before now. After they parted lips, she said, "Remembering something is fartherest thing from my mind." She looked deeply into John's eyes. She saw a wanting that thrilled her. She looked away and thought about his question. It came to her in a flash of recall and said, "The date was four years ago when the Cherokees first attacked the fort. The hand holding was when you grabbed my hand and pulled me over the fort wall to safety. And once again, I am truly grateful for your saving me in the face of bullets and arrows. I get cold chills when I think of that time."

It was about two weeks later, around August 1, when they were seated on the porch of John's home on Limestone Creek. They talked about a lot of things and when there was a silent moment, John took her hand and said in a low voice, "Catherine, I love you and I'm asking you to be my wife."

Catherine was, once again, struck speechless. She took his other hand, looked deeply into his eyes and in a moment of fading breath, said, "John, I want you to be my husband, and, yes, I'll be your wife."' John's smile could light up the darkest room. He took a deep breath and yelled, "The Lord has truly blessed me!" He jumped up to tell others in the house the good news. The children ran up to Catherine and gave her hugs. She had become knowledgeable about each of John's children and knew their emotions were heartfelt.

After the whooping, hollering, and hugs, John said, "Let's get married in two weeks. I know that is a Monday."

"Seems to me that you have been planning this for some time," said a smiling Catherine.

"Unhhhh ohhhh. I was so excited by your answer that I almost forgot this." He reached into his vest pocket and withdrew a ring. He gently took her hand and slipped the ring on her finger. "There now, we are engaged."

John and Catherine "Bonnie Kate" Sherrill were married, August 14, 1780. They were enjoying the congratulations and helping with the final preparations of a barbeque. The men were sampling some of the best distilled spirits and metheglin produced in the region. Someone said, "Here comes Shelby. Mighta known he wouldn't miss a party." The other men laughed about the comment.

"John, I gotta talk with you. We got trouble aplenty comin' at us. Let's go in the house and talk."

"Thanks, Isaac. And another thanks for coming so far to our wedding barbeque."

"Wedding? I didn't know about it even though a lot of people thought you and Catherine would tie the knot some time. But you know that I've been over in the Carolinas making that English Major know he isn't messing with some pushovers," said Isaac.

John soon learned that Isaac's cousin, Samuel Phillips, who was captured during the Battle of Camden and somehow or other they found out about his relationship to Isaac. He was brought to the Tory camp and told by Ferguson to carry a message to Isaac.

Isaac said, "He says something like if we didn't lay down our arms, he would come over here and hang some of us and then burn out and kill the rest of us with his sword."

John and Isaac soon agreed that they had to defend themselves and the way to do it was to find Ferguson first rather than wait for him to attack their forts and homes. "He's got a bunch of Tories with him and, if he got the Cherokees to help him while attacking us, then we will be in a lot of trouble," said John.

John and Isaac walked onto the porch and John said, "Boys, we got some trouble to get rid of."

"Trouble? What kind? Cherokees at it again?" said Samuel.

"Nope it has nothing to do with the Indians this time. It's the English and their Tory friends. Seems they are set on running us out of here," said John.

"Who and when and how?" said Samuel.

Samuel soon learned what happened when John said, "This English major, named Ferguson, had captured some Patriots that included Samuel Phillips. Ya know, he's a cousin of Isaac Shelby." Everyone soon learned what Phillips had told Isaac.

"Sounds like this Ferguson wants to do what that murdering butcher Tarleton did at Waxhaws back in May," said Samuel with the Sherrill glare. "What's our plan?"

John said, "Let's get some men to ride out and tell our neighbors that the men have got to get together at Watauga. We're gonna find us that Major Ferguson and show him that we are the best fighters who know how to fire a rifle better'n anyone and that we are gonna make him wish he never heard of us."

Samuel and Samuel Jr. headed back to their home. "Mary, we've gonna make a long trip down to the Carolinas and whip some English and Tories."

Samuel, Samuel Jr., Adam, and George readied their rifles, powder, lead balls, food, and blankets for the mustering at

Watauga. Mary said, "I'm not in favor of you and the boys leaving again to fight. But, I know it has got to be done."

Samuel said, "We gotta protect our places. Been fighting the Cherokees for years around here. But this time, we'll fight the men who still think living under King George's rule is the best. They ought to know they'll never be free because it is always some English officer, like Ferguson or that devil Tarleton, leading them."

Adam said, "Sure wish we could let Uncle Mode know what's going on. If he knew, then I bet he'd try to meet up with us."

"Yep, you're right. Do you know if Boudroe has left yet?" said Samuel.

They found that Boudroe and the boys had just left since their fire ring was still warm. "I'll find 'em, Pa. Want them to come back here?" said George.

"That'll take up a lot of time. Just tell him what you know about what's going on and that we wanted to let him know so he could let Mode know what's goin' on. He can then tell the other brothers. Just tell him to tell Mode to wait for more information before heading off over here," said Samuel.

"I'm on my way!" said George.

The closer the Sherrills got to the fort, the more neighbors they saw heading in the same direction. "As they topped a hill close to the fort, they were surprised at the number of men gathered in small groups around and in the fort. As they rode onto the fort grounds, there were numerous waves to them and shouts of greetings. It was apparent that some of the men were enjoying some of their still makings and others were exuberant in sampling their version of metheglin.

Samuel observed a number of women at the fort and further investigation into why they were here came as a surprise to him. *I didn't think of that. The Cherokees will rise up and attack our homes.* "Adam, get back to the house and tell your ma, John, and Phillip to be on the lookout for the Cherokees. And if they don't feel safe doing that, then hurry to the fort."

"Yes, sir! I'm on my way. Hope George gets back soon to help us out," said Adam as he pulled himself into the saddle.

"How many we got here?" said Samuel to John Sevier.

"More or less a thousand. And every man I've talked with is eager to get on the way and settle this once and for all," said John. "You seen Isaac? We've gotta do some figuring."

"Nope, sure haven't, but I'll find him. You gonna be here for awhile?" said Samuel. "By the way, you know if Boone is here?"

"Don't know, haven't seen him. The last I heard he was over in the Kentucky territory. I'm sure he'd be here if he has heard anything about this muster."

"Yeah, you're right. He wouldn't want to miss this. I'll get Isaac for you. Ohh, by the way, I meant to say 'Happy Birthday' to you yesterday. So to my daughter's husband I say 'Happy Birthday!'"

Isaac, who had joined the group, said with a slight smile, "Heck of a way to spend your day. That plus you were in the midst of a wedding party. Hope Bonnie isn't too upset."

After John and Isaac discussed the plans for getting to where they hoped to find Ferguson and his Tory army, Isaac said, "I think we have enough men to stop that Ferguson."

"I agree. But it came to me this morning that if we take all these men with us that leaves our back door open."

"Whatcha mean?"

"Every able bodied man is going with us. You know darn well that the Cherokees will find out that all the men are gone. Dragging Canoe is a smart one and you well know what most likely will happen."

"You got that sharp mind of yours working. Yep, you're right," said John. Got any idea of what we need to do?"

After checking with other leaders they arrived at a plan to have each leader assemble their men and start counting off. Then, after counting off, the leaders were to tell each seventh man to assemble at a designated spot. Those men were the ones who could not go on the march and had the duty to protect the territory from the Cherokees.

John assembled the 240 men from the Nolichucky area. He asked them to start counting off and to remember their number. When they finished counting off, John asked those who number could be divided by seven to assemble in front of the others. After counting off, thirty-four men stepped to the front and looked at John with a "what's next?" attitude.

John said, "All right, men. The others have assembled just like you and counted off. Those of you standing in front will be staying here to guard our wives, children, and homes!"

The initial response was so still you could hear a pin drop. Then the number 7s started shouting that they were not going to stay back. They wanted to fight for their rights. John let the shouting go on until he had to calm them down. He waited for the cussing and shouting to subside before saying, "We've thought long and hard about how to keep a guard against Cherokee attacks. We just can't all leave here without some of us staying to make sure our families and homes have some protection. Do I need to mention what the Cherokees will do." Then he shouted to the top of his voice, "And y'all know what I say is true!"

Once again, silence reigned. Samuel started clapping his hands to show his agreement with John's words. Then ever so slowly, other men joined in the clapping while others started shouting their support. The noise was almost deafening when John started trying to calm them down. After the shouting slowly subsided John shouted, "Georgie boy is gonna find that he can't have his way by saying it or signing his name on a piece of paper telling us what we have to do! Let's get rid of him and his kind!"

The men from Nolichucky roared their approval.

The remainder of the day was taken up but the men, women, and children preparing the men for the march over the mountains. There never was a statement made about the difficulty of climbing the high mountains following old buffalo trails. There was a general concern about finding Ferguson and his army of Tories and other British sympathizers.

John, Isaac, and other colonels were discussing when to leave and make doubly sure of the route they had agreed would be the best to get to the Carolinas. "Looks like everything is ready to go in the morning," said one of the men. "Guess we best get to our men ready to move out."

John asked Samuel to make sure the Nolichucky men were getting ready. "Might be best if we had someone who would lead us in prayer before we leave," said Samuel.

John said, "Excellent point! We can't leave without Doak saying a few words and prayer for our success and safety. Samuel, do you know where he is?"

"I'm fairly sure he is over around Limestone and, for all I know, he is on his way here," said Samuel. "I'll get a couple of men to find him."

"No need in that," said Isaac. "Here he comes now!"

Reverend Samuel Doak's comforting presence coupled with an attitude that he was doing God's work made him a much sought after minister. "Good afternoon to each of you. I want to go with you, John. Since I'm settling around the Nolichucky River area, I thought it best to go with you."

"Mighty fine, Reverend, but you are needed here rather than going over there. Would you please get before the men and pray for their success in defeating that English lovin' crowd," said John.

The next morning, Reverend Doak gave a stirring sermon describing how badly England was treating the men in America. Taxation without representation and quartering English soldiers in the settlers' homes without permission. He then said, "Let us pray." His stirring and force filled voice asked, "Almighty and Gracious God! Thou hast been the refuge and strength of thy people in all ages." He continued with the prayer asking for infinite mercy in saving the Patriots to come back to their cabins after showing Ferguson they could fight and win against his army. His final words in his stirring prayer were, "Help us as good soldiers to wield the sword of the Lord and Gideon."

Doak looked over the men who with bowed heads and said, "Amen." After a few moments, the men started looking up and some looked at each other barely shaking their heads, signifying that this was the time to mount their horses and leave.

John said, "Reverend Samuel, your words are of much comfort to these men."

∽

Major Ferguson sat for a long time watching the fire dance its various colors of gold, yellow, and an occasional popping that sent brief sparks flying into the air. *Why is it I haven't heard anything from that Shelby?* He had been told that an army of the men from across the mountains were preparing to track him down. He also knew the message he sent to Isaac Shelby was the catalyst that stirred the men over the mountains to action.

Lt. Anthony Allaire watched his major and knew not to disturb him while he was in obvious thought. Ferguson looked from the fire to his lieutenant, "How are the men?"

"They are in good spirits, but some are wanting to get back to their homes to finish up their harvesting," said Allaire.

"Might not happen, Tony. We're going to leave this Gilbert Town place and march to Charlotte to meet General Cornwallis. I will ask him to give us more men to march over those mountains and show those rebel traitors to the king the error of their ways. We've got to finish this war and get those rebels to recognize the Crown rather than someone like Washington as their leader."

Captain Abraham DePeyster had just arrived from his evening rounds of inspection. "Well, Captain, what is your thinking about our position?"

"All I know, sir, is what our friends who left those men coming over the mountain told us. Judging by the number of men they are said to have, I think we should make plans to attack them."

After discussing the situation, it was decided to break camp and march toward Charlotte. The next morning found the men up and on the march by five o'clock. One of the men asked about the day's date. He was told it was Wednesday, September 27.

At that time, the Overmountain militia was starting their climb to Yellow Mountain Gap. The fall colors of the wide assortment of trees were at their peak.

Samuel said to Samuel Jr., George, Uriah, and Adam, "Ma sure would like to see all these colors from way up here." As he turned to continue the march to the gap, he was a little surprised to see snow on the ground at the gap. "Kinda early for snow."

Adam said, "Yeah, those colors are such that Ma and Kate would really take to them. And against the blue sky, it almost makes you think the colors are just painted by some unknown artist."

"That artist is God," said Samuel Jr.

"Got a point, my brother,"

"Just look at the men we've got." Samuel looked down the mouintainside to see the line of men walking and riding up the trail. "I hope all of us can make it over this gap before dark."

47

Boudroe had gotten to Mode's cabin and told him that Samuel had wanted him to know what was going on with the men coming over the mountains. Mode then rode to the rest of the brothers and told them about the men looking for Ferguson's army.

"You know, I've heard talk about men coming from our area. Seems they are going to meet with those men over at Quaker Meadow," while Mode pointed to the west.

"We best get a move on and help Samuel. I've been wanting to get rid of those British for a long time and this may be it," said Jacob as he sighted down the barrel of his long rifle.

"When we going?" said Isaac. "Tomorrow is the second of October. I figure our kin is close to here. Let's head out tomorrow...crack of dawn."

The next morning, William, Uriah, Adam Jr., Aquilla, Isaac, and Jacob met at Mode's cabin. "Lead the way, our youngest brother!" said William. "Since we got some creeks to ford, I guess we best be calling you Moses on this trip." All the brothers gave a quick smile and started to find their way to Quaker Meadow.

On the way, they learned from others heading to the same place that the militia had gone on to Gilbert Town. They joined the rest of the men who were riding hard to catch up with the main body.

The Sherrill men, along with others from North Carolina and Georgia, arrived at the camp site. After being told where they

could possibly find Samuel and his sons, they were told the men of Sevier's company had left for a place called Cowpens.

"Our horses need feed and rest," said Isaac. "I think we best give them a few hours before we head out."

Uriah said, "I'm for going on. They may need us if they are getting close to that Ferguson. Sure would hate to see him get to Charlotte. If he gets there, then he can start action against us like he and his kind have done down in Carolina."

They arrived at the Cowpens camp only to find that almost half of the militia had been chosen to ride during the night to a place called Kings Mountain. They had been told that is where the enemy was making camp. They also learned that they were not to go forward until word was sent back from the main attacking body.

"Pa, do you think we'll find them on that mountain? This rain shows no sign of stopping," said Adam.

"Gotta look on the bright side. At least Ferguson won't think we're after him in the dark and rain-soaked night," said Samuel.

The next morning started with little let up in the rain and then it started to clear up. "Sure is good to see the sun. I haven't been so wet in a long time," said John Crockett.

"I sure agree with ya, John. We best be checking to make sure our powder is dry," said Samuel Jr.

Word was passed among the men that their destination could be seen on the eastern horizon. Each man began checking his rifle, powder, and shot. There was an unusual quietness to the men and horses. Some mentioned the wet path they were on made the hoofbeats quieter plus made no dust.

John Sevier rode next to Samuel who said, "Looks like Ferguson is going to find out that we won't allow his kind to come visiting."

"Yeah, that's the truth. Ya know something? I can't believe you are my father-in-law," as he patted Samuel on his back.

Samuel gave a quick smile and said, "We'll do more celebrating of y'all's wedding when we get back. I hope all these Nolichucky men can come to the party. Now, let's get us some of those Tories and that Ferguson."

Nine colonels—Sevier, Campbell, Shelby, Williams, Lacey, Cleveland, Hambright, Winston, and McDowell—led the charge up the mountain in the afternoon. The fighting raged up and down the mountainside. Bayonet charges were ordered by Ferguson against Sevier's and Campbell's command who were pushed down the mountain. The Tories then climbed back up to their original position. The militia started back up the mountain using every tree and rock for protection and their long rifles continued to take their toll on the Tories.

The militia made it to the top of the mountain after many of the Tories had been killed or wounded. They saw a man on his horse blowing a whistle in attempts to rally his army.

"Hey, Pa! Look there! It's a white flag! They gonna surrender!" shouted Adam. They saw Ferguson on his horse knocking down the white flags of surrender. He wasn't ready to accept defeat.

The Sherrills along with the rest of the men from the force in the mountains kept firing their rifles at selected targets. The Englishman, trying to rally his troops from his horse, stood out from his troops which made a fine target. *If only I had the men with my rifle*, thought Ferguson as he tried to rally the men. It was obvious to nearly all the men of the Tory army that they were not going to win this battle.

"We've got to take that man down!" shouted Samuel as he aimed his rifle at the man on the horse. Just as he was about to pull the trigger, he saw the man jerk backwards and drop his sword. Samuel immediately knew the man had been shot and watched him slowly fall from his saddle.

Major Patrick Ferguson felt the sharp impact of a rifle ball when it penetrated his chest. The sudden hit made him stiffen his body in an effort to stay on his mount. Other shots hit him. As he fell to the ground, his final thought was: *Can't wait to smell Mother's roses.*

As the battle on Kings Mountain was being won by the men from over the mountains, Catherine was looking across a majestic hidden valley high in the mountains above the Nolichucky River. *I hope and pray that my husband, Pa, and brothers are safe and will return as soon as they can. I will help John in whatever he chooses to do and I know that together we can be people who will help others in making this land a truly wonderful place to live.* She reached down and patted Betsy on the neck saying, "Let's go home, Betsy."

Epilogue

Reports about the news of the victory at Kings Mountain gave the delegates to the Continental Congress in Philadelphia the enthusiasm to finish their work. Thomas Jefferson said it was "the turn of the tide of success." And many years later, he recalled this battle as "the joyful annunciation of that turn of the tide of success which terminated the Revolutionary War."

CPSIA information can be obtained at www.ICGtesting.com
Printed in the USA
BVOW11s0515260116

434255BV00040BA/1295/P